A Place to Run Free

A Place to Run Free

Michael LaReaux

Stormbird Press

Stormbird Press

Stormbird Press is an imprint of Wild Migration Limited.
PO Box 73, Parndana, South Australia.
www.stormbirdpress.com

Cover Stormbird Press.
Typeset by Alice Teasdale, Big Quince Print.
with Antique Olive and Kazimir.

NATIONAL
LIBRARY OF AUSTRALIA

National Library of Australia and State Library of South Australia
Legal Deposit
LaReaux, Michael 1972 – Author
A Place to Run Free
ISBN – 978-1-925856-51-4 (hbk)
ISBN – 978-1-925856-52-1 (pbk)
ISBN – 978-1-925856-53-8 (ebk)

*The publishing industry pulps millions of books every year when
new titles fail to meet inflated sales projections—ploys designed to
saturate the market, crowding out other books.*

*This unacceptable practice creates tragic levels of waste. Paper
degrading in landfill releases methane—a greenhouse gas emission
23 times more potent than carbon dioxide.*

*Stormbird Press prints our books 'on demand', and from sustainable
forestry sources, to conserve Earth's precious, finite resources.*

We believe every printed book should find a home.

*This book is dedicated to pets
and the people who love them.*

Chapter One

The world was on one side, and Jake was on the other. Two fallen white pines, their trunks half buried in the earth, marked the boundary of his tiny kingdom on the riverbank. Above him, the buds on some of the birches had already opened, tiny leaves waving against the brisk air coming off the river. He hadn't thought to bring a jacket with him, so he sat huddled against one of the fallen trunks with his knees against his chest. Patches of white, icy winter still clung to the moist earth. Some of the birds had returned, so the silence was broken by the occasional bird call or the flapping of wings in the branches above.

Golden light broke through the treetops and dappled the thick carpet of pine needles that lay exposed where the snow had melted off. Jake always thought his special place was like church, except not the way church was, but the way church should be. Beautiful and peaceful, like someone inviting him to rest, even if he was suspended from school.

Two days suspension for ripping Peter Nichols' essay off the bulletin board, spitting on it, then sticking it back to the bulletin board using the wet side to make sure it stayed there. "That," Mr. Meyers said, "was the last straw." Jake didn't know what straws had to do with being suspended, but that's what Mr. Meyers said, leaning over the big metal desk, jabbing his finger in the air with his right hand while he dialed the phone with his left.

Principal Meyers never bothered to ask him his side of the story. It didn't matter that Peter had hit him in the back of the head three times with paper clips. It didn't matter that Peter lied about Jake calling him a pecker. Jake's uncle told him that Peter was just another word for pecker, and he had simply repeated it when they were out on the playground. Mr. Meyers probably didn't even read far enough down the referral form to see his side of the story. Jake spat on Peter's precious South Dakota report, so he was suspended, and that was that.

Precious Peter, already on the eights. Mrs. Collins loved to point out that Peter was already on his eights. Peter could spell big words like "excavator", and Peter could type forty-five words per minute. Even if she had seen Peter shooting paper clips, her precious little favorite wouldn't have been punished. She probably would have found a way to blame Jake for allowing his head to get in the way of Precious Peter's precious paper clips. Because Peter was already on his eights.

At least it was too early for the mosquitoes and black flies. Jake could sit by the river and stare at the water without being eaten alive. If he had just remembered to bring a coat before he slipped out of the bedroom window, being suspended wouldn't have been bad at all. Almost perfect, in fact.

Except that Sebastian wasn't next to him. Jake felt his absence a hundred times a day; Sebastian wasn't there in the morning to leave a wet streak across his face when his room was still dark and cold. He wasn't at the door, bouncing in circles and barking, when Jake arrived home from school. He wasn't there to crawl up onto the bed with Jake in the dark while his parents fought in angry, hushed voices when he was supposed to be sleeping.

"You'll see Sebastian again." That's what Jake's father told him when he took Sebastian away. "You'll see him again. I promise. And when you see him, he'll be the Sebastian you played with when you were little." Then he picked up Sebastian and looked down at Jake with a strange, glassy-eyed, faraway expression, as if he were trying to see the future and Jake was in the way. When Jake asked to go with him, his father told him, "No, Jake. Not this time. You'll see him again, I promise." The last thing Jake saw was a wisp of a white tail as his father turned and left the kitchen, closing the door behind him.

Dad came home alone.

All Jake had left were pictures in a faded green photo album Mom kept under the coffee table in the living room. He envied the sandy-haired little boy in the photos. He envied the bright smile on the boy's face, his mouth a patchwork of missing teeth, because in most of the photos Sebastian posed with him, eyes sparkling from a sea of white fur across his muzzle, receding into a rich gray along his back. Near the back of the album was a picture of Sebastian chasing a ball, all four legs off the ground. In the picture Sebastian was flying, his lolling tongue and wide eyes captured in a moment of pure joy.

Jake had been looking at that photo when his mom finally took a break from her studying to come in and lecture him about controlling his anger. He tried to control his anger at having to listen to it again by looking up to the ceiling and breathing, but that only made things worse. "Don't you roll your eyes at me," she said. "I've put up with just about as much of your attitude as I can stand." He tried to make her understand that he was looking at the ceiling, not rolling his eyes, but that only made her angrier, and he had to listen to ten minutes of *I Am Tired Of Your Excuses*, followed by a litany of everything he'd ever done wrong since he'd spoken his first word. Then he made the mistake of looking at the ceiling again.

When she told him to get out of her sight, he shoved the photo album across the coffee table. Maybe he shoved it a little too hard; it slid right off the opposite side and into his mother's shin. He didn't wait around to see if he had hurt her; he stomped down the hall and slammed the bedroom door, but not before throwing his Xbox into the hallway, the cables still attached to the back. She was going to take it anyway.

Jake hadn't climbed out the window until Dad came home. It wasn't that Jake was afraid of what his dad would do; he'd heard the "Respect Lecture" at least a hundred times, and he could probably predict his punishment word for word. *No Xbox, no bike, no four-wheeler, no nothing until you smarten up. Jake, you're better than this.*

What he hated was the fights. *Brad, you have to do something,* his mother would say, in that strange, perfectly clear whisper that carried out into the yard. Dad didn't whisper. *I'm out there every day busting my hump trying to keep food on the table.* That was how it always started. *Brad, you have to do something.* Once Mom said it, Jake knew what was next. He slid the window open, dropped onto the soft grass, and headed for his special place by the river.

It didn't take long for things to get too quiet. Jake missed Sebastian; together they could have sat there for hours by the river, watching the water flow past, him telling Sebastian about everything. Sebastian was probably the best listener on the entire planet. But Sebastian was gone, gone to whatever place dogs go when they don't come back from the vet.

Jake looked up at the sky, thankful that he could finally look up without causing a meltdown, and wondered how long he'd been out of the house. It seemed like hours. He stretched his legs and felt the cold air raise goosebumps underneath his shirt. His room was warm, at least, and he did have colored pencils and paper. Not as good as an Xbox, but better than sitting alone in the cold. If he was lucky, the fight would be over, and he could sneak back into his room before they knew he was gone and draw until it was time for dinner.

He clambered to his feet. The cold air forced a shiver from his body. He took one last look at the river before turning to the trail that led up the hill.

A strangely shaped chunk of ice floated lazily past him through the dark water. He had to look again. As he climbed over the pine trunk, he lost sight of it but spotted it just as it was about to round a bend in the river.

It looked exactly like a ship.

Nature had somehow created an ice ship. It had a pointed bow and a flat stern, and Jake imagined tiny ice sailors working below the deck.

He had to have it.

Jake darted after it, weaving through the pines and cedars that grew along the riverbank.

"Sebastian—"

He felt a stab of loss.

The ice ship had already covered a good distance, but the river curved to the north, giving him a chance to cut across through the woods and get ahead of it. Jake ran as fast as he could, scratching his arm on a hawthorn and nearly tripping over a fallen sapling still hidden in the snow. He shook off the obstacles and pushed on, determined to get his hands on the prize adrift in the icy water.

When he reached the place where the river flowed back toward him, the ship was nowhere to be seen, and he feared he'd lost it. Then it sailed into view, slicing through the water under full steam, hugging the opposite bank.

A sheet of ice still extended out from the next bend in the river. Jake hesitated as he stepped off the bank. He'd only have one chance to get his hands on that ice ship, if the ice was even thick enough to hold him that far out. A glimpse of the ship's hull convinced him to try. As he neared the edge, he got down on his hands and knees, and finally on his belly, inching his way across like a soldier beneath barbed wire.

It seemed solid enough. His dad had always told him not to trust ice. River ice was never safe, he said, but especially in spring. Jake considered turning back, but there was the ship, only a few feet away. A little more, and he'd be able to grab it and pull it out of the water. The ice chilled his belly, but the prospect of getting his hands on the ship overrode his discomfort. Only a few feet now.

The ice ship was gone.

Not the ice itself; the chunk floated past him, but something had happened to it. Jake lay on the ice and watched what had been his ship float by, nothing more than a miniature iceberg, like a thousand others he'd seen on the river.

Disappointed and suddenly very cold, Jake reversed course and crept back toward the bank. His arms and legs felt numb, and he could no longer feel his fingers. Creeping on his belly wasn't getting him to the bank fast enough. He decided to stand up.

Drawing his legs underneath him, he struggled into a kneeling position and attempted to stand. An ominous crack sounded beneath his feet, and Jake froze, his heart racing. Slowly, he got back to his knees, doing his best to distribute his weight evenly across the ice.

Stupid, Jake, Stupid.

The ice cracked again, and Jake launched himself toward the bank. The ice gave way beneath him, and the river reached up through the shards and wrapped cold tendrils of water around his waist. The frigid water closed over his head and ripped the breath from his body. He tried to fight his way back to the surface with arms numbed in the freezing water. Blind, mindless panic robbed him of any conscious thought, and when his face splashed through to the open air, he choked down a single, ragged breath before the river pulled him back under.

Darkness closed around him. All at once his vision seemed to blend into a gray mist. He kicked for the surface again, but with less energy than he had before. His body tingled and then he felt nothing. His head broke the surface once again. He sucked in a final breath.

He had time to cry out for his mother once before the river took him.

Chapter Two

Other than a vague sensation of drifting with the current, Jake felt nothing. The terror that gripped him subsided, leaving behind a sleepy, languorous feeling. He felt light, at peace, content to go wherever the river carried him. He was no longer cold, nor did he feel any particular need to breathe. It was a dream, he decided, and he'd wake up in his own bed to the sound of one of Mom's morning news shows and the aroma of coffee and toast in the air.

It would be all right.

He drifted for what seemed like a long time. Sometimes a thought would try to form in his mind, but would dissipate as quickly as it came, like a bubble in the water. Jake surrendered to the feeling, content to float in the darkness.

Something snagged on his shirt, tightening it around his neck and armpits. Water flowed through his fingers and toes and through his hair. Absolute darkness turned to gray, and then to a sparkling aquamarine, and then Jake's head burst through the surface into warm, bright light.

Heaviness returned to his body. He coughed, vomiting water through his mouth and nose. After a few seconds of terror, he took his first breath and opened his eyes.

Jake lay on a grassy riverbank beneath a canopy of tall trees. Broad leaves quaked and shimmered where the slight breeze touched them. The pale green in the leaves, the rich, vibrant grays and browns in the branches, and beyond them the deep blue of a cloudless sky all glowed with a clarity that left Jake gaping in stunned silence.

Those were not his trees. They weren't like any trees Jake had ever seen; even the smallest of them was as wide as he was tall. Branches spread in all directions, twisting and arching in intricate patterns, almost as if the canopy was woven from wood.

Wonder and fear mingled in his mind; as beautiful as it was, it wasn't familiar. He had no idea where the river had taken him.

"Mom? Dad?"

He remembered calling out to his mother before the water sucked him under. Perhaps she had noticed his absence and started after him. Maybe she'd plunged into the icy river and pulled him out just as he was about to—

Jake chose not to finish the thought.

"Mom?"

He sat up. The river ran in a wide, meandering path, forming the border of a vast forest. The river was much wider than his own, so wide that he could make out very little of what lay on the opposite bank. Nothing was certain.

His body warmed, shaking off the river's icy chill. The ground beneath him was covered in soft, fragrant grass, curiously warm. His shoes and socks were gone, and his clothes were different; he was dressed in a plain white t-shirt and brown denim pants with no pockets.

Possibilities crept into his mind. He'd been fished out of the river by a psychopath, thrown into a van, and carted off where his mother would never find him. He'd been captured by aliens and placed in some kind of huge habitat, like a fish tank for boys. A terrarium, where people kept pet lizards and turtles. Maybe the ground was warm because there was a heating pad underneath. Maybe he'd end up finding trays of food at regular intervals.

"Hello?" he said again, a little louder. His speculation wasn't getting him anywhere. He needed the person who pulled him out of the water.

"Hey!"

The silence was beginning to close in on him, the peace almost oppressive. He struggled to his feet. It was difficult to stand, as if his arms and legs had been asleep and were still waking up. He felt unnaturally heavy and clumsy. He took a step and stumbled. It felt like his body had forgotten how to walk, and he had to learn all over again.

"Who's there? Anybody?"

Only the low rush of the river and the quiet ripple

of air through the leaves above disturbed the quiet.

"You do not belong here."

It came to Jake as a deep, vibrant growl and seemed to come from everywhere at once. Startled, Jake hauled himself to his feet, searching the trees for the source.

"I don't even know where 'here' is," Jake said. "I was in the river—"

"I pulled you from the river. You are a Giver who does not swim."

"I swim good. It's just that the water was cold."

He could almost hear his teacher saying *You swim well, Jake. Not good.* Jake couldn't remember her name or her face.

"You are a Giver who does not swim. Now you are on dry ground. It is good to please the Givers."

Jake realized where the voice was coming from, and why he couldn't pinpoint its direction. He didn't hear the words or think them but felt them, the same way he could sometimes feel his mother's disappointment when he came home with another failed spelling test or his father's disapproval when the report cards came out.

"If you pulled me out, where are you?" Jake said. He spoke out loud; it felt more natural that way. There was no response.

"So you pulled me out of the water and now you're just going to leave me here? Where am I supposed to go?"

Then the voice spoke again. The feeling of it in Jake's mind was jarring.

"Givers know all. All Givers know the Calling-Place."

"Why do you keep calling me Giver? My name is Jake."

"You are a Giver. You have the Giver's scent. This is not the place for Givers."

"Do you have a name?" Jake asked. At least that would be something.

"They call me Ursus at the Howls."

"What are the Howls?"

Jake scanned the forest again, hoping for some movement; a rustle of a branch, anything that would betray the presence of another person. Ursus, whoever he was, said Jake had the Giver scent. He sniffed his arm, wondering if perhaps the river or his time on the grassy bank had given him a strong odor, but he smelled nothing.

"What do you mean I smell like a Giver? What's a Giver?"

His question hung in the air, unanswered, and Jake grew tired of waiting. Rivers always lead somewhere, he decided. What he wanted to do now was find his way home, and downriver seemed as good a direction as any.

Jake picked his way down the riverbank in the direction of the current. He walked for a few hundred feet, glancing around him, hoping to catch a glimpse of Ursus. He saw nothing but the trees, crowding the bank as far as he could see, up and down the river. He wondered what kind of a person Ursus was, rescuing him and then leaving him.

"The Calling-Place is not that way."

"Maybe you could show me where it is," Jake said. He spoke his words loudly, not knowing how far his voice would have to carry. He waited for a moment, watching, but Ursus didn't answer, and the forest remained as still and silent as a painting. He marveled again at its beauty; the magnificent trees, ancient and majestic, their colors so rich and deep that even his own idea of color paled in comparison. It was as if he had been blind for a lifetime and then by some miracle been given the gift of sight. Yet even as he stood in rapt amazement, he felt a sliver of fear in his mind. Fear, and a question, one that he almost dared not ask.

Where was he?

His memories began at the river. Even his name felt a little strange to him, a collection of sounds without meaning, but undeniably part of him. If he concentrated, he could come up with facts; stop signs were red, sometimes 'Y' was a vowel, the capital of Pennsylvania was Harrisburg. But about his own life, everything seemed shrouded in a thick fog, impenetrable. He felt lost, alone, as much adrift now as he had been before Ursus had pulled him from the river.

"Hey, Ursus," Jake said. His voice quivered. He swallowed to ward off the tears. "I think I'm lost."

From between two twisted roots, something moved. At first, its color seemed almost indistinguishable from the bark of the trees, but it moved closer, and Jake was able to get a better look.

Ursus was a dog.

Jake was sure that dogs were not supposed to be

that big. Ursus stood at least a head taller than Jake. He doubted his head would come up to the dog's shoulder. If he wanted to, Ursus could have split Jake in half with one snap of his massive jaws.

He came within twenty feet of Jake and stopped, regarding him with eyes the color of dark amber. Short, black hair stretched over rippling muscles that bunched around his forelegs and massive chest. His head was wide and heavy, with a thick snout and an upper lip that dipped down just underneath the lower jaw. Jake sensed no aggression from it; the dog regarded him with a strange, quiet sadness, something Jake felt more than he saw.

Ursus looked away, glancing down the wide curve of the river, then looked back at Jake.

"It is good to please the Givers," Ursus said.

Now that Ursus stood before him, Jake could see without a doubt that the dog didn't speak in the sense that he was familiar with. Somehow they were connected, closely enough he could sense the dog's pure thoughts, and his mind was able to form the dog's thoughts into something understandable.

"I'm lost, Ursus," Jake said. His voice caught in this throat. Saying it made it feel much more real.

"I will take you to the Calling-Place," said Ursus. "I will take you to where the Givers call the dogs."

"Thank you, Ursus."

"I will take you. Follow me," Ursus said. He turned toward the forest.

"Is it far?"

Ursus looked back at Jake. "Near and far is the same."

Jake didn't have time to ponder the dog's strange answer. Ursus plunged into the forest at a brisk trot.

Chapter Three

It felt more like flying than running. The dappled light through the treetops made the forest sparkle. The air was cool and filled him with renewed vigor each time he took a breath. He waited for the fatigue, for the burning in his legs and lungs that inevitably came when he ran too fast or too long, but it never came, and its absence was euphoric. There was no undergrowth, nothing to scratch his skin or catch his clothing, nothing at all to slow him down. Jake had nothing to do but run, and Ursus ran ahead of him, poetry and power with each spring, bunched muscles rippling beneath the short coat that glowed in the broken light from the canopy.

Jake wished he could run forever. If he could just keep running, he could leave behind the things that made him worry or made him cry. When he was running, he was alone but never lonely; the beating of his heart and the regular rhythm of his feet kept him company.

Gradually, the spaces between the trees lengthened until the light crowded out the shadow and the moss gave way to a thick carpet of springy turf. Ursus slowed down to a trot, and finally a walk. Ahead, the last of the trees clustered in small copses at the edge of a great, grassy field that sloped gradually downward and terminated at a vast canyon. From the forest's edge, the deep azure of the sky plunged down to meet it.

"The Calling-Place," said Ursus, without ceremony. He scratched at the turf for a moment and then hunkered down.

Jake saw nothing remarkable about the field; aside from the impossibly intense colors, it contained nothing that set it apart from the rest of the scenery.

"Where? I don't see anything. It's just an open field. Isn't there supposed to be people—Givers—here?"

"There are Givers at the Calling-Place." Ursus lay perfectly still, his massive head propped up on his left paw.

"Ursus, I don't see anything. Am I looking in the wrong spot?" The dog's answers began to frustrate him. If it was the Calling-Place, like Ursus implied, there should be someone doing some kind of calling. He ventured out a little from the edge of the forest and looked around. As far as Jake could see, the forest stretched on either side, a few hundred yards of flat grass separating the cliff edge from the woods. The cliff bent around, its curve so distant and so gradual that Jake could see nothing beyond the edge.

"What am I supposed to do? Throw myself off the

cliff? What's down there? More water? Look, if you just wanted to get rid of me, you could have just walked off before I saw you. You didn't have to trick me into coming out to a cliff. It was your idea to come to this stupid Calling-Place. I didn't even know there was a Calling-Place until you told me. I don't even know where I am or what I'm doing here. I just want to find my way home, ok? So could you just tell me what I'm supposed to do?"

Ursus rolled over onto his side and let out a contented sigh through his nose. The air whistled a little as his barrel-chest rose and fell.

"Ursus, come on!"

The dog's sudden lethargy was worrisome. Jake hoped the dog hadn't run himself to death on his account, but the dog's apparent disinterest meant that he was either too tired to help or he didn't intend to do anything else. Either way, Jake would be alone again and without even the river to provide any guidance.

"So what are you going to do? Just lay there?" Jake's voice cracked a little.

"You go to the Calling-Place. You find the other Givers. Go to the place where you can run free. I will stay here."

"What's that supposed to mean? There's nothing here!"

Ursus scratched at his ear with a front paw.

Jake left Ursus at the edge of the trees and ventured out all the way to the cliff's edge. His eyes widened. It wasn't a cliff at all but the top of a long ridge that gradually sloped into a wide valley. Tall grass shrouded the slope, interspersed with exquisite wildflowers that shimmered and changed color as they moved in the shifting breeze.

The grass rippled in long, languorous waves as the wind moved through it, and at times it took on the appearance of a vast green waterfall. All around the valley's edge was the ever-present forest. The slope was gentle enough for Jake to descend easily, but he could see nothing at the bottom of the valley but more grass and wildflowers. There were no people, no buildings, and no paths—nothing that would suggest any kind of human presence. It was beautiful, but the sight of it only disappointed him. He stalked back to the gigantic dog, who hadn't budged from his spot.

"There's nothing down there. There's nothing up here, and there's nothing in that forest. I would have been better off just following the river until it led somewhere instead of coming here with you."

"I will stay here," Ursus said.

"You said that already," Jake replied. "It's not like I have a lot of friends here, but I have to be honest. You're not really helping."

"You are a Giver. This is the Calling-Place," said Ursus.

"Oh, my God! What does that even mean?"

A memory flashed through his mind. It was only a flash, a bare sliver that whispered to him without words that it wasn't the first time he'd lost his temper with someone. He tried to think of who it might have been, but nothing came. Tears stung his eyes, and he stomped at the turf.

"Can't you at least point me in the right direction? Is it down the hill? Is it this way? Is it that way?" Jake wagged his finger in each direction as he asked his questions.

"There is much noise in you," Ursus said. He rolled back upright but didn't stand. He leveled his gaze at Jake. He seemed calm; unaffected by Jake's tirade.

"I just want some directions here!" Jake said. "I wish you would just tell me where I'm supposed to go!"

"You have much noise," said the giant dog. "That is what I know."

"So, you want me to be quiet? Is this one of those moments where you say something like 'as soon as you're quiet, you can go,' like a teacher or something?"

"You are a Giver. If you must bark, bark. If you must howl, howl."

Ursus flopped back down on his side and sighed again.

Jake thought hard, trying to come up with something, some way he could criticize the dog, to get him back for calling him a loudmouth. As he pondered his next salvo, the gentle, regular sound of Ursus's breathing and the rush of the wind through the broad leaves were all that disturbed the stillness.

The wind shifted and took on a different tone as it flowed down the valley's slope and caught the tall grass. Waving in the wind, the grass roared almost imperceptibly, like the breaking of surf in a seashell.

Jake took a deep breath. The smell of the forest mingled with the faint smell of grass and the rich, loamy smell of newly turned earth.

As beautiful and peaceful as it was, there was something wrong with it. Something missing. He sat down in the grass and closed his eyes. It came to him after a while.

There were no birds. Jake hadn't heard a single bird call since Ursus had dragged him up on the riverbank. There wasn't a bird anywhere. He looked at the grass that brushed against his bare feet. No insects either. And there was something even more strange about the place, something he hadn't noticed until he searched the sky for birds.

The sky stretched from horizon to horizon; a perfect, unbroken dome of deep azure. There was not a wisp of cloud as far as Jake could see, and there was no sun. He glanced around him in the grass and found that he cast no shadow. Somehow, light just seemed to radiate from everywhere at once, bright enough to illuminate everything it touched in fine detail, yet so gentle it was hardly noticeable. Jake craned his neck, certain that he must be wrong, that the sun must be hiding behind some copse of trees or a faraway hill.

"Ursus," he said, but before he could complete his question, he heard the faint but unmistakable sound of a dog barking. It was deep and resonant but high-pitched; the sound of happiness, of excitement, a welcome-home bark.

Out of the trees burst a German shepherd, large for his breed, but not as large as Ursus. The shepherd shot past Ursus and Jake at a full run, plunging headlong down into the valley, instantly lost in the high, waving grass. His voice carried in the wind and lingered after the dog disappeared. Jake stood and stared, unsure of what to do. He wasn't even entirely sure he hadn't imagined the whole thing.

"Go," said Ursus. "Follow the dogs. Follow them to the Calling-Place. I will stay here."

The German Shepherd's excited bark was like the bursting of a dam. All at once, a chorus of excited barks filled the air. Dogs, hundreds of them, emerged from the forest, dashing toward the canyon rim.

Jake rose to his feet. The dogs continued to pour from the forest, flashes of paws and fur sprinting for the canyon, intent on whatever lay in the tall grass beyond the rim.

He took a last look at Ursus. He breathed easily, lying on his side, appearing to take no notice whatsoever of the sudden appearance of so many of his kin.

"Sorry for yelling at you," Jake said. "And thanks for showing me the way."

"It is good to help the Givers."

"I wish you'd come with me, though. We could go check out the Calling-Place together."

"I will stay here," Ursus said.

Jake patted Ursus on the shoulder. "Well. See you around, I guess."

Ursus glanced at Jake and then gazed off into the distance. Jake patted Ursus again as the last of the dogs disappeared into the valley.

Jake followed.

The grass was much taller than it looked from the top of the ridge. If it hadn't been for the dogs trampling a path through, Jake would have lost sight of the sky. As it was, he could only see a few feet ahead, which forced him to slacken his pace.

All around him the joyful cacophony of barks and shifting grass filled the air. Jake caught a glimpse of a swatch of tail or the corner of a floppy ear, but otherwise saw nothing of his companions. They paid him no notice at all, dashing headlong toward the bottom of the valley.

The slope gradually leveled out, and Jake increased his speed a little, though he could still only see a few feet ahead. The dogs must have sped up as well; judging by their barks, they had opened a sizable lead on him.

The tall grass abruptly came to an end. Jake burst through. The German shepherd sprinted across a wide, green field toward a hill. The other dogs, spread in a ragged line, followed. Jake peered across the field, straining to see what or who the dogs were rushing toward.

People.

Hundreds, perhaps thousands of them. Jake couldn't begin to count them; the hillside vanished into a gray mist to either side. Some waved their arms, some knelt with their arms outstretched, and some clasped their hands together as if they were in prayer. Jake caught sight of the German shepherd. A man in the crowd separated himself from the others, waving the big dog in toward him. They met. The dog thrust its head between the man's knees, and the man bent over, wrapping his arms around the shepherd's chest, his head pressed into its back. The dog's tail wagged back and forth. The two stayed that way for a while. The man released his dog and knelt down so that the dog could sniff him and lick his face.

Jake wasn't close enough to see the man's expression, but he could guess that it was pure joy. It looked to Jake as if the dog and the man hadn't seen each other in a while. Jake wondered what had separated the two.

Now that he could see, he accelerated to a full sprint across the wide field. The man and his shepherd finished greeting each other, and they headed back up the mound until they were lost in the crowd. Jake ran and watched as dogs and their people met, embraced, and moved together back up the hill to disappear. It occurred to him as he ran that there weren't any other people running toward the hill, nor were any dogs running down.

Something was wrong.

"Hey!" he cried, hoping to catch the attention of one of the waiting owners. None made any indication that they heard him. In fact, they made no indication that they noticed any of the other people either. Fear twisted his gut, and he slowed down. Dogs rushed across the field toward the people who waited with open arms to welcome them. They were still so far away that Jake couldn't distinguish one person from another by their faces.

He stopped and turned around, wondering how far he'd come. The tall grass waved and rippled into the distance, masking his passage.

"Hello! My name's Jake! I'm lost! Can anyone help me?"

But there was no answer from the people on the hill. Jake's run slowed to a walk. He was no closer to the Calling-Place than when he'd started. Still walking, he watched the reunions unfold like a pageant on a distant stage.

Drenched in the light of an endless summer afternoon, the people gave their dogs hugs and kisses and belly rubs. Dogs leapt from the grass into their person's waiting arms or spun around in circles, overjoyed. One by one, each dog found a human companion, and together they wandered back up the mound's gentle, grassy slope until the last dog and his person met and embraced. Jake stopped and watched as they too made their way up the slope and disappeared.

"Hey! Don't leave me out here!"

The hill was deserted. The golden light that washed it was gone as well.

The ocean of tall grass and wildflowers rippled into the distance, sloping back up to the forest through which he and Ursus had passed.

Jake wished that Ursus was here; at least he would have someone he could talk to. But Ursus was somewhere at the top of the canyon taking a nap, or doing whatever dogs did in this strange place when there weren't ghost people calling for them.

Ghost people.

It was a silly idea, just something that popped into his mind, like a hundred other thoughts he had on a normal day.

But this was anything but a normal day. There weren't any such things as ghosts. But the more he thought about it, the less silly it became. That scared him; seeing one ghost would have been bad enough, but there were more people than he could count on that hill. Not one of them had made a sound. Not one of them noticed a boy running among the dogs. He was the only human among them; Jake should have stuck out like a pig in a chicken house.

Where am I? The thought repeated over and over in his head.

"Where am I?" he asked. As if in response, a puff of breeze tickled at the blades of grass at his feet.

"Where am I?" he asked louder. But the valley had no response for him.

"Where am I?" He shouted. His voice carried across the grass and dissipated. He shouted again, and again, but the wind and the grass paid him no attention.

This is a dream, he thought, and the idea comforted him. A dream! All he had to do was lie down in the grass and close his eyes. He'd wake up and everything would be all right.

He stretched out on the cool grass and stared up into the deep azure of a sunless sky. He wondered where the light came from. It was such a beautiful color, the sky, and he hoped he would remember that color, all the colors of this place when he awakened from his dream. He took a deep breath, relaxed, and closed his eyes.

His body felt light, and he began to drift. Images appeared in his mind, images of trees and a snow-covered trail that followed the course of a river. They were different trees, with needles for leaves and cones instead of fruit. Moss and pine needles covered the ground, visible in places where the snow had melted. Jake followed the trail down to a place where two of the trees had fallen. There was something familiar about it; he'd been there before, though he didn't know when or why.

He saw himself.

He sat in the snow in nothing but a stained white t-shirt, a pair of faded blue jeans, and his old gym shoes. There was a tear in the fabric near the toe, which is why his mother had gotten him new ones.

He huddled against the tree, his head buried in his arms, and every once in a while, glanced up toward the river. Finally, he got up, stretched, and took another look out across the water.

Something caught his eye.

He leaped over a fallen pine, running along the riverbank. Watching himself, Jake felt a sense of foreboding. Go home, Jake. Go home and forget whatever you're chasing. It isn't worth it.

Jake climbed out onto the ice shelf that protruded into the river. He crawled all the way out to the edge and reached into the water.

The ice boat.

No!

The ice cracked, and Jake plunged into the frigid water. He was no longer watching himself. He felt the icy tendrils of water curl around his arms and legs and chest, force its way into his mouth and nose; he felt the ache in his lungs for one more breath; felt his limbs tingle and watched the light slowly fade into darkness.

He sat up; his mind gripped in sheer panic. His breaths came as sobs. He opened his eyes.

Green grass rippling in the wind. Wildflowers. An azure sky. He understood.

He was dead.

Chapter Four

Jake had mixed feelings about being dead.

He wanted to be afraid. He wanted to cry. He wanted to call out to his mother, but even though he was sure all those things were what he was supposed to feel, he didn't really feel any of them. He felt numb, with only traces of sadness and loss lingering around the edges. Fear didn't make sense; he was already dead. The worst had happened.

Gazing out over the serene beauty all around him, he admitted that it could have been a lot worse. It hadn't hurt to die, and he still had all his fingers and toes.

The wind tumbled down the canyon and rustled the tall grass in long, majestic waves across the slope that led back to the forest. Overhead, the sunless sky stretched, without a wisp of cloud to interrupt. Wildflowers burst through with splashes of color; deep reds, bright yellows, and a few that seemed to change color as they waved back and forth in the wind. It was a desolate beauty; what was the point of going to Heaven if there was no one to share it with?

If it was Heaven.

He sat for a while in the grass and gazed out over the meadow toward the Calling-Place, though without the sun Jake had no way of knowing how long. He thought perhaps a new crowd of people would emerge, and he could try again to reach them.

No one came.

Jake forced his way back up the hill, pushing the thick stalks and broad blades of grass out of his way. If he couldn't find Ursus, he'd make for the river. The ground began sloping gently upward, which heartened him; at least he wouldn't end up walking in circles if he followed the slope.

As he walked, he tried to remember something about his past life, but beyond his name and the plunge into the river, it was entirely blank. He reassured himself by thinking of the things he did remember. He named the features of his face—these are my eyes, here are my ears, my nose, my mouth; named his arms, his legs, his feet. Beneath his feet was grass, and above his head was the sky. These things he knew, and he clung to that knowledge the way a drowning child might clutch to its father's neck. But no amount of concentration could bring back a single memory of who he was before the icy water and the darkness. The silence and the solitude surrounded him and settled on him like a heavy coat and, without consciously deciding to do so, Jake began to run.

His pace quickened as he felt himself nearing the top. The joy he'd felt earlier returned. The cool air in his lungs and the spring of his feet against the turf energized him and lifted his spirits. He felt hopeful, though he had no idea where he was going, unsure if he were running toward Ursus or away from the Calling-Place. It didn't seem to matter while he was moving.

He was deep in thought about what he would say to Ursus when the tall grass abruptly ended, and Jake found himself back on the high ridge overlooking the valley.

Ursus was nowhere to be seen.

Jake called to him, but there was no answer. Either the dog had moved off, following some scent, or Jake had emerged far from where he'd gone in.

"Ursus! I couldn't make it to the Calling-Place. Ursus?"

The dog's voice wasn't in his mind. Only the light brushing of wind in the broad leaves and the sound of rustling grass disturbed the quiet.

"Ursus? I really need help." The last part came out as a whisper. He expected tears, but none came. He called out for Ursus a couple more times, but they were half-hearted cries. He suspected the dog was gone, plodding through some remote section of the forest. If he hadn't forgotten Jake already, he probably thought Jake had joined the people at the Calling-Place, and his job was done.

Jake sat down against a nearby tree and waited, hoping that perhaps the dog had heard him and was heading in his direction. He tucked his knees into his chest and wrapped his arms around his shins. The horizon seemed terribly far off, but its beauty held no awe or joy for him. It just was, as he just was, something that happened to be there, an object without purpose or reason.

Jake wished the grass would just grow into his skin and melt him away. He tried drifting again, the way he did when he saw his own death, but his mind remained a blank. All he remembered was the river, and its icy water closing over his head, sparkling and deathly silent.

A dog barked in the distance. Jake leaped to his feet and ran out past the trees.

"Ursus!"

One bark was followed by another, and still another, and then dogs filled the forest, running toward the slope that would take them down to the Calling-Place, down to where their people waited for them. There was unbridled joy in their bodies as they vanished over the canyon rim and plunged into the tall grass. Watching them, knowing what was to come, Jake found an emotion that he thought he'd lost. He envied them, a thousand dogs running toward a sweet reunion with people who loved them.

Why them and not me? Jake thought. Isn't there anyone over there who wants to see me? A mother? A father? A grandmother? Anyone?

He made his way back into the darkness of the forest. He walked at first, watching the branches twist skyward, their ends covered in wide, deep-green leaves. He had no clear destination in mind; he just wanted to put some distance between himself and the Calling-Place. It would get more painful each time he had to watch. The walking helped, and before long, he stretched out his stride and ran as fast as he could, weaving in between the trees and watching the dappled light sparkle across the forest floor. He savored the cool, springy moss against his feet and the scent of the forest in his nose and mouth. The Calling-Place was somewhere behind him, farther and farther away with each step.

The farther he went, the more difficult it became to choose a path between the ancient trunks. He slowed down and finally stopped.

The trees were becoming more difficult to see. He looked up into the canopy; perhaps there was simply less light getting through the branches. But there were still traces of dappled light on the forest floor, and there were plenty of open places in the canopy for light to penetrate. The light was waning, there was no mistake, and seemed to be accelerating, as if someone had been playing with a dimmer switch.

So, Jake thought, there's night in Heaven.

A pale, silver light bathed the forest through the gaps in the branches. He could see the outlines of the trunks around him, not well enough to risk running, but enough to make his way without hurting himself. He didn't feel sleepy or tired, so he set off again at a leisurely walk. The silver light danced against the tree trunks, revealing details Jake hadn't noticed before. Some of the trees had scaly bark that resembled skin. Another trunk had parallel ridges that wound their way around the trunk in a delicate spiral pattern. The more he looked, the more he realized that each tree had its own unique beauty, and the idea captivated him so much that he barely noticed stepping into a clearing where the silver light shone almost as brightly as the day.

He looked up into a sky filled with stars that danced through the blackness as if they were alive, moving with perfect joy to a rhythm that only they could hear. They flowed in currents and swirled together in eddies, only to suddenly burst into motion in all directions before joining the vast flow once again.

Jake fell into the soft moss, transfixed. He lay on his back as the stars flowed past his vision in a silver river. They seemed close enough to touch, though his outstretched hand met only the cool air. In the stillness, Jake imagined that space had come closer, close enough to feel and be a part of, and if he just wished hard enough, he could disappear into it, and the stars would all welcome him back, and he'd be looking down instead of up.

Maybe he could do just that.

He stared into the silvery blackness and relaxed. He began to feel lighter, almost light enough to float above the moss, above the branches, and away. He heard music, distant and very faint, a sweet, pure harmony, beckoning him.

And he wanted to go.

Jake willed himself toward the stars, toward the music, to the silver river just beyond his reach. Upward, a little higher, and the music swelled within him. Voices, joyous voices, faint behind the music, sang. If he could just go a little farther, he would hear their words, though he already knew what they were telling him.

Welcome.

A growl rent the air, and the music shattered like spring ice. Jake fell back, heavy once again in his body. He opened his eyes. The stars were cold and distant, their song silenced.

The awful, screeching wail still hung in the air, nothing in it but rage. Exposed, abandoned by Ursus and the stars, Jake pressed himself against a tree.

Silver light still spilled through the clearing, but it was somehow colder, its brightness waned, and the shadows beneath the trees deepened to impenetrable darkness.

Another growl pierced the stillness, followed by the groan of metal scraping against metal. Both sounds seemed to come from Jake's left, beyond the clearing. Jake crawled, determined to put distance between himself and whatever was growling at him. He froze when he heard the creaking of old hinges and the thump of a heavy footstep coming from the right.

He was surrounded.

He cast about for somewhere to hide, but the clearing was broad and flat, offering no cover or concealment. Across the clearing, other noises rang out from the darkness. Jake couldn't identify them all, but they all sounded vaguely mechanical, like a machine with broken parts. They came from all sides, lurking in the dark.

The trees loomed around him. Until the noises began, Jake had thought them benign, their twisted, ancient trunks and broad leaves beautiful. In the wan light they looked misshapen instead of merely twisted, diseased instead of old. It was probably a trick of the light, made worse by his fear, but they seemed to be leaning, almost grasping at him. All around him, the harsh mechanical sounds grew louder, closer, answered by the low, baleful shriek that first disturbed the night. He cast furtive glances at the trees, wondering whether they would get him before the things lurking behind them closed in. Their branches dipped close to the ground and lingered there, waiting.

The trees were offering him refuge.

Jake stood and jumped for the nearest branch. He caught the end with one hand and pulled himself up into the safety of the higher branches, where the broad leaves and the darkness offered concealment. From his vantage point, he could see the entire clearing. He hoped that whatever was coming hadn't seen him.

All was still and quiet, as if the forest were holding its breath, and then an explosion of noise poured from out of the darkness, a terrible din of growling and thumping, metallic screeches and hurried movement. It rose to a crescendo and then something large and heavy emerged and landed hard on its side.

It was a cat. It struggled to its feet and peered back in the direction it had come, its low, angry growl loud enough to vibrate the branches of Jake's tree. It was at least as long as Jake was tall, with a massive head and a long tail. Its hair was erect, making it impossible for Jake to see how large it actually was, but its movements expressed a powerful, dangerous grace. Scratches and cuts marred its sides, visible where tufts of fur were missing, and a turn of its head revealed its tattered left ear. The cat remained defiant. Despite its wounds, there was still plenty of fight left in it.

If the cat knew Jake was in the tree, it gave no sign; its attention was fixed on what lay beyond the light. Neither the cat nor Jake had long to wait. Tall shambling things that walked like men emerged from the shadows, their bodies the source of the terrible, mechanical din.

The creatures had been pieced together out of junk. A bike frame formed the body of one, while another had a leg made of a ski pole, its head an old radio. They were tall, probably twice as tall as Jake, and fashioned from auto parts, kitchen appliances, belts, aluminium pallet straps, broken pieces of furniture, electrical wire, and other objects that Jake couldn't make out or didn't recognize. With each step, their bodies seemed to moan and cry out in protest, as if their very existence was painful.

Their bodies had been assembled haphazardly; some had one leg shorter than the other. One had something resembling an arm protruding from its back like a scorpion's tail. The junk-men, seven in all, formed a circle around the cat, who tried in vain to keep them all in sight.

They closed in, stepping almost in unison toward the angry cat in the center. Its eyes flashed yellow, catching the pale starlight. It bared its teeth at its enemies, hissing and spitting, its tail held high. The cat seemed to sense that for good or ill, the fight was coming to an end. It let out a long, loud cry, full of rage and defiance. The shambling junk-things gave no outward signs of fear, moving inexorably closer. Then, for a brief instant, they paused.

Jake tensed, dreading what was coming. It didn't take long.

The shambling figures surged forward, faster than Jake expected, and with one final battle cry from the cat, the fight was on. The cat tumbled and rolled, lashing out with its powerful hind legs, while the junk creatures lashed out with blows of their own. One by one, four of the junk-men fell to the cat's power, exploding into heaps of metal, plastic, and wood. The three that remained circled warily, mindful of the cat's deadly power. The closest had a toaster for its head, and another moved around on a pair of broken hockey sticks, bound together by leather and door hinges. The third was the one with the protrusion coming out of its back, a strange contraption of cables, pulleys, and weights taken from an exercise machine.

Jake stayed high in the tree. It seemed to be a fair fight, and he worried that if he showed himself, the cat might mistake him for one of the junk-men and attack him. The junk-men, on the other hand, might think him an ally of the cat. He tightened his grip on the branch and watched.

The creature with the scorpion tail circled around behind the cat, while the other two made feints, keeping its attention fixed on them. The ploy worked; with a spring, the scorpion-back looped a length of wire around the cat's tail and wrapped the free end around the trunk of a nearby tree. The cat whipped around, lashing out at the wire to no effect.

The toaster-head looped a wire around the cat's head, while the other managed to snag its hind leg. The cat fought, clawing with its free paws, but it was futile; the creatures had it securely bound.

Despite their advantage, the junk-men were at a stalemate. The cat was largely immobile, but in order to keep it that way, they had to maintain tension on the wires. The cat struggled and hissed, swiping at them with its free paws, but they kept themselves out of range. It looked to Jake as if the junk-men were prepared to wear the cat out before they approached it. Gradually, the cat's struggles became less pronounced. It was only a matter of time.

"No!" Jake shouted.

The word escaped from Jake's mouth before he could stop himself. Something else inside him had taken over. He dangled from the branch and dropped to the forest floor. All three of the junk men turned to look at him.

His first urge was to run into the darkness and find a place to hide, but another look at the cat kept him rooted in place.

"Why don't you leave that cat alone?" The fearful tremor in his voice embarrassed him. The junk-men peered at Jake, as if sizing him up, and then turned their attention back to the cat. The toaster-head began to lean backward, tightening the noose around the cat's throat.

"Hey! Let the cat go!"

But the creature ignored him. The cat let out a terrible, choking cough.

"Leave him alone, I said!" He grabbed at the nearest creature's arm. It was much more substantial than it looked. A flick of its rusted elbow sent Jake tumbling backward into a pile of the creatures' fallen comrades. Seething, Jake scrambled to his feet.

Sitting next to him in the rubbish was an ax-handle fashioned out of some light-colored wood. Silver starlight played across its length. Jake picked it up. It was heavy and solid, its surface polished smooth. He tapped it against his palm, hard enough to feel a sting.

He lifted it over his head and chopped down into the creature's knee. It shattered in a satisfying spray of wood and screws, sending pieces of rusted hinge across the clearing. The junk-man toppled sideways, and the wire around the cat's leg went slack.

With its leg now free, the cat rolled back to its feet and lunged at the toaster-head, stopped short by the wire on its tail. The toaster-head scurried backward, adding tension on the cat's throat.

Jake ducked under the wire and took a swing at scorpion-back. This creature was larger and much stronger than the first one, and it blocked Jake's strike easily with an arm fashioned from a fireplace poker. Jake wasn't prepared for the creature's power; the blow sent pain through Jake's hands, and the ax handle flew from his grasp, landing somewhere in the shadows on the clearing's edge.

Now he had their attention.

The scorpion-back had an old portable television set for a head, and Jake caught his own reflection in the darkened screen. He saw himself as they saw him, a skinny, barefoot thing, small and terribly, terribly afraid. He backed away. Every pore in his body screamed run, but before he could obey, something closed around his ankle and jerked him from his feet.

Jake's ankle was caught in a fallen junk-man's grip, its hand a c-clamp that slowly tightened. It was already painful; a few more turns of the screw and it would be unbearable. He kicked out with his free foot. It connected, but the blow did nothing to extricate his ankle.

The pain intensified. The junk-man dragged him closer. Its bulk blotted out the stars, and Jake smelled metal and grease. He cried out in pain as the thing tightened down on his ankle again.

Jake's fingers searched the ground for another weapon. He reached down and grabbed the clamp around his ankle, hoping to relieve some of the pressure, but he couldn't budge it.

The thing pulled back, trying to dislodge Jake's hands. Jake held on tight, but the creature was strong, and Jake's fingers slipped down the smooth metal until they became wedged against a tab protruding from the clamp's underside. He pulled against the tab with his fingers until it gave with an audible pop. The pressure on his ankle was gone. He kicked his leg, and the clamp slid free.

He tried to roll to his feet, but his ankle wouldn't support his weight and he went down on his backside.

The junk-man, undaunted, crawled after him. Jake retreated. It came on, implacable, pulling itself along on its arms. Jake's entire world narrowed to encompass only the thing dragging itself inexorably forward, gaining ground on him with each pull of its makeshift arms. Time slowed, and Jake was powerless to quell the panic that rose inside his chest. His hand bumped against something. Something wooden.

The ax handle.

It hadn't flown as far as he thought, landing between the exposed roots of a tree on the edge of the clearing. He snatched it up and used it to help him regain his feet. Panic drained away, and where the panic had been, rage filled the void. Jake felt the weight of the ax handle as the junk-man closed the space between them.

He struck the creature again and again, smashing it into pieces. He was blind to everything else, his anger uncaged, suddenly free to rush where it will, destroying what lay in its path with terrible, indiscriminate power. He struck the remnants until the ax handle cracked and split in two. He relaxed his grip, allowing the lower piece to slip from his fingers and land in what remained of his adversary. His body felt heavy, and he sank down into the soft moss.

A warm breeze stirred the air near his right ear. He turned and gazed straight into the pale, yellow eyes of the cat, whose nose was no more than an inch from his.

Chapter Five

Jake dared not move. The cat eyed Jake with a mixture of curiosity and disdain. A glint of starlight fell upon a piece of wire still wrapped around the cat's neck.

Its long, shaggy coat was a pale, golden color, ending with a strip of white running down the breast to its underside. The eyes were yellow; they had an otherworldly glow, as if they reflected more starlight than they took in.

Old scars crisscrossed its face, and Jake got a better look at the cat's torn left ear. There was no blood; like the scars, it was an old injury, long since healed, one small episode in the long record of violence recorded on his body.

The cat broke the silence between them.

"You are not dog. You are not cat. You are not one of them."

Jake was relieved to learn that it didn't consider him an enemy. As it had when Ursus spoke to him, the cat's voice seemed to come from somewhere deep in his own mind.

"My name is Jake."

He relaxed a little; if the cat meant him any harm, it could have easily done it by now. But it seemed more curious and confused than angry.

"You are a Giver," said the cat. "This is not the place for Givers."

Jake bristled at the cat's remark. He glanced around the clearing, where pieces of the junk-men lay scattered in haphazard piles.

"I don't think it's the place for cats, either."

"I will not stay," said the cat. "I will return to the grasslands."

"Hey, you still have a piece of wire around your neck." Jake pointed but didn't touch. "I can take it off for you if you want."

The cat dropped down to its belly. "You may."

It sat perfectly still and waited for Jake to get rid of the wire. The cat had an imperial bearing, as if he were accustomed to being served in such a manner. Had he not seen what the cat was capable of in a fight, he might have been offended. As it was, he thought it better to do what he could to stay on the cat's good side.

Gingerly, he ran his fingers through the long, wavy hair on the cat's neck, following the wire to where it was attached. It was thin and firm. There was no insulation covering the bare metal; it was more like baling wire than anything electrical. Jake located the knot on the other side of the cat's head. The cat's struggles left the wire hopelessly tangled and twisted, like a twist-tie on a bag of bread, and Jake simply wasn't strong enough to pry the wire apart and reverse the twist.

"It's on there pretty good."

"If you are too weak, I will find help in the grassland," said the cat.

"No, wait," said Jake. He thought of the cat going to its friends in the grassland and telling them about the weak, pathetic Giver he rescued in the woods, and he decided he wasn't going to give the cat that kind of satisfaction.

"Stay here for a minute. I'll bet there's something in all this junk I can use as a tool." He searched around the piles for something he could use to pry the wire apart. He tried a broken pair of scissors, the fireplace poker, and a garden trowel, but none of them worked. The c-clamp didn't work either. Finally, he located a leather work glove at the bottom of the pile. He put it on and tried again. He pried, as hard as he could, but the glove offered him no real advantage apart from protecting his hands from being cut. His frustration got the better of him, and he bent the wire sideways, growling.

That was it!

He bent the wire back and forth, thankful for the leather glove. The cat tensed, likely because the wire was growing hot, but it didn't flinch or ask Jake to stop what he was doing. The heat was a good sign; it meant that the wire was probably about to break.

"Hold on, cat. It's about to go."

"It is burning my neck," the cat said, but he remained still.

"Almost there," Jake said, feeling the tension

mounting in the cat's body. If the wire didn't give way soon, Jake would have to stop, or he'd risk having the cat turn on him. Despite the danger, Jake bent the wire back and forth until finally it gave way with a loud snap, taking most of the tangle with it.

"Hey, I got it!"

But that wasn't entirely true. A closer inspection revealed that the break left the wire still looped around the cat's neck. The tangle had broken unevenly, leaving enough wire for Jake to get his thumbs around. He regretted it immediately as a searing pain shot through his hand.

"Hot!" Jake said, slapping his hand against his leg. He expected the cat to give him an "I told you so," but the cat remained silent. Jake spit on his thumb and gave it another try but the saliva made the wire too slippery. He dried it off with the bottom edge of his shirt and made another attempt. This time he was able to twist the remainder of the wire apart, and the cat's erstwhile collar slipped away from its neck.

"There, you're free."

"Almost free," said the cat. "There is something around my back leg. I wish to have it off." The cat rolled to its side, giving Jake access to both its hind legs. He looked but found nothing.

"Are you sure? It looks fine to me."

Jake got down on all fours and inspected the cat's rear legs from the paws up to where the legs joined the body. The wan starlight revealed nothing he hadn't seen before. He tried inspecting it with his fingers and he was rewarded with a stinging pain.

Gingerly, he felt around for it and finally located it. Thick, matted fur obscured the site and Jake brushed it to the side to get a closer look.

Embedded in the back of his leg was a fishhook. It was a large one, the curve about as big around as Jake's big toe. The barb was buried in the flesh in the back part of its leg. He tugged on it gently, eliciting a surprised twitch from the cat's leg. Jake was no veterinarian, but he knew he couldn't pull it out without taking a sizable chunk of meat with it.

"I found it. I think I can get it out, but you're not going to like how I do it."

"Do what you must," said the cat. "I will stay quiet."

"You sure? This is probably going to hurt a lot."

He took the cat's silence for acquiescence. He couldn't yank it out, but he thought he might be able to push it through the skin and get it out that way. The ring that would have connected a fishing line to the hook had broken off, so once he pushed it through the skin on the other side, the hook would slide out easily.

He took a deep breath. He'd seen the full range and power of the cat's claws, and he didn't want them being used on him, especially when he was trying to help. He sat there for a minute or two, unwilling to proceed.

The cat's golden eyes flashed in the starlight. "You have done nothing."

"It's going to hurt," said Jake. "I have to push it back through your skin and then pull it out."

"It hurts now. Do what you must. I will stay quiet."

Jake took another deep breath. The fishhook

protruded from the flesh halfway, like an ax embedded in a stump. There was no trace of blood on the hook or around the wound. Almost shaking with fear, he grasped the hook between the thumb and forefinger of his right hand, but that was no good; he'd have to bend his wrist at an unnatural angle to push it through. He switched hands, took a deep breath, and swallowed hard.

"All right. Here goes. Remember, you promised."

He steeled himself. With the thumb and forefinger of his right hand, he stretched the skin out and with his left, pulled hard on the straight section of the hook. He watched as the skin distended, then broke as the brass barb burst through. The cat's breath came sharp and fast, but otherwise, it remained perfectly still.

Jake grabbed the barb on both sides and pulled. The hook slid out through the new hole, and he found himself staring at the large fishhook held between his thumb and forefinger, the cold metal glinting in the pale starlight. He found it ugly and obscene, especially in the light of the stars, and he cast it away.

"I got it." It didn't seem real until he said it.

"Now I am free," said the cat. "And that is how I shall stay."

Its ears twitched and turned backward, and the cat sprang up to its full height once again. Jake clambered as fast as he could away from the cat, terrified. But its motion wasn't aggressive; its attention seemed fixed on something behind Jake, in the darkness beyond the clearing.

"They are coming," he said.

"More?"

Jake peered into the darkness. He hadn't heard anything. The junk-man he fought had nearly broken his ankle. He didn't want to consider what would happen if he had to fight two or three.

"Climb the tree," said the cat.

"What about you? Aren't they hunting you?" As he said it, he made his way back toward the tree he'd occupied earlier. The cat stretched, revealing ten long, sharp, curved claws.

"They are not hunting me now," it said. "I am hunting them."

Jake clambered back up into the tree. The cat looked up, boring into him with its large, yellow eyes.

"I am Samuel," the cat said. "And I will not forget."

Samuel turned and vanished into the darkness beyond the clearing.

Chapter Six

Jake found a place where a large, thick branch cradled his back so that he could almost lie down against it. The branch faced out over the forest, but Jake didn't mind the view; the last thing he wanted was to be reminded of the monsters that lay broken and scattered across the moss.

He kept his gaze fixed on the swatches of sky visible between the branches overhead. From beneath the treetops, Jake could still see stars flowing through the night sky like a silver river, but that was all. He tried to close his eyes and will himself closer to them, closer to where the music had beckoned him, but he could not force the images of the junk-men from his mind. They towered over him, reaching for him with hands of metal and wire and wood. Gradually, the music faded entirely from his memory, and he was left with an unbearable longing.

He stood up, using the branch above him to balance.

"Hey!" he shouted. "I want to go! I don't belong here! Hey! Aren't you listening?"

There was no answer.

"What am I doing here?" His question ended in a long, desperate scream. The stars flowed impassively by in distant eddies and whorls, and Jake could do nothing but watch them pass.

His rage spent, Jake sank back down, leaning against the trunk of the ancient tree, and stared off into the darkness.

"What am I doing here?" It came out as a whisper this time, a final, dejected plea for guidance. His limbs felt heavy and weak. He closed his eyes again, expecting the junk-men to be there waiting for him, but they were gone. In their place was only darkness, as deep and cold as anything he'd ever felt. The cold washed over him, numbing him. He could no longer feel the bark of the tree through his shirt or against his feet. He was adrift, unattached, somewhere between the forest and where he should have been, and through the darkness, he heard voices.

He could not separate them, nor make out what they were saying. They tumbled over each other, like water over rocks, some pleading, some calm, some terse. He tried to will himself to the voices as he had to the music, but his body was heavy and cold and would not obey him. He hovered there in the dark for some time, until gradually the voices melted and coalesced into a single word, repeated over and over.

Jake, Jake, Jake—

"Jake."

Overhead, broad leaves fluttered in the breeze under an azure sky. A few paces away, Ursus loomed over him, sitting on his enormous haunches and looking intently in his direction. Jake realized that he was no longer in the tree and that somehow, he'd missed daybreak.

"There was a cat here," the dog said.

The dog's presence was a profound relief. Without thinking, Jake scrambled to his feet and threw himself against Ursus, pressing his face into the dog's muscular shoulder. If Ursus disliked it, he made no sign. Jake stayed there for some time; the dog's presence was like an anchor, a familiar face in a forest of strangers.

"How did you find me?" he asked, finally pulling away.

"Your scent was in the forest," Ursus said. "I followed the scent. You cried out. I found you under the tree. You smell of cat. And something else."

Jake told Ursus of his flight from the Calling-Place, and all that had happened since. The dog offered nothing; he lay down in the moss and rested his chin on his paw. The dog's lack of concern galled Jake. Ursus hadn't even asked him if he was all right.

"So?" Jake said.

Ursus said nothing.

"So what am I supposed to do?" Jake prompted.

"You are the Giver," said Ursus. "Givers know all."

"I got news for you. Givers don't know all. Givers don't know half the stuff you think we know. At least I don't. I can't even remember who my parents are. I can't remember anything except my first name and falling in the river. I don't know why I ended up here. Maybe if I could just remember who I was, I'd know where I'm supposed to go. But I can't remember a thing, so I guess I'm just supposed to wander around this forest until one of those junk-men gets me."

Jake stood up and motioned for Ursus to follow him.

"Come on. They're right over here." Jake wandered into the clearing, expecting to find the wreckage of the previous night's battle. "The one that almost killed me was—"

Jake's voice trailed off. Deep, rich, green grass warmed by the light was all there was to see. He dropped to all fours and searched through the blades of grass for something, a bit of wire or a screw or a piece of torn hinge, anything that would prove that there had been a battle. His search turned up nothing. All the while, Ursus watched him from his vantage point near the tree.

Jake's frustration boiled over.

"They were right here!" he shouted. "Samuel was tangled up in wires right here. I'm telling you, there was a fight here last night. I'm not crazy. I know there was a fight here. How come you're just laying there? Don't you believe me? Why don't you do something? I hate this place. It doesn't make any sense! I can't even remember who I'm supposed to be!" He collapsed into the grass and rolled over on his back. He stared into the blue until it filled his vision. He tried to cry, but no tears would come.

A shadow passed over him, and for a second, Jake

thought the forest had once again descended into night until he saw two huge brown eyes looking down at him.

"I will take you to the Howl," Ursus said.

"Is it far?"

"Near and far is the same."

"Yeah, you said that before." He sat up. Though he had no idea what a Howl was or how it could help him, the dog's offer made him feel better. At least for a short time, he had a destination. He still didn't completely understand what Ursus meant by near and far being the same. There were more important things to ask about.

"What's at the Howl?" Jake said.

"The Howl is where the packs gather. Many packs. Many dogs."

Jake was disappointed. "I already saw many dogs, remember? The Calling-Place?"

"Not like the Calling-Place."

"Well, what do they do there?"

"They remember."

That was enough for Jake. He rose to his feet. He expected a little pain in his ankle, but it felt fine. In fact, his entire body was pain-free, despite the long-distance running and the battle with the junk-men. Even his hands displayed no signs of struggle. He had certainly swung the ax-handle enough to cause at least a little raw skin, but his hands were none the worse for it.

Maybe the dogs could help him remember who he was. He wasn't sure how they would be able to do that, but it was worth a try. Far better than wandering around in the woods, waiting for the junk-men to come back.

"Let's go to the Howl, then."

"I will take you. Follow me." Ursus sprang from the grass and burst into a ground-eating run. His speed took Jake by surprise, and he had to sprint to keep the big dog in sight.

Ursus was already a hundred yards ahead and growing more distant with each step. The dappled light, which had seemed beautiful to Jake the day before, now carried with it a sense of concealed danger, as if the shadows created by the branches harbored some hidden evil. Light and dark shifted so quickly that Jake's eyes had no time to adjust. Twice he nearly ran into a tree trunk while trying to locate Ursus far ahead.

Eventually, Jake lost him entirely. He slowed down to a walk and finally stopped.

The canopy blocked out most of the light; the shadows and the thick trunks made it impossible for Jake to see more than a few yards in any direction. The forest was absolutely still and silent; there was nothing to suggest the presence of the junk-men or the cat, but Jake's imagination put them behind every tree. His fear gave way to frustration, and finally, anger. For the second time, Ursus had left him. Perhaps the big dog just wanted to be rid of him, but was too afraid to come out and say it.

"Great. By myself again. What am I supposed to do now, you stupid dog? It's not like I can sniff out your trail on the ground. You couldn't look behind you and notice that I was five hundred miles back?" He stretched his arms, exasperated.

"Don't worry about it," Jake said. "I'll find the stupid Howl myself. It can't be far. Near and far is the same, remember? Maybe it's right behind this tree over here."

He found nothing but moss and a view of the tree next to it.

"Nope!"

Jake paced between the trees. His anger spread past Ursus and to whoever or whatever had caused him to end up all alone in a big forest filled with dead dogs and cats. He must have been a terrible person in his past life to be sent to Dog Heaven instead of People Heaven. Or maybe, he thought, whoever made decisions on where to put people was really an idiot, and the reason for his being among dogs instead of people had nothing to do with punishment at all. Maybe it was just some kind of stupid office error, or worse, dumb luck. The thought of being a victim of random chance was almost too much for him. He kicked at a tree trunk before remembering that he wasn't wearing any shoes.

There was a sharp crack, and then a searing pain shot up his foot and continued through his ankle and halfway up his leg.

"Ow!" He hopped around, rubbing his injured foot.

"I hate this stupid place!" Jake shouted into the canopy.

"This is not the Howl."

Jake turned, and there was Ursus, sitting on his

haunches. The dog's proximity startled him.

"Where did you come from?"

"I came from where I was."

"No. I mean, how did you sneak up on me like that? You're not exactly hard to miss."

"There is much noise in you," said Ursus. "I did not sneak."

"Fine, whatever. So, could you take me to the Howl? Maybe a little slower this time? I kicked a tree and hurt my foot."

"I will run slower," said Ursus. He trotted off again, but this time Jake was able to keep up fairly easily. The forest slid by, but Jake couldn't recapture the joy he'd experienced when they first ran through the forest. Jake regretted calling Ursus stupid. Ursus was the only person, dog or otherwise, who'd offered him any kind of assistance since he had fallen into the river.

"So, what are all the dogs trying to remember?"

"Our names," said Ursus.

They ran for a time in silence. The forest stretched on and on, lush, beautiful, and in Jake's mind, terribly empty. Not a bird or a squirrel broke the silence. The longer they ran, the more oppressive it became, but Jake could think of nothing to say that would fill the silent void. An ache began to form in him, a vague but persistent loneliness for the presence of another human being. He wondered as he ran about the people he had known before he had fallen into the river. He must have had friends, parents, perhaps brothers and sisters. It made him sad that he might never know if anyone cared that he was gone.

The ground began to slope gradually upward. Outcroppings of gray stone jutted out from the forest floor, and the broad-leafed trees gave way to tall conifers, their needles long and soft. The slope became increasingly steep. Jake marveled at the resilience of his body; he felt just as fresh as he had when he and Ursus set off. The hill seemed to make no difference at all in the state of his muscles. Jake felt that if he wanted to, he could climb indefinitely. He looked down the hill and noticed that the last of the broad-leafed trees was below him. Thick stands of tall pines obscured his view, much to Jake's disappointment; he would have liked to see the view of the forest from a high vantage point.

On and on they climbed, and Jake wondered if they would ever reach the top. Up ahead, a jumble of tall gray boulders lay strewn against the hillside, blocking their path. Ursus reached the first boulder and stopped.

"Climb," Ursus said. "At the top you will find the Howl. Many dogs, many packs. You will see."

Jake looked up at the rocky hillside. The boulders weren't as close together as they seemed to be from a distance. Jake saw several paths that would easily lead him to the top without having to climb any boulders at all.

"So, let's go," Jake said. "Lead the way."

But Ursus had already hunkered down in the moss.

Jake leaned against a boulder. "Why are we resting? I don't feel tired."

"I will stay here," said Ursus.

Jake rolled his eyes. "Again? Well, what if I want to stay here too?"

"You are the Giver. If you wish to stay, stay. If you wish to remember, climb. I will stay here."

Jake stood for a moment, watching Ursus. The dog rolled on to his side, apparently ready for a nap. His muscles bunched and corded beneath a short, shiny brown coat, so deep and rich that it was almost black. Jake had seen the dog move, and there was no reason at all that Ursus could not make the climb.

"Why can't you come with me?"

"I will stay here."

Jake knew he wasn't going to get any more information out of the dog. Once Ursus' mind was made up, there seemed to be no changing it.

Jake sighed and then began making his way up the rocky slope. Before he got too far, he stopped and turned around. He could just see the dog's paws sticking out beyond a nearby rock.

"You're not going to wander off, are you?" Jake said.

"I will stay here."

"Thanks for taking me here. You're a good friend. Well, sort of."

"It is good to help the Givers."

The climb was easy at first; the gaps between were wide, creating winding paths up the hill, and it didn't take long for Jake to become lost in the twists and turns. Gray boulders loomed over him, the stone cool and smooth to the touch. The ground was covered with the same soft grass he'd walked through near the Calling-Place. His excitement grew as he climbed. Somehow, just having a destination made him feel better, and he gave himself over to the joy of the climb.

The paths gradually narrowed, converging until there was only one, continuing upward as far as Jake could see. He briefly considered giving up and going back down to Ursus. Perhaps there was another, easier path to the Howl, but he didn't want Ursus thinking he was a weakling.

Ursus told him that near and far were the same. He climbed, expecting his strange new endurance to eventually fail him, but it seemed he could keep going as long as he cared to. His mind was made up; he would go as long as necessary to reach the top.

Once he glanced downward to measure his progress, but the ground beneath him was shrouded in mist. He wondered if he wasn't going to climb right into the silver river of stars he'd seen the night before.

The slope began to lessen, imperceptibly at first, but before long, it was gentle enough for him to regain his feet. Just before he reached the crest, he heard the barking of a dog and then another. Mixed with the sounds of dogs was the low roar of rushing water. He ran the rest of the way.

"Hello!" he shouted. "I'm friendly!"

It sounded strange coming out of his mouth, but it was the only thing Jake could think of to say. At the top of the hill was a wide, thickly forested plateau. From somewhere beyond the tree line came the answer to Jake's call. First one, then another, and finally a chorus of barks loud enough to make the trees tremble.

He paused, unsure of himself. Just because he was friendly didn't mean that they would be. He thought of the climb he'd just made. He doubted he'd be able to get down the same way he came up. The only way open to him was through the trees. He took a deep breath and stepped into the thick stand of pines.

The woods became quiet again; apparently the dogs had lost interest. Jake expected at any moment to come across one or two of them lounging in the soft grass that covered the ground, but he found none. A short time later, the woods abruptly came to an end, and Jake looked out over an enormous hollow, dominated in the center by a pool of water fed by a waterfall, its source obscured in deep, silver mist. It was spectacularly beautiful. Jake stood for a moment, paralyzed by a sense of overwhelming awe. So much was he overcome by the view that it took him a while before he noticed the dogs.

There were hundreds of them, lounging by the water, sleeping in the grass, chasing, playing, sniffing. There was plenty of room for all of them, though some preferred to cluster together in groups. There was an air of contentment about them, mixed with a sense of expectation, an excitement barely held in check. The roar of the waterfall filled the air, carrying with it a deep, abiding sense of peace. It was the first time since Ursus pulled him out of the river that Jake believed he'd found Heaven.

A Saint Bernard napped about twenty yards from where Jake stood. Its ears perked up, and the dog's massive head rose from out of the grass. He turned and locked eyes with Jake. For an instant, Jake was seized by fear, and he nearly bolted for the hillside. Then the dog leaped to its paws and spun around in an expression of joy.

"A Giver!" it bellowed. Jake's mind rattled with the force of it. "A Giver has come to the Howl!"

Chapter Seven

Dogs surrounded him. Jake was inundated with a torrent of individual requests. "Giver, I am called King!" "Giver, a belly-scratch!" "Giver, throw something, I will chase!" "Giver, I am called Bear! I wish to play tug-of-war! Have you brought a chew-toy for me?" "Giver, I am waiting for Daddy to call my name from the Calling-Place! Do you know Daddy? He is a Giver, like you." "Giver—

"Hold on," said Jake, "I can't hear—"

"Giver! I can shake!"

"Giver! I wish to wrestle! I wish to play!"

"Please!" Jake's voice was drowned out by the cacophony of questions and greetings that echoed in his mind; his body immobilized by suffocating press of canine bodies.

"I need your help!"

But the dogs were too immersed in their own excitement to hear him. They jostled and crawled over one another, forgetting everything else in their desire to see him, touch him, smell him. Something struck him from behind and he went down, lost in a sea of furry legs and snouts and tongues. It was worse than the river, worse than the junk-men, and in his fright, he cried out as loud as he could.

"Ursus said you could help me. Please help!"

The hollow was instantly silent. The dogs scrambled away from him and dropped to their bellies. The nearest dog, a large Irish Setter, cowered at least ten yards away from him. Many of the dogs lay on their backs, exposing their undersides, their tails tucked between their back legs. Here and there in the crowd, dogs whimpered. None dared speak.

At first Jake thought it was the word please which drove the dogs away, but that didn't make any sense. It was something else.

Ursus.

Some of the dogs had simply run away and now lingered along the edge of the forest or by the waterfall. The rest remained on their bellies or on their backs, neither speaking nor moving.

Jake picked himself up off the turf, relieved to have some space to move and breathe again. Along with the relief came guilt; he had never expected such a reaction, and he was sorry to see the dogs so terrified.

"Hey, it's all right. No one is going to hurt you. I'm friendly, I promise."

The dogs didn't move.

Jake wasn't sure what to do. If they stayed on their bellies, they weren't going to be any help at all. He could not have known that Ursus would inspire such a reaction, but he felt responsible nonetheless.

"He's not coming up here. He told me he was going to stay down there at the bottom of the hill."

Jake looked out over the sea of fur, and a lone snout poked up into the open air. It belonged to a black and white border collie, who eyed Jake with a mixture of fear and distrust. It seemed to believe him, however; it did not look away when Jake met its gaze.

"Ursus is not coming?"

"No. You don't have to be afraid of him anyway. He's a nice dog. He rescued me from the river, and he took me to the Calling-Place, and then he brought me here. But I promise, he's not coming up here. It's just me."

"No Givers come from the Calling-Place." The border collie backed up a step.

"I didn't come from the Calling-Place," said Jake. "I came from the river. Ursus pulled me out. He told me you could help me remember. Then maybe I'll know where I'm supposed to go."

"Ursus is not here to take the rest of us?"

"What do you mean? Ursus hasn't taken anybody."

The border collie dropped to her belly at the mention of Ursus. Jake tried to calm her down and keep her talking. He wouldn't get anywhere if all the dogs were afraid of him.

"I'm Jake. What should I call you?"

"I am called Sarafina at the Howls," she said.

"Come on, everybody. Get up," Jake said. "It's all right. No one is going to hurt you."

One by one, the dogs slowly got back on their

paws. Many still hung their heads, their ears pinned back. Sarafina trotted up and accepted Jake's hand against her muzzle. A few of the braver dogs did the same. Most of the other dogs wandered off and before long were busy sleeping, playing, or following a scent trail, apparently none the worse for their experience.

"Many dogs are missing. Many packs," said Sarafina. "I think. I remember."

"And you think Ursus had something to do with it?"

"Many dogs are missing. That is what I know,"

"I saw lots of dogs at the Calling-Place. That must be where they went." He couldn't bring himself to believe that Ursus was worthy of Sarafina's fear. Ursus hadn't shown any aggression at all, even when Jake raised his voice at him. Ever since Ursus pulled Jake from the river, the dog had done nothing but help him.

"No," said Sarafina. "Givers call from the Calling-Place. The dogs hear them at the Howl. Those dogs are not missing. Other dogs, other packs came to the Howl. Now they do not."

"You think something took them?"

"They are not here. That is what I know."

"It's not Ursus," said Jake. "There's something else out in the forest besides—" He almost mentioned Ursus. "Besides dogs. I found a cat."

"Cats do not belong in the forest," said Sarafina. "Cats stay in the grassland. Dogs stay in the forest. That is what I know."

"If you don't believe me, smell my clothes," Jake said. "You should be able to smell cat on them."

Sarafina sniffed around Jake's body. Jake tried to stand still, even when the border collie sniffed between his legs and around his backside. Dogs are different than people, he reminded himself, even dogs who can talk.

"There is the smell of cat on you," said Sarafina. "And something else."

"See? Urs—I mean, dogs aren't the only things in the forest. And I think those other things are taking the dogs. I know because they were trying to take that cat when I ran into them."

Jake told Sarafina about his encounter with the junk-men.

She and the other dogs seemed to be listening, but every so often a dog would wander off, his nose pressed into the grass. By the time he was finished with his tale, Sarafina and a handful of other dogs were all that was left of the group. The rest had gone back to what they were doing before Jake arrived.

"Tell us what to do, Giver. I do not wish to be taken. I wish to answer when my Givers call. They are called Sarah and Donovan at the Howls. I wait and listen. When they call, I shall go to them."

Sarafina looked at Jake, her gaze intent. He realized that she was waiting for a command, that she believed that Jake knew exactly what to do, and she stood poised to act. He stood and watched her, completely unsure what he should do or say next. No one had ever placed such blind trust in him before.

"I don't know," Jake said. He tried to think of something wiser, but it was the truth, and there was nothing he could do to soften it.

"Givers know all," said Sarafina. Jake wished it were true. He didn't tell Sarafina; there was nothing to be gained by trying to explain it to her. "Well, maybe back when we were alive," said Jake, "But not here. I don't even know who I am. I don't remember anything except my name, and falling into the river."

"We sing, and we remember," said Sarafina. "You sing, and you will remember. Then you will know what to do."

"I don't know any songs," said Jake.

"When the darkness comes, we sing, and we remember," said Sarafina.

There was no way to tell when it would get dark, and so Jake wandered among the dogs, petting them, scratching bellies, and answering questions. Though the dogs weren't clustered around him, they hadn't lost interest. They had simply accepted his presence and moved on. As far as they were concerned, he had always been there among them.

He sat down by the pool and watched the water fall in a vast sheet, tumbling into a rich lather as it struck the surface of the pool. Its sound was almost hypnotic. Around him was the cool scent of wet rocks and fresh grass, and for a while, he thought that perhaps he didn't want to remember anything, that it would be better if he just stayed in the hollow with Sarafina and the other dogs. He looked down into the water but saw no reflection; only the smooth, round rocks that lined the bottom of the pool stared back at him. He cupped his hands and put the water to his lips, but it seemed to dissipate into nothing before it hit his tongue. Jake felt a little disappointed. It was good that the dogs suffered no hunger or thirst, but there was some pleasure to be had in eating and drinking, and the feeling of cool water against his throat was something he would miss.

A dog barked, and Jake caught a glimpse of a gray coat with a thick, bushy tail. It paused and looked at him, cocking its head to the side. Something about the dog captivated him, though Jake did not know why. A moment later, the dog bounded off, its attention stolen by something Jake couldn't see.

All at once, the blue sky faded into darkness, replaced by a silver river of stars. A hush fell over the hollow. Jake waited, listening. Droplets of water caught the starlight and turned the falls to silver fire as if the sky itself flowed into the pool at Jake's feet. One by one the dogs padded to the edge of the pool and sat down on their haunches; their eyes trained toward the sky. In the half-light he could see them, hundreds of them, their eyes trained upward, watching the stars flow in their eddies and whorls, their dance mirrored in the mist coming off the water.

Then they began to sing.

They cried to the stars, each voice mingling with the others in haunting, plaintive harmony, a one-note melody that rang through the hollow and washed over everything in it. Jake felt it; it passed through him and lingered in the deep parts of his soul, and he did not know at first that when the song touched him, he added his voice to it as well. Their song washed over him, and his over them, and he forgot entirely that he was Jake, only that he was one voice of many, seeking, remembering. They sang, and in their song the dogs and Jake were one.

The stars sang back.

Faintly at first, but stronger and clearer as the song went on, the stars sang, their voices like frozen rain falling against a skin-thin sheet of ice. Jake remembered the voices but not the song; it was not welcome they were singing, it was something else, something that Jake did not yet understand.

He began to hear names. Lady, Duke, Digger, names woven into the tapestry of the star song, Wolf and Hollie, Bridget, Lucy, Onyx, Champ, hundreds of names, and with them, memories. They passed through his mind, brief glimpses of warm hands caressing a floppy ear, of big, bright puppy-eyes gazing up at the Giver, of tugs-of-war and tennis balls, of grass and trees and a thousand unfamiliar scents, of warm sand and salty water that stretched so far it touched the sky. Days and nights tumbled and blurred together, a thousand early morning walks and late-night strolls under moonlight, a thousand car doors thudding shut and front doors opening to cries of Giver! The Giver is returned! Scratches and belly rubs, food, water, treats, and kind words, half-dozes under the Giver's gentle brush, and the sound of the Giver's breath as she slept in the high bed, too high now for old bones to reach. A thousand last stokes and kisses, and tearful partings, a prick on the skin and then darkness.

But that was not the end. The stars sang on. They sang to Jake.

There was a baby resting against the skin of his

mother's chest, warm and content. "Congratulations, Mrs. Phillips, you have a beautiful son." And there was the baby again, this time in the arms of a man. He touched the baby's nose to his and beamed, his long brown whiskers tickling the baby's cheek.

"We'll call him Jake."

Jacob Allen Phillips. That was his name.

He was one or two, stumbling around the hardwood floor in nothing but a diaper, leaning on an old Tonka cement mixer. Sebastian was there too, much younger, not much more than a pup himself. Jake fell when the truck slipped out from under his arms. He climbed back to his feet using Sebastian's hair as handholds. The dog did not object.

Jake rolled the truck around the living room, bumping into the worn couch by the window. A breeze blew through and rippled the lace curtain, revealing a glimpse of Dad outside mowing the lawn with the rusty old lawnmower Uncle Ryan gave him for ten dollars. Somehow Dad managed to keep the thing running. The old Tonka truck was Jake's lawnmower, cutting imaginary grass growing around the coffee table.

He was four, sitting in a regular chair; his chin was just visible over the edge of the table. Mom brought out a cake and there was singing. She was wearing her favorite white tank top that said Old Orchard Beach on it and whenever she wore it, she and Dad looked at each other funny and Jake didn't know what that was about, but for some reason it was ok because moms and dads should love each other and that's what Jake thought it meant.

He blew out the candles and his mother clapped. He never noticed how pretty his mother was. She cut a piece of cake—vanilla with strawberry frosting because that was Jake's favorite even when he was four—and he ate it without using his hands. Most of it he wore on his face. Mom laughed and wiped at his face with a towel. Sebastian crouched at the base of Jake's chair, ready to snatch up anything Jake dropped.

He was seven. His room was a maelstrom of Legos and dirty laundry and action figures. He was angry, his face beet red with the effort of screaming. He threw his skateboard at the door, gouging a hole near the bottom hinge.

He was eight, and Dad was on the day shift finally. Jake was walking home from school with his Patriots backpack loaded with stuff. The straps were too long, and the bottom of the backpack bumped against Jake's backside with each step. On his head he wore a dirty Red Sox cap turned backward. He talked and talked, barely taking his eyes off Dad.

Sebastian was with them. Dad had him on the leash, but Jake didn't think they needed a leash because Sebastian would walk on Dad's left side, right by his leg. Sebastian was a smart dog. Jake almost had to run to keep up with Dad, but he didn't mind because finally, Dad was walking home with him instead of being asleep every afternoon.

He was nine, out in the backyard playing soccer with Sebastian. The dog chased the ball, snapping at it, unable to get the big soccer ball between his jaws.

Jake saw himself through a layer of smoke. Dad

was grilling burgers and shish kabobs because Mom wasn't too crazy about hamburgers and shish kabobs were the next best thing. The sun was beginning to set. Jake and Sebastian ran back and forth across the grass, so fast that the shadows flickered across their moving bodies like a strobe light. There were black flies and mosquitoes in the air but they weren't bothersome enough to stop the game. Only the burgers and tater tots and cold root beer set on the old picnic table could do that.

He was eleven. It was dark, but the door opened and let in light from the hallway. Jake was asleep on the bed, still in his clothes. His room was a war zone. Every piece of clothing he owned was strewn across the floor, the drawers ripped from the dresser and cast haphazardly about. There was an empty space underneath the television where the Xbox was supposed to be. Mom had taken it again because his grades weren't good, and he had blamed his twenty percent homework score on Precious Peter.

He had called his mother a dumb housewife who couldn't even figure out how to make macaroni and cheese even if she watched it on Youtube, and maybe she should go back to school herself so she could learn how to be a better mother instead of taking his stuff all the time.

Now his mother entered the room and gingerly picked her way through the wreckage until she arrived at the bed. She pulled a blanket over his body and bent down to kiss him on the side of the head. And as she did it, she whispered in his ear, "Jake, I love you."

The singing faded, and along with it, the images until all was quiet and only the stars danced in Jake's vision. He lay against the stone, feeling the waterfall's spray on his skin. The memories that crowded his mind paralyzed him. It was too much in too little time, as if he had waded into the pool and tried to drink from the waterfall. Relief and longing and regret swirled and roiled within him, fighting for dominance, leaving him weak and cold and confused.

His mother's voice lingered in his ears, so vivid he could almost feel her breath against his skin. Jake savored the sound as it faded into nothingness. Tears brimmed against his eyes and spilled down his face.

"I'll do better," he whispered. "Mom, I'll do better, promise." He knew that she couldn't hear him, and the realization plunged him into a deep despair. He was crushed with the certainty that any promises he made, any attempts at apology, any love, any forgiveness he might receive or give meant nothing now. He was too late. There was a vastness between him and everything he left behind. He lay on his back, unable to move or think. None of the dogs approached him. Even in a sea of fur, Jake was alone.

But something gnawed at him, some faint hope that he could not immediately understand. One word emerged from the maelstrom of his memories, calling above the tumult, foreign at first to Jake's ears. The memory of it was like a thread that wove its way through all the others. His mother? No, it wasn't her, and the realization saddened him. It was a name, a familiar name to which sorrow and joy were attached in equal measure, joy in the knowing and sorrow when the thread had been suddenly and irreparably cut. When it finally emerged, he leaped to his feet.

"Sebastian!"

Many of the dogs sat up and turned their heads when he called out his friend's name, but none responded. Jake called out again, terrified that Sebastian was not here, that he had been taken by the junk-men or had simply wandered off to be alone as Ursus had.

"Sebastian!"

The crowd of dogs watching him shifted uneasily, some turning their heads, others dropping back to the grass. Jake took no notice of them; he was consumed with the name, with the dog that wove through all his memories, the one thread in his life that sustained him and anchored him. He must be here.

"Sebastian!" he called out again. He thought of a thousand games of tug-of-war, a thousand surreptitious treats slipped underneath the table, a thousand games of catch and chase. He thought of the smell of his friend's coat, the brightness of his eyes and the sloppy warmth of his tongue. If he were here, Jake could bear it. Sebastian would make it all right.

Out near the treeline, Jake caught sight of a wisp of silver-gray darting among the shadows. He thought it might be his imagination, a mix of starlight and wishful thinking, but he saw it again, closer this time. Then, there could be no mistake, and Jake rushed for him, dogs scattering to clear his path until he threw his arms around his friend's neck and buried his face in Sebastian's soft coat.

"Jake." His voice was soft, almost effeminate, nothing like the voice Jake would have imagined in his head. "Where is Bradhun? I am waiting for Bradhun to call me to the Calling-Place. Bradhun is not here."

"Bradhun?" Jake said, confused. "Who? Who is Brad-hon?" For a second, Jake feared that he'd found someone else's Sebastian until a memory came to him in the sound of his mother's voice, calling from her bedroom upstairs. *Bradhun, I think Sebastian needs to go out.*

The realization fell on him like a weight. Sebastian wasn't waiting for him. He was waiting for Dad.

Chapter Eight

Light filled the sky and bathed the hollow, but the daylight brought no inspiration to Jake's mind. His memories were supposed to tell him what he should do next, but he felt no wiser than he had been the day before. All he'd done was trade confusion for regret. Now he knew what he had lost when the ice broke and the river sucked the life from his body. Sebastian sat next to him; the dog hadn't left his side since they were reunited, but seeing his friend again felt hollow, as if he were petting a friend's dog instead of his own.

Jake had spent the nights since Dad took Sebastian to the vet thinking of what he would say to his friend if Dad was right and they met again. Now that he was here, there wasn't much to say. He tried to talk to Sebastian about the fun they used to have, but most of the memories he'd gained from the Howl were already fading, his old life slipping back into darkness.

Sebastian remembered almost nothing from their old life but his name and the sound of Dad's voice.

He seemed overjoyed that Jake was there, but he was focused on whatever was happening at the moment, with no need to reminisce and no desire to think about the future. With nothing to talk about, Jake sat on a rock next to the pool and idly stroked Sebastian's back. Sebastian had been his best friend for ten years, and no one had ever bothered to tell Jake that Sebastian was Dad's dog. All the time Jake had spent playing catch, all the time he'd fallen asleep to the dog's quiet snuffles, all the treats, and all the backdoor soccer games meant nothing. Jake felt a strange sense that he'd been betrayed.

The question was by whom.

His dad seemed to be fine with letting Jake take his dog out for walks and games of catch and tug of war in the backyard. It galled Jake that even though he did all the work and spent all the time with Sebastian, the dog was still attached to his dad. He wanted to steal Sebastian away, so when the call finally came, Jake and Sebastian would answer it and then calmly explain to Dad how Jake had been there to keep Sebastian company and that Sebastian was his now. Dad would understand, and they'd all go off to the real heaven together.

And what about that? How had the church people gotten Heaven so completely wrong? Somebody wasn't telling the truth, and Jake didn't have the inclination to try to figure out which church person was lying. They said Heaven was supposed to be perfect, with all these happy people floating around greeting each other and singing songs of praise. Instead, Jake had been shut out of the real Heaven, if there even was one, and sent to some kind of gigantic backyard. He probably could have been a nicer person back at home but he hadn't killed anyone or done anything all that terrible. At least not terrible enough to spend eternity camping without a tent and surrounded by hundreds of dogs that weren't even his.

Maybe he could make them his.

Not just Sebastian, but all of them. An entire pack of dogs, just for him. If they wouldn't let him into the real Heaven, he'd make his own right here. The dogs would all warm up to him eventually, and Jake was sure that once he became King, he could even get Ursus to join them. What he needed was a way to impress them. He watched them lounging in the light, following trails across the meadow, chasing each other around the edge of the forest, or sleeping in the grass. None of them looked particularly interested in either being a king or a subject. If he wanted to become their king, he would have to show them once and for all why Givers are in charge. It would have to be something that all the dogs could agree upon, and that was a tall order.

His eyes widened and he slapped the water in triumph.

"Sarafina, I know what to do!"

Sarafina leaped to her paws and trotted over, sitting on her haunches at Jake's feet.

"You said there are dogs missing, right?" The plan that he was forming in his mind was simple, so simple in fact, that he didn't know why he hadn't thought of it sooner.

"Many dogs are missing," Sarafina said.

"I think I know what is behind it. If we all work together, we can hunt down the things that are taking dogs. When we find them, we can destroy them."

"A Hunt!" called Sarafina. "The Giver is taking us on a Hunt!"

The cry went up among the dogs, most of whom were now listening to Jake. He looked over the hundreds of noses and eyes and swishing tails, and he already felt like a king.

"A Hunt! A Hunt! The Giver is going to take us for a Hunt! What shall we hunt, Giver? Tell us!"

Jake reminded them of the story of his fight with the junk-men, and his encounter with Samuel. He didn't get far when he noticed that many of the dogs lost interest and began following their noses or wrestling or napping again. That would never do; if he wanted to be King, he decided, he needed to start leading right away.

"All right, everyone, here's what we have to do. We have to go into the woods and follow my scent back to this big clearing where I met Samuel."

"I am called Reba at the Howls! I am a tracker! I will track your scent," said a beautiful hound.

"Good," Jake said. "Now—"

Reba didn't wait for any more instructions. She began to track Jake's scent across the meadow toward the treeline. The dogs followed her, barking and howling in their excitement.

"Wait!" said Jake. "We can't go that way. There's no way down!" But the dogs had already made up their minds. Most of them had already begun following Jake's scent into the woods. Among them was Sebastian, who was one of the first to dash away.

"Ursus is that way!"

The dogs stopped and turned around. Reba trotted back to Jake's side.

"I will track your scent," said Reba, "But I will not track your scent to Ursus."

"You can't go down that way anyway. There must be another way down. Once we get down there, we can circle around and you can pick up my scent, and follow it all the way back to where the junk-men are hiding."

"There is another way down," said Sarafina. "I remember."

Sarafina dashed around the pool and toward the far side of the meadow. The other dogs charged after her, ecstatic. Jake smiled and sprinted after them, catching up to the stragglers before Sarafina made it to the far side.

It occurred to him as he ran that he ought to tell Ursus what he was planning to do. He knew the giant dog would probably just turn onto his side and say, "I will stay here," but he should at least be given a choice.

But stopping his new friends now would be nearly impossible. With any luck, he would see Ursus when they circled around, and he could tell him what they were planning to do, and Ursus would decide to join them.

They crested the hill, and Jake looked out over the vastness of the forest, an unbroken sea of green that melted into a haze at the horizon. He'd never seen anything so magnificent. When he and his army got rid of the junk-men, he would explore it all; every tree, every rock, and he'd have Sebastian by his side. Someday, Dad would call from the Calling-Place, and Sebastian's ears would perk up, and he and Jake would run back to the valley where Dad would be waiting. They would all be together again, and Jake would have a thousand stories to tell his father and time enough to tell them all.

Dogs streamed into the woods, and Jake followed. The joy he'd felt on that first run returned, but there was something even more wonderful. Exuberance and wild anticipation seemed to flow from the dogs as they ran, and Jake soaked it up like a sponge. He worked his way to the center of the pack and reveled in the chase. He ran, invincible, weaving among the trees in the center of a moving, undulating whirlwind of fur and claws and wagging tongues, and he glimpsed just for an instant what it felt like to be a god.

By his side ran Sebastian. Before he died, the dog would spend hours and hours chasing down tennis balls, and Jake would spend hours throwing them just to see Sebastian run. He was pure exuberance, each stride an expression of joy, a verse of canine poetry. But Sebastian had gotten old, and toward the end, could barely manage a trot. Heaven had restored his youth, and he ran with reckless, joyful abandon, just as before.

But Jake was no god. When they reached the forest below, he called a halt; he wanted to tell Ursus what happened at the Howl and invite him to join them in the hunt. Reba continued on without breaking stride. She had already picked up his trail, and she ignored his pleas to stop. On either side, he watched dogs peel away from the pack, finding interesting scents of their own to follow. Jake could do nothing to stop them.

Perhaps they didn't need a leader after all. Maybe all Jake had to do was run with them. There were more than a hundred dogs in Jake's army, more than enough to tear apart the junk-men.

But after a while, even Sebastian's presence wasn't enough to reassure Jake. The longer they went, the more dogs peeled off the sides and rear to follow their own noses. A few stopped in their tracks, their ears suddenly alert to some faraway sound, and they bounded off, their bodies shifting from solid to translucent as they vanished into the deep woods.

"They heard their names," said Sebastian, in answer to a question Jake hadn't even had time to ask. And so it went; the day wore on, and the farther they ran, the fewer they became. The dogs had been too numerous for Jake to count when they set off from the top of the hill. Now, those bringing up the rear were practically at Jake's heels.

"We have to stop! Reba! Sarafina! Stop!"

They did. The pack came to a halt. The trees towered overhead, blocking out most of the light. Jake didn't recognize the place. They had passed through pine stands and rocky outcroppings, and those had given way to the thick, ancient broad-leafed trees that covered the lowlands. Jake still found it beautiful, but he knew that somewhere ahead lurked the junk-men.

The trees seemed to know it too, and Jake got a distinct sense that they wanted him to leave.

The dogs clustered around him, apparently content. There couldn't have been more than fifteen or twenty. Aside from one fairly large Rottweiler, none of them reached Samuel's size, let alone Ursus'. Sarafina, Reba, and Sebastian sat down at Jake's feet, watching him, waiting for direction, but he didn't know what to do. His plan called for an army, and he no longer had one.

"Where did they all go?" Jake was only thinking out loud, but Sarafina answered him.

"They hunt."

"We were supposed to stay together."

"They follow until they forget," said Sarafina. "They run, they hunt, they sleep. They do not remember why they follow us."

"I will stay with Jake," said Sebastian. Jake gave him a scratch behind the ears.

The other dogs crowded him, looking for attention as well. Jake scratched and petted them all, but he couldn't shake the terrible feeling of dread that grew in his mind. He felt exposed, unprotected. What he needed was to get as many dogs as he could back to the safety of the waterfall. There he would reconsider his plan and come up with a way to keep his army together. It wasn't a retreat, he told himself. They hadn't seen any junk men. He needed to regroup.

"Ok. This is what we're going to do. We're going to go back to the waterfall. Back where we started."

"The hunt is over," said Reba. "Now we go back to the Howl."

Reba led the way, and this time none of the dogs strayed from the group. Jake hoped that the other dogs had come to a similar decision, and they would all be back by the time he reached the waterfall.

Thankfully, his strength still seemed boundless; no matter how long he ran, he never felt even a hint of fatigue. Next time he came out to hunt the junk-men, it would be different.

Just as hope returned, the world plunged suddenly back into darkness. The forest was utterly black, and only the feel of Sebastian's flank against his leg told him that the dogs were still with him. The stars burst forth, drenching the forest in pale silver, but the sky's beauty was lost on Jake. All around him, the dogs dropped down to their bellies. Some had rolled over to their sides as if they were preparing to sleep.

"What are you doing?" Jake's voice cracked with the panic in his throat.

"It is dark," said Sarafina. "We sleep until the light."

"What about the Howl? We have to make it back—"

"No howl in the forest," said Reba. "In the forest, we sleep when the dark comes."

"You don't need to sleep! You need to get up! We have to get away from here!" Jake tried to get them up, but not even Sebastian would budge.

They follow until they forget. That's what Sarafina told him, and now, they had all forgotten why they had come out into the forest. He shook Sebastian until he sat up.

"Sebastian, listen to me. There are things out

there that take dogs! We have to move. Sebastian, up!"

To Jake's relief, Sebastian sprang to his paws.

"Help me get the others up."

Before Sebastian could obey, the baleful screech of metal grinding against metal rent the silence. All the dogs scrambled to their paws, their heads darting back and forth. The Rottweiler let out a low growl.

"Something is coming," he said.

"Run!" Jake shouted.

It was too late. Reba howled in pain and surprise; one second, she was standing next to the Rottweiler, and the next, something dark and shiny wrapped around her hind legs, pulling her backward into the shadows. She whined and scratched the moss uselessly with her front paws.

"I am caught, I am caught!" she cried. Some of the dogs bolted, and the sound of their capture, a mixture of creaking metal and terrified howls, echoed through the darkness. One by one, the dogs vanished into the dark, wailing piteously. Sarafina and Sebastian cowered next to Jake, paralyzed with fear. Only the Rottweiler stood his ground. He let out another long, low growl.

"I am called Cy at the Howls. I will not run. You will not take me. I will bite. I will bite and shake until you show your belly."

Cy was as good as his word. The junk-men emerged from the shadows, shambling amalgamations of wire and plastic and wood. The closest tried to tangle Cy in a jumble of lamp cords and power cables, but the big Rottweiler shrugged them off and charged. He hit the junk-man in the center torso, and the force of his charge tore the thing in two. Cy bore down on the upper half, ripping and shaking until there was nothing large enough to bite. More came, and Cy turned to face them.

Three came at once. The first managed to get a noose around Cy's gigantic head, while the others attempted to circle around behind. Jake had seen the tactic before; they had done the same thing to Samuel.

"We have to help him!" He snatched up the lower torso of Cy's first kill and pulled away a hockey stick that had been one of its legs. Sarafina and Sebastian crouched low to the ground, trembling.

"Sebastian! Sarafina! Cy needs our help! Come on!"

But the two dogs were overcome with fear, and Jake could spare no more time trying to motivate them. He charged at the junk-men, his hockey stick at the ready. He reached the first one and swung hard, smashing the creature in the back. The stick snapped in two, but the blow was hard enough to dislodge the rope. Cy was free. The Rottweiler turned his attention to the creatures behind him, knocking both of them over in a single charge. Four more junk-men appeared, and Jake put himself between them and Cy.

"Jake! Jake! I am caught! Jake! Free me! Jake!"

Sebastian slipped away into the darkness, his paws tearing into the moss, his eyes wide with fear and pain. Sarafina was nowhere to be seen.

"Sebastian!"

Jake ran headlong into the darkness, following Sebastian's cries, but they became weaker and died out altogether before Jake could catch up. He dropped the hockey stick at his feet. His limbs felt heavy, and his mind seemed to fill with sand.

"Sebastian!" He shouted. Behind him, Cy howled. There was a clattering noise, another howl, and then silence.

Chapter Nine

Jake counted four of them emerging from the shadows. They shambled toward him. It was too dark to see any details, except for one red bike reflector that floated in the air and shifted back and forth as the thing hobbled through the dark woods.

In those shambling figures he saw something worse than death, worse by far than slipping away from one world and waking up in another. They limped toward him, filling the air with the din and clatter of failing machinery and the sharp metallic scent of an old junkyard.

The red reflector approached, swinging from side to side hypnotically, trailing a streak of red in Jake's vision. Jake tried to back away, but with one step backward he found himself against the trunk of a tree. He was trapped. The junk-man shuffled, his body a patchwork of refuse, none of which Jake could identify in the dim light. Its silhouette was barely distinguishable from the dark. Only the reflector was recognizable, coming closer with each passing breath.

Jake attempted to slide around the trunk, but the other junk-men spread out, intent on preventing his escape. He watched as the cyclops—for that was how Jake thought of him—stalked forward another few paces, its red eye bobbing back and forth, the thump of its makeshift feet muffled by the moss. It came within a couple of yards of Jake and then stopped.

"Where did you take my dogs?" Jake whispered.

The creature took another step forward. It moved slowly, as if it were more curious than angry or afraid. It paced back and forth in front of him, its red eye never leaving Jake's. Jake noticed that its head was built from a cracked goldfish bowl wrapped in baling wire, through which the bike reflector was threaded.

"I said, where did you take my dogs?"

The cyclops moved closer, leaning in, inspecting Jake's face. Only an inch or two separated his face from the strange tangle of glass and wire that made up the cyclops' head.

He realized the creature was just as confused as he was.

The others began to tighten the circle, with Jake in the center. There was still a large enough gap between them that Jake could flee, but he was too frightened to move.

He cast about for something, anything he could use as a weapon, but there was nothing useful, and the nearest tree branch was too high for Jake to reach. He was at their mercy. If he went quietly, they'd probably bring him to wherever Sebastian and the other dogs had been taken.

The junk-men inched closer. They were going to take him whether he liked it or not.

"All right. If that's the way it's going to be, come and take me."

The cyclops looked him over one more time, and then turned around and shambled a few steps toward the deep shadows from which he had emerged. Jake watched them with a mixture of confusion and relief. He prayed that they would keep going, that they would forget about him, and leave him alone in the dark. Please, please, please, Jake thought. The other creatures shambled a few paces as well, following the cyclops' lead. The cyclops turned to face him again.

"So, you're just going to stand there and stare at me?" His question came out more as a squeak than a challenge.

As if in answer, something dark and fast shot out from among the trees and wrapped around Jake's legs. It went taut, and Jake was thrown to the ground. His hand slapped painfully against an exposed root. He grabbed with both hands, ignoring the stinging on his palm, and held on with all his strength. The bindings tightened against his legs as the junk-men attempted to haul him off.

He held fast to the root as the junk-men pulled. The cords went taut, and Jake's body was lifted from the ground. His grip weakened. Gradually his fingers opened against his will. Fear coursed through him. His half-open fingers slipped, little by little, off the root.

A growl pierced the night air, followed by a crash, and the bindings around Jake's legs went limp. Jake tore at them, desperate to free himself. The old netting clung to his feet and legs. Behind him, the crashing continued. Jake rolled on to his back, fighting with the net. Something large and white shot past him, and the night shook with a violent clatter. Jake worked one foot out of the netting and then the other and clambered to his feet.

Samuel stood over a pile of refuse. The light of a red reflector shone between the cat's front paws. He cocked his head upward, toward the maze of branches overhead. His body tensed.

"Wait," Jake said. He tried to speak, but he didn't know what he should say. Samuel turned his attention back to the canopy, and Jake stopped him again.

"Wait, Samuel. Please." He searched for something to say that would keep the cat near him.

"You killed all four of them. Thanks for helping me."

"I do not forget," said the cat. Between his paws, the red bike reflector gleamed as though its wearer were still alive.

Samuel's jaw seemed set in a perpetual frown, and his eyes reminded Jake of a leopard or a tiger. Jake got the sense that for Samuel, life and death had never been all that far apart. Jake felt a pang of sadness for him; Samuel hadn't found the peace that Heaven was supposed to offer. Then again, perhaps the giant cat preferred it that way.

"You do not belong here," said Samuel. "Go home."

"I don't have a home. Not anymore."

"You will be taken away like the dogs. Many dogs were taken."

"I know that. I'm the one who brought them here. We were going to fight them. I thought if we kicked them out, everything would be all right."

Samuel didn't need to know that he wanted to be King. Even the thought of it embarrassed him. Samuel said nothing.

"One of them was my dad's dog. His name was Sebastian. He was my best friend, and I just let them take him. I didn't even try to stop them."

If Samuel had any sympathy for Jake, he didn't show it. The big cat watched him, his yellow eyes reflecting some of the starlight. Samuel's indifference nettled Jake; if he hadn't helped, Samuel would have been captured by the same things that took Sebastian and the others. The cat was only free because of him. But the cat made no offer of comfort or encouragement, and his silence felt like a rejection.

Jake kicked a jumble of wires and refuse into the shadows. Samuel didn't move.

"Don't you even care? I want my dog back. He's gone forever and it's my fault! I'm the only kid in the world who has a dog that died twice! They dragged him away, and all I did was watch! And you, you were probably up in a tree watching the whole thing. Just leave me alone." He sat down heavily against the tree. The bike reflector flickered in the starlight like a candle flame, splashing Samuel's chest with pale, pink light.

"Your friend is not dead. There is no death here," Samuel said.

"How do you know?"

"There is no death here."

"But how do you know? Just because you haven't seen anyone die doesn't mean there's no death."

"There is no death here. Malbinocks do not kill."

"Malbinocks?"

"They are called Malbinocks on the grassland. The horses named them. For the sound they make when they come."

"What do the Malbinocks do?" Jake wasn't entirely sure he wanted to know the answer, but something compelled him to ask.

"Make dogs suffer. Make cats suffer."

"Suffer? Suffer how?" The thought of Sebastian suffering sent a shudder through him.

"Cages. Sticks. Fire. Claws. Rope. Water. Many ways."

"Why? Why would they do that here?"

"I know what they do. Not why."

Jake's mind whirled. The enormity of what he had done crushed him. Sebastian's fate, and the fate of all the other dogs he had foolishly led into the woods, was his fault. He curled up against the tree, guilt and sorrow washing over him like a tide. He longed to cry, but he could not get the tears to come. After a while, he gave up and studied the Malbinocks' remains. Cold starlight sparkled against the pieces of the fishbowl near Samuel's front paws. The reflector no longer resembled an eye; now it reminded Jake of blood.

Samuel never moved. He sat in the pile of Malbinock junk, regarding Jake with impassive, golden eyes. Jake's guilt gave way to cold rage.

"I'm going with you," Jake said. "I'll help you hunt them down. We'll hunt them all down."

"You are no hunter."

"Teach me. I can learn. I have to do something."

"Free them," said Samuel.

Jake sat up. Samuel came closer.

"There was a dark place." Samuel said. "Small. No way to turn around. Then a big place. In the light, the Malbinocks do not come. They come in the night. They come with the stars. They bring pain."

Samuel blinked. He stared past Jake into the night, remembering.

"There was a dog. Small. Black. The dog found a way. The light came. We ran."

"Show me where they are. I'll help you. We'll rescue them together."

"I do not remember the way."

"Try," said Jake.

"I can not remember. Gordon remembers. Find Gordon."

"Gordon?"

"We ran. At the Mountain, he hid. The Malbinocks followed. Day, night, I ran. No sleep. Left Gordon by the Mountain. I swam the river. They followed. They caught me in the forest. You found me in the forest. Now I hunt them."

"Where is the Mountain?" Jake said. It was a sliver of hope, no larger or brighter than any of the stars overhead, but hope nonetheless. Jake clung to it with grim, focused desperation. There's a way, he said to himself. There's a way to get Sebastian back. To get them all back. It was only a sliver of hope, but enough to get Jake on his feet.

"Where is the Mountain, Samuel?"

"I will take you to the river. The Mountain is on the other side. That is what I remember. Find the Mountain. Find Gordon. Free them."

"Take me to the river."

Chapter Ten

Samuel and Jake reached the river just as the night ended. All at once, the stars melted into a bright, sunless blue sky. Beneath it lay the river, catching the light in the slow, languid waves that rose and fell as they flowed past. It was vast, impossibly vast, larger than any river he had ever imagined. Since the last time he'd been near it, the water had taken on a sinister cast, a roiling ocean daring him to enter.

Samuel sat near the riverbank. He was not the cat he had been in the dark; like the river, Samuel had changed. Starlight had given Samuel the bearing of a king, but in the full light of day, he was thin, almost emaciated, with patches of fur missing from his belly and hind legs. Despite his frailty, he held his head high. He surveyed the water, and the grasslands beyond, as if it were his personal domain.

"The Mountain is on the other side," he said, never taking his eyes from the far bank.

Jake looked across the water as well, and the

distance unnerved him. Swimming the river was something entirely different than splashing around near the shore or doing backflips in his grandmother's pool while his mother watched from a lawn chair on the deck. He imagined the river's current strengthening as he waded into the deep, the water tugging at his legs until his feet could no longer find the bottom, and then the river would be in charge.

Somewhere out there he'd lose sight of the far bank altogether, and the near bank as well, and he'd be swimming blind, like a sailor thrown overboard in a terrible storm. That prospect terrified him even more than the current, more than the depths beneath. The thought of being lost in so much water filled his mind with unutterable dread, and he could think of nothing that would dispel his fear. Even if Samuel was correct, and there was no death in this land, the water would still have him. Would he float forever, or swim until his strength gave out and be swept under the waves? How many dogs and cats lay buried in the depths? Jake cast the thought away; he didn't want to know.

He had another thought almost too terrible to contemplate, and that was the possibility that Samuel was wrong. If there was death in this place, he would find it in the river, and he was just as certain there wouldn't be trees and dogs and cats in whatever came next. Nothingness was what he would find. The more he thought about it, the hungrier the river felt.

"You must swim," said Samuel. He took his large, yellow eyes off the river and studied Jake. Jake wondered if his fear was showing. He decided it probably was.

"It's too far," said Jake.

"Near and far mean nothing here."

"Look at it! How am I going to swim across that?"

"Get in the water. Swim until you reach the other side."

Samuel was right, of course, but the thought of being alone in all that water robbed Jake of his reason. There had to be another way. Somewhere downstream, there must be a bridge or a boat, or a place where the river narrowed. There must be something. Fear and shame mingled together, and he felt as he had the night before when Sebastian slipped away into the darkness, calling out for him.

"You must swim, Jake."

"Come with me," said Jake. "You swam it before. You know how to do it."

Samuel cast his gaze over the water again. "I will swim with you," he said. He rose to his paws, and Jake saw once again how frail he was in the light. He hadn't recovered from what the Malbinocks had done to him. It was a wonder that Samuel could walk, let alone fight or swim. If Samuel did get into the water, Jake wasn't sure the cat would emerge on the far bank. Courageous as Samuel was, the river would likely get the best of him.

Samuel betrayed no such misgivings. He made his way down toward the water. Jake's unease grew as Samuel neared the water's edge.

"Samuel, wait. I'm not sure this is a good idea."

Samuel turned, the water lapping around his back paws. "I do not forget," he said.

"This is not the place for cats."

The voice came from the trees. It rolled through Jake's mind and temporarily overwhelmed the low, constant rush of water. Samuel left the water's edge to stand between Jake and the edge of the forest. Something large and dark moved among the trees. Jake recognized the voice.

Ursus.

"Cats go where we please. I am Samuel. I fear nothing. Not cat. Not dog. Not Giver. Not Malbinock. Not you."

"Samuel, I know him—" Jake said, but it was too late. Ursus emerged from the trees. His muscled forelegs rippled; his dark coat iridescent in the light. He moved with a fluidity that belied his bulk; there was deadly strength and power in the dog, barely contained beneath his calm demeanor.

Samuel did not move. His ears lay flat against his head, his body arched, and his tail curved downward. He bared his fangs.

"You. I have heard your name. All other dogs fear you. All cats fear you. I am not afraid."

Ursus stopped a few feet from Samuel. For a moment, their eyes locked. Jake kept silent, afraid that a single word could set them off. He took a deep breath that felt like an eternity. He hoped that Samuel was telling the truth, that there was no death here, for if there was, Jake had no doubt that Samuel would be the first to meet it. If Samuel chose to fight, Jake could think of no scenario that enabled the cat to survive, let alone win. Samuel would be torn to pieces, crushed, thrown into the river to drift away on the current. He seemed almost eager for it.

Ursus blinked and looked away.

"I have no fight with you," he said. "I do not wish to fight."

"You say this is not the place for cats. I say cats go where we please," Samuel said. His voice was a hiss in Jake's mind, his words spat out with contempt. His eyes found the dog's again, and once more the two were locked in a stare. For an instant, a subtle change came over Ursus, a tensing of the muscles, a slight flicker of his ears toward his skull, an almost imperceptible twitch of his upper lip. But it passed like a cloud on a windy day, so quickly that Jake thought he may have imagined it. Once again, Ursus blinked and looked away.

"I have no fight with you," said Ursus. He sat back on his haunches, blinked, and then yawned.

"Cats go where we please," said Samuel.

"You are a cat," said Ursus. "If you wish to roam the forest, roam the forest. If you wish to roam the grassland, roam the grassland. I have no fight with you."

With those words, Samuel relaxed. His ears lifted, and his back lost its arch. He sat back on his haunches.

"I have no fight with you, Ursus of the Howl."

Jake finally breathed again, and thanked God for whatever had prevented Ursus from launching himself at the cat. Samuel probably didn't know how lucky he was; he probably believed that he would have come out the winner. Jake was glad none of them would have to find out.

He looked at both of them, gigantic specimens of their respective species. Ursus' muscles rippled beneath his coat, and the power they projected was somehow muted by the gentleness in his eyes. The cat's eyes were hard, cold, gleaming a pale yellow, sharp as broken glass, and the power in them was muted by the wasted state of his body. It was astonishing that the cat could move, let alone hunt and fight as he did. Samuel was a warrior, a fighter, a survivor. Jake admired him, and he was glad that Ursus had backed down.

"Something in the woods," said Ursus. "Not cat. Not dog. Not Giver."

"Malbinock," said Samuel.

"Not cat, not dog. That is what I know."

"Junk-men," said Jake. "They took Sebastian, and Sarafina, and Cy, and who knows how many others. I'm going to swim across the river to look for them. Samuel is coming with me."

"No dogs came this way. No Malbinocks," said Ursus. He raised himself to all fours and sniffed at the riverbank.

"Samuel says there's a dog hiding at a mountain across the river. The dog can show us where the Malbinocks took Sebastian. We have to swim across to get there." Now that the tension had lifted, his dread returned. The river still lay between him and the Mountain, and even with Samuel's help, Jake wasn't sure he'd ever see the other side.

Ursus stood at the water's edge, his dark coat reflected in the surface. If Samuel was the size of a dog, Ursus looked like a Clydesdale horse in comparison.

"Maybe you could come too," Jake said. The words left his mouth before he realized he'd said them. He hadn't much hope that the dog would accept; Ursus seemed to shy away from the company of other animals, and despite his size and power, he was reluctant to fight. Though Ursus had pulled Jake out of the river once, there was no reason to suspect he'd do it again. Jake guessed the dog would probably decide to stay where he was.

At the worst, Jake would wave goodbye to Ursus when he finally got up the courage to wade into the river, while the dog flopped over on his side and watched them swim away.

Samuel busied himself with grooming, licking a paw and wiping it across the top of his head. He took no further interest in either Ursus or Jake.

Jake stayed quiet; he was in no hurry to go swimming, and as long as he could pretend to wait for Ursus to decide, he could stay on dry land. Samuel didn't appear to be in any hurry himself. But as time wore on, Jake's thoughts began to turn to Sebastian and the other dogs, and he knew that he couldn't sit on the bank forever.

Free me, Jake! Free me! Sebastian's plea echoed in Jake's memory. Now it sounded less like a plea for help and more an accusation of cowardice. The river joined in the chorus, mocking and beckoning Jake at the same time. The water flowed past and seemed to say, *Prove it, Jake. If you think you can. Prove you are not a coward. Prove you are not a greedy, selfish coward. Prove it.*

Before he realized what he was doing, Jake was ankle-deep in the water. The current at the bank was relatively weak; he could barely feel the flow across his feet. His toes sank into the fine, soft sand that lined the riverbed. Fear crept into him and hid in the corners of his mind, unwilling to reveal itself, but undeniably present. Jake swallowed hard and took another step. The water lapped around his shins.

"Jake," said Ursus.

Jake turned around. "I'm sorry, Ursus. I have to go. Sebastian is out there somewhere and he needs my help. I don't know if I can do it, but I have to try."

Samuel stretched and stood before following Jake into the water. Jake could see by the way he jerked his paws that the water made him very uncomfortable.

"I will follow you," Samuel said.

"Thanks, Samuel. Guess we better get started." He waded out a little further until the water came up to his waist. He felt the tug of the current against his midsection, much stronger than it had been only a few feet back. The fear that had been sitting dormant came to life, and Jake fought the urge to head back to the safety of the bank. His feet sank into the sandy bottom, making the way more difficult.

The water was up to his chest. Samuel was a few feet behind. He craned his neck to keep his head above the water.

"Do not go," said Ursus.

Jake turned around again. Ursus seemed even larger from the bank. "I have to," he said. "Sebastian needs me."

"You must go," said Ursus. "Samuel must stay. That is what I know."

"Samuel? Why?"

"I am not afraid," said Samuel.

"Samuel is a fighting cat," said Ursus. "But the river is too strong. Samuel can not fight the river."

"I am strong," said Samuel. "I am not afraid."

The cat pushed ahead. As he did so, the current swept him off his paws and sent him drifting helplessly downstream. Samuel thrashed and fought, but he could not overcome the strength of the water. In the space of a breath, several yards separated Samuel from Jake.

"Samuel!"

Jake dove after him, his run instantly turning into his best crawl stroke through the water. Samuel kicked and pawed at the water to no avail. Jake was aware of a dark shadow slipping past him on the bank, but he was focused on swimming, on catching up to Samuel. A great splash erupted in the water ahead. A ripple struck Jake in the face, temporarily blinding him and filling his mouth and nose with water. When his eyes cleared, he searched the water for Samuel, but there was no sign of him. He was gone.

"Samuel!" Jake cried out. He thrashed toward the bank, hoping to get a better vantage point from which to locate the cat. Ursus was there, water glistening on his coat, and at his front paws lay Samuel.

He lay on his side, his wet, matted fur clinging to his thin body. Ursus stood over him, watching him.

For a moment, Jake feared that Samuel was wrong, that there was death here, but as he looked closer, the barely perceptible rise of Samuel's ribcage showed that the cat was breathing.

Jake looked into the sky and closed his eyes, overcome with relief. He sat down beside the two animals and stroked Samuel's head. His eyes were closed.

"How did you know?" Jake said, looking up at Ursus.

"His wounds have a strong scent," said Ursus. "His wounds make him weak."

Samuel did not open his eyes again that day. Ursus and Jake waited with him on the riverbank. Night came again, blanketing the sky with its own river of silver, and the starlight danced across the water like cold flame, and still, Samuel slept. Jake watched over him through the night while Ursus sat with his back to the river, watching and listening. They didn't speak. As the night wore on, Jake feared that Samuel might not wake up again, but he kept his fears to himself. Instead, he prayed.

"I've done a lot of bad things since I came here," he whispered into the dark. "And there are a lot of good dogs who are suffering because of me. Please don't punish Samuel for what I did. He was only trying to help."

Dawn came, and the stars vanished behind a veil of blue. Samuel opened his eyes. Jake didn't take the time to ponder if it was coincidence or the answer to his prayer. Relief supplanted all else in his mind. He called out to Ursus, who continued to stand guard a few yards away.

"Ursus! He's awake! He's awake!"

Samuel managed to pull himself partially upright. His gaze passed from Jake to the river, and finally, to

Ursus, whose massive head now loomed over Jake's left shoulder.

It was Samuel who finally broke the silence.

"It is still day. We can swim. Make it to the other side before dark," he said. He tried to lift himself to his paws, but only succeeded in getting his hind legs underneath him. Jake fought back a wave of sorrow and guilt. An image filled his mind of Samuel bathed in starlight, standing over the shattered Malbinocks, and Jake could hardly believe that such an animal could be reduced to the thin, broken creature that lay before him. And it was all because Jake had been too afraid.

"No, Samuel," Jake replied, "That was yesterday. Don't you remember? We tried to swim. The river almost took you away,"

Samuel stared out over the sparkling water. When he spoke again, his voice was distant.

"The river was too strong. I fought. I am not stronger than the river." His words came slowly, laden with sadness and defeat. Samuel had been captured, tortured, chased, and hunted, but Jake suspected that there on the riverbank was the first time he had ever admitted to being beaten. Jake wondered if it would have been more merciful to let Samuel go.

"You are a brave fighting cat," said Ursus. "Rest and sleep. Become strong again."

"I must cross the river with Jake," said Samuel.

"I can do it," said Jake. "I can make it across. I'll find the Mountain. I promise I won't stop until they're all free. Every dog, every cat. All of them. I promise you I'll do whatever I have to do to get them out."

"I will not forget," said Samuel.

Jake stood up and faced the river, and he was struck again by its vastness and its beauty. A fingernail-thin brown line was all that prevented the water of the river from melting into the deep azure of the sky, so far away that even in a boat Jake would have been daunted by it. Nevertheless, he stepped off the bank and into the water flowing cool over his feet, feeling the fine sand settle between his toes. He took one look back. Samuel and Ursus watched him from the bank.

"I'm just a kid," Jake said. "I don't know how far I'll get. But I'm going to try."

Somehow, it didn't feel right to say goodbye. He turned his back to them and waded deeper into the water. The current tugged at his clothes. Fear took hold of him again, familiar as his favorite shoes, but Jake did not give in to it. The water rose to his chest, and his feet slipped off the soft sand and drifted in the current.

He kicked his legs and pushed through the water, cupping his hands and breathing the way his father taught him. Strength coursed through his body with every breath. Soon it felt less like swimming and more like flying. The water lost its weight and seemed to Jake like nothing more than a cool wind flowing over and around him. He exalted in the sensation and laughed at himself for ever having been afraid.

He could have been well on his way through the grassland if he had just started swimming yesterday. It was only a river, after all. Just water and sand and rocks, like his river back home. Water and sand and rocks. He glanced down in the middle of a stroke to watch the sand and rocks pass beneath him, to banish the last of his fear. Sand and rocks and water, a river like any other. Nothing special.

But there was no bottom.

There were no rocks and no sand. Jake peered into the depths, letting the current take him while he searched for the riverbed. He was so transfixed by the darkness that he barely noticed when the water closed over his head.

There was nothing beneath him but a limitless, unutterable void. In its depths he would never again see sunlight or feel the wind against his skin. The river would take everything, starting with his body, then his mind, and finally, even his name. It was already happening; he could see the sparkling surface far above, so far that he couldn't imagine reaching it, and he questioned whether it was really the surface at all. Darkness closed over him, and Jake's senses returned. His body wanted to breathe, but the surface was far, far above his head.

He felt a tug against his shirt. He was being pulled, inexorably, toward the light. His head broke the surface, and he breathed again, sucking in the pure air as deeply as he could. He blinked away the water in his eyes and basked in the vivid blue of the sky and the feel of the breeze on his face. There next to him was Ursus, churning through the water like a battleship, massive and steady. Droplets of water glistened against his dark coat before slipping back into the river.

"Swim, Jake," he said, "Swim."

Jake swam.

Chapter Eleven

On the other side of the river, the world turned to gold.

Jake lay on the riverbank, thankful to have solid ground beneath him again. He didn't know how much time had passed since he'd waded in or how far the current had taken him. As he swam, his world consisted of nothing but the rush of water in his ears and the feeling of his legs and arms working through the cool current until he forgot what it felt like to move any other way.

It was possible he had swum through the night, or perhaps two; somewhere along the way his mind had melted into the thought that he had always been in the river and that the river was all that there was. It was Ursus, swimming along beside him, steady and certain, that kept him going. It never occurred to Jake to ask Ursus how far it was or how long it would take to get there. He simply swam, his stroke and breathing as regular as a heartbeat. The feeling of sand beneath his fingers had been a surprise, almost a shock, and he barely remembered pulling himself up the bank and out of the water, rolling onto land, soft but gloriously solid.

He reveled in the curious, foreign sensation of stillness, a feeling that he lost whenever he closed his eyes. With his eyes shut, he felt the gentle rise and fall of the water despite the grass that tickled his neck and ankles. He didn't mind, however; all that mattered was that the river was behind him. Stretching as far as he could see was an ocean of golden grass, rippling in great waves where the breeze moved through it.

Ursus lay next to him, up on his belly, a canine Sphinx rising from the grass. As far as Jake could tell, Ursus seemed none the worse for the long swim. Jake envied him; though he wasn't physically tired, he felt weary, as if he'd spent too long concentrating on his math homework without a break. What he wanted to do was close his eyes and think about nothing for a while, but he had questions that wouldn't let him rest.

Ursus had saved him twice, but Jake could not shake a sense of despair whenever he was near the giant dog. He wasn't sure if Ursus intended to accompany him in his search for Gordon. Part of him hoped that Ursus would lie on the riverbank and watch him disappear into the golden sea of grass. But something else told him that the dog was there for a reason, and he would be a fool to wander into the grassland alone.

"Thanks for saving me again," Jake said.

"It is good to help a Giver."

"Why are all the other dogs afraid of you?"

The words seemed to hang in the air for an instant

before the rustle of the grass swallowed them up. Jake felt a terrible, icy feeling take hold in the pit of his stomach. Behind the sadness in the big dog's eyes was some terrible truth, and part of Jake hoped that Ursus would simply turn his head and refuse to answer the question.

Ursus did not turn away. He gazed out over the sea of golden grass and said nothing.

Jake closed his eyes and listened to the wind and the low, constant rush of water flowing past them. If he stopped now, he was sure that the question would simply fade into the recesses of the dog's mind until it was lost. All he would have to do was lie back and stare into the sky, and they could both forget. It would be easy.

But Jake needed to know. He couldn't explain why; he only knew that Ursus was hurt, deep inside, and the dog was carrying his pain around like a weight strapped around his neck. In his way, the dog was no freer than Cy or Sarafina or Sebastian.

"Why didn't you come with me to the Howl?" His voice came out in a whisper.

Ursus turned his gaze on Jake.

For a brief second, Jake was afraid. Ursus' gaze was cold, hard; Jake had seen it flicker across the dog's features when Samuel challenged him. But it melted away just as it had before, only a flicker, like distant lightning, gone so quickly that Jake wasn't sure it had ever been there at all. In its place was the familiar, quiet sadness Jake knew.

"I will show you," Ursus said.

Ursus sat up, gazing up into the deep, impenetrable blue of the sky. Everything around them went silent at once as if even the wind held its breath.

It began as a low growl, so low and deep that Jake felt rather than heard it, rising from somewhere in the dog's cavernous chest, and by the time it reached his throat, it was a howl, and with it came a tide of sorrow, loneliness and regret that washed over Jake like the river. The feeling overwhelmed him, and he begged Ursus to stop, but the howl did not abate, and the sound washed out the soft rush of the river and the rustle of grass and his own plaintive cries. The grassland itself melted away, and Jake was cast into total darkness.

Jake felt enveloped in soothing, quiet warmth. The clean scent of newborn puppies hung thick in the air, and gradually he became aware of the sound of snuffling, scratching, whimpering. There was still darkness, and Jake tasted something sweet and warm. It coursed with life, and he drank deeply, feeling the warmth in his throat and belly, and finally his limbs.

Around him, he felt the jostling of paws and tails, searching for the same sweet taste. Jake drank his fill and then curled up in perfect safety, his littermates pressed against him. He slept.

His eyes opened to a world blurred and indistinct. He could make out the shapes of his littermates, and the smell of pups still overwhelmed any other scent save that of his mother. There was bliss and peace, and mother's milk. Four brown walls made up his world; beneath him, a softness against his paws and belly. He drank, and he slept.

Each time he stayed awake a little longer, each time his eyes and ears and nose sensed a little more. Flies, landing on the edge of the box, watched him with oversized, iridescent eyes. Curious sounds beckoned to him over the brown wall. Every now and then, a shadow would pass over the box, linger there for a moment, and then depart, leaving behind a strange, thick, slightly acrid odor. There was nothing to fear; mother was calm, and if she had nothing to fear, neither would he.

Time flowed, broken up by sleep and warm milk and wrestling with the others. His body grew stronger. His eyes were clear and his hearing sharp. A breeze stirred the air inside the box, and carried with it the crisp sweetness of cut grass and the rich aroma of cooking food as it drifted in from beyond the walls, and even the walls themselves exuded a peculiar smell; wood and urine and, very faintly, the strange, acrid odor of the shadow.

There came a time when the shadow lingered over the brown walls of his world. Its odor washed over him, and then he felt smooth, warm hands gather him up and lift him.

The cardboard box that held his mother and his littermates seemed impossibly distant. From his vantage point, Jake saw a wide, carpeted area. Bookcases lined the walls, and a pair of couches formed an l-shape in front of a large-screen television. Then he stared into the face of his first Giver.

She was a little girl, but in Jake's estimation, she was a giant. Her hair was curly and raven-black, spilling down her shoulders, partially obscuring the rims of her glasses. She smiled, the wonder in her eyes magnified by the lenses, and Jake found himself captivated by her, as filled with wonder and excitement as she appeared to be.

She said something in Spanish. Jake could not understand the words, but he recognized the sentiment: you are a beautiful little puppy, and I love you. She drew him close and nuzzled his ears, his paws, his belly, her strange scent clinging to his black coat. A voice beckoned the little girl in Spanish from another room. The girl answered back, gently replaced him in the box and disappeared. Now he understood why Mother had nothing to fear; the Givers were wondrous and beautiful.

Every day he and his littermates grew more robust, and he noticed that he was stronger and larger than any of the others. They knew it too; though they wrestled with him, it was always he who ended up the victor, and their games with him were more often games of chase than tests of strength. One by one, his littermates were taken away by the Givers until he was alone with Mother. She was calm, and if she was calm, he would be calm as well.

A Giver came. It wasn't the girl but a man. His features were severe, his eyes cold. A tattooed spider web in faded green ink spread from his left ear across the side of his head.

When the Giver picked Jake up, his hands were surprisingly gentle, though the skin was rough and knobby. The man lifted him to eye level and then smiled. He said something quietly, in words that Jake could not understand, but there was hope, malevolent hope in his whispers as if he were examining a new weapon and imagining what terrible deeds he would do with it.

The man placed him in a plastic crate with a wire mesh door and carried him out of the house. The world was magnificent through the spaces in the mesh; vast houses loomed against the expanse of the street, broken up by lawns that looked to Jake's tiny eyes like patches of a dark green meadow. The crate bounced and swung in the man's hand until they reached his car, an old Camaro painted a shade of red that reminded Jake of fresh blood. Jake could see nothing but black upholstery. The inside of the car was a miasma of acrid Giver odor, old food, and cigarette ashes. Then the engine roared to life, and the car lurched into motion.

The scene shifted, and Jake found himself in a kennel. He was cold, and all around him rang the barks and whines of other dogs, the air thick with fear and sorrow and hopelessness. He howled for his mother, but she did not come, and the Givers did not bring him to her, no matter how loud his cries.

A Giver came eventually, but it was not the Giver who had taken him from his mother. This one was younger; his black hair pulled back tight against his scalp, a wisp of a mustache underneath his sharp, thin nose. Seeing the Giver made him howl louder, calling for Mother until his cries echoed from the kennel walls. The young man peered into the cage. Jake thought that perhaps the boy might give him a little comfort, but he did not. He slammed his hand against the kennel door and shouted. Jake could not understand the words, if indeed, there were any. But he understood the young man's meaning.

There was no more calling for Mother after that.

Mother was not there to give him milk, so he had to eat what the Givers pushed into his kennel: hard, cold bits of powdery kibble that irritated his throat on the way down. He did not like it, but it was worse to feel the emptiness in his belly, so he ate it whenever the Givers provided it.

Mother faded from his memory until even her scent was lost. His world was the kennel; four walls, a wire floor, a bowl of water, an empty bowl where the Givers put his food.

Time flowed, but nothing changed except the food and the newspapers that lined the underside of the kennel. Loneliness and boredom were his only companions, and even the other dogs ceased to matter, their barks and cries merely part of the background noise, their scents bleeding into the kennel-smell that infused every breath he took.

The bald Giver came. Jake remembered the sour mixture of sweat and tobacco and the tattoos and the coldness of his eyes. The bald Giver peered into the cage, appraising the pup inside. He seemed satisfied. He opened the kennel door, but instead of shoving in a ration of food, he reached in and gently put his hands around Jake's little body. Jake felt the strange knots of dead skin on the bald Giver's palms, but he was not afraid; at least it would be something different than the walls of the kennel.

When the Giver pulled him out, Jake could see the long rows of kennels, stacked three high. Some were occupied by dogs, others by cats, and still others empty. They paraded past the kennels and into the blinding sunshine. The air smelled like grass and fallen leaves, but also of fear and blood.

The Giver opened a gate and stepped through. All around them was a tall, chain-link fence. The Giver set him down on white concrete, rough and cool against his paws. Training, Jake thought. But instead of giving the pup a command, the bald Giver struck him. Jake felt the blow, but shock and surprise kept him from running. The Giver struck him again. The pup yelped in fright and pain and tried to move away, but the bald man advanced, hitting him again and again.

Jake felt the pup's anger and heard a growl rise from his throat. The sound of it was hardly scary; it would have been comical in another situation, but the anger was real.

The bald Giver smiled. He offered Jake a treat.

Time flowed, and the pup learned. The Givers wanted his anger. His growl made them happy; his bite earned him meat and praise. They gave him a knotted rope, and he learned to bite and shake, and clench his jaw so that he would not let go. The harder he bit, the longer he held on, the happier the Givers were. He learned to keep his anger close, so he could make the Givers happy. It was good to help the Givers. He did not know why the Givers wanted his anger or his bite, but they gave him meat and praise when he showed it to them, and that was enough.

Now he was inside the enclosure again. But there was no Giver this time. Instead, a calico cat was pacing the length of the wire fence, searching for a way out. The pup had smelled cats but had never seen one. It was small, like a pup, and it was beside itself with fear. He knew what the Givers wanted, but he could not give it to them; a heavy chain attached to a leather collar held him back. He strained against it. The cat arched its back and then shrank away. It tried to jump free, but the fence was too high, and it could gain no purchase on the metal. From outside the cage, the Givers laughed.

There was no anger, only a sense of anticipation, the rush of the hunt. The Givers released him. The cat eluded him twice, but he caught it in a corner and clamped his teeth across its hind end. Fur and the taste of warm blood filled his mouth, dripped off his tongue. The cat struggled, but its claws were nothing; the Givers had shown him pain, much more than any cat could. He held on, shaking the cat back and forth until its limp body hung still, draped against the sides of his mouth. The Givers laughed and praised him, but still, he would not relinquish his prize. The Givers laughed even louder. They let him keep it until he lost interest. The cat was not for eating; it did not taste good, but the Givers gave him good meat, and so he let them take the cat's mangled carcass away.

Time passed, and Ursus was no longer a pup. He knew his strength and power. The Givers stopped giving him cats and gave him dogs instead, small ones at first, but as he grew, so did his prey. Dogs fell beneath his jaws, whining in their death-agony, the taste of their blood in his mouth. Jake had seen enough, but he could not look away.

They took Ursus and put him in a car. He rode with the Givers, not in a cage, but next to them, part of their pack. There was wind in his face, and with that wind came new scents; the sharp stink of newly poured asphalt, the hot, dusty smell of dry concrete, the stink of old beer and discarded French fries, and the pervasive Giver-odor, which seeped into everything. The sun warmed his back through the windows, and the Givers sang along to the music blaring through the car radio. It was the first time Ursus had felt something akin to happiness since being taken from Mother.

The car ride lasted a long time. The shadows stretched across the pavement, and the sun approached the horizon by the time they stopped. The sharp tang of gasoline told Jake exactly where they were; the Givers had stopped at a gas station, but not like any Jake remembered; there were too many people, their cars packed closely together, and no one seemed to be buying gas. Instead, the people threaded their way between the cars toward the rear of the building. As they moved away from the car, Ursus smelled dogs.

The closer they came, the more distinct their smell, and the air grew thick with the metallic taste of blood. The familiar anger rose up in Ursus; he wanted to please the Givers, and he felt the hackles rise across his neck and his ears press flat against his head. He strained against the chain until it choked him.

Behind the building stood a makeshift arena

of plywood and chicken wire, surrounded by crude bleachers. People milled around, leaning over the rim to witness what was happening inside. Ursus could not see what was taking place behind the plywood, but he could hear the snap of jaws and the tearing of skin. An anguished howl sent the Givers scrambling over the sides of the arena, and all was quiet.

The Givers made an opening in the arena. One dog walked out next to the Givers. He was covered in blood. His eyes were golden brown behind a red, wet mask. The anger came over Ursus, and he lunged at the dog. The dog lunged back, snapping and growling. His Givers dragged him away, a trail of red pawprints tracing their path. Another dog was carried out, its body limp and dripping blood.

The Givers led Ursus through the opening. Across from him was another opening, and through it stepped a Giver and another dog. This dog was not like the ones Ursus had killed at the kennels. This one was like him. His eyes were narrowed into slits, ears flat against his head, his teeth bared.

I will please the Givers, it seemed to say, though Jake heard no words. *I will growl deep. I will bite hard. I will make you die.*

There was no fear in Ursus, only the anger he had been taught. He answered the same way. *I will growl deep. I will bite hard. I will make you die.*

The Givers let go.

For Jake, the fight was a nightmare from which there was no waking. He felt the searing pain of the bites and scratches, tasted the blood in his mouth, felt the crunch of flesh and bone in his jaws. He heard the anguish of the other dog, felt the last, rasping breath and the limp weight of its body against his neck and shoulders. Ursus shook the carcass until the Givers came and forced him to let it drop. It made a horrible, wet slapping sound when it hit the concrete, and the sound echoed in Jake's mind.

The Givers were pleased.

Ursus went back to the arena many times, more than Jake could count, and the fights bled into one another, a long, steady river of violence, pain, and fear. A sick, listless feeling came over Jake. All he could do was keep watching and hope for the end.

The end came.

In the arena, four dogs faced him. They were smaller than Ursus but powerfully built and unafraid. They seemed to say, *We are many, and you are only one. Our pack will make you die.*

Ursus answered them, growling deep, showing his teeth. *I am Ursus. I have killed many dogs, many packs. I will make you all die. I will lap up your blood.*

The Givers let go. Jake and Ursus fell into a maelstrom of gnashing teeth and searing pain. In the end, four dogs lay still on the concrete. Ursus lay among them. Agony ripped through his body when he tried to move. The other dogs had done their work, even as Ursus had done his. The Givers came, and he begged them to make the pain stop. Jake begged along with him, for he felt everything, just as Ursus felt it. The bald Giver with the tattooed head leaned down. He shook his head. His hard features softened, and Jake saw something like genuine sadness pass over his face. He stepped back.

In his hand was a gun.

The bald Giver said something in a language Jake could not understand, but he knew what it meant. It was goodbye. A flash, one last pain, and then darkness.

They drifted, their bodies light. Then they felt heavy again. Ursus took a breath. All was darkness and warmth, as it had been before the Givers. He tried moving his legs, and they obeyed. The searing pain was gone. Gone also was the smell of blood, the acrid stench of the Givers. He could no longer smell the arena, not even on his own coat.

Ursus opened his eyes.

He lay in a patch of soft grass. Beside him, a river flowed, wide and cool. Behind him were trees; he did not have to look to know they were there; their aroma infused every breath he took. Above the river was a vast, empty sky. A thin golden line marked the boundary where the river and sky met.

But there were no Givers, and Ursus did not know what to do. He had displeased them, and so they sent him away, and now he was alone. He tried standing, and his legs felt young and strong, as they had when he was still with Mother. He paced back and forth. He took a drink from the river, but the water disappeared as soon as it entered his mouth. He found that he wasn't thirsty, nor did he feel any hunger. He could make no water to mark his presence or pass the old food from his body.

He followed the river. The water was going somewhere; there were ripples and froth where the water ran over submerged rocks. Follow the moving thing, the thing that was going somewhere, he thought, and he would find the Givers. He would find a way to please them again. It was enough.

He followed the river for a long time. All was wondrously new; each bend and curve brought something unexpected; the tumbling babble of water over rocks, the fresh scent of damp grass and warm sand. From the other side of the river, the air carried the rich, earthy smell of tall, golden grass. Even the scent of his own skin, warmed in the daylight and suffused with moss and rich earth, was new to him. The memory of the Givers faded from his mind, and he was not sad to let them go.

He walked until it was night, and the sky filled with a strange, milky brightness against the dark. He had never seen such a thing before, and he sat for a while and watched the sky, how the light drifted and moved, just like the water. It spilled down in the water itself until the river and the sky became the same. He stepped closer, curious, but the sky had no scent; the place still carried the day-smells; river and grass, moss, and earth and tree.

From a distance, he heard it, faint but persistent. Howling.

Dogs!

The sound stirred anger in him, but it was weak, like a breeze rippling through the leaves of a tree, gone before he even realized it was there. From far away the howl called, and in the call came the promise of comfort, of walks in the woods and warm nights curled up on a blanket, of games and baths and gentle scratches behind the ears. From somewhere deep inside, he remembered the warmth of his littermates and the taste of sweet milk and the deep peace of falling asleep nestled against his mother.

He broke into a run, plunging into the forest toward the sound of the howls. He darted between the thick trunks, weaving among them, using the wan starlight as a guide. He ran for a long time, but he could not run enough to get tired. He did not think of stopping; as long as he could hear the howls, he would come. The Givers were good. He had done all they asked. They hadn't sent him away but rewarded him. He would see Mother again.

After a while he caught their scents; many dogs, many packs of dogs, all gathering, howling together. The memories grew stronger as the sound grew closer, and he could almost see her in his mind and feel the warmth of the fur and the steady beat of her heart. Anger and confusion melted away, and he doubled his speed.

The ground sloped upward, and the sound of the howls grew louder in his ears. They were close; their scent was in the air, fresh. He burst through the edge of the woods and into a great clearing. Jake recognized the waterfall and the rocky pool. Silver fire poured from the cliff above and filled the pool with light. The dogs sat clustered together in a large, ragged knot in the center of the clearing, their heads craned toward the sky. Ursus did not hear their howls anymore, though they washed over him like an ocean wave. He took a deep breath and called to her, adding his voice to the howl.

Mother!

It was not Mother who answered. All the dogs in the clearing turned to face him, fangs bared, ears pulled back, and all around him was the stench of the arena. One after another they charged, snarling. Once again, he heard their challenge. *I will growl deep. I will bite hard. I will make you die.* He felt once again the brush of coarse fur against his tongue, the snap of bone, and the rasp of a last breath. Agony, a flash of light, and then darkness. He opened his eyes.

He was still surrounded.

Ursus growled deep, his ears pinned back against his skull, his teeth bared for all the dogs to see. They turned when they heard his growl, hundreds of heads at once. Some fled. Others dropped to their bellies. Ursus bounded after one of the runners, a black and white Great Dane, closing the distance between them in an instant. He snapped at the Dane's hind legs, missed, and then the Dane slipped to the right and vanished among the trees. Standing in his place was another dog, and the sight of it sent Ursus skidding to a halt.

It was as large as Ursus, its deep brown eyes stared through him, unafraid. Its body was gray, its coat thick and long and wolflike. Ursus met his gaze, challenging him.

"What is your name?" the dog said. Ursus did not answer. The dog's question came not in bark or growl, but he understood nevertheless. Ursus growled instead, deep and menacing.

"I am called Nikita at the Howls," the dog said.

This time Ursus answered. "I am Ursus. I will please the Givers. I will shake you until you are still. I will make you die."

But the gray dog did not meet his challenge. It did not make a threat of its own, not did it back down or lie on its belly. It stood motionless, regarding Ursus with what seemed more like sadness than anything else.

"You will be called Ursus at the Howls," came the dog's response.

Ursus hesitated. It pleased the Givers when Ursus made dogs die, but Ursus could not bring himself to growl deep or bite hard. In the clearing, with silver fire pouring from the sky and milky light dancing above, Ursus could do nothing.

"There are no Givers here," said Nikita. "You are free."

Ursus did not know what that meant.

"There are no Givers here for you to obey. There are no Givers here for you to please. You are free. Howl with us, Ursus."

Ursus did not know what to do. He looked at Nikita once more. A terrible sadness gripped him. Before Nikita could speak again, he turned and fled.

He wandered a long time, careful to avoid the Howls. He came across the Calling-Place, watched as the dogs rushed joyously toward the calls of the Givers. He left that place, afraid that the Givers would call him. But no amount of wandering would take away the lingering sadness that clung to him like his own skin. Day and night came, but to him it made little difference. Finally, he returned to the river.

He stared into the water. He saw his own reflection distorted by the rippling current. The water beneath the surface was dark and inviting. He could find peace there. And so Ursus waded into the river, allowed it to lift him and carry him away from the bank, allowed it to pull him under, into the darkness. He sank, slowly closing his eyes for the last time, when something white flashed just ahead of him. He peered into the dark, searching. It was there, a little way in front of him.

A Giver.

Jake.

Ursus stopped howling, and Jake came back to himself. He opened his eyes, expecting to see Ursus still sitting next to him, but the dog was gone. Jake sat up, searching the grassland around him. He was seized with a terrible fear; Ursus would go back to the river and sink into darkness. Jake would be left alone on the grassland, wandering forever, the Mountain always just out of sight.

"Ursus?"

But the dog was gone.

"Don't go," Jake begged. "Stay with me. I need your help."

Jake cast about for some sign. He saw a faint, deep footprint in the sandy soil and then another. Ursus was following the river. He leaped to his feet and sprinted up the bank, following Ursus' trail. Before long, Ursus came into view, standing on the riverbank, staring out across the wide swath of the river, his front paws submerged.

Jake splashed into the water, putting himself between Ursus and the deep.

"It wasn't your fault. That was the Givers. It wasn't you."

Tears welled up in Jake's eyes. Ursus stared out over Jake's head into the swirling depths of the water. Jake put his hand on Ursus' shoulder. His skin was warm and damp.

"I killed many dogs. Many packs of dogs," Ursus said.

"That was before! You're free here. You don't have to listen to those Givers anymore."

"I am not free," said Ursus, and he took another step into the water.

"Ursus, wait—" Jake said, but the dog, it seemed, had made up his mind. He waded out into the river. Jake splashed ahead of him, the water nearly up to his neck.

"If you go, I'm going too."

Jake had never felt such clear resolve about anything. It was suddenly, immediately clear to him. If Ursus kept going, Jake would follow, to whatever end lay in store for them in the cool darkness beneath the surface. The water felt cold, and his feet sank into the soft sand. Jake felt every grain against his skin as if his body knew it might not ever have the chance to feel again.

Ursus hesitated. "You must find the Mountain."

"I can't do it by myself. I need you with me."

Ursus tried to step around Jake, but Jake blocked his path again.

"You did some bad things. So did I. Everybody does bad things. But when you do something bad, you have to try to fix it. My dad taught me that. He said everyone makes mistakes, and when you do, you have to try to make it right. My friend Sebastian got taken by those Malbinocks because of me, and I want to make it right. If you come with me, we can do that together. Or you can give up, and we'll do that together too."

Ursus became very still. The water lapped around his massive legs, and he gazed out over the water. Finally, he shifted his gaze down to Jake.

"I will follow you, Jake. We will find the Mountain. We will find Gordon. We will find the other dogs."

Jake threw himself against the big dog's body, pressing the side of his face into the dog's muscular chest. Relief and joy almost overwhelmed him. Jake imagined the entire world around him relaxing. They waded back out of the water, and Jake reveled in the breeze that stirred the tops of the grass and blew against his wet skin.

Before them lay the grassland.

Chapter Twelve

In the grassland, Jake got his first real glimpse of eternity. Across the river lay the forest, nothing more than a thin line of green on the horizon, at the very least a promise of a destination. The grassland was something entirely different. With his back to the river, Jake could not make out a single landmark, let alone a mountain peak. Flat, featureless ground stretched out into the distance, the grass undulating in golden waves stirred by the breeze. There were no paths through the grass, as if no paw or foot had ever disturbed it.

He felt like a tiny speck, looking out across a vastness he couldn't comprehend. At least he had Ursus and solid ground under his feet. The dog sat and looked out over the grass, his coat still shiny from the river. His manner hadn't changed. Jake still felt his friend's quiet sadness, but now that he understood its source, he found it easier to accept.

"I guess we should get going," Jake said. Ursus came up to his side and stopped.

"Lead the way, Ursus." Jake gestured out into the grassland.

"I will go with you."

"Well, you know your way around here."

"I will go with you."

Jake rolled his eyes. "We'll never get anywhere like this. You're kind of from here. I mean, not exactly, but you've been here longer. So you should pick."

"I will go with you."

"Oh my God!" Jake balled his hands into fists. "Look. We have to pick a direction, all right?"

"I will follow you. Givers know all."

"Who told you that?"

"Givers know all. That is what I know."

"Well, then you don't know anything. How could I know the way? I just got here!"

Ursus blinked and lay down in the grass.

"What are you doing? We're supposed to be looking for the Mountain! I hate this place! How am I supposed to find a mountain in all of this? And you're not even helping! Couldn't you at least sniff around?"

"No dogs have passed this way. That is what I know."

"Well, let's follow the river then. Maybe they crossed somewhere else."

They followed the river for some time, and Ursus' answer was always the same: no dogs have passed this way. As they walked, Jake watched the water roll past. He was caught between two seas, and he could navigate neither one. He felt hopelessly inadequate. Any minute he expected Ursus to wander away, just as the other dogs had, but Ursus remained by his side, plodding across the sand with the same steady rhythm as he had in the river.

"This is getting us nowhere," Jake said. "Are you sure you can't smell any dogs?"

"No dogs have passed this way. That is what I know."

"Well, fine." Jake turned his back on the river. "Samuel said there are supposed to be cats in here. Maybe we can find a cat and ask for directions."

"Many cats have passed this way."

Jake stretched out his arms, exasperated. "That would have been good to know! Why didn't you tell me that before?"

"Many cats have passed this way. That is what I know."

"Could you track one down for me?"

"I will find a cat. But cats fear dogs."

"Yeah, but they're not afraid of Givers. I'll talk to them once you find them."

Ursus set off into the grass, his nose pressed to the ground.

The grass beyond the river was nothing like the tall, stiff blades Jake had encountered at the Calling-Place. That grass was almost sharp as if it were designed to keep things out. Here the grass was much thinner, each stalk topped with a tuft that reminded Jake of a woolly caterpillar. The ground was spongy but not soft; it pushed back when he set his feet down. With each step, it seemed that the ground itself was helping him along.

It occurred to Jake that he was seeing something that perhaps no other person had ever seen, and so he tried to memorize the view. But he also considered the possibility that he'd never see anything else, that he would never see his parents or Sebastian again. Once more, he thanked God that at least he had Ursus along.

The big dog kept pace behind Jake, stopping periodically to sniff the air or sample the ground for signs of other creatures. He said nothing, but Jake sensed a lightness in him, perhaps an extra spring in his step that had nothing to do with the ground beneath his paws. Now, Ursus at least had a place to go.

They walked along in silence for a long time, each lost in his own thoughts. The boundless golden waves hadn't lost their beauty, but the sameness of it wore on Jake, and the longer they walked, the more he hoped they'd encounter something different. It was a relief when day abruptly ended and the world plunged into darkness.

The darkness in the grassland was far different from what Jake had experienced in the forest. There, everything had been bathed in pale silver, the starlight lending a different kind of beauty to the trees. Jake waited for the stars to burst forth, as they had over the woods, but there was nothing in the sky but inky blackness.

"Ursus, where are the stars?" Jake said. It was so dark he could not see the dog, though Ursus was so close that Jake could hear him breathing.

"Rain is coming."

That was the last thing Jake expected to hear.

He took a deep breath, intending to use it to lecture Ursus about saying foolish things, but in that breath came a scent that reminded Jake of wet sidewalks on a summer afternoon. Everything became very still and quiet. The air took on a warm, moist feel, like the air in the bathroom after a hot shower. Then, all at once, the sky let loose a torrent of rain, so intense that it sounded almost like a jet engine in his ears. Instantly, he was soaked to the bone, and he had to bow his head to keep the rain out of his mouth and nose while he breathed. Jake took some solace in the temperature; it was neither too hot nor too cold, so at least he wouldn't boil or freeze.

Jake decided he could write an entire book about how the people in church had gotten Heaven so wrong. The water pounded the grass in a steady roar, and it was all Jake could do to keep his feet.

"How long is this going to go on?" Jake raised his voice over the rush of the storm.

"It is raining. That is what I know," said Ursus. "Sit under my belly. I will block the rain for you."

Jake quickly did as the dog suggested. He was still soaked to the bone, but at least he could sit up without water running over his face and getting into his nose.

"What about you?" he shouted.

"I will sit and block the rain."

Jake ran his hand against the dog's coat. He felt the warm water spill over his hand and run down his forearm in little rivulets until it dripped from his elbow. There was no way the dog could be comfortable. Even sheltered underneath Ursus, Jake continued to get wet, so it was probably much worse for the dog.

"Ursus, I'm glad you're with me. Glad you're my friend."

"I am called Ursus at the Howls. I am not called Myfriend."

Jake was surprised at first, but when he thought about it, Ursus' answer soon began to make sense. There was nothing like friendship in the world Ursus had left behind, and the dog had kept to himself since arriving. Jake decided it was up to him to try to explain it.

"It's not a name. It's ..." he trailed off, trying to think of a way to explain. The more he thought about it, the more confused he became. Ursus wasn't going to know anything about trading Pokemon cards or playing tag or switching places in line in the gym to be on the same team, but that wasn't friendship. Maybe friends did those things, but there was something more to it, and Jake wondered how he had gotten to be eleven years old without ever really thinking about it.

"It's like this," Jake said. "A friend is someone you'll go anywhere with because you want that person to be happy. And you know that person wants you to be happy. You went into the river to get me, and I went into the river to get you. That makes us friends."

Ursus was quiet for a while, and Jake listened to the steady drum of rain against the dog's flank and wondered if he had explained it well enough. He probably hadn't; he barely understood what it meant himself. Maybe he, like the people at church, had gotten a lot of things wrong. Maybe a lot of the things he thought he knew weren't right after all once he really thought about them.

"I am a friend," Ursus said, as if trying it on, getting its scent before taking it in his mouth.

"That's right. You're a friend."

"I am a friend," Ursus repeated.

The patter of rain sounded like a drum roll in the darkness. Beneath the sound of the rain was the measured rush of air flowing in and out of the dog's lungs just above Jake's head. The air smelled of wet dog and grass. Ursus did not move; he was as still and solid as a marble statue. Jake tried to think of something to talk about, but nothing came to him.

The darkness and the steady, driving rain made him drowsy. He realized his eyes were closed, but he wasn't sure when it had happened. He drifted. His body felt cold, far colder than the rain, but it was more an observation than a feeling. He drifted on.

In the darkness he heard voices. Faint at first, they grew louder as Jake drifted closer. There were many voices, all talking at once so that he couldn't understand any of the words. It reminded Jake of the school cafeteria when everyone had something to say at the same time, but no one was listening, so the words tumbled together between the tables and were lost.

He thought he heard "hypothermia", but the word was strange and meant nothing to him, and he quickly gave up thinking about it.

Eventually, the voices began to quiet down, one by one, until there was only one voice left. It was a woman's voice, and her words felt very close as if they were being whispered into Jake's ear.

One misty, moisty morning,

When cloudy was the weather,

I chanced to meet an old man dressed all in leather.

He began to compliment, and I began to grin,

How do you do, and how do you do?

And how do you do again?

Jake remembered the song. It was something his mother used to sing to him to get him to fall asleep. He had a vague notion of climbing out of his crib and hitting his head, and then the crib was gone, and a regular bed was in its place. He remembered Mother being very angry with him for getting out of bed, and then she sang the song. The song was the one thing that always worked, though his mother hadn't sung it to him in years. Jake did not recognize the voice. It was a weak, haggard sound, more of a croak formed into words than the voice of someone singing. Jake thought that perhaps the woman had been crying. She finished the song, her voice trailing off into silence.

As he drifted, he wondered what had made the woman so sad. He wished there was something he could do to help her, but he could think of nothing. Other voices broke the silence until they once again filled his head with a mad jumble of words. Somewhere in the tumult, he thought he heard his name, whispered in the sad woman's creaky, tremulous voice.

"Jake!" she called, but Jake could not answer her. The sad woman called two more times, almost begging, but Jake could only drift and listen and feel sorry for her.

"Jake!"

The last time it was loud enough to wake him. His

body felt heavy again, and he opened his eyes. The rain was gone, and he clutched at the grass beneath him to make sure it was still there. His mind felt sluggish. He blinked, rubbed his eyes, and sat up. Stalks of golden grass waved in a light breeze, their strange, tufted tops just above Jake's head. It took him a moment to remember where he was. He and Ursus had crossed the river.

Ursus was gone.

Jake cast about, his concern turning to panic. He was just about to cry out when Ursus emerged from the grass.

"Jake!"

It hadn't been the sad woman calling him, Jake thought. Ursus had found something. Jake clambered to his feet. The air was warm, and his clothes felt dry.

"What is it? What did you find?"

"Cats," said Ursus.

Ursus plunged back into the grass without another word, and Jake followed.

Chapter Thirteen

Ursus carved a meandering path through the grassland, occasionally stopping to locate the scent again. Jake didn't object. He plodded on, grateful to have someone else making decisions for a time. The great golden waves stirred up by the breeze gradually lost their novelty, and Jake's thoughts turned inward.

The sad woman's song haunted him. It played through his mind in the same raspy, raw voice that sang it in his dream. It lingered at the edge of his memory, hiding like a ghost in his peripheral vision, only visible when he focused on something else. Every time he tried to remember where he'd heard it before, it would vanish.

His memories from before came and went, hidden and elusive, like dishes in a sink of soapy water. Familiar things pushed through the bubbles and gave him a glimpse of his past life before disappearing into the depths, but he couldn't control what emerged or how long it remained in view. The sad woman remained hidden from him, except for her song, lingering quietly beneath the soft rush of wind through the grass.

Ursus stopped again. He leaned forward, pressing his nose into the golden stalks between his paws, his sides moving in and out like a bellows.

"They are close," Ursus said.

"Where? I don't see anything."

"Their scent is strong. They are close. That is what I know."

"Which way?" It didn't really matter; anywhere he looked he saw nothing but more grass.

"All around."

They waited. Jake strained his eyes, peering across the tufted tops, hoping to catch movement against the wind, something that would indicate the presence of animals moving below.

"Dogs do not belong in the grassland."

The words were spoken in a silky, imperious voice, and Jake got the impression that the speaker considered it a chore to address them. He cast about for the source of the voice until he remembered that the dogs spoke without sound. If it was a cat speaking to him, it probably worked the same way. He would have to draw it out of hiding if he wanted to see it.

"What about Givers?" Jake said aloud.

"This is not the place for Givers," the voice answered. "Givers go to the Calling-Place and wait for their dog servants to come running when they call. We are cats, and we will not be called."

Jake bristled at the cat's tone. But he needed the cats more than they needed him, and so he held his temper.

"We're not here to cause trouble," said Jake. "We're looking for the Mountain."

"You do not belong here. This is the place for cats. Go back to your Calling-Place and take your servant with you."

"He's not my servant."

"He walks at your side. He takes the rain on his back, so you will remain dry," countered the cat. Jake peered into the grass, searching. The cat had been watching him since he and Ursus had crawled out of the water onto the riverbank, toying with them all day.

"I'm not going to argue with you," Jake snapped. "We're supposed to be on the same side."

"There are many cats missing, and now a dog prowls the grassland. You and your servant have been taking cats. Now we have found you. You have taken many cats, but we are still enough to drive you back into the river."

"What would I want with a bunch of cats?"

"What would cats want with a Giver who follows a dog?"

"I'm following him because he can smell you and I can't! I told you, we're trying to find the Mountain—"

"Go back to the river."

"We're not going back."

"Then you will be hunted," said the cat.

Jake stared out into the grass, stunned. He looked at Ursus. The dog sat, relaxed and apparently unconcerned with the cat's threat. A chilling thought crept into Jake's mind.

What if all the cats were as large as Samuel?

They probably wouldn't be a problem for Ursus. Jake doubted that any of the cats, even those as large as Samuel, would attack him. But Jake was a different story. He had nothing but a pair of jeans and a thin t-shirt to protect him and no weapons to defend himself. Ursus couldn't watch him every second. Eventually, the cats would get an opportunity. The situation made Jake feel a little like a mouse.

"Come on, Ursus. If they don't want to help us, we'll find the Mountain ourselves." He didn't like the idea of being hunted by a cat, but he refused to let them know it. He started forward again, with Ursus at his side. Jake sensed no anger in him.

"Didn't it bother you, what the cats were saying?" Jake asked.

"They are afraid."

"That's good, I guess. They won't come after us then."

"They are not afraid of us."

"We are not afraid. We wait for the dark," said the cat. There was a quiet malevolence in the cat's voice this time, a sense of anticipation, like a school bully watching his victim, counting the minutes until the bell rang.

Jake scowled and raised his arms over his head. "You know what? If you think you can take us on, here we are. Come out and push us back into the river. Or leave us alone."

Jake stopped and waited. Ursus stood at his shoulder. The grass waved in the breeze, but nothing emerged to face them.

"You're right. They are afraid. These cats aren't like Samuel. Samuel would have come out and took us on face to face."

"Samuel?" the cat said. "What do you know of Samuel?"

"Samuel's a cat. But not like you. He's brave. He's the one who sent us here."

"You have seen him? He is not taken?" Much of the insolence had faded from the cat's voice. Jake heard only concern, and underneath, hope.

"He was, but he escaped," Jake said. He recounted his battle with the Malbinocks and how they parted with Samuel at the riverbank. It felt a little strange to Jake that he was telling his story without knowing exactly who was listening. Ursus made himself comfortable, stretching out in the grass, his head resting on his front paws.

"Dogs are missing too," Jake said. "That's why we need to find the Mountain. Samuel said there's a dog there who knows the way to the Malbinock hideout."

A rustle in the grass sent Ursus' ears up. A gray cat emerged, quite abruptly, as if it had stepped out from behind a curtain. It was only a little larger than a regular cat, and standing next to Ursus made it seem unnaturally small.

"I am called Smokey," the cat said. "I have never seen the Mountain. But I know of one who has. He is called Blue. I will allow you and your servant to follow me."

"Well, thank you," Jake said. "You're a real pal."

Smokey crept through the grass without disturbing a single stalk, and Jake admired him in spite of his arrogance. Ursus followed a little behind. Though Smokey was leading them somewhere, he did not appear to be in any particular hurry to get there. He ambled rather than walked, the way a person might wander from one room of their house to another. The slow pace bothered Jake, and before long he couldn't contain himself.

"Do you think we could pick up the pace a little?" Jake said. "The sooner we get to Blue, the sooner we can get all the cats back."

"I do not take orders from Givers," Smokey said. "If you do not want my help, leave me and find Blue yourselves. I will watch and be amused."

Jake took a deep breath, resisting the temptation to land a foot squarely into Smokey's backside. The cat walked regally ahead of him with his tail raised high. Jake forced himself to calm down. Smokey was their only link to the Mountain. Sebastian was depending on him, as were the other animals the Malbinocks had taken. Ursus plodded along beside him, unconcerned.

"So this cat Blue, he'll take us all the way to the Mountain?" Jake asked. He had already had enough of cats. If Blue was anything like Smokey, Jake wasn't sure it would last all the way to the Mountain. He would either kill the cat himself or feed him to Ursus.

"Blue? Blue is no cat." Smokey's reply was aloof and dismissive. Fine, Jake thought, so Blue isn't a cat. Whatever he is, it couldn't be worse than having Smokey leading them. Jake dropped his questions and trudged on in silence, parting the soft grass and marching along beneath the cloudless, sunless blue sky.

Jake bore it for as long as he could, but eventually, the silence was too much for him. Ursus was right; there was still noise in him, and he had to get it out. Unfortunately, the only one who had anything to say was Smokey.

"How long has Samuel been gone?"

"Cats do not count days. But the grassland is not the same without him."

"He wanted to come with me, but he couldn't get back across the river."

"That is what you said."

"I think he'll be back as soon as he feels better," Jake said. "You should have seen him fight. He must have taken out ten of them."

"There is no better hunter or fighter than Samuel," said Smokey. "It was Samuel who decided to fight back against them."

"So what happened?" Jake said.

"Samuel fought. Many cats joined him. He did not like being hunted, and so he hunted them. I did not join him at first. I thought we should run. I thought that we should find another place, a safe place. Many cats thought this way, but Samuel did not listen to us. Samuel did not blame the dogs as many cats do. One night we were resting in the grass, and Samuel came to us. He had something in his mouth, things we recognized from the old world, the Givers' world."

"A Malbinock," said Jake.

"He dropped it into the middle of our gathering. It was a pile of old Giver things, metal and wood and things that were good to scratch to keep claws sharp.

He told us they could be killed. Many cats followed him, and they hunted the Malbinocks. Some Malbinocks were killed, but cats still went missing. I told Samuel that if we moved farther away from the river, we would be safe, but he would not listen to me. He and the others pushed the Malbinocks all the way back to the river, but it was a trap. They were waiting.

"We heard their fight from where we hid. We listened to the Malbinocks take cats. I went to the river, but I was too late. There were no cats left."

Smokey's voice was tinged with shame and regret.

"We tried to fight them too," said Jake. "I tried to do the same thing. It wasn't your fault."

"I did not ask for comfort," said Smokey.

"You know what, Smokey? I knew plenty of cats back home, and they were all friendly. They got along fine with their owners. You don't have to put me down every time you say something. We're supposed to be on the same team."

"Cats have no owners. We come and go as we please. When we wish to see the Givers, we go find them. Dogs are envious. Givers are envious too. If you wish to give orders, you have your servant."

"He's not my servant! But if that's how you want it, fine. I'm a Giver, and Givers make rules all the time. Just lead us to Blue, Smokey, before I lose my grip and feed you to my dog."

"I do not eat cats," said Ursus.

"Ursus!"

"I do not take orders from Givers," said Smokey. "Find Blue yourself." Without another word, Smokey slipped into the grass and disappeared.

"Smokey, come back! Didn't you hear him? He doesn't eat cats! Smokey!"

But Smokey was gone.

Jake and Ursus wandered until dark descended on the plain. According to Ursus, the scent of cats was all around them, and they discovered just before the darkness fell that they had walked in a gigantic circle, coming across their own trail as the stars began to swirl and dance overhead. Jake flopped on the springy turf next to Ursus, defeated. He had no one to blame but himself. It was he, not Ursus, who drove Smokey away. The only thing Ursus had done was tell the truth.

"I'm sorry, Ursus,"

Ursus rolled over on his side, and Jake leaned on his belly, rising and falling gently as the big dog breathed. "I should have kept quiet. You're right about me and noise."

The dog seemed content to rest. But Jake's thoughts swirled in his head, and it was all he could do to sit still.

"Didn't anything Smokey said bother you?" he asked.

"The cat has much noise in him."

"Like me?"

Ursus stayed quiet, and Jake let it go; he'd had enough truth from the dog for the time being. It stung a little to be compared to Smokey, but Jake had to admit that what bothered him most about the cat was his refusal to obey. Unpleasant memories swirled to the surface. He remembered shouting matches and the

big, hard chair outside Mr. Meyers' office where he'd
waited so many times. He watched himself slip out of
the bedroom window and down the path through the
woods to the river—

He shook himself and stood up. Ursus lifted his
head.

"Hey, Smokey. I know you're out there. I'm sorry I
threatened you. That was stupid."

Jake's voice vanished into the night, and the wide,
dark space closed in on him. "We really need to find
the Mountain. There are a lot of dogs and cats and who
knows what else counting on us. I promise if you come
back, I'll be nice and I won't order you around."

Dejected, Jake sank back down and leaned against
the dog's massive belly. The stars danced overhead,
forming whorls and eddies that shimmered and
melted back into the silver flow. For all of their beauty,
they felt distant and cold, and Jake found no comfort
in them.

"Not all cats are the same." It was another cat,
its voice so close that Jake whipped his head around,
expecting to see something right next to him, but there
was nothing but grass drenched in silver light, and
beyond that, darkness.

"Not all Givers are the same either," Jake replied.

A cat emerged, slipping through the golden stalks
as if through an open door, appearing quite suddenly
at Jake's feet. This one was larger than Smokey, its coat
dappled in patches of black and white. His belly was
rounded, and he had the look of a cat who enjoyed
napping more than hunting. His face was wide and

friendly with big, yellow eyes that sparkled a little in the starlight. It padded up to Jake and rubbed its forehead against Jake's foot.

"I am called Elmo," the cat said.

"I'm Jake."

"I know your name, and the name of your servant," said Elmo. "We have been stalking you since you climbed out of the river. I wanted to help, but Smokey said it was a trap."

"What changed your mind?"

"You did not turn back when Smokey abandoned you. And you did not stay where you were or beg for help. I wish to help the ones who were taken. That is why you and your servant—"

"Friend."

"Your friend," the cat repeated, "have come."

"What about Smokey?"

"Cats do not take orders."

"That's what Smokey said."

"Smokey is not always wrong," said Elmo. "Come, I will take you to Blue."

"Is it far?"

"What is 'far'?"

Jake didn't know how to answer. He only had a vague understanding of it himself, and even that understanding seemed to have little practical use on the grassland.

The cat shrugged it off. "Follow me, I will show you the way."

Ursus stood, and Jake scrambled to his feet as well. The cat set off at an unhurried pace through the grass, and Jake was careful to make no objections. They walked through the night, each of them keeping to his own thoughts. Elmo led the way, his belly swaying to and fro as he walked. It was almost comical to watch him waddle along. Ursus followed along behind without complaint.

They stopped just as the light burst across the sky and washed out the stars. The ground rose gradually ahead of them, forming a long ridge that stretched across the horizon. There was no sign of the Mountain.

"Where is Blue?" said Jake. "There's nobody here."

"You will find Blue beyond the rise."

"You're not coming with us?"

"I must rejoin the others." Elmo rubbed his head against Jake's legs, and Jake reached down to scratch behind the cat's ears. He could feel the thrum of Elmo's purr against his fingertips. Ursus paid no attention; he looked upward, toward the top of the ridge. Whatever lay on the other side had captured his interest, and he gave no further thought to the cat.

"Thanks, Elmo," Jake said. He scratched Elmo under the chin.

"Find the others and bring them back."

"We will."

Elmo turned and melted into the grass.

Ursus sniffed the air. "Something is close. Not dog. Not cat. Not Giver. Not Malbinock."

"Let's go see."

Ursus broke into a run, and Jake joined him. Before long they reached the top of the ridge. Jake's eyes widened as he took in the view.

The land sloped sharply downward from the top of the ridge. Light sparkled across the waters of a long oxbow lake that curved away from them and receded into the distance. At the bottom of the ridge, a sea of brown, gray, and white blotted out the grass. The mass undulated and shifted, almost iridescent, like a film of oil spread across a puddle of water. As he looked closer, he saw that it wasn't a liquid at all. It took Jake a moment to understand what it was.

Horses.

Chapter Fourteen

If the cats were telling the truth about Blue, Jake and Ursus would be searching for a very long time. Thousands of horses crowded along the lakeshore. Individuals emerged, silhouetted against the waters of the lake for a split second before disappearing back into the herd.

Ursus sniffed the air, his nose pointed skyward. Jake watched him. He hadn't seen his new friend express such interest in anything.

"Horses," Jake said.

"Their scent is new to me." Jake could smell it too. With so many horses, the air should have been thick with the smell, but only a hint lingered in the air.

"People ... Givers, that is, ride them. The Givers climb up on their backs and the horses carry them around."

"My Givers did not do this," said Ursus.

Jake shook his head. "Not everyone. Now most people use cars. But some people still keep horses and ride them for fun. They're also used for racing and rodeos and some other sports. There are even some police officers in big cities that ride them. But a long time ago, that's how most people got around. Now it's more of a hobby."

"There are many in their pack," Ursus said.

"Too many. We're never going to find Blue in that crowd."

Ursus wasn't wrong about the numbers. But there was something wrong with a word he used. Pack. It wasn't right. Jake thought of old cowboy movies, saddlebags, and pack horses lumbering on a dusty trail behind a ragged line of riders, all going in the same direction. But there were no saddlebags here, or people who needed supplies. Horses didn't travel in packs. Jake's eyes lit up, and in his excitement, he gave Ursus a friendly slap on the shoulder.

"That's it!" Jake said. "This is going to be easy."

Ursus cocked his head and waited for Jake to speak.

"You called them a pack. Well, that's close. I mean, it's the right idea, but a bunch of horses is called a herd, and they pretty much go everywhere together. Don't you get it? We don't have to find Blue. Blue is just one horse! There's about a million of them down there, and any one of them should be able to tell us where the Mountain is. If Blue has been there, they've all probably been there too."

Ursus eyed the vast herd. "There are too many. We must find one away from the rest."

"You sound like a wolf," Jake said.

Ursus blinked, uncomprehending.

"That's how wolves hunt. But we're not hunting, we're asking for directions." Jake patted Ursus on the shoulder again, admiringly, and set off down the steep slope to where the horses gathered on the plain. Having Ursus at his back was like being the only person in the world with a machine gun; no one was going to try to pick a fight with him. He headed down the slope at a fast trot, buoyed by excitement. He looked back once, and found Ursus sitting on his haunches at the crest of the ridge.

"Come on," Jake called. "Let's go talk to them."

"I will stay here," Ursus said.

"How come? What's the matter this time?"

Ursus did not answer. He hunkered down in the grass overlooking the valley.

"How about if you come with me halfway?"

Ursus rolled over on his side.

There would be no convincing him now. Frustration seeped into Jake's shoulders and settled in the back of his neck. Thoughts crept into his mind, whispering to him about the dog's cowardice. Some fighting dog he was, afraid of just about everything. What was the use of having a big fighting dog with him if he stayed behind every time Jake might need some protection?

"Fine," he said. "I'll go down and talk to them, and then I'll come back and tell you what I found out."

"I will stay here."

"Yeah, you said that already."

Jake descended the ridge alone. He looked back

more than once, hoping that Ursus had changed his mind, but he was in the same place Jake left him, a large, dark shape jutting up out of the grass, his side silhouetted against the ridgeline. At least it would be easy to find him again.

The scene changed as he descended. The horses weren't as densely packed as they seemed from up above, and Jake began to see the horses as individuals. Every kind of horse Jake had ever seen or heard of was there on the low plain. Giant working horses, strong enough to drag trees, mingled with slim, graceful racehorses. Scattered in the throng were ponies, some no bigger than large dogs. They wandered around each other seemingly at random, with no apparent preference for breed or size or color; each horse appeared perfectly comfortable in the company of all the others.

Jake was still too far away to get their attention, and he was in no hurry. Ursus' refusal to come along still rankled him. Jake cursed him under his breath.

Each step carried him closer to the herd, and the horses themselves loomed larger and larger as he descended. At the top of the ridge, Jake had focused mostly on the sheer number of them, but here he could see their hooves and their leg muscles rippling with speed and power, and he thought about them as individual animals, capable of taking off his head with a kick, or running him down and trampling him into the churned field.

Perhaps Ursus had been wise to stay behind; Jake didn't want to think about what would happen if the big dog's presence panicked the herd. He glanced back up the ridge, wondering how quickly he could cover the distance to the top.

If the horses sensed him, they paid him no mind at all. Without Ursus, he felt small and vulnerable. He paused, searching the herd. He wasn't sure what he was looking for; perhaps a horse that seemed kinder than the others. He couldn't find any of the ponies; they had either melted back into the herd, or perhaps their smaller size had just been some kind of optical illusion.

The grass at the bottom of the ridge was no longer golden; the blades were wider and had been beaten into a dirty brown, crushed flat beneath the horses' hooves and mixed with churned-up soil. The air was still and smelled of turned earth and the rich scent of horses. Despite the herd's vast number, it was largely quiet, save for the sound of hooves thumping against the turf or an occasional snort or whinny.

He chose a tall, graceful gray horse directly ahead of him. It noticed him before he could address it, its large, black eyes fixed on his. Jake froze. For the space of a heartbeat, time ground to a halt. The horse took a tentative step toward him and then another. Jake found himself backing up, seeking the safety of the high ridge and Ursus.

"You are a Rider."

There was wonder and disbelief in the horse's voice, rich and deep and sonorous in Jake's mind. The horse's voice calmed him. There was no malice or ill will in it, only a sense of confused awe, the way one might sound after witnessing a miracle. Jake took a deep breath.

"My name is Jake."

"I am called Gunnar," said the gray. Several of the other horses turned their heads toward Jake.

"Rider!"

That one word, Rider, spread through the herd like a gale, and horses began to jostle against one another for a look at the boy in their midst. Before long, they had crowded in so close that Jake was forced a little way up the ridge to avoid being accidentally crushed.

A deluge of questions inundated Jake's mind, swelling like a storm, blotting out any chance of understanding. He tried to quiet them down, but the force of their voices in his mind was too much for him, and any resolve he might have had was torn away in the torrent. He ran. The echo of their questions followed him halfway up the ridge, a roar in his mind that blotted out all sound and turned his vision into a red haze, and he nearly tripped over Ursus when he finally reached the top. He threw himself over the dog's body and hid against his belly. Gradually, his vision cleared, and the roar in his mind dissipated to silence.

"You did not find Blue," said Ursus.

"No. They were all talking at once. I thought my head was going to explode. They're not coming up here, are they?"

Ursus rolled over and pushed himself upright. He turned a little and gazed out over the ridge.

"No horses are coming this way," he said. He hunkered back down in the grass.

"Good." He leaned against Ursus' massive shoulder, keeping the dog's body between himself and the ridge. He looked out over the grassland instead, taking refuge in its emptiness. It was like looking into a great, golden ocean, the daylight scattered and sparkling across the stalks like seafoam, and the sound of the breaking waves came to him quietly, a whispered crash against the hillside. Jake watched and listened and tried not to think about what he should do next.

There was no help for it. He would have to go back down, but just the thought of so many voices clamoring for his attention kept him crouched at the top of the ridge. Ursus lay next to him; his gentle, regular breathing almost made Jake feel as if he were in a rocking chair.

"I'm sorry," Jake said. "I was hoping I could bring one of the horses up here so you could meet him."

Ursus said nothing.

Jake was out of ideas. He stood up and surveyed the valley below. The horses remained at the bottom of the ridge, just as they had been before they took notice of him, as if they had already forgotten him. That, at least, was encouraging; Jake could simply start over when he came up with another plan. He thought of sneaking back to Gunnar and calling him a little way from the others, but there was no way he'd be able to recognize a particular horse in the crowd. His next thought was to have Ursus charge halfway down the hill and catch one of the slower horses before it got too far away. He rejected that one too. Ursus probably wouldn't agree to do it, and Jake was worried about the horses injuring one another in their haste to get away.

"I don't know what to do."

"Givers know all."

"Yeah, except the way to the Mountain."

"Blue knows the way."

"Maybe. Maybe they all do. But how am I going to find out when they're all talking at once?"

Jake looked back at Ursus. He lay with his head toward the valley, relaxed and alert. Jake marveled again at the power contained in the dog's dense, rippling muscles, at his head, contoured and sharp like the head of a spear. An idea flashed through his mind, and the simplicity of it startled him so much that he leaped to his feet and pressed the palms of his hands against his temples.

"You could get their attention!"

Ursus' head snapped to where Jake stood, the way he might if he caught something small running past his peripheral vision. He didn't reply, but his ears cocked forward, and he didn't look away. The dog's reaction heartened Jake; he hoped it meant that Ursus would help as long as it didn't involve fighting. He paused a few seconds longer to make sure. The dog's eyes remained fixed on Jake.

"I used your name to get the dogs' attention at the Howl. Not on purpose, but it still worked. This time, you're going to do it."

"They will not know the name of a dog," said Ursus.

"No, but they called me Rider," said Jake. "If you told them to listen to the Rider, it might distract them long enough for me to talk to them."

Ursus gazed out over the grassland for a time.

"I will tell them," he said.

Jake suppressed the urge to jump up and shout. "You might have to tell them really loud," he said.

"They will hear my bark."

Jake believed him. Ursus rose and shook himself, and there was a sense of purpose in the dog's step, like a coiled spring before its release. Something of the fighting dog remained in Ursus, and Jake watched with a mixture of admiration and dread as Ursus brushed past him and stood silhouetted against the top of the ridge. Ursus had power the way a thundercloud or a volcano had power, and Jake could hardly wait to see it.

If any of the horses were still searching the hillside for Jake, they would see Ursus instead. He stood against the top of the ridgeline like a monument, and Jake took a position to Ursus' right.

"I'll go down about halfway, and then you get their attention."

Jake made his way back down the hillside. The dog's ears leaned backward, almost flattened, his eyes staring out into the vast, teeming herd below him. Jake descended the hill as fast as he could go without tumbling. He felt like he'd just lit the fuse of the biggest firecracker ever made, and he had to get far enough to be safely away before it went off. Anticipation and a tinge of fear formed a sublime mixture in his chest, and he breathed little heavier as he neared the halfway point. Below, the horses milled around the base of the ridge, oblivious to Jake's descent. He slowed down, expecting at any moment to hear Ursus call from above.

Jake knew it was coming, but it made no difference. A deep, low growl rose in pitch, growing into a staccato bark that rang across the valley, loud enough to force Jake to his knees. Even the turf beneath his hands vibrated with the sound. And somewhere inside the dog's roar were words.

"Horses! I am called Ursus at the Howls. You will listen to the Giver Jake. He wishes to speak to Blue and find the way to the Mountain. Hear him!"

The rumble of Ursus' call was matched by the rumble of untold thousands of hooves. Jake looked up to see the entire herd turn and flee, dispersing across the plain. Jake tried to shout over the tumult, tried to get them to stop, but his pleas were useless. His heart sank as the herd shrank into the distance. At last, the plain was quiet. Where the herd was, only two horses remained.

Jake took a couple of deep breaths before he got back to his feet. To his relief, the two horses held their ground. Jake waited for Ursus to make his way down the hill, and together they crossed the ground churned black by the fleeing herd.

Memories of horses bubbled up from the murky depths. Horses, through the window of a bus, watching him roll by on his way to school. He'd seen them so often that they had long since become part of the scenery, no more noteworthy than clouds or white pines or the occasional eagle circling high over the lake. But as he reached flat ground and his feet sank into the dark, aromatic soil, he knew he was seeing horses for the first time.

The two that waited for them in the field were not the docile creatures he remembered, content to crop grass or plod along the roadside while its rider bobbed up and down in the saddle. Jake could feel their presence from across the field, a majesty so palpable that it brushed against his skin like a warm breeze.

On the left stood the mare, black as the moon's shadow. Her mane poured across her neck in long, wavy tresses, and her eyes, small in comparison to her head, blazed with a fierce intelligence. Next to her stood a dappled gray stallion, his legs as thick as the trunks of trees, his mane close-cropped to his broad neck. He gazed down on them as if from heaven, his ears erect, and the same intelligence that illuminated the mare's eyes burned in his as well. Both of them dwarfed Ursus. Standing in the midst of the three of them made Jake feel almost insignificant.

Jake and Ursus came to a halt several yards short of where the horses stood. Jake tried to think of some apology, but the words sounded used and plain in his mind. He felt the horses' eyes gazing fixedly on him, but he kept his gaze on his feet, now half-buried and caked with dark loam. He reached out a hand and pressed it against Ursus' flank, profoundly grateful for the dog's presence.

"Welcome, Ursus of the Howls," said the mare. Her voice was gentle but rich and full of untapped power, like the sound of the sea on a calm day. "Welcome, Rider. Your place is on the other side of the water. How is it that you come from the grass, from the place of cats?"

Jake opened his mouth to respond, but his mind was empty. He strained for words, but for that instant, they had abandoned him.

"I am called Freya," said the mare, "and this is Jarl."

Freya's prompt shook only Jake's name from his paralyzed mind, and he forced it past his lips. The horses looked on impassively.

"How have you come to be on this side of the water?" said Jarl. His voice was deep and resonant, a heavy wind through the forest.

"You're not mad?" Jake asked. His mind began to thaw. It was clear that they meant him no harm. Their voices rolled through him, but instead of panic or fright, Jake began to feel a sense of calm.

"Dogs bark," said Freya. "Horses run. Riders ride. Each does as it was born to do."

"What did you mean about 'this side of the water?'" Jake asked.

"The Riders come on the other side of the water and call us to them," said Jarl.

"A Calling-Place!" Jake said. "The dogs have one too!"

"But you have not answered us," said Freya. "How have you come to be on this side of the water?"

Jake told Freya and Jarl the entire story, including the battle with the Malbinocks and the loss of Sebastian and the other dogs, and finally, his swim across the river and the trek through the grassland. He told it as best he could, though he suspected that he hadn't gotten everything in the right order. The horses stood still, listening. Neither attempted to interrupt.

"That is why you wish to have Blue show you the way to the Mountain," said Jarl. "You are a brave Rider."

"Not really," Jake said. "If I was brave, we wouldn't be in this mess."

"You are only one. The Malbinocks are many," said Freya.

"So can you show us the way?"

"No."

Jake shook his head as if someone had splashed cold water in his face. He found himself struggling for words again. He took a deep breath.

"What? Why?" The questions came out much harsher than Jake intended, but he didn't apologize.

"We do not know the way to the Mountain. It is outside our borders," said Freya. "Only Blue has been to the Mountain."

"Well, can I talk to him?"

"We cannot allow it."

Jake stamped his foot into the soft soil beneath his feet; it sank in up to his ankle but made little noise.

"Why not? Don't you care what's happening? The Malbinocks might have horses too!"

"Blue is not a strong horse," said Freya. "He was very afraid when he crossed the Black and came to our herd. He would not come near us. When I tried to approach him, he galloped away. The stars came and went many times, and he did not return to us. More came, and some of the herd were called back across the water, and still, he did not return."

"So, Blue ran away and never came back?"

"He came back to us, only a short time before you arrived," said Jarl. "Now we must help him. We must teach him not to be afraid. He must stay with the herd."

"How do you think he's going to feel when the Malbinocks come and drag him away?" Jake said. He was yelling now, shouting at the top of his lungs, though it seemed to do little good. Whatever noise he made seeped into the churned field or spread into the wide plain and was lost. Freya and Jarl watched him impassively, not even twitching an ear at Jake's angry display. Ursus stood as still and quiet as the horses.

"The Malbinocks do not attack the herd," said Jarl. "We are sad to hear about the others, but we must look after our own."

"Maybe they don't attack you right now, but how do you know they won't start tomorrow?" Jake said.

"We are many," said Jarl. "And the Malbinocks are frail."

"That's what the dogs thought!" said Jake. "Now there are only a few dogs left. They hide out by the waterfall because they're too afraid to go anywhere. There are only a few cats left too, hiding in the grass up there." He pointed up toward the top of the ridge. "How do you know they won't come after you once they have all the dogs and cats?"

"We are many," said Freya.

"But how do you know? Maybe they have a few horses right now."

"The herd is safe," said Jarl.

"It's a big herd," said Jake. "You just said so. You can't keep track of all of them."

"We keep the herd safe," said Freya.

"Did you keep Blue safe?" Jake said.

"Blue did not stay with the herd," said Jarl.

"So how did you keep him safe if you didn't even know where he was? What if there are other horses out there that you don't know about? What if the Malbinocks have them? Even if they just had one horse, wouldn't you want to do something about it?"

Freya didn't answer.

"I just want to talk to Blue, that's all. You can let him talk to us, can't you?"

"We cannot split the herd," Freya said. "If we allow Blue to go, others will wish to go. One by one. That is how the Malbinocks feed. They cannot harm the herd if we stay together. Blue must stay. We must all stay."

"But that isn't going to solve anything!" Jake cried. "Sooner or later, they're going to come for you. You can't just stay here and hide!"

"Jake," said Ursus. His attention was fixed on something beyond Freya and Jarl.

A lone horse plodded across the ruined turf. It seemed reluctant; it skulked toward them a few yards and then stopped. Jake waited and watched. He stayed very still and quiet as if he were watching a bird that would fly off at the slightest hint of danger. Ursus followed Jake's lead and remained where he was. Freya and Jarl watched the horse as it made its way across the field, allowing it to come forward in its own time.

"Is that Blue?" Jake whispered.

"That is Blue," said Freya.

"Can I please just talk to him?"

Freya bowed her head a little. "Talk. But Blue must stay with the herd."

He was small, at least compared to Freya and Jarl, with a stout neck and muscular legs, much more like the horses Jake remembered from the school bus window. His coat was a deep, lustrous brown, and a small white diamond filled the space just above his eyes. His eyes remained, for the most part, fixed on the ground in front of him; he seldom glanced up. As he came closer, he began to move sideways, putting a healthy distance between himself and the other horses. When he got within a hundred yards or so of Jake, he stopped and would come no closer.

Jake glanced over at Ursus and gestured for him to stay where he was, and then he set off very slowly across the field toward Blue. The dog made no attempt to follow, nor did Freya or Jarl. He tried to walk as slowly and calmly as he could, praying with each step that Blue wouldn't bolt. Blue glanced up every now and then, but he seemed far more concerned with Freya and Jarl than he was with Jake.

Blue wasn't nearly as large as the other two horses, but he still towered over Jake, and yet Jake's only fear as he approached was that he would scare the horse away. It seemed a little odd that something as big as Blue might be worried about a little barefoot boy who barely came up to his belly, but Jake wasn't taking any chances. He stopped several yards short and introduced himself.

"Hey there, Blue. My name's Jake."

"I have not seen a Rider before in this place," said Blue.

"I think I'm the only one. I need your help."

"You wish to go to the Mountain."

"There's somebody there, someone we're looking for. A dog named Gordon. We really have to find him. It's important." He decided not to elaborate; there was no telling what might set Blue off and send him galloping in the other direction.

"I'm here with my dog Ursus. Well, he's not my dog. More of a friend. A companion. He's right over there." The distance and the size of the horses nearby made Ursus look small.

"I have not seen a dog since I crossed the Black."

"Don't worry. He's friendly."

"Dogs do not frighten me," said Blue.

The comment surprised Jake. He was under the impression that Blue was afraid of everything, but that didn't seem to be the case. Blue appeared calm enough in Jake's presence. Jake moved a few steps closer, and the horse didn't flinch or shy away. In fact, he seemed to pay Jake and Ursus very little mind at all, preferring to maintain a furtive, sidelong watch on Freya and Jarl.

"Will you help us?" Jake said. Blue's eyes snapped back over to him.

"I have not been to the Mountain," said Blue. "I have only been close enough to see it, far in the distance."

"Close enough. Which way is it?"

Blue did not answer immediately. He glanced over at Freya and Jarl, twitched his ears, and snorted, pawing at the broken turf. "I cannot explain," he said.

"What do you mean? Just point. With your head

or something," Jake said, craning his neck in a crude imitation of a horse.

"I cannot show you that way," Blue said. "You must climb on my back." Blue hunkered down, offering Jake a way to clamber up. For a moment, Jake paused, daunted by the horse's size. There was no saddle, no reins, and no bridle; he would be completely at Blue's mercy once he climbed on.

"Don't be afraid," said Blue. "I have never lost a Rider."

"But I told Freya I just wanted to talk to you."

"There is no other way. I will take you. But you must climb on."

"How am I going to stay up there? I don't know how to ride."

"Hurry. Climb on and hold my mane. Hurry, Jake, before they stop us!"

Jake glanced over his shoulder. Freya and Jarl were on the move, closing the distance between themselves and Blue.

"You must climb on now!"

It took Jake a couple of attempts, but he managed to throw himself up onto Blue's wide shoulders. The ground pulled suddenly away, and Jake found himself looking down from a dizzying height. He felt unsteady as if the horse's back were slick with grease and the slightest movement would send him tumbling back into the churned field. The horse took a few tentative steps backward.

"You are safe, Jake. Do not fear. I have never lost a Rider."

But Jake didn't feel safe at all. He lurched back and forth over Blue's shoulders, expecting at any second to be on the ground, staring up into the blue sky.

Freya and Jarl broke into a canter, eating up the distance.

"Blue—" said Freya. Her voice was calm, but in the undertone was the sharp edge of command. Blue spun around. Jake's free arm flailed behind him like a ribbon, and the world lapsed into a momentary blur with the speed of Blue's turn.

Freya kicked into a gallop, with Jarl close behind. Ursus also launched into motion, sprinting toward them.

"Hold on," said Blue.

"Wait! What about Ursus?"

With a spray of grass and mud, Blue launched forward, running with all the speed and power in his body across the empty field. The lake glittered and lost focus, only a silvery blur on Jake's left side. Behind him, he heard the thump of their pursuers' hooves. A low, deep bark drowned out the sounds of their pursuit, and Jake glanced back to see Ursus dash out in front of Freya, so close that Jake was afraid the giant horse would run Ursus down and trample him. Freya changed directions instead, doing her best to get around the dog and make up some of the growing distance between herself and Blue. Every time she moved, Ursus moved as well, hindering her progress. Jarl brought up the rear, far too slow to keep up. Gradually, Blue began to pull away, but Freya did not give up the chase. She galloped on, hard on Ursus' tail.

"Wait!" Jake cried, "Wait for Ursus! We're leaving him behind!" But his words tumbled out into the empty air and were lost in the rushing sound of their wake. Blue surged forward, picking up speed until the dirty gold of the tattered grass and the black soil bled together into a single color, and the wind in Jake's ears left all other sounds behind.

Jake shouted with all the power in his lungs, but it was nothing, the sound of a mosquito's wings in a tornado.

Over his shoulder, Jake watched as Ursus shrank and finally melted into the dark blur of the plain. There was nothing he could do but hold on and watch the empty landscape slip past him through eyes blurred with tears.

Chapter Fifteen

Jake no longer felt the rhythm of Blue's hoofbeats as if the horse had found a way to run without making contact with the ground. The world melted into a kaleidoscope of earth tones; brown bled into swathes of green and gray, which gave way to powder blue, until all the colors collapsed into a small, perfect circle of pure white light in the center, made even more brilliant by the shifting colors surrounding it. The light was warm and carried with it the touch of comfort, a mother's touch, and he hungered for more. For a while, he tried to steer Blue into it, but the light never came closer, dancing just out of Jake's reach, a mirage flickering, a pupil of light in an iris of constantly changing patterns that burst and collapsed, folded, and burst again.

Blue slowed. The light waned and finally faded into the wide, slate-gray sky, and when it was gone, Jake found himself at the mouth of a canyon that meandered between low, rounded hills. All around them, the hills rolled into the distance, blanketed in rich, green heather. The air was cool and heavy with the plant's fragrance, a sweet scent that reminded Jake of both licorice and mint. The steady tumble of water over rocks announced a stream hidden in a nearby draw.

Jake slipped off Blue's back. The soft heather cushioned his landing. Aside from the distant rush of the stream, nothing stirred. Around him, the hills pushed against the gray sky in all directions, but Jake could see no sign of the Mountain. He paced back and forth a few times, peering through the breaks in the hills for a glimpse of a peak or a rough sliver of mountainside, but there was nothing but more heather as far as he could see.

"You said you were going to take me to the Mountain! There's no mountain here. There's no mountain and no Ursus. What am I supposed to do now?" He shouted the question into the sky.

Blue took a few steps backward. He hung his head. His ears twitched, and he licked his lips several times, mechanically, as if he wasn't aware it was happening.

"Well?" Jake said.

"I told you I would take you where you could see the Mountain," Blue said.

"So where is it?"

"You must climb the hill. You can see the Mountain from the top."

"First take me back so we can find Ursus."

"Freya will not let me go with you again."

Jake glared at Blue and then started the climb. What began as a gentle slope became steeper as he neared the top as if the land itself was trying to prevent him from reaching the summit. Jake's anger fueled him, and he paid little mind to the steep grade, dropping to all fours when standing became too difficult. Abruptly, the slope leveled out again, and Jake clambered up to the top.

The rolling hills stretched to the horizon. Jake was seized with the thought that perhaps Blue merely wanted to get rid of him and had dropped him deep into the maze of hills, hoping that Jake would never find his way out. He dashed back to the edge and looked down. Blue hadn't moved. Jake studied the horizon again, peering into the gray depths for some shred of hope.

There it was.

Far beyond the hills lay the jagged outline of a mountain, its peak obscured in a strange black cloud.

Relief and joy mixed with shame and loss, and for a while, Jake could do nothing but sit down in the thin heather on the hilltop and stare wordlessly into the gray distance. It was there, all right, just as Blue said it would be, but without Ursus at his side, he felt paralyzed. No, not paralyzed, he decided. He could still move. It was something else.

He felt small.

All around him, the hills rose and fell, and between them ran a maze of deep draws and canyons. There could be a thousand routes through them to the Mountain or none at all, and even if he found a way, what then? Without Ursus to guide him, Jake had no hope of finding Gordon and no hope of rescuing anyone.

Since he crossed the river, the thought of rescuing Sebastian and the others had been a distant goal, something to work out later, but later had caught up with him, and now he looked down at his own thin arms and feet still stained and blackened with dirt, keenly aware of his own uselessness. Above him, the strange, sunless sky swept low across the hills and on past Jake's sight. He was nothing, a speck of dirt on a rough ocean of green heather.

He would apologize to Blue. The horse had been true to his word. If he could do nothing else, he decided, he could do that. He rose, stretched his legs and descended. The horse remained where he had been standing. When he saw Jake, he lowered his head again.

"It's there," Jake said. "Just where you said it would be."

"This is what you wanted."

"I thought it was. But now I don't know."

Blue lifted his head and studied Jake. "You miss your dog."

"We were supposed to do this together," said Jake. "I want to go back and look for him."

"It would not be good to go back. Freya will be angry." He rolled his eyes and snorted. "She is fast and strong. Faster than me."

Jake remembered the last glimpse he had of Freya, her powerful legs sending a spray of grass and dirt high into the air, her mane a mass of whirling tendrils dancing in the wind. He thought of Ursus, running just ahead of her, inches away from hooves that could crush his legs like dry leaves. Blue would never get another chance to leave the herd, and without intervention from Ursus, they likely wouldn't have escaped in the first place.

Jake couldn't fault Freya for protecting the herd. Had he been in her position, he might have done the same thing. But not going back meant that he wouldn't have Ursus with him when he reached the Mountain. He would be alone.

He lay back on the heather and stared into the sky. The clouds were low and dark, threatening rain but delivering only a vague sense of foreboding. They roiled past his sight, heedless of the insignificant creature watching them. Indecision gnawed at him. His mind ran over the same thoughts again and again, a merry-go-round of choices that led nowhere. Can't go, can't stay, can't give up, which meant either going or staying, on and on the thoughts whirled like the pattern traced by a top that had lost most of its energy and was just about to tumble over on its side.

"You are afraid."

Blue's voice startled him, and he sat up. He had, without realizing it, rolled to his side and tucked himself into a ball. He took a deep breath and stretched his legs and back. Blue was standing directly over him, looking down at Jake with one eye, his head cocked to the side.

"What are you talking about? I'm not afraid."

But he knew the words were a lie before they ever left his mouth. He was afraid, more afraid than he had ever been.

"I am afraid," said Blue. "I am always afraid. And you are afraid too."

"You? What do you have to be afraid about?"

"I fear the other horses," said Blue. "And I am afraid that I will be so afraid that I will forget what it means to be a horse, and then I will be nothing. I will not be Blue and become part of the grass and the sky, and I will not hear the call when my Rider comes."

Jake stood up. Blue was practically on top of him. He reached out and ran his hand along the horse's smooth, glossy coat. Blue's admission wasn't all that surprising when Jake thought about it. It was probably the reason why he had left the herd and traveled on his own for so long.

"So you liked your Rider?"

"My Rider was kind. She never did any harm to me. I carried my Rider and walked among the trees. Sometimes she wished to run, but she never used the whip. When the days were warm, my Rider gave me a cover to keep the tiny things from biting my face. I had bedding, clean and soft, and a paddock with soft green grass and all the water I could drink. When the days grew shorter, there were the colors on the trees, cool mornings and mist, and when the coldest days came, hay in great piles and a dry place to stand out of the snow."

"That sounds pretty good," said Jake. It reminded him of home, but a more exotic version, like something from a dream. Jake's home hadn't been all that different. Memories flashed in his mind of lying in his bed playing Xbox games when he was supposed to be sleeping, with the smell of pine and fresh-cut grass drifting through the screen on summer nights, and fireflies lighting the bedroom in staccato flashes of pale green. He thought of all the times he'd spent the long bus rides to school poring over Pokemon cards or looking over someone's shoulder while they played games on a phone or sent text messages to people sitting in the next seat. It seemed so important at the time, but the memories felt empty now as if the most precious part of them was lost.

"My home was good. My Rider was kind. But I was not the only horse who lived there. There was another with her own Rider. The horse was called Siri, and she was very cruel. She was strong and tall. When the Riders were not there, she chased me away from the best grass. She bit and kicked. One night we were shut in the dry place, but her Rider went away without keeping Siri apart from me. I could not run away. She kicked, and something in my belly began to hurt until I could not stand. Another Rider came and looked at me. I could not get up, and I could not see; I could only smell Siri nearby. I was afraid she would kick me again. Then the other Rider helped me cross the Darkness, and I could see again. I saw many horses. Some of them approached me, but I did not wish to be kicked again, and so I ran."

"I didn't know horses could be like that," Jake said. "I always thought horses were nice."

"Siri was good to her Rider. But not to me. To me, she was very cruel," said Blue.

"But you went back to the herd. Freya said so."

"I wandered a long time. I saw the Mountain. I visited the grassland, and there I saw the cats. Most of them were too afraid to approach me. But some did. They told me there were cats missing and asked if I had seen them. I could not help them. I wandered until I could not remember Siri or my Rider. It felt like it was time to sleep. I was afraid again. I did not want to forget, and so I went back to the herd. I told them of the missing cats, and Freya said the Malbinocks were angry with the cats, and they would be angry with the herd unless we stayed together. And so I stayed with them while I waited for my Rider to come. And I was afraid, always afraid. Afraid to run away and afraid to be with the herd. But I waited for my Rider to call. She would take me back to the green grass and the soft bedding and the walks among the trees."

Jake did not speak for a while. He ran his hand idly along the horse's flank, thinking.

"I guess I'm afraid too," Jake said. "It's like I got a bad cut on my arm. I don't want to look at it, even though it hurts and I can feel the blood coming out, because if I look at it, then I'll know it's bad. Does that make sense?"

"I do not understand."

"What I mean is that if I go to the Mountain and look for Gordon and I can't find him, I'll know what a loser I am. I'm afraid I'm no good to anybody. That's what I've always been afraid of, and I just don't want to go there and fail because then I'll know for sure it's true."

"If you do not look, you will not find him."

"I know."

"And if you do not find him, you will be sure that you are not good?"

"Yeah, that's what I just said."

"So, if you do not look, you will be sure you are no good."

Jake tried to work his way out of Blue's trap, but he was caught, and he knew it.

"I have to go look for Gordon, don't I?" Jake said. A smile played on the edges of his lips.

"You are the Rider. I am only Blue," the horse replied.

"Seems like you have a lot more sense than I do. Thanks for taking me this far. I'm going to get moving again."

Jake patted Blue on the neck, rubbed a palm gently over his soft nose, and then started for the top of the hill. He'd get his bearings and then begin searching for a route through the maze of valleys that separated him from the Mountain. Even as he began to climb, he felt Ursus' absence.

"May I come?" Blue said. Jake turned around. Though he hadn't expected the offer, it was a welcome one.

"Won't you be afraid?"

"I will be afraid."

"Guess I will be too," said Jake. "I would love to have you with me."

Jake scaled the hill again and lingered at the peak for a time. He found the Mountain again, a dark blot against the gray sky, taunting him. Jake took a long look at it, listening to the voice in his mind whispering all the reasons why he should turn back, all the reasons it was hopeless to try, all the ways he was small and weak and useless. He listened to the whispers, every one of them passing through his thoughts like migrating birds, calling out as they flew by.

He listened to them all. Then he made his way back down the hill, where Blue stood waiting, and together, they set off in the direction of the Mountain, their footfalls leaving no trail through the fragrant heather.

Chapter Sixteen

Jake could not recall how many days had passed since he and Blue began their trek through the green hills. When there was light, they wandered through valleys covered in soft heather, each much the same as the last. They spoke little. Every so often, when the sameness and the quiet got the better of him, Jake would climb one of the hills to make sure their path still led toward the Mountain. He suspected they were getting closer, but the Mountain didn't seem to be getting much bigger. The strange, black cloud still swirled around the peak, surrounded in the blanket of gray that covered the sky. Each time was the same; Jake would climb the hills full of hope and return a little more discouraged.

At night, the thick clouds held back the starlight and made the darkness complete. Jake could do nothing but lie down in the heather and wait until the light returned. It made him nervous at first, exposed as they were with the hills looming above them, out of sight but still there, but they encountered nothing more dangerous than the heather, and gradually Jake forgot his fear. But that only made Jake dread the nights even more; the fear gave his mind something to do when the dark robbed him of his sight. In the dark he lay awake, staring into the void with nothing for company but fleeting memories of his life before. Sometimes he would think of Ursus, and his face would flush with shame, and he would tell himself over and over again that there was nothing he could have done. Each night he fought the same battle until the light filtered through the clouds, and it was time to get moving again.

On one of those gray mornings, he trudged up a low hill, expecting to see the next set of hills beyond them and the peak of the Mountain, wrapped in that strange, black cloud, jutting up behind them. His eyes widened as he reached the top.

The land sloped gently upward in a wide, undulating plain. The heather thinned out, giving way to broken patches of shrubs and scattered copses of tall, thin trees. In the center of the plain stood the Mountain, its wide base swathed in mixture of purple and green. Farther up, the green faded into a pale yellow before vanishing into the baleful black cloud that swallowed the peak.

"Blue! Blue! I think we made it!"

Blue trotted up the hill and stopped at Jake's side. He gazed out over the plain toward the Mountain.

"The Mountain is not a place for horses," said Blue.

"We're not going to stay there. We'll find Gordon and go."

Blue gazed into the distance. After a while, he snorted and turned his head away.

"It's not that scary," said Jake. "Look. The bottom is covered in grass. How bad could it be? It's not like we're going to have to climb to the top or anything. Gordon is down there somewhere." He gestured toward the Mountain's verdant base.

"That is not grass," said Blue.

"It looks like grass to me."

"I know it is not grass."

"What is it, then?"

Blue remained silent. After a moment, Jake lost his patience. "Come on, Blue. We should get going." He started down the opposite side of the hill, toward the Mountain, and Blue followed. Jake was relieved; he'd grown accustomed to the horse's steady, quiet presence. It was a comfort, especially at night. If Blue decided to turn back—

Jake decided to put that thought out of his mind. The two made their way down the hill and started across the open scrub between them and the Mountain. The going was easy; the heather thinned and finally disappeared as they moved ahead, replaced by a reddish hardpack that reminded Jake of sandstone or clay. Thickets of shrubs with broad leaves of variegated shades of green pushed out of the soil like islands. Jake approached them carefully at first, suspecting that something might be lurking inside, but found nothing.

In some places heavy rains had washed away the soil, leaving deep arroyos and channels in the hardpack. Jake glanced up at the gray sky, hoping that the dry weather would continue. He remembered the rainstorm in the grassland. There, it had merely been inconvenient, and the grass absorbed the water like a sponge. On the hardpack, it would likely be different.

They pushed farther up the slope, and an uneasy feeling settled in the pit of Jake's stomach. As they ascended, the shrubs became more numerous. Thin, tall trees sprouted up in places between them, alien things with smooth, almost rubbery bark, segmented like bamboo. Wide, elongated leaves sprouted directly from the tops of the trunks, giving them the appearance of green dandelions. Jake didn't like them; all the other trees looked like something he might have found in the world before. The unfamiliarity of these new trees felt like a warning.

The ground had changed as well. Instead of the hard, red clay that supported the shrubs, the ground was springy, more brown than red. Eventually the shrubs gave way completely to the trees. The dandelions were joined by larger, thicker trees with rough, brown bark. Their branches soared overhead, creating a canopy that broke up the gray light filtering through the clouds. The stands of trees grew denser and more numerous until it was obvious to Jake that what he'd seen wasn't grass at all.

Jake and Blue had stumbled into another forest.

"Well, go ahead and say it," Jake said. When Blue didn't answer, Jake prompted him.

"Tell me 'I told you so.'"

But Blue just shuffled nervously beside him and said nothing.

The high spirits that propelled him since daybreak abandoned him, and he peered into the forest. Patches of shadow lined the ground between the trunks, and beyond them, Jake could see no farther. Even the air was different; warmer, humid, like a breath, beckoning them forward, ready to swallow them whole. He leaned against the trunk of a tree and rested his forehead on his arm. Blue waited a few feet away, stamping nervously.

Jake dug his foot into the soft ground and pressed his forearms into the sides of his head. "What was I thinking? I should have known. How are we supposed to find a little dog in all of this? How are we supposed to find anything in this?"

He looked up at Blue, but the horse was no longer paying any attention to him. His gaze was fixed on something ahead of them. Jake tried looking at the same place Blue was focused on, but he saw nothing suspicious.

"What is it, Blue?"

"Something moving. That way."

"What? What do you see?"

"Not see," said Blue. "I hear it. Something growling."

"Growling? It could be a dog! Let's go check it out."

Blue stamped a foot and took a step backward. "We should go. Go back and find Ursus. This is not a place for horses. Not a place for Riders."

"Come on. Just a little way. Maybe we'll see something."

Jake crept forward. The soft earth cushioned the

sound of his steps. His apprehension grew as he moved nearer to where the woods made pockets of deep shadow. Every few steps, he paused, held his breath, and listened, but he heard nothing. Blue followed a few paces behind him.

"I don't hear anything," Jake whispered over his shoulder.

"It is there," said Blue.

The woods loomed in front of them. Jake could see none of the dandelion trees; this was the forest proper, and the dandelion trees were too small to survive beneath the canopy. The roots flared out from the trunks like fins, spiralling around the trunks until they disappeared into the soil. The roots of one tree crossed over those of another, forming low, natural barriers. Some of the roots rose over Jake's head. He could manage it if he were alone, but the way was impassable for Blue.

"We have to find a path," said Jake. "There's no way we're getting through right here."

"The trees do not want us here."

"Blue, they're trees. They don't care. It's just how their roots grow."

They skirted the edge of the forest, searching for an opening wide enough for Blue to enter. Before long, they found it, a break in the trees that flooded the place with diffuse light. The soil had worn away in places, revealing a layer of pale, yellow rock the same shade as Jake had seen on the Mountain's upper reaches. The clearing pushed into the forest for quite a distance before a rise hid what lay ahead.

"This isn't so bad," said Jake.

"It is the same forest."

"Well, the sooner we find Gordon, the sooner we can leave."

Jake led the way into the clearing, and Blue followed a few steps behind. Jake glanced back every few steps to make sure Blue was still there. He seemed to be handling the forest well; his head was up, his ears cocked forward, but his gait was relaxed, and Jake didn't get the impression that the horse was prepared to bolt at the slightest noise.

Neither he nor Blue spoke, and nothing broke the silence except the occasional scrape of a hoof on stone.

At the top of the rise, the forest closed in again. The light dimmed, and the air became thicker, suffused with the aroma of wet wood and mushrooms. The tangle of roots made walking treacherous, especially for Blue, and their progress slowed.

Blue guided them through the labyrinth of twisted roots. The horse's keen night vision and sense of smell were far more reliable than Jake's senses. Giant, ancient-looking trees surrounded them, their tops lost in the dense canopy, but Jake never quite felt at ease. The forest, beautiful as it was, didn't have the same welcoming feeling as the forest around the Howl. At best it was indifferent to them, though Jake had the feeling that the farther they penetrated, the more hostile it would feel. The canopy blotted out most of the light. All that grew beneath Jake's feet was a strange, pale moss. On the roots grew yellow fungus that gave off a pungent odor, like the inside of a bandage that had been left on for too long.

The enormity of the forest filled Jake with a sense of futility. Finding Gordon in such an immense place would be like finding a penny at the bottom of a lake.

"Blue, we're going in circles." Jake sat down on the edge of a tree root and rested his chin on his palms.

"We have not passed this way." Blue pawed at the moss, searching for tracks.

"No, that's not what I mean. I mean, we're not getting anywhere. We have to figure out some kind of plan. Flush him out somehow."

"I do not understand."

"Well, when you're hunting something that's hiding, sometimes you have to get whatever you're hunting to move. You know, like hitting the trees to flush birds. But sometimes you can use a call to make them come to you. You can call in deer, or ducks, or moose. There was this time that my dad took me to this camp up in Weston—that's back home—and there was a guy. I think his name was Don or Dave, or something like that. But there was this guy who taught us how to do moose calls. You just cup your hands over your mouth like this and try to sound like a moose."

Jake demonstrated, but it didn't sound as impressive as he'd hoped. He thought he sounded more like a wounded dog than a moose. His call travelled only a few yards before the trees stifled the sound, which was probably just as well.

"If you call them, they will know you are there. They will run away."

"They would if they thought you were a hunter. But they think you're like them," said Jake. "The guy who taught us the moose calls knew all kinds of outdoor tricks. He showed us how to make a survival whistle ... oh, wait!"

Jake rolled his eyes and smiled. What he needed was a dog whistle, and there was plenty of material right over his head. Jake hopped down off the root and faced the trunk of the tree. The bark was rough and riddled with indentations, cracks, and thick protrusions. He tested it, gently at first, then with vigor. He climbed until his head was level with Blue before jumping up and down on the bark in an attempt to break a piece off. He hung off the side, his fingers wedged in a crack, and dangled there for a minute or two before letting go and dropping back to the ground.

"I think it's safe. What I mean is, I'm going to go up there and get some leaves."

"Leaves? Gordon is a dog. Dogs do not eat leaves."

"I learned how to make an emergency whistle out of a hollow stick when I went to that camp last summer. Those leaves have pretty thick stems. I figure I might be able to make a whistle out of one of them. That way we can call Gordon and make him find us."

"Other things will hear the whistle. Other things will come. It is better to stay quiet."

"You're not worried about me climbing the tree, but you're afraid of me making a whistle?" said Jake. "Look how tall this tree is. If I fall out of it, I'm not going to ... well, I don't know what would happen, but it wouldn't feel good to hit the ground from way up there."

"It is better to stay quiet."

"I don't have any other way," said Jake. "Stay down here while I'm up there."

"Horses do not climb trees."

"You know what I mean."

Jake began his climb, scaling the tree's wide, rough trunk. After a few minutes of climbing, Blue was barely visible; his dark brown hide well-camouflaged in the murky shadows. Upward and upward, he climbed, and as he moved, gray light from above chased away the worst of the gloom. His heart raced, and the warm air rushing into his lungs carried with it the scent of the rainforest, a strange blend of coconut and loam and warm wood.

His skin tingled with exquisite, sublime joy. He exulted in the texture of the bark against his fingertips, in the bottomless endurance in his muscles. He no longer knew or cared how high he was; the canopy surrounded him and obscured any view of the forest floor. Cloud-filtered light shone down, bright and warm after the prolonged darkness. He stretched his face toward the sky and let the light splash against his skin like water on a hot day.

He chose a wide, thick branch and clambered on. The bark on the branch was far smoother than the trunk. Here, Jake moved with much more caution. He inched his way out on his belly, though the branch was easily wide enough for Jake to stand up and walk. He came to a place where he could reach out and grab a leaf. They grew in abundance on the smaller branches. Each leaf was a long strip of deep green, waving like a pennant in a medieval army.

He stretched out a hand and hesitated. Something flashed in his mind, a dim memory of a night bathed in silver starlight when trees leaned and stretched out their branches to offer him shelter from the Malbinocks.

"Hey, tree," Jake said. He spoke out loud as usual, but his voice was so soft it was barely audible. "I'm trying to rescue my friends from the Malbinocks. There's a dog here, somewhere in your forest, who can show me where they live, but he's hiding. Would it be all right if I had one of your leaves?"

Jake felt no objection from the tree. All he had to do was reach out and pluck a leaf, but still, he held back. He kept his gaze firmly in the treetops, unwilling to catch a glimpse at how far he would fall.

"I want to use your leaf to make a whistle, so I can let that dog know I'm here, and he'll come and find me."

If the tree was listening at all, it was doing so in stoic silence. The leaves were there, easily within reach, and yet, Jake's hands remained on the branch.

"The truth is, I wanted the forest all to myself. I wanted to get the dogs to come kill all the Malbinocks for me so the forest would be mine. But it didn't happen that way. It was my fault my friends got caught. I'm just trying to make up for what I did wrong."

Jake held his breath.

He felt a gentle rustling in the branches above his head. Where he lay, clinging to the smooth bark, the air was still. Motion sent his gaze upward, and a single leaf drifted through the air, slipping between the thin branches near the tree's crown. It fell in a gentle spiral moving as if borne up by the air surrounding it. Jake was transfixed by it, descending gracefully from high above him, and he nearly forgot to stretch out his hand and catch it before it drifted past him. His hand closed around it, gently, and he drew it to his chest.

He scooted back to the trunk, where the limb was thickest, and gingerly sat up, his back against the rough bark. He dared not look down; the transcendent joy that propelled him through the climb had abandoned him. Now the edge of the branch felt like the edge of the world, and it was hard to think about anything except what would happen if a sudden gust of wind sent him plunging into the abyss. Jake could almost feel the darkness tugging at him as if it resented him being out of its reach.

The leaf measured from the top of Jake's head down to just above his knees. The stem was surprisingly stiff. He tried breaking off the end of the stem to see what was inside. Tough fibrous pith filled the stem's interior. The blade felt thick and supple, almost leathery. With some difficulty and a little help from his teeth, Jake tore a section of the blade away from the stem. He tried wrapping it between his fingers, the way they did with blades of grass on the playground, but the stuff was too thick. The only sound he was able to make was a low humming sound that tickled his mouth when he tried to make it louder.

After several more failures, Jake finally hit upon an idea that had some potential. He wrapped a piece of the leaf blade around a section of the stem. The result was a thick green tube closed at one end, which he tied off with stringy sections peeled away from the stem's outer layer. His fingernails were just long enough to help him cut a hole through the wrapped leaf. He took a test blow and lost a section of the stem when it shot from the tube like a blowdart and landed somewhere on the forest floor.

Still plenty of stem, he told himself, and he started over, wrapping it even tighter and tying it down with more material from the stem's skin. A second test blow yielded a similar result, as did a third. Desperation began to set in; he was almost out of stem, and Jake wasn't sure the tree would give up any more of its leaves to help him.

It was his pants that saved the day. The bottoms were hopelessly frayed as if they'd been dragged across miles of paved road. Carefully, Jake tore a number of long strands from among the frayed edges. They turned out to be much stronger than the crude string he'd made from the leaf, and he wrapped all of them tightly around the tube, the stem shoved firmly inside.

This time, it held. He carved out a hole near the top with his fingernail and blew again. It didn't make a sound. The urge to toss the contraption into the treetops and just shout at the top of his lungs nearly overcame him, but he glanced over his feet at the open air beyond the branch and thought better of it.

It took several more attempts before he remembered the mouthpiece plug. He split the last piece of usable stem in half and inserted it into the open end of the tube, positioning the flat part toward the hole.

It was finished.

He took a deep breath and raised the whistle to his lips. If it didn't work this time, he decided, he'd throw the whistle away and head back down the trunk.

Jake blew hard. At first, he couldn't get any air at all into the mouthpiece, and it nearly shot from his hand. He tightened his grip and blew as hard as he could.

The whistle screamed so loud it felt like the tree had shoved its longest branch into Jake's ear. It took a few seconds for the agony to register in his brain, and when it did, he dropped the whistle and clapped his hands to the sides of his head. The whistle rolled slowly toward the edge of the branch. For an instant, it lingered there, and then, to Jake's horror, it dropped off into the void. Forgetting his fear, he leaned over, watching the small, green tube as it floated down among the branches and dropped out of sight.

Chapter Seventeen

Jake hadn't considered the return trip when he clambered up into the canopy. Progress was painfully slow; he couldn't see what lay beneath his feet, and so each step required him to seek out a foothold with his toes. Even climbing back out onto the trunk had been a challenge. He made several attempts to grab hold of the rough bark and swing out directly from the branch, but when he tried, he caught a glimpse of the darkness and retreated to safety.

In the end, he had to climb up and sideways before he could start his descent. It was the only way he could do it without a visual reminder of how high he had climbed.

The climb down held no fascination for him. With his ears still throbbing, he made his way down the trunk, pausing every so often to scan the nearby trees for the whistle. There was no sign of it, and Jake wasn't altogether certain that he wanted to find it again.

Finally, his feet touched the damp soil between

the tree's high roots. Blue remained just where Jake had left him, none the worse for his solitude. Jake was glad to see him.

"I made a whistle," Jake said. "Did you hear it?"

"I heard a noise. I do not know if it was a whistle. If you make the noise again, I will know."

"I can't do it again. I lost it."

"Making noise will bring danger. Your whistle made much noise. I am happy your whistle is lost."

"Hey! I spent a wicked lot of time on that thing," said Jake. "I almost fell out of the tree, too, it was so loud. And now my ears are ringing. But we should look for it anyway. Come on, Blue. Help me look."

Jake bent down and canvassed the area immediately in front of the tree, but he found nothing but a few footprints scattered in the soil.

"It is better to leave it," said Blue.

"If we don't find that thing, we're going to be living in these woods for a long time."

Reluctantly, Blue joined in the search. They did a circuit around the tree, but they saw no sign of the whistle. Jake feared that it hadn't survived the fall, that the various pieces lay scattered across the jungle floor or draped across a tree branch high above them. After a while, Jake suggested they split up and head in opposite directions, walking until they could no longer see each other between the close-packed trunks. It proved to be a fruitless search as well. When Jake grew tired of searching the dirt, he called out.

"Blue! Did you find anything?"

Blue answered back, faint in Jake's mind. "No," he said.

"You sure you're telling the truth? You don't seem like you want me to have it."

"I have not found your whistle."

Jake believed him. "Well, let's meet back at the tree I climbed. I don't want to sit around in the dark by myself all night." The prospect of spending the night on the forest floor by himself was vaguely terrifying, though they hadn't encountered anything more dangerous than a growl.

A few minutes later, they arrived back where they started. The dim light made it difficult to see, but Jake was just able to make out his own tracks in the damp soil, and he used those to find his way back to the tree where Jake intended to hunker down for the night.

"I didn't see a thing," said Jake.

"I saw many things. But I did not see your whistle."

"That was our best chance." He looked around for a comfortable place to spend the night. He didn't relish the thought of sitting around in complete darkness again, haunted by his many failures. It occurred to Jake that guilt might be the least of his worries if Blue was right, and there were other creatures in the woods who might not be as friendly as the animals he had met so far.

"Hey, Blue. Mind if I climb up on your back before it gets dark? I don't want you stepping on me if we have to get away."

It wasn't entirely true, but it was as good an explanation as any.

"You are the Rider. If you wish to ride, ride."

"Thanks, Blue. Come on over here. I'll climb up on that root so you don't have to lay down."

Jake pulled himself up on a tall section of the tree's root until the top half of his body dangled over the other side, and there on the ground in front of him lay the whistle. Between the darkness and his eagerness to right himself, Jake almost missed it, wedged perfectly between two roots. He stretched his arm out and leaned down deep into the little wooden canyon, and then a little more, using his left arm to keep from slipping down face-first into the crevasse. With one final stretch, his fingers closed around it, and he drew himself up, quite pleased.

Jake slid onto the horse's wide back and made himself as comfortable as he could. Blue's back was warm and smooth against his skin and broad enough for Jake to stretch out. He stared up into the canopy, searching for a view of the sky, but the branches and leaves formed a dark green vault over his head and showed him nothing. He held the whistle at arm's length, studying it. It seemed none the worse for its fall.

The forest was quiet and dark, and the gloom pressed in on him. Blue's reassuring warmth beneath Jake's back wasn't enough to ward off the loneliness. He tried to start a conversation with Blue, but he couldn't think of anything to say, and so he sank into himself, longing for the sound of his mother's voice or the feel of his father's calloused hand ruffling his hair. Soon after, night plunged the forest into complete darkness.

Jake drifted.

His body was light, and he no longer felt Blue's presence. He floated, warm and comfortable, as if he were lying in a pool of bathwater with his eyes closed. From somewhere distant came the sound of voices. Jake could not recognize them, nor could he make out what they were talking about, but he sensed in them terrible desperation.

Gradually the voices became clearer, but he still could not understand them. A man and a woman, no, two women were speaking in hushed tones about something important. The words were still gibberish, falling over each other and tumbling through the air like smoke, but behind the words were feelings that Jake could understand, and he focused on them. One of the women spoke calmly, but it felt forced. Jake remembered cutting his hand on a tent stake, how the sight of so much blood made him panic. The woman's voice had the same quality as his mother's when she wrapped his hand in gauze and ushered him out to the car. "It's only a scratch," she told him, "but we'll let the doctor see just to make sure there are no germs to make you sick."

Jake remembered clinging to those words like a drowning sailor. He understood then that she had been just as terrified as he was. All he could stammer out was, "Mom, I'm hurt, I'm hurt."

Words clattered out of the dark, filled with desperation and horror. They were pleading. For what, Jake didn't know.

He drifted closer, and the voices seemed to be coming from somewhere just beyond Jake's feet.

"What does that mean? What are you telling me?"

"It means that right now, the machines are keeping him alive."

"So he is alive? Is that what you are telling us? Can you please, please tell me exactly what is happening in there."

"I understand how difficult this is—"

"I need the truth."

"It's still too early to tell—"

"Tell what? Tell what?"

"Doctor, please—"

"Right now, we aren't reading any brain activity, but that could change."

"Oh, dear God."

"It's possible the hypothermia might have preserved the brain despite the hypoxia ..."

"Oh, dear God. Oh, dear God."

That was all. The voices swirled once again into a maelstrom of confusing sounds, no longer recognizable. Jake was borne away again, and the tumble of voices receded into silence. A thought flitted through his mind, but Jake could not seize it, and the voices slipped away like the memory of a dream just after waking, and in their place, Jake heard music, far above; faint but distinct. He had heard it before, a vast chorus raised in song, beckoning him.

He opened his eyes.

Jake remained on Blue's back, exactly as he had been when he stretched himself out. The trees loomed around him, carved out of the darkness by pale, silver light that seemed to come from everywhere at once. Jake held up his hands, and they too were visible.

"Blue," Jake whispered. "Did I sleep all night?" Sleep wasn't really the right word, but Jake wasn't sure there was a right word for what he had been doing.

"It is still night," said Blue.

"But there's light. How—"

Jake didn't need to ask. He knew.

He slipped off Blue's back.

"I'm going back up."

"It is still night."

But Jake was already scaling the rough, broken bark. The silver light threw everything into sharp relief, and Jake, guided by the song that swelled as he ascended, climbed without a trace of fear.

It was the song, and not his arms and legs, that propelled him up into the leafy canopy until it was no longer a song but a flood of peace and joy, the very essence of love made whole and real. Silver light broke through the leaves and lit up the canopy as brightly as the day, and then Jake himself emerged into the open air to look upon the vast sea of stars in their full glory, so close his hand stretched out of its own accord to touch them.

The song lived in him and through him, and all else became trivial. His life before, the journey with Ursus and Blue, and even Sebastian's plight slipped away like the vestiges of a dream. He would abandon it all if the stars would accept him, if they would only tell him through the song how to slip away to shine and dance and learn the tune for himself. But he remained, tethered against his will, listening and watching helplessly until the stars faded once again into the deep azure of the morning, and all was silent.

He sat for some time in the crown of the tree. Beneath him spread the vast swath of canopy, a tide of green that washed across the Mountain and broke in a wave beneath the peak. Above him, the sky was deep blue, and the Mountain shone pale gold against it. The black cloud was gone, revealing the Mountain in all its majesty, its summit a jagged, irregular triangle, so tall and distant that it seemed to be holding up the sky.

For all its wonder, it did little to drive away the sadness that held Jake against the rough bark of the tree. He felt small, powerless, trapped in a place he didn't belong, and the panorama before him, vast as it seemed from his vantage point, felt like nothing more than an elegant cage.

Fragments of the song still echoed in his memory. Jake fought to keep them, but they slipped away like water through his fingers. The silence frustrated him.

The stars should have taken him. He was ready, but they either didn't hear him, or they didn't want him. That thought was too much, the silence too heavy and oppressive. He reached down beneath his shirt and found the whistle. It was still intact, though the mouthpiece was frayed.

"I wanted to come with you!" Jake shouted. "Can't you hear me? I wanted to come with you!"

The need to find Gordon took on a new desperation. He put his right palm over his right ear and pressed his left ear against the tree's trunk, and then he sent another shrill blast that shot through the rainforest like an arrow. The measures he took to protect his ears had little practical effect, and he nearly dropped the whistle again.

The forest answered.

The closest thing Jake could think of was rain, the kind of rain that poured from a mile-high thundercloud and pounded the roof with such wrath that the house rattled, so hard that Jake would feel the vibration through the soles of his feet. But it was not the same; the forest's answer didn't come from above but from all around him. A great, fluttering mass poured from the tops of the trees, spots and wisps at first, then growing into thick columns that wound their way into the air like waterspouts. Jake wondered if the forest had caught fire, but then columns of black erupted close to his perch, and he realized what it was.

It was not smoke at all, but birds. Untold millions of them, their plumage sparkling in the sun as they took wing and flew. Parrots, lovebirds, falcons, pigeons, and a thousand other kinds that Jake could not name spun, plunged, and climbed, each bird a wisp of brightly-colored smoke taking wing, glorying in the morning air.

He received no memories from them as they darted into the sky and rose high overhead, winging their way toward the peak of the Mountain, but he guessed what their lives had been like, deprived of flight, forced to live out their days behind the bars of a cage. No room to fly, no room to be a bird, but instead an ornament, a music box that ate seeds from a bag and stained newspapers white, flapping useless wings and watching the sky through windowpanes. But here, they soared, trees and mountains beneath them, and they were birds again. They swerved and shifted direction in gigantic flocks, the black clouds that obscured the mountain peak. Before long, the peak was once again lost to view.

Sebastian was in a cage, and Jake pictured him languishing against makeshift bars, miserable. Jake felt a stinging shame. If he could have abandoned Sebastian, he would have, and he would not have given him another thought. He would have left Sebastian to rot for the chance to join in the song.

No wonder the stars didn't want him.

Jake sat for a while longer and watched the birds. They swirled and danced like the stars, and something of the stars' joy lived in them. He thought about Sebastian and the other dogs and cats held captive somewhere beyond the Mountain. Their joy had been stolen from them. It was unfair; not only had they been robbed of their freedom, but they had to depend on Jake to set them free again; small, stupid Jake. The right person wouldn't have left Ursus behind. The right person wouldn't beg to be taken away because it was easier.

He climbed down again, giving little thought to the placement of his feet or to the dizzying height and the danger of falling. If he fell, it would serve him right.

A furtive movement in the canopy overhead shook him out of his guilt. He stopped and surveyed the surrounding branches and saw nothing out of the ordinary.

Jake had already descended into the gloom beneath the canopy, and so his first impulse was to ignore it as a trick of the fading light, but it happened again as soon as he began to move, nothing more than a faint orange blur against a field of green dappled in faint light and shadows, following him as he climbed downward.

The hairs on the back of his neck tingled. He peered into the darkness, hoping to catch a better look at his pursuer. Again, he strained his eyes in the dim light and saw nothing. After a few seconds pause, he resumed his descent, slower this time.

Again, a blur of orange flitted in and out of sight.

He resisted the impulse to speed down the tree as fast as he could go. That was the most likely way for him to fall, and he'd never catch a decent glimpse of what stalked him. Aside from Smokey, every creature Jake had met during his travels had been friendly, even reverent.

"Hey," Jake called. "I know you're over there. Why don't you come out? I'm not going to hurt you."

A rustle in the branches across from him betrayed the presence of something that was alive and listening. Whatever it was, it seemed content to stay hidden.

Jake climbed down to the next thick branch and edged out onto it. It was wide enough for him to stand on and walk comfortably without fear of slipping. He sat down against the trunk.

"I'm out here looking for a friend. Maybe you've seen him around? He's a little dog, maybe this high." Jake raised his hand a short distance above the branch. "Actually, I don't know how big he is, but he goes by the name of Gordon."

The branches across from Jake shook again.

"So, it's true. It is a Keeper." The voice was deep

and powerful, laced with malevolent amusement. Three figures emerged from hiding, hulking shadows only barely distinguishable from the darkness that surrounded them. They were large, much larger than Jake, and too fleshy to be Malbinocks. Dark, reddish-brown fur covered their long arms. One by one, they swung across the divide that separated Jake's tree from theirs and landed on the branch.

Orangutans!

The first one dwarfed the other two, and he stared at Jake with close-set, dark eyes sunk deep into its wide, round face. There was only enough room on the end of the branch to stand single-file, and the other two peered out from behind the first, gawking at Jake with strange, almost human expressions of wonder.

"A Keeper," the orangutan repeated. "Here, in our forest."

"My name is Jake." The ape's size intimidated him, but he tried to mask it with a smile.

The one in the front advanced a little, moving smoothly on all fours, perfectly at home in the trees. Jake envied him. The orangutan only moved a few steps before the one behind him spoke.

"Don't touch it, Spence. Where there is one Keeper, there are others."

Jake didn't like the way they said "Keeper". They spat the word, as if it was something unclean that they wanted out of their mouths.

Spence loomed over him, a few feet away. He was probably strong enough to tear Jake apart if he wanted to. But the orangutan didn't advance further, content to remain where he was, peering at Jake. Whatever Spence saw in Jake must have given him courage; the orangutan edged a few inches closer.

"What are you doing in our forest, Keeper?" Spence said.

"I'm looking for a dog named Gordon. Maybe you've seen him. I—"

"Dogs do not climb trees," said Spence. The two behind him laughed, but there was no mirth in his voice.

"I know that," said Jake. "I climbed up here to call him. I made an emergency whistle—" Jake paused to fish the whistle out of his shirt. He held it up for Spence to examine. "I thought he might come if he heard it."

"Careful, Spence," said one of the two behind him. "Keepers know things. They know tricks."

"I know their tricks, Wigwig. I know all of their tricks."

"It's not a trick," said Jake. "I'm telling the truth."

"Where there is one, there are others," said Wigwig. "They will come and take us back."

"It's just me and my friend Blue. No one else. We just want to find Gordon so we can help the other dogs."

Spence glared at him. "Help dogs? How? By climbing trees?"

"No. Well, possibly. I told you. I climbed up here to use this whistle. I need to find where the Malbinocks come from. They've taken a lot of dogs and cats. I'm trying to get them back."

"He is trying to trick you, Spence," said the third orangutan. It pointed a long, crooked finger at Jake and looked at him as if he were something poisonous. Jake pressed his back into the trunk of the tree. The orangutans, especially Spence, frightened him; not so much because of their size, but because they seemed frightened of him. The best thing he could do was get away from them.

"Listen to Bobo," Wigwig said. "He knows."

"What is a Malbinock?" said Spence. Jake stopped and looked at him. He couldn't read the expression on the orangutan's face, but Jake got the sense that it had become more curious than afraid. He decided to answer.

"They look like people. Like Keepers," Jake said. "But they're made out of junk."

"Junk?"

"Garbage. Trash. You know, like old mop handles and broken car radios and toasters."

"I have not seen any of these," said Spence. "And I have not seen the dog."

"I'm sorry I bothered you." Jake shifted a little to the side, searching the bark for a handhold. "I'm just going to go back down, all right? It's not like I'm going to find Gordon in a tree."

He turned toward the trunk, careful to keep Spence in view. Spence only watched him. The other two peeked out from behind his red fur like nervous children clinging to their mother's legs. Spence made no attempt to stop Jake when he grabbed the bark and gingerly descended. Whether it was old memories, or fear, or habit, Spence remained rooted to his spot on the branch, but Jake felt the ape's small, brown eyes follow him as he made his way to the forest floor. He moved as fast as he could down the tree, not daring to stop or look up. Instead, he kept his eyes fixed on his feet. The ground was still a long way down, but he was more afraid of Spence than he was of falling, and now he welcomed the gathering darkness beneath him. Handhold by handhold, foothold by foothold, he sank deeper into the gloom, leaving the orangutans far above.

Blue scraped the dirt with his hoof and snorted when Jake reached the ground.

"Jake! I have heard things. Many things moving around us. This is not the place for horses or Riders."

"You got that right. Let's get moving."

Jake led the way, finding paths through the labyrinth of tall, arched roots that anchored the giant trees in place. He was hopelessly lost, but he didn't care, as long as he put distance between himself and the orangutans. Gradually, the terrible, crawling sensation of being watched from above lessened, and Jake relaxed a little.

Jake and Blue threaded their way between the trees until night fell. The clouds rolled back in as they walked, removing what little light managed to reach the forest floor. The darkness was impenetrable, and so they settled down to wait. Jake climbed up onto Blue's back and lay down and listened to a forest so absolutely quiet and still that it felt to Jake like a second death.

Chapter Eighteen

The voice pierced the darkness, whispered, yet clear and distinct, as if someone had spoken into Jake's ear. The voice wasn't full and strong, like Spence. Its pitch was higher, timider. Jake sat up. Blue shifted underneath him.

"Blue, you hear that?"

"There are animals. Many animals. Above us in the trees," said Blue. "This is not a place for horses."

"Keeper!"

Jake was afraid. He hoped that the darkness would conceal him, despite Blue shuffling and stamping his hooves. If he didn't answer, perhaps whatever was calling him would give up and go away.

"Keeper, do not be afraid."

Jake stayed absolutely still. Blue scraped the dirt with a hoof and snorted.

"Keeper, you have told the truth. I wish to help."

It had to be the orangutans. Aside from the birds, Jake had come across no other creature during his time in the rainforest. Jake wanted nothing to do with them. He didn't like the way Spence watched him with barely concealed revulsion, and he didn't like the way Spence's smaller friends were so terrified. Frightened animals were the most dangerous.

"I have seen your dog. I have seen Gordon."

The offer was too much for Jake to ignore. "Where?" he whispered.

Blue shook his head and took a step to the side. "Do not answer," he said. "They will find us."

"It's ok, Blue," Jake said. And then, to the other voice, "Where did you see him?"

"Near. Very near,"

"Wigwig? Is that you?"

"It is," said Wigwig. "Now, you must follow me. I will take you to Gordon."

"It will do us harm," Blue said.

"I don't think so. I think he's trying to help."

Jake slid off Blue's back and landed in the soft, loamy soil.

"Stay here, Blue," he said.

"Do not trust the animals in the tall forest. They wish to harm you." Blue's warning was so cold with fear that Jake nearly changed his mind. What did he really know about the orangutans? Spence was certainly one to steer clear of, but Wigwig and the other orangutan didn't feel like a threat. He had to take the chance. If he didn't, he could be wandering the rainforest forever in his search. Sebastian and the others probably didn't have that long.

"All right, Wigwig. Which way?"

"Follow me. I will lead you to Gordon."

From above, Jake heard the branches shake, and he crept toward the sound. He felt vulnerable, walking in the dark with only the sound of Wigwig's signals to guide him. The scent of the trees hung heavy in the humid air, and all was still save the sound of his hands brushing against the high roots and Wigwig's signals, urging him to follow.

"Yes, just that way. Keep going, Keeper! Gordon is near!"

Wigwig was eager, almost giddy in his excitement, and Jake could feel the malice behind the ape's joy. He stopped.

"I don't believe you."

"I only want you out of our forest," said Wigwig. The excitement had been replaced by a touch of anger and righteous indignation. But even that seemed feigned, and Jake refused to take another step. He thought about turning back, but the darkness would make any such attempt futile. As quietly as he could, Jake climbed over one of the tall roots and hunkered down behind it. There were roots in front of him and behind him, and he scrunched down into the narrow cavity to wait.

Wigwig called out a few more times.

"Keeper! You are almost to Gordon. Do not turn away! Keeper!"

Jake made himself as small and as quiet as he could. Nothing that Wigwig said would budge him. He would wait for the light, and then find his way back to Blue. That was another worry, but one that would keep until morning.

Boredom and loneliness proved to be more formidable than Wigwig. Every breath felt like an eternity, and Jake wondered if the night would ever end. He tried to drift and make his way back to the place where the sad woman was. It didn't matter that they mostly spoke in gibberish or that he could not speak to them; it was enough that they were human. His efforts came to naught; try as he might, he remained between the roots, fully aware of the oppressive darkness surrounding him like a prison cell.

Part of him hoped that Wigwig and the others would come looking for him, to use force where trickery had failed. It would have at least given him something to occupy his mind, but the apes, it seemed, had abandoned him too. His body ached for movement.

The darkness wore him down. He imagined himself getting stiff, his joints freezing, his body tucked into a ball between the tall roots. He wouldn't be able to get away from Spence, much less make his way back to Blue if his joints stiffened up. That he hadn't experienced any kind of fatigue or soreness since his arrival never entered his mind, and he threw away every other consideration but his desperate need for movement.

He closed his eyes and strained to hear any sign of Spence and the others, but he heard nothing. Cautiously he extended his left leg, then his right, and sat up. Movement was just the thing; his joints were as flexible as ever, without a hint of stiffness in them, but he immediately felt better.

He didn't dare call out for fear that they were

simply lying in wait, testing their patience against his. He imagined moving like a hunting snake, first his left arm, then his right, sliding up the tall root to the upper edge, and then he pulled himself up to his feet. Had there been any light, the apes would have seen only his eyes and the top of his head protruding from behind the root, but there in the dark it made little difference.

They were gone, he was sure of it. He would have heard them searching if they were still in the area. Jake climbed back over the top of the root and landed lightly on the other side. Even the gentle thump of his feet on the soil sounded like a bass drum in the darkness. He listened. Nothing stirred.

As he felt his way along, he felt a certain satisfaction at having outwitted Wigwig and his companions. I might have been born at night, but it weren't last night, he told himself. If they wanted to lure Jake Phillips into a trap, they would have to try a lot harder than that. Blue had been right about them, he admitted, and he intended to tell the horse exactly that when he got back.

Somewhere behind him, a dog barked.

All his confidence vanished like smoke in a strong wind, replaced by fear and paralyzing indecision. Competing voices, each with their own theory and plan of action, tumbled through his mind. Another ruse, or his mind playing tricks, adding noise because there ought to be some, or maybe Wigwig was telling the truth, and the object of his quest was only a few paces away from him, waiting, while Jake crept in the opposite direction. Go back. No, run. No, wait.

Jake waited.

The sound of his own breathing filled his ears, and Jake feared he might miss it if the dog barked again. He held his breath and closed his eyes.

Another bark, louder this time. Close.

A trick! It had to be a trick.

Another bark pierced the darkness, cut off with a thud and a terrible, keening whimper. Jake rushed toward the sound, forgetting the tall trees and the maze of roots that loomed around him, forgetting the apes and the way they spat the word Keeper with such hatred, thinking only of what would happen if he didn't reach Gordon. He grazed a rough trunk and nearly bounced off another and finally stopped, listening. Another cry, this one practically at his feet, launched him back into reckless motion.

The world opened up beneath him.

Terrifying weightlessness lasted only a second or two, and he landed roughly on all fours, his hands and feet sinking into fetid mud. He was unhurt; the soft mud cushioned the impact. He pulled his hands out of the mire and tried to stand up. As he did so, his arms brushed against something solid. High walls surrounded him on all sides.

He was in a pit.

The walls crumbled when he tried to climb them, and they were too far apart for him to brace his body between them and use the purchase to inch his way back to the surface. After a few attempts, he gave up. He'd never find the answer in the dark. He stood ankle deep in the mud, waiting for his captors to reveal themselves, until he could no longer stand the silence.

"Hey!" Jake called. "Wigwig, are you out there? I know you did this to me. Let me out!"

Jake received no response.

"Wigwig! I never did anything to you! Let me out! Bobo! I'm just a kid! I never had a pet monkey or a bird or anything like that. Let me out! My friends need my help!"

Again, Jake hunkered down. He tried to find the voices or hear the stars, but the clammy mud added to his misery and prevented him from drifting off. He had never been so uncomfortable. The mud smelled awful, like week-old garbage, and refused to dry. Water must have been coming from somewhere; he could feel it pooling around his ankles where his feet sank straight down into the mud.

He didn't bother to call for Gordon. It was clear to him that Gordon was never there. The whistle still lay beneath his shirt, but it was sodden and caked with mud. No one except Blue would have heard it, and he wouldn't be able to come to Jake's rescue in the dark.

Jake was testing the limits of his prison, counting paces along the wall when the gray light streamed through the treetops high above. The first thing he saw was his feet, covered in thick, ochre-colored mud that reminded Jake of bruised bananas. The pit wasn't nearly as tall as Jake had imagined in the dark; the edge was only two or three feet above his outstretched fingertips. He made another attempt to climb out, but his hands and feet could find no purchase in the soft soil. No matter how deep he shoved his feet into the wall, the soil refused to hold his weight. A dark shape moved overhead, and Jake looked up into the silhouette of an orangutan.

"It was dug by them," said Spence. His words dripped with malevolent triumph. "The creatures made from Keeper things."

"You're going to give me to them?" Jake said.

"No. You are not for them. We killed them all," said Spence. "And now we have you."

"Why do you want me? I never did anything to you."

"You made us forget!" said Spence, pointing an accusing finger at Jake. "Your kind puts birds and apes in cages! You take the treetops, take the sky, take the songs! What is a bird when it cannot fly? When it cannot sing? What is a tiger when it cannot hunt? What am I without the trees?"

Jake didn't know what to say.

"Your kind made us forget."

"I'm sorry," said Jake.

"It is too late," said Spence. "You belong to us now. We are the Keepers and you are the Kept Ape."

"How long are you going to keep me down here?" said Jake. A wave of terror rose inside of him.

"Until you forget," Spence said.

Spence vanished beyond the rim of the pit.

Chapter Nineteen

Spence came back a short time later, this time flanked by Wigwig and Bobo. Triumphant, they watched him from the edge of the pit.

"You are smart, Spence," said Wigwig. "Smarter than the Keeper."

"What will we do with it, Spence?" said Bobo. "It is not happy in the pit. It sits in the mud and looks up at the sky."

"It will never see the sky again. Now it belongs to us. We will teach it tricks," said Spence.

"Yes, it will learn tricks," said Wigwig. "When it learns tricks, we can play with it."

"It will be happy if it learns some tricks," said Bobo. "I know many tricks. I will teach it."

"And we will show it to the others," said Spence. "The others will see that we are Keepers now."

Jake snatched up a handful of wet mud and hurled it at Spence. Most of the mud splattered against the pit wall, but a little managed to clear the rim, and Spence was forced to leap sideways to avoid it.

"I'm not an 'it'. I'm Jake Phillips. And another thing, I'm not your pet. So stop talking about me like I'm not down here listening to everything you say."

"It is not happy in the pit, Spence," said Bobo.

"When do we get to play with it?" said Wigwig. "You said—"

"It will stay in the pit!" Spence snapped. Bobo and Wigwig edged away from him.

"First, we will teach it tricks and show it to the others, and then we will play with it," Spence said. He glared at Bobo and then at Wigwig. Neither met Spence's gaze.

Spence leaned down over the pit. He pointed at Jake. "You will learn tricks. Bobo will teach you."

"I'm not doing any stupid tricks," Jake said. He grabbed another handful of mud and sent it over the edge of the pit.

"You are a Kept Ape," said Spence. "You will learn tricks."

"Come on—"

Jake almost said, "Come on down here and make me", but he thought better of it and cut himself off before the words escaped his mouth. The last thing he wanted was Spence down in the pit with him. The orangutan was no doubt strong enough to wrench his arms out of their sockets—or worse. He would have to cooperate, at least until he could figure some way out.

"Fine," Jake said. "What kind of stupid tricks do you want me to do?"

"Bobo will teach you," said Spence. "You will learn before the others come."

"What others?"

Spence vanished from the pit's rim, along with Wigwig. Bobo remained. He was much smaller than Spence, his face narrow, without the flanges that wrapped Spence's features. Perhaps it was the lack of flanges or just the set of his eyes; whatever it was, Bobo had a pleasant, friendly look about him. It was something that Jake thought he might be able to use when the time was right.

The sound of Spence's call filled the air, a staccato series of whoops that carried with perfect clarity from the treetops. It was loud, even in the pit. After a moment, it sounded again, a little farther off. Jake cocked an ear and listened, hoping for one more call. He was not disappointed; the call came once again, farther off than before.

"Is that Spence?" Jake asked.

"He is calling the others," said Bobo.

"Other orangutans?"

"Some. There are many of us. Not just our kind, but many other kinds. Cats. Bears. Large beasts with noses that curl, beasts so large that they shake the ground when they walk. Spence wants the others to see that we are Keepers now. He wants to show them we are not Kept Apes anymore. When he returns, he will show them. But now it is time to teach you a trick. It is time for you to bark like a dog."

Bobo covered his mouth with his hands and made a short, yapping bark. It was the same bark Jake had heard the night before. Jake felt a curious mix of vindication and disappointment; even in the daylight

Bobo's impersonation was convincing. Anyone might have fallen for the ape's ruse.

Despite his predicament, Jake couldn't bring himself to feel angry at Bobo. The orangutan was only doing what Spence told him to do.

"I can't do a dog," said Jake.

"Spence will be angry."

"What about you?"

"I do not hate the Keepers. Not like Spence. Bark, now, or Spence will be angry with us."

"I told you. I can't do a dog. But I can do a moose."

Jake cupped his hands over his mouth and did his very best bull moose call. Bobo clapped and bounced up and down, sending a shower of loose dirt raining down into the pit. When the applause stopped, Jake demonstrated the call for a cow moose to Bobo's enthusiastic praise. The orangutan slapped the rim several times, with predictable results. Jake retreated to the far side of the pit to avoid the debris cascading from the pit wall.

"Now you do one," said Jake.

Bobo slapped the ground one more time, obviously excited by the game. "Yes! Yes! I will show you a long call! This is the sound of my kind!" Bobo took a deep breath and howled. It was a higher pitch than Spence's had been, but it sounded similar in tone, starting off low and ending in a loud, ear-splitting screech. Jake cupped his hands around his mouth and did his best to imitate Bobo's call. The result was an awful noise that sounded more like an injured cat than an orangutan. The effort gave Jake a tickle in his throat, and he resolved to limit himself to moose calls for the time being. Bobo, however, was delighted in Jake's attempt, slapping the ground and whooping with amusement.

"How was that?" Jake said.

"You do not sound like one of our kind full grown. You sound like a baby crying out for mother!"

"It was my first try," Jake said. Bobo was beside himself with glee, rolling back and forth along the edge of the pit. Jake noticed something off to Bobo's left. Just below the edge of the pit, Jake caught a flash of white protruding from the soil. He looked closer.

The object was a long, thick root buried deep in the ground. It was only a couple of feet out of reach, but with his feet sitting in six inches of thick, foul-smelling mud, two feet may as well have been two hundred.

"Do not make the long call when Spence is near," Bobo said. "It will make him angry. Make your moose sound."

"I'll remember."

It was enough. Bobo clapped his hands together. "See? You know some tricks and now you are happy!"

"Sounds like you're the happy one."

"Spence will be pleased."

Jake leaned against the pit wall and squatted down. He was already slathered in mud; it didn't make much sense to bother about it anymore. Above him dangled the root, a sickly, pale yellow only a shade lighter than the ochre soil surrounding it. Bobo perched on the rim, his right hand resting on the ground just above the root.

"He isn't going to let me out of here, is he?" Jake asked. "He's going to keep me here for good."

"When you are tame, we will let you out. Then we can play with you."

"How long will that take?"

"When you do what Spence wants."

"What does he want?"

"He wants you to forget you are a Keeper."

"But I didn't do anything to him!"

"Learn tricks. Show them to the others when they come. Then Spence will be happy and let you out. Then we can all play together."

Jake tossed a handful of mud at the pit wall. "Spence isn't going to let us play together. He hates me. He's just keeping me here to hurt me because he wants to get back at the people who kept him locked up. But he can't do anything to them, so he's taking it out on me because I'm here. He's never going to let me out of this hole."

"Spence is very smart," said Bobo. "He would not do such a terrible thing."

"You'll see."

There didn't seem to be anything more to say. Jake glanced up at him once or twice and then fell to brooding. He sat with his knees tucked up under his chin. The whistle, still nestled inside his shirt, lay pinned between his leg and his belly. Jake tried to ignore it, the way a hiker might try to ignore a pebble in his shoe, and like the pebble, the whistle would not allow itself to be ignored. Jake reached into his shirt and pulled it out. It was still intact, and the wrapped leaves felt solid and reassuring against his palm. He intended to just toss it into the mud, but the thing had weight, and the weight lent it some power.

He inspected it and discovered that it wasn't as damaged as he thought. Just some mud on the body especially caked around the cloth strips he'd used to wrap it. The windway was clear; that was something, at least. Blowing it would do him no good; he doubted that Blue would hear him, and, while loyal and kind, he wasn't the type of horse who charged in with flying hooves to mount a rescue. Even if he had been more like Freya, he would have been powerless to help Jake climb out of the pit.

Jake idly rolled the whistle across his knees and contemplated the humiliation that Spence had in store for him when he returned with the others. Time was impossible to gauge from the inside of a muddy hole, so Jake had no way of knowing when Spence would lead the first of his audience to the pit and show everyone that he was no longer a Kept Ape, but a Keeper. Then he would try to force Jake to do tricks.

And what better trick could Spence ask for than whistle-making?

The thought came to him in a sly whisper, more like a feather-light tickle in his mind, as if the very idea itself required utmost secrecy. With it came the seed of a plan.

"Hey, Bobo," Jake said. He did his best to keep his voice calm and even. Bobo leaned over the pit, regarding Jake with a mixture of curiosity and pity.

Jake glanced up at him for a second, then focused all his attention on the whistle. "Do you think Spence will be back soon?" he asked, pretending to make a minor adjustment on the cloth strips that held the whistle together.

"He will be back when he has called all the others," said Bobo.

"Oh. There probably isn't enough time, then."

"Time? Time for what?"

"Well ... no. Never mind. It would probably just get us both in trouble."

It was like fishing, in a way. It felt a lot like tugging a lure in front of a brook trout. It had to be done delicately, with patience, or he would lose the fish. He had to dangle the bait just right; too little and Bobo would lose interest, but too much, and the orangutan would probably sense a trap.

"Tell me!" Bobo pleaded.

Jake picked up the whistle between the thumb and forefinger of his right hand and pretended to gauge its strength and quality. He tugged at the knots again.

"You must! You must!" Bobo wailed.

"Well, I was going to show you how to make an emergency whistle, just like mine. But no. I think I'll just wait for Spence to come back. It would be a good trick. I could show everyone."

Jake held up the whistle again, pretending to admire its form. Bobo peered into the hole, his eyes lingering on the mysterious, muddy-green tube in Jake's hand.

"I was just thinking that if you already know how to make them too, then you could ... no, that's stupid. They would never go for it. And there's not enough time, anyway."

"What? If I knew how to make one, what? What could I do?"

"It's nothing really. Forget I said anything."

"Tell me! Keeper!"

Jake put the whistle back underneath his shirt.

"Jake! Please tell me!"

Hooked.

"Well," said Jake. "I guess it wouldn't hurt to tell you. I was thinking that if you knew how to make emergency whistles, you could help me teach the others. I bet the sound of my whistle goes a lot farther than your calls. You and the others could communicate better. And in case those things, the ones that dug the pit, came back, you could warn each other a lot faster. But I guess I can't since you aren't allowed to let me out of this pit. It would have been wicked cool, though."

Bobo hesitated, his body vacillating in time with his thoughts.

"I will let you out if you promise you will teach me to make the whistle," Bobo said.

"Deal."

Bobo peered down into the pit, wary of being trapped inside himself. Jake pointed to the exposed root beneath the ape's foot. "What about that root right there? Would that hold you?"

Bobo felt around for it and grabbed it when it brushed against his hand. With a yank, he tore a long, thick section of root away from the surrounding soil. Jake almost panicked until he saw that Bobo's pull had only lengthened it rather than tearing it away completely. Bobo gave it a tug, decided it was steady enough, and then swung down, gripping the exposed root with his left hand, while beckoning Jake with his right.

"Climb," Bobo said, "I will help you."

Jake climbed, and with Bobo's help, he soon found himself sitting next to the orangutan, looking down into his former prison.

"Now, teach me," Bobo said.

"A deal's a deal. First, you need to get a leaf. One of those big, long ones way up there."

The battle taking place in Bobo's mind played itself out on his face. His eyes darted up and then settled back on Jake. He looked back up into the treetops. His eyebrows arched up, his upper lip wrinkled, exposing the tops of his sharp teeth, but it was his eyes, darting back and forth between Jake and the canopy high above, that showed Jake the course of the battle. Each time, they lingered less on Jake and more in the treetops.

"I'm telling the truth," Jake said. "Look. It's made out of one of those leaves." He held the whistle up, pointing to the base so Bobo could see the green layers wrapped tightly around the thick stem.

Bobo studied it for a moment. His brow furrowed. Again, the battle raged across the ape's features as he struggled to decide his next move. Jake's efforts were bent entirely on maintaining an air of nonchalance. He reserved most of his attention for the whistle, only glancing up occasionally.

Then the battle seemed to take an unexpected turn. Bobo's eyes widened, and he clapped his hands together. He leaped to his feet and pointed at the pit.

"I will climb. You will go back into the pit."

Jake's heart sank. He tried to stammer out some

kind of excuse, some reason why he ought to stay out, but his mind deserted him.

"But, wait. No. I—"

"I will climb. You will stay in the pit."

Jake hesitated for a second but soon acquiesced. He rolled over on his belly and lowered himself back beneath the rim and let go. The foul smell of the mud rose like an invisible hand and surrounded him, and he landed with a sickening, fetid slap, his feet buried to the shins in the foul mess. A wet, sucking sound accompanied Jake's efforts to pull his feet free. He leaned against the pit wall and tried to breathe as shallowly as he could until his nose became accustomed to the stench again.

Bobo leaned over the rim of the pit. He looked down at Jake.

"I will climb. You will stay until I come back with the leaf."

"I'm not going anywhere." Jake gestured toward the pit walls.

Bobo gave him one last look and then disappeared.

Jake tried to convince himself that there was still a chance, but his efforts were only cursory, more a matter of form than anything else. He had had freedom in his grasp, and it had slipped away. The fountain of lies and excuses that Jake had always drawn on to get himself out of trouble had dried up, and at the worst possible time. He stared up at the rim of the pit and chided himself for his failure.

There was the root.

Jake shot to his feet and dragged himself through

the deep mud in the pit's center to where it dangled, now only a few inches out of Jake's reach.

"Yes!"

Jake leapt for the root, but the mud sucked at his feet and bled away the power in his jump. He tried climbing, but the walls collapsed, carving deep furrows where he dug into them. Powerlessness and frustration got the better of him, and with an anguished shout, he threw a hard kick at the pit wall. Pain shot through his foot as it sank deep into the crumbling soil about eight inches from the bottom. He hopped around, pressing his hands into the wall to keep from losing his balance, and he realized that the wall wasn't crumbling. He allowed himself the tiniest fragment of hope as he tested it with more of his weight.

It held.

Pushing off with the buried foot, he thrust himself upward toward the root, reaching as high as he could until he felt it, rough and fibrous against his palm. First one, then the other hand made contact, and he hauled himself upward. The soil around his foot resisted, and for a second, Jake was caught in the middle of a tug of war, but with one final pull, his buried foot came free, and Jake clambered up the root and threw an arm over the rim of the pit. A moment later, he lay on his back, breathing the free air once again.

He allowed himself only a moment to rest and rejoice in his victory, but even that was cut short. Through the trees came the deep, staccato whoops of Spence's long call. First once, then again.

And it was coming closer.

Chapter Twenty

Jake ran.

Behind him and above him came the calls of his pursuers. Spence urged them on, and his deep, throaty whoops pushed Jake to run even faster, dodging this way and that through the labyrinth of tree trunks and tall buttress roots. Jake had no idea which direction he was heading; the only thought that his mind could conjure up was away, and the foliage slipped by him in a blur. From the canopy, he heard the rattle of branches. He tried to push himself harder, to run faster, but the trees blocked his path and kept him from reaching a full sprint. He glanced off one trunk to his right and scraped his ankle against a large one on the left, and all the while came the sound of his pursuers, leaping from branch to branch above his head, calling out to one another as they came on.

Jake could not tell how many. Four? Ten? Twenty? One hundred? The forest erupted in a tempest of rattles and howls as the others made a move to encircle him. Jake's pace lagged, not with fatigue but with hopelessness. He was just one boy; he couldn't fight his way out, and running to safety was looking more unlikely with each passing moment. He thought briefly of surrender, but he pushed that thought out of his mind. There was no way he was going to back into the fetid darkness voluntarily.

He cast about for some solution, but nothing presented itself. Only the trees and their endless maze of tall buttress roots filled the landscape. With his attention diverted, he missed a root directly in front of him, and Jake struck it painfully with his toes and his shin. The world spun around, and Jake landed hard against a tree trunk, the wind driven from his body. Behind him the rattle and chatter of his pursuers grew ever louder; they were almost upon him, and Jake could do nothing but fight for breath. He lay on his side against the trunk of a tree, sucking air into uncooperative lungs and dreading the inevitable. He had given his best effort, but Spence would have him again. Even as his breath returned to normal, he couldn't bring himself to run. He stayed beneath the tree, his breath stirring up bits of red soil, and waited for Spence to collect him.

The soil was damp and loose and warm between his fingers. Idly, he lifted his hand, peering through the gloom at the red patina the soil left behind. The orangutan's calls came louder. He looked at his hands again. A thin hope, perhaps, but better than no hope at all. Jake reached down and scooped an armful of dirt across his legs and up over his belly, as if he were drawing a sheet over himself on a cool summer night. He pushed a handful of dirt over his face and through his hair and then lay completely still.

Dead and buried, he thought. Finally.

Above him, muffled by the dirt in his ears, came the sounds of his pursuers. For an eternity, they passed over his head while he lay still as a corpse beneath the churned soil. Jake didn't even dare breathe as the branches shook above him. He lay there beneath a fingernail-thin layer of dirt, terrified they would find him, almost willing them to look down and see him lying there.

As the din of the pursuers receded into the forest, he could stand no more. He sat up, clawed the red dirt from his face and sucked in breath after breath. Around him, the forest was silent, save for the occasional long call somewhere up in the canopy. He clambered to his feet. The dirt cascaded around him in a red cloud as he brushed it from his hair and clothing.

Hope, thin as a spider's thread, remained.

All around him, the forest stretched, hemming him in. He couldn't begin to guess where he was in relation to the Mountain, or to the pit, or to the place where Blue was likely still waiting for him to return. He peered into the gloom for anything that might resemble a path. Ahead lay a break in the roots. It was as good a place to start as any.

He made it four steps before a hand clapped over his mouth, and he found his arms pinned to his sides with a grip so tight he could barely breathe.

"That was a good trick."

Jake recognized the voice. It was Bobo. He struggled, but he knew it would do no good. The orangutan had him. All his efforts had come to nothing. Jake stopped fighting, and Bobo released his iron grip on him.

Jake turned to face his captor. He expected anger or smug triumph, but Jake saw none of that in the orangutan's features. Bobo was calm, his expression serene and peaceful. He regarded Jake with something akin to admiration. Jake was thoroughly confused.

"I will not take you back to the pit," said Bobo, in answer to Jake's unasked question.

"You won't?"

"No."

"So, you're just going to let me go?"

"No."

Jake's hope dashed again. "What are you going to do with me then?"

"I will show you the way back."

"Really? You're really going to take me back to Blue? You'd do that for me?"

"I will show you the way back. But not for you. For Spence. For Wigwig. For me. We are not Keepers. I will not become a Keeper. I will not let Wigwig and Spence become Keepers. It is not for us. The Mountain is for us. To be free, to roam the treetops. To feel the wind on our backs and the daylight in our face. To feel the rain on our skin. That is for us. That is enough."

"I never was a Keeper. I'm just a kid."

"You did not keep us, but you are a Keeper. I will take you back. Follow me. No tricks now. Now we understand, you and me. Now we trust."

For a moment, Jake looked into the orangutan's eyes. The wistful, calm sincerity he saw there was enough to convince him.

"I trust you," Jake said.

"Follow me. I will take you to your friends."

They passed through the forest again, and none of it was familiar to Jake. Bobo kept to the trees, low enough that Jake could see him. The orangutan moved through the canopy with surprising grace, and Jake was reminded of the birds, taking to the air with pure, unfettered joy. Bobo, it seemed, had found some of that joy for himself there in the treetops. Jake was glad to see it.

Soft rain fell, and quickly intensified into a downpour. The rain was a welcome change, washing the dirt from his hair and his filthy clothes. The wet trees gave off an exotic, spicy smell, a mix of cinnamon and clove and coconut. Jake had gotten hints of it while in the canopy, but now the smell hung, thick as a mist, over the entire forest.

Though his body had never tired, his stay in the pit had sapped his confidence. Moving through the warm rain, Jake felt vigor and hopeful energy return to him. Perhaps it was the relief of escaping Spence's pit, or perhaps the strange, cinnamon-scent of the forest tapped some hidden strength in him, but regardless of what it was, Jake navigated the trunks and buttress roots of the tall trees with renewed purpose. Somewhere ahead, Blue waited for him, and they could resume their search for Gordon without any more interference from the orangutans.

The thought came to him that Bobo could easily be lying, leading him to some place of captivity worse than the pit. But watching Bobo move through the trees with careless grace put Jake's mind at ease. He moved now as Ursus moved, fast but without urgency. The orangutan glanced down only occasionally, slowing from time to time to ensure that he wasn't lost from Jake's view.

The rain eased off a little. Bobo, high in the trees, stopped on a low branch. He pointed out to his left.

"Your friends are there," he said.

"Thanks, Bobo. I'm sorry. For what the Keepers ... for what we did to you."

"Listen," Bobo said. "Do you hear it?"

Jake closed his eyes and focused. At first, he heard only the light patter of rain against the leaves. But beneath it, there was something else, something he hadn't noticed before. It was a shushing sound, like static on a radio or the buzz of a large crowd from far away.

"I hear it."

"Follow that sound. That is the waterfall that flows from high on the Mountain. There is a passage behind the water. Go through the passage. Your dog is on the other side."

"I'll never forget you, Bobo. I'm glad you're free. Here. Take it." Jake held up the whistle, now a filthy, broken mess. Jake doubted it would ever make a noise again.

"I do not need it," said Bobo. "Go to your friends. Hurry before Spence comes."

The orangutan shimmied up a trunk and disappeared.

"Hey, what do you mean by friends? I just have Blue," Jake called. There was no response from the trees except the distant sound of a long call. He broke into a run in the direction Bobo had given him. It wasn't long before he stumbled into a clearing. Blue stood in the center.

"Blue!" Relief overwhelmed him, and he threw his arms around the horse's neck and held tight.

"Jake. I am happy to see you again."

"You have no idea," said Jake. The distant roar of the falls beckoned to him. He wondered how he'd missed the sound before.

"Jake," said Blue, "We must not stay here. We are in danger. The forest creatures do not want us. I heard them in the trees. Before you came, they passed overhead. They are hunting you."

"I know," said Jake. "Bobo warned me. But he also showed me a way out of here."

Jake listened. Beneath the sounds of his own breathing, and the nervous stamp of the horse's hooves against the red soil, Jake heard it. The steady, distant thrum of the water tumbling from some high place on the Mountain, and for Jake, it was the sound of freedom. Bobo seemed to think of the waterfall as a border beyond which Spence and his companions would not cross. Jake hoped it was the case.

In the distance, he heard the long call of an orangutan.

"Blue, come on, we have to get to that waterfall

before Spence gets to us." Jake gestured toward the faint sound.

"But that will take us deeper into the forest," said Blue. "There are many enemies here. If we go deeper into the forest, we will find more of them."

"If we don't go deeper into the forest, I'll end up back in that pit, and who knows what Spence will do to you."

It took a little more cajoling to finally get Blue to follow Jake toward the sound of the waterfall. The way was surprisingly easy; what seemed little better than a maze widened out into a path large enough for the two of them to walk side by side with room to spare. Jake heard Spence's call again and quickened his pace.

"Come on, Blue! Spence is going to catch us!"

"I am faster when you are riding," said Blue.

"It's too dangerous," Jake said. The ground here is covered in roots. You could trip and throw me."

"I have never lost a Rider," said Blue.

With the aid of a nearby tree, Jake struggled up onto Blue's back. Off to the side, in the shadow of a stand of trees, something moved.

"Did you see that?"

"There are many things in the trees. This is not a place for horses. Not a place for Riders."

"Hello?" Jake called.

Jake began to doubt he had seen anything at all. He chalked it up to imagination. It wasn't surprising that he would start seeing Spence or one of his ape friends behind every tree. But they would be, soon enough, if he didn't make it to the waterfall before they reached him. He patted Blue on the flank, and Blue set off with Jake on his back.

The ground was rough and uneven, riddled with exposed roots, but Blue deftly avoided them without slowing down. Behind them, the branches shook, and the calls of their pursuers grew louder and louder, even as the sound of the waterfall grew. Jake chanced a look upward. He caught a glimpse of a shadowy figure high in a tree, crouched on a stout branch, watching him. A second later, Jake heard the shrill cry of a monkey, high pitched and insistent, and his call was answered by a dozen others. Jake leaned over Blue's neck and spoke into his ear.

"Blue, you'll have to run. If you don't, they'll catch us for sure."

"This is not good ground for running," said Blue. Jake could feel Blue's lungs work underneath his legs.

"You've never lost a Rider. Blue, please."

Blue's trot turned into a brisk canter. Not quite a full gallop, but the trees began to whip by, and the sound of their pursuers receded a little.

Jake saw it again. Off to the side, hidden in the dense trees, a shadow. Someone or something was mirroring their movements.

"Hey! Bobo? Is that you?"

But Blue was moving too quickly for Jake to receive an answer if there was anything out there to reply. The sound of the waterfall grew louder until it dominated everything but Blue's heavy hoofbeats. The pursuers howled and crashed through the branches until they were nearly above him.

Jake urged Blue on, glancing over his shoulder into the treetops. Before long, the sound of the falls was so close that Jake could practically feel the cool spray on his face, and still his pursuers followed. Strange, he thought, that Spence and his troops hadn't caught him. They had been close for what seemed a long time, but Jake couldn't see them, and they had made no attempt to snatch him from Blue's back or block his passage. It nagged at him, but he could spare no time to ponder it.

Blue burst from the trees into a wide clearing. The ground was strewn with rocks and the remnants of fallen, moss-covered logs. Beyond them, a white mist rose, obscuring the sky. The same thick, leafy moss that covered the logs spread like a green carpet across the clearing floor. Patches of pale, yellow stone glimmered in the mist, marking the position of the Mountain.

They had made it. The waterfall loomed over them, just as Bobo said it would.

Jake pointed to the waterfall. "There's a tunnel or something up ahead. We're here!"

Jake dismounted and led Blue forward. The mist enveloped them, and Jake's skin became clammy with condensation, and his ears rang with the deafening rush of the falls.

A few more steps and the air began to clear. Jake saw the Mountain, or rather a spur of it, loom up out of the mist like the hull of an approaching ship. It terminated with a steep drop into a white cloud, and over the edge poured a vast, deafening torrent of water. Light danced across the falls, and in the mist played a moving kaleidoscope of rainbows, spilling across a canvas of white before fading and breaking out anew in brilliant color. For a time, the falls held him transfixed, and Jake could not rouse himself back into motion. Deep in the roar, Jake heard echoes of the stars' song.

It was Blue who broke the spell. "Jake, something is there in the mist. Dark. Large."

"It's the passage. Bobo said it would be there. That's our way out. Come on." He began moving again, but turning away from the sight of the falls left a keen, lingering ache in him.

Ahead, the rock had worn away, creating a massive, arched overhang, hidden from the outside by the wall of water tumbling down from above.

They started toward it, but a closer look froze them in their tracks. Jake sighed and hung his head. "I should have known."

Standing between them and the tunnel was Spence.

Chapter Twenty-One

Through the mist, Jake could see Spence's sharp teeth protruding past his upper lip. Spence shifted a little, leaning forward on his massive arms, daring Jake to try to get past him.

"Bobo," said Spence. He spat the name as he spat the word Keeper. "Bobo pulled you out of the pit. Bobo made you free."

"Bobo had nothing to do with it," Jake said, as much to himself as it was to Spence. The orangutan's accusation meant that Bobo hadn't betrayed him, and that gave him a little comfort.

"You are still a Kept Ape. You are still mine!" Spence growled. His voice carried, despite the constant rush of water over the falls. Startled, Jake took a step back before he could stop himself, and Spence leaned forward a little more. Every muscle in the orangutan's body was tensed, ready to spring on Jake and exact whatever revenge he had planned for him. But something held him back; he stayed in place, rooted to the patch of glistening, mossy soil that stood between Jake and the wet stone of the tunnel.

"You are not going anywhere. I will keep you here until you forget."

Spence craned his head toward the sky and let out his long call. Several times he did it, louder each time. The apes that had been pursing Jake emerged from the trees. They dropped to the ground and formed a wide arc, cutting Jake off from escape.

Chimpanzees, orangutans, Rhesus monkeys, bonobos, and a number of silverback gorillas filled Spence's ranks. Leading them was Wigwig. A look of satisfaction, even glee, played across his features. He clapped his hands together and pointed at Jake.

"It was just as you said, Spence. We caught him. This is a good game!" Wigwig said. The apes behind him did not share his levity; they eyed Jake with a mixture of fear and disdain. Blue pawed the stony ground nervously, his ears pinned back against his head. Jake wondered if Blue would fight if the monkeys tried to take him. It was strange that they hadn't tried; Jake and Blue were outnumbered at least twenty-five to one, and yet, the apes and monkeys seemed reluctant to press their advantage.

"Let us go," said Jake. "We didn't do anything to you."

"Jake, you are making it angry," said Blue.

The arrival of the others emboldened Spence, and he stalked toward Jake, his gums pulled back to show Jake a set of long, sharp fangs. Blue tried to insinuate himself between Spence and Jake, but he was too late; the ape stopped, his face only inches from Jake's.

"You belong to me now," Spence hissed.

Wigwig and other apes edged forward. Jake cringed away from Spence, turning his face to the side to avoid staring into the orangutan's gaping maw. Spence watched him, his face a mask of sadistic joy. He glanced at Blue, who was shifting this way and that, looking for an opportunity to run. He huffed and snorted, throwing out a short kick at a chimpanzee that ventured too close. The chimp shied back, unharmed but wary of Blue's power.

"I think I will have your friend too," Spence said, gesturing toward Blue. The other apes hung back, in no hurry to try to capture a horse.

"Let him go!" Jake begged. "Blue didn't do anything to you. He had to do what people told him, just like you did!"

"They will not let us go, Jake. They mean us both harm."

"No more talking," said Spence. He grabbed Jake by the arm and dragged him away from Blue. The orangutan's long fingers wrapped around Jake's upper arm so tightly that he could already feel a tingling in his hand.

Wigwig and the others moved to surround Blue, but they refrained from touching him, wary of the horse's strong right rear leg, which was poised to kick the first monkey bold enough to attack. Blue started after Spence, but two of the silverbacks blocked his passage, baring their teeth. Blue kicked out with his front legs, driving the gorillas back, but they remained in his way. The rest of them tightened the circle, forcing

Blue's attention away from Jake and Spence. A couple of the chimps moved in a little too close. Blue kicked out, grazing one on the shoulder and narrowly missing the other's head. They skittered backward, rejoining the line.

Spence dragged Jake across the stony ground and stopped just short of the cliff's edge. The thick, humid air was saturated with the smell of water and wet stone. He thrust Jake to the precipice, a smile of grim satisfaction playing across his features. Jake was petrified; he could do nothing to loosen the ape's iron grip, and anything he said would simply be overwhelmed by the roar of the water over the falls. His toes rested on the edge of the precipice, and he felt the cool spray against the soles of his feet.

A dog barked, deep and ominous. It sounded familiar, but Jake remained wary; he remembered how he had been tricked before. The apes broke ranks and retreated, leaving a wide gap.

Indistinct shapes rippled in the silver haze, and Bobo emerged from the mist. The bark was only a trick, one that Bobo must have perfected since the last time. He advanced slowly, coming to a halt near Blue.

"You," Spence said. "You helped it. You let it go."

The orangutan's grip on Jake's arm remained painfully firm.

"This is not a place for Keepers," Bobo said. "Where there are Keepers, we cannot be free."

Another figure emerged from the mist, and Jake's eyes widened. At first, he dared not believe it, but somehow it was true.

Coming to a halt just behind Bobo was Ursus.

He seemed none the worse for his journey and carried himself with the same quiet sadness Jake had come to miss in the days since their parting. His eyes were fixed on Spence, but there was no malice in them. Understanding, perhaps, or pity. Bobo stood next to him, watching Spence with the same expression.

"I told you to keep it in the pit," said Spence. As he did so, he squeezed a little on Jake's arm, sending a jolt of pain up into his shoulder.

"It wasn't happy there," said Bobo.

Spence turned his attention to Ursus. The dog matched him for size and power, but Spence showed no fear. He pointed a finger in Ursus' direction.

"And who are you, slave-thing? Keeper's pet? Why have you come to the Mountain? This is not the place for your kind."

"I am called Ursus at the Howls. I followed Jake's scent."

"Do not give it a name," said Spence. He hauled Jake close to him and wrapped a protective arm across his chest. "It is mine. It is my Kept Ape. Go crawl back to your forest beyond the river. You cannot have it."

"Jake is my friend," said Ursus. I will go where he goes."

Spence's eyes lit up. "We will see."

The water, cool and dangerous, flowed just over the top of his head. Jake looked down into turbid foam raging at the waterfall's base. He wondered what would happen to him if Spence loosened his grip and let him fall. It would be the nothingness, Jake guessed, the empty, dark void he'd seen in the depths of the river. That was where he would go. He thought of Sebastian and Samuel and the other dogs, dragged off into the darkness. He shivered a little.

"Come and get him," said Spence. He lifted Jake off his feet and dangled him over the edge of the cliff, shaking him, daring Ursus to make a grab for him. "We will see who is stronger."

"We are not Keepers, Spence," said Bobo.

Bobo took a step forward. He held out his hands in supplication. "This is not our way. If you drop it into the falls, you will become like them. You will be a Keeper, then. But you will not be happy."

Spence loosened his grip just a little, letting Jake's arm slide a few inches downward. Jake cried out in terror; the sound of his voice lost in the water.

"It will not help," said Bobo. "You must forget what the Keepers did to you. You are here now, here at the Mountain. The Keepers are far away. They cannot harm us anymore. Forget them, Spence."

"Far away? Far away! This is not far away!" he thrust Jake higher into the air.

"Spence. I am free. Wigwig is free. You are free. Be free with us."

If Spence heard anything Bobo said, he made no indication. His eyes were fixed on the dog's.

"What will you do, slave-thing, if I let go?" There was a mad, reckless glee in Spence's voice.

"I will go where he goes," said Ursus.

"No!" Jake cried. "Ursus, no!"

"You will not," said Spence. "You will remember!

You will remember what I did and you will come for me. We will see who is stronger. I will make you my plaything."

"Don't fight him," Jake shouted. "Take Blue! Get out of here!"

"I will go where he goes," Ursus said.

One by one, the other apes closed ranks again, dark, foreboding shapes in the mist. Whether they intended to fight or to bear witness, Jake did not know. They came no closer, spread out across the ledge in a wide arc, watching.

Spence bared his teeth, his face brimming with barely suppressed violence. A hush fell over the assembly, a sense of calamity made worse by the sound of the water plunging into the pool far below. But Ursus blinked, looked to his right, and then met Spence's eyes again. The ape frowned, confused and disappointed with Ursus' response.

It wasn't something Jake could see, but he felt it; a shudder in Spence's body that ended in a sigh, an almost imperceptible drop in the shoulders. Water condensed on Jake's pants and dripped down his legs.

Wigwig laid his hand over Spence's free arm. "Spence, put it down. This is not fun anymore." Spence shrugged him off and glared down at Jake. His grip loosened a little more, and Jake's arm slid through Spence's palm. The mist condensed on his skin and in his clothes. He feared the nothingness, but it was almost preferable to dangling above it, waiting to die.

"I am the Keeper now. You are the Kept Ape. I choose. I choose!" Spence said. Jake felt the ape's hot breath in his ear.

"I'm sorry! I'm sorry!" Jake cried. "I wish you were never in a cage! But it wasn't me!"

"Your kind are all the same," said Spence.

"I never kept anything in a cage!" Jake pleaded. "I never even had a fish!"

It was true, but only because aquariums and cages were expensive. Jake had asked many times for caged pets, but the answer was always the same. *Jake, when things get better, we'll see.* It was his mother's way of saying no when she didn't want to deal with Jake's temper.

Jake felt a flush of shame. He wished he could take back his desire to have something in a cage, something he could watch and control. Spence was right, he was a Keeper. But before he could admit his sin, Spence pulled him up until Jake's face was level with his own, and the dark, leathery skin of the orangutan's flanges made a gaping, hideous maw of Spence's entire face.

"Your kind are all the same!" Spence shouted. "You take, always take, you put the ones that please you in cages and kill the others. You see us as pretty things, or food, or enemies. You make your cities grow until most of us die, and the ones who are left must stay in the cage. And now you follow us here to make us Kept Apes again. But you are not strong without your metal and your smoke. Here I am strong. I will show you how weak you are. I choose. I choose!"

"Spence, put it down. Let it be free. It will go away and you will forget. If you do not let it free you will always be a Kept Ape." Bobo put a hand on Spence's arm.

"You were born a Kept Ape. You do not know."

"Listen to him, Spence," Jake said.

Spence turned him and pulled him close until his face eclipsed the waterfall.

"Mother and I wandered for days. Wandered through the Keeper-trees. Many trees, all the same, and nothing to eat. Why do you keep trees with no food? Why do you make a place that looks like a forest but is not?" He paused. Jake had nothing to say. Though their eyes were separated by only the space of a fingertip, Spence's gaze was elsewhere, somewhere distant.

"Then the trees stopped. There was an open place. A flat place. Mother was afraid to cross. We could see trees. Real trees, food trees, on the other side, but she would not cross the open place. We stayed there for a day and a night. I slept. Mother woke me. She was moving again, down. Down to the ground. There was food at the edge of the open place. I did not remember seeing it before."

Spence closed his eyes. His shoulders sagged, and Jake thought that Bobo had gotten through to him. But his eyes opened again, narrow slits, and his grip tightened painfully around Jake's arm.

"They came while Mother ate. They came and hit mother from far away. She fell on the food, and I could not wake her. Then they put a net on me and dragged me away. I remember how Mother got smaller and smaller until I could not see her. I remember."

"I can't remember my mother at all," Jake whispered.

"They kept me in a box. A box like the pit. They

brought little Keepers like you to look at me and poke me with sticks. The large ones beat me when I showed them my teeth. They kept me in a box until I became old. I never saw the trees again. I never saw any of my kind again. But I never forgot. Never. Even when I came to the Mountain. I never forgot."

Spence looked into Jake's eyes. A thousand useless apologies flashed through Jake's mind. None of them were enough. No matter how much he ached for the ape's pain, no matter how responsible he felt, his words would accomplish nothing. He closed his eyes and turned his head away, feeling the cool spray against his forehead.

Any second now, he thought, but Spence did not let go.

"I am free," he said. "I will not drop my Kept Ape into the water. I will keep it. I will keep the grass-eater and the slave-thing too. I will learn to ride the grass-eater, and the slave-thing will follow me."

"You are not a Rider," said Blue. "I have never lost a Rider. But I will not carry you."

"I will go where Jake goes," said Ursus.

"The other apes will take you, and they will be Keepers too," said Spence. He pointed to Wigwig.

"Take the grass-eater to the pit," he said. But Wigwig did not move.

"Take the grass-eater to the pit!"

Wigwig looked at Spence, and then at Ursus and Blue. He turned his back on them and joined Bobo at the cliff's edge.

"Who will take the grass-eater to the pit?" Spence bellowed. None of the apes came forward.

Ursus moved a few steps closer. His ears were pinned against his head, his eyes narrowed.

Jake struggled against Spence's grip. "Ursus! No! You're not a fighting dog anymore!"

"I will throw it in," Spence said. His lips curled back. "Then you will want revenge."

Ursus took another step forward. He growled, low and ominous, audible even over the rush of the falls.

"Ursus!" Jake cried.

The dog's eyes fell on Jake.

"Your Givers can't touch you here," Jake whispered.

Ursus blinked. His ears relaxed, and the tension melted away.

"I will go with Jake," he said.

Spence howled. Long and deafening, it echoed against the Mountain, lingering on the cliff like the mist. The other apes retreated. Blue rolled his eyes and scraped the moss with his hooves, but the apes surrounding him left him no avenue for escape.

"Move!" Spence howled, but Wigwig and Bobo held their ground.

"You are not a Keeper!" Bobo pleaded. "You belong with us!"

"It was a good game," said Wigwig, "But it is not a game anymore. Come with us back to the trees. Come with us. We will be free apes again."

Jake looked down at Bobo and Wigwig, and he understood. He had to get away, or Spence would never be free. What he did to Jake, he would do to others, again and again, trying to fill the emptiness, trying to assuage a hunger that nothing could satisfy.

Bobo and Wigwig grabbed Spence's arm and tried to force Jake from his grasp, but Spence knocked them away. Jake wrapped his legs around Spence's arm, clinging to it like a shipwrecked sailor on a spar. Spence roared in frustration and grabbed Jake by the face. He was no match for the ape's strength, and Spence pried him off the way a boy might pry a clinging kitten from his arm. He felt his legs pull away, but something stayed Spence's hand, and Jake managed to recover his grip. He looked up to see Wigwig and Bobo wrestling with Spence's free arm. Spence was strong, but together, Bobo and Wigwig nearly matched him, and try as he might, Spence was unable to free his other arm to pry Jake off so that he could send him plummeting into the waters beneath the falls.

"Spence, let the Keeper go free!" said Bobo.

"No!" Spence wrenched his body, pulling his arm with all his strength to free himself from their grasp. Bobo and Wigwig held on, and their bodies lifted from the wet stone, and it was them, not Jake, who dangled over the waterfall. The force of it was enough to dislodge Jake from Spence's arm, and he tumbled in the air, landing in a heap against the stone wall of the tunnel.

He felt a sharp pain, and his head swam. He watched through a blurry curtain as Spence and the other orangutans tottered on the edge of the falls, orange blots against the sparkling water. Then, in an instant, they were gone.

Jake got to his knees and crawled toward the edge of the waterfall. Ursus and Blue arrived almost at the same instant. Jake peered over the edge.

Spence was nowhere to be seen. Wigwig and Bobo clung to the gray stone a few feet below the cliff's edge. They appeared unhurt, but their faces were haggard with grief and fear. Bobo looked up at Jake. He extended one long, disdainful finger in Jake's direction.

"You, Keeper. You killed him."

Jake said nothing. He could think of no words of protest, no defense, no condolence that would help. He looked down at them, his mind a maelstrom of horror and shame.

"Go," Bobo said. "Take your friends and go. Never come to the Mountain again."

Still, the words would not come. Jake could only nod, his mouth open, his breath coming in short, strained gasps.

"Go!" Bobo shouted.

Jake obeyed. He scuttled back from the edge, regained his feet, and started into the tunnel. He didn't look to see if Blue and Ursus were behind him, but the sound of hooves echoed against the tunnel, barely audible beneath the water's constant dirge, flowing eternally against the gray stone.

Chapter Twenty-Two

The tunnel sparkled with an unworldly beauty that on any other occasion would have stopped Jake dead in his tracks, but he took only passing notice. His only thought was to get away, to wash Bobo's despair and loathing from his mind, to wipe away the single, accusing finger that had been leveled at him from the cliff face.

"You killed him," Bobo said. "You."

The stone was rough and cold, and Jake could just make out the sound of his feet and the click of Blue's hooves over the rush of water coursing across the overhang and into the maelstrom below.

Muted, diffuse light shone ahead, and it wasn't long before Jake, Blue, and Ursus emerged from the far end of the tunnel into the jungle beyond. The tunnel must have sloped downward, for the waterfall was high above, still audible but no longer overpowering.

"You would have done it," Jake said. "You would have followed me over that waterfall."

"I will stay with you," Ursus said.

Jake didn't know what to think about that. He doubted Blue would follow him over a waterfall, kind and loyal as the horse was. The responsibility was too much for Jake to comprehend. In his mind, he saw the frothing water roiling beneath the mist. Ursus would have followed him there, into the darkness, the nothingness beneath the surface.

Beyond the Mountain, Sebastian and Sarafina and the other dogs suffered. They had put their trust in him, as Ursus had. He looked out into the rainforest, overcome by the enormity of his task.

"I can't do this. I'm just a kid." He slumped down in the shadow of a gigantic root and hugged his knees. He swept his arm across the horizon, across the expanse of woods around them. "How are we going to find Gordon in all of this?"

"Givers know all," said Ursus.

"Don't you get it? I don't know all. I don't know anything. I don't know what I'm doing! I don't even know how I made it this far. If you two keep following me, you'll just end up like the dogs that got captured. Or maybe like Spence."

"We cannot go back," said Blue. "The orange ones are there. They will harm us if we go back."

"I go where you go," said Ursus.

"Why?" said Jake. "I'm probably just going to screw it all up, like I screwed it all up back home."

"I am a friend," said Ursus.

Jake didn't know what to say. He felt unworthy, wholly inadequate to accept something as valuable and pure as the friendship Ursus offered. There was no way Jake was going to lead them into whatever terrible fate lay in store if they managed to reach their objective.

Above them, the water flowed, its constant rush already a part of the background noise. He wondered where all that water was going. And then it occurred to him, suddenly, like a cuff to the side of the head, where they were.

This was where the river started, and they had crossed back to the other side through the tunnel. If he followed the river, he'd end up back at the forest where he and Ursus had met. Blue and Ursus would be safe. Then, it would just be a matter of convincing the two of them that he had to make the trip alone. Jake felt a sweet sense of relief come over him.

"I guess you're right," Jake said. "We'll just have to keep going and hope we get lucky."

"If Gordon has passed his way, I will know," said Ursus.

"How did you find us?" Jake said. He put on his best smile. The plan he buried deep in his heart. There would be time for that when Blue and Ursus were safe.

"Blue has a strong scent. I followed," Ursus replied.

"I'm sorry we left you."

"You did not leave me."

"But we did! I watched you disappear behind us. We've been apart for days. Maybe a week."

"You went to the Mountain. I went to the Mountain. Near and far is the same."

"I think I like near better," Jake said. He reached up and ran his fingers along the dog's snout. "I missed you."

"Now we must find Gordon," said Ursus.

"Bobo said that we'd find him on the other side. Well, this is the other side."

The rainforest spread out before them, a shadowy maze of trees and buttress roots that continued in every direction, interrupted only by the rocky spur that lay behind them. Jake felt the familiar sense of helplessness come over him again; the area was unutterably vast. They might search for a hundred years and not cover it all. That, of course, didn't matter anymore. Jake would have time enough, after.

"Well, I have an idea," said Jake. "I bet the waterfall flows down into the river. I think if I were Gordon, I would stick close to it instead of going deep into the jungle. We'll probably have a better chance of finding him if we do that."

"I will follow you, Jake," said Blue.

Jake felt a pang of sadness. He couldn't have asked for better friends, not back home with Mom and Dad, not in any world, and he had to remind himself again that letting Ursus and Blue go would be the best for all of them. Jake couldn't bear the thought of bringing them any more pain or sorrow than they'd already faced. It was for the best.

He scrambled to his feet. "Might as well get a move on," he said.

There was no clear path down to the water. Jake picked his way through the maze of roots, searching for a path downward, but each choice seemed to lead him farther and farther into the forest. They went on that way until the rush of falling water became nothing more than a whisper.

Green-tinged, diffuse light offered the only illumination, revealing nearly barren soil between the trees. Before long it became difficult for Jake to find gaps in the roots large enough for Ursus and Blue to pass between, and they were forced to turn back. He tried to retrace his steps, but in the shadowy half-light, Jake could see nothing that indicated the direction from which they had come. There were no footprints.

"So much for my idea," Jake said. "We're lost again."

He hunkered down near the ground, scrutinizing every inch of soil for a track or some disturbance, but he saw nothing. Then he crawled, touching the ground with his fingertips. He circled around, through Blue's legs, and eventually stopped near an opening that Jake was sure he'd recognized on their way in.

"Here it is," Jake said. But Ursus was preoccupied, his nose pressed into the soil.

"Ursus, I think I found the way back. Didn't we come through here?"

Ursus didn't look up. He wandered among the trees, sniffing at the ground, blowing small puffs of loose soil.

"Ursus, come look. This is the way out."

But Ursus again ignored him. He took in the scent of every tree around him, pausing, and then repeating the strange procedure over again a few steps later.

"Ursus, I think this is the way."

"This is the way," said Ursus.

"I don't think so," said Jake. "I'm sure we came through there. I remember the tree."

"Samuel came this way," Ursus said. "Malbinocks followed him. This is the way to Gordon."

In front of him was the trail that would lead them to Gordon, but Jake felt no joy, no sense of accomplishment; only a vague foreboding, as if the trail were a decaying bridge that might not hold them up. In his mind, the turbid water beneath the falls roiled and bubbled, and once again he saw his feet, dangling in space. Somewhere below the tumbling water lay Spence, drifting quietly, deeper and deeper, toward the darkness.

"Jake," said Blue. "Ursus has found the way. Shall we follow?"

Jake wanted to say no. But he couldn't form the word. Instead, he nodded silently and followed Ursus down the narrow trail between two massive trees, their buttress roots as high as church walls. Blue brought up the rear. It was slow going; Ursus had to stop every few minutes to reacquire the scent, and the trail wound in a haphazard, almost random fashion through the labyrinthine roots. Samuel had led the Malbinocks on a long, difficult chase. Jake could almost envision the cat running, twisting this way and that between the trees, Malbinocks shuffling behind, relentless.

The trail led them gradually downward, toward the sound of trickling water. The fear that had gripped Jake earlier eased a bit; he told himself that there was still time to convince Blue and Ursus to remain behind. He'd do the same for Gordon; as soon as Gordon gave him directions to the Malbinocks' hideout, he would turn the dog loose. They could start a new pack, the three of them, two dogs and a horse, and wait out their time together until they heard their Givers' calls.

Ursus came to a root unlike any they had encountered. Its top was broken in several places, and wedge-shaped cuts in the wood gave it a jagged appearance, like broken teeth. The cuts were too regular and deliberate to be accidental; someone had swung an ax at the trees. Ursus paced in circles, doing his best to try to reacquire the scent, but it was to no avail. The dense canopy blotted out so much of the light that the forest floor lay in perpetual darkness.

"It's no use, Ursus. The trail's gone cold," said Jake. Part of him was relieved. The sound of tricking water remained enticingly close.

"No dogs came this way," said Ursus. "Samuel did not come this way." There was no distress in the dog's voice. Jake became hopeful again. They had managed to narrow the area down, which would make it easier upon Jake's return, and the damaged root marked the spot.

"What happened?" Jake said, feigning disappointment.

"Samuel did not come this way,"

"Which way did he go, then?"

"Up."

Jake looked up. It made sense; Samuel would have taken to the treetops, given the opportunity, and there were a few branches close enough to the tops of the roots for Samuel to make the leap.

"Down," said Blue. "This is where he came down."

Jake looked up into the canopy. Blue was right. They were following Samuel's back trail, and they had no idea how long he'd moved through the trees. It wasn't a starting point they'd discovered but another dead end. This time, Jake didn't have to feign his feelings. Even with Ursus' sense of smell they were no closer to Gordon now than when they had begun. So much for Givers knowing all, he thought. Ursus cast about, his nose in the soil, searching, but Jake held out little hope that the search would turn up anything useful.

He hated himself a little for it, but a tiny sliver of gratitude worked its way into his mind. The loss of the trail was another chance for him to get his friends out of danger before resuming his search. There would be safety across the river if he could just find it again.

"All right," Jake said, "Let's try to think like Gordon would think." The animals watched him expectantly.

"If you were Gordon, and you escaped from a terrible place, wouldn't you want to go back to a place you remembered? A good place?"

"I am not Gordon. I am Blue."

"I know," said Jake. "Use your imagination."

Blue blinked twice and pawed at the ground.

"I will follow you, Jake," said Ursus. "You are the Giver."

Jake threw up his hands. There was no need to convince them, or trick them. Blue and Ursus would follow him regardless of his reasoning, and the responsibility settled on Jake's body like a weighted vest. Their faith in him was entirely unearned; he hadn't done a single thing right since he arrived. Being leaderless would have been safer for them than following him, and yet here they were, waiting patiently for Jake to decide.

Jake didn't want the job, but there was no one else.

"All right," he shrugged. "If I was Gordon, I would have gone looking for the river. Once I found it, I could follow it all the way back to the Howl. So, what we should try to do is follow the river, like he probably did."

It had all sounded much cleverer in his head.

"There is water this way," said Blue. "I hear it flowing over the rocks."

And so, it was settled. Jake let Blue take the lead since his hearing seemed to be the best of the three of them. He was all too happy to let one of the others lead for a while. He thought it would give him time to think, but instead he merely drifted, content to follow the horse's tracks and let his mind go blissfully silent. For a long time, he simply walked, letting the trees slip past his view. His eyelids grew heavy, and a strange, sweet, languid feeling came over him, leaving just enough will to keep his feet moving.

But it didn't seem to matter how far they walked; the water remained nothing more than a distant trickle, barely audible to Jake. Blue led them on, picking his way between the roots and trunks, his tall ears flicking this way and that, while Ursus, his nose to the soil, brought up the rear. Once in a while, Blue would halt, listening intently at some noise Jake could not hear, but each time, he dismissed it as nothing. It went on that way until the meager light that managed to break through the thick canopy finally disappeared, and the woods were once again plunged into total darkness.

Jake no longer found the darkness unsettling. He had spent enough nights with Blue to become accustomed to it, and having Ursus back only made him feel more secure. The coming of night was nothing more than a chance to lean against Ursus' belly and close his eyes. The dog's warm coat against his back made Jake even more grateful for his return. A slight breeze carried the lush, vibrant scent of the leaves down from the canopy.

Only swatches of memory remained from those Jake had seen at the Howl. When memory did come, it came in bursts, explosions bubbling up from his unconscious mind, always too jumbled to make any sense. He might hear the tune to Monday Night Football, or catch the moist, soapy smell of the bathroom when he stepped out of the shower, or see the face of Mrs. Collins or Precious Peter or his dad, eyes weary, staring out into the backyard through the dining room window with that desperate, quiet expression his face had when he thought no one was looking.

Ursus scrambled to his feet, knocking Jake sideways in his haste. Jake covered his face, sure that Spence's long, slender fingers would close around his arm or his leg and drag him screaming into the dark, away from his friends.

"There is a scent in the air," Ursus said.

Jake's fear ebbed a little. "What? What kind of scent?"

"Dog."

"A dog?" Jake struggled to his feet as well, reaching

out with his fingers to make contact. He searched until his hands reached Ursus' smooth, warm coat.

"Gordon is close," Ursus said.

Jake felt the dog's smooth coat slide across his fingers as Ursus tracked the scent. He moved quickly, his nose snuffling as he searched the air.

"Ursus, slow down. I can't see anything. I'll get lost."

"Take hold of my tail," said Blue. "I have never lost a Rider."

Blue's tail was only a few inches outside his grasp. Jake snatched it from the air and held it tightly against both palms. As soon as he felt Jake's grip, Blue lurched forward into a brisk trot. Jake could barely keep up. A couple of sharp turns almost sent Jake careening into whatever lay just outside of Blue's path, but he managed to keep his grip and the two of them hurtled through utter darkness. Foreboding and excitement consumed him, but he focused on running absolutely blind through the labyrinth of roots and trunks that lay in their path.

Ursus let out a strange, low huffing sound; neither a growl nor a bark, and Blue surged forward, quickening his pace until Jake found himself in an outright sprint with his hands locked in a death grip on the horse's tail. The dim outline of his own hands faded into view, and the trickling water, so distant before, now sounded as if it were only a few yards ahead.

They emerged from the cover of the trees into the dazzling silver light of the stars. Jake let go of Blue's tail and stared in abject wonder.

An outcropping of rock, a deep massive root of

the Mountain, descended from among the trees and plunged into the water of a magnificent lake. Starlight glittered and danced on the rivulets that trickled from some unseen source across channels of rock worn smooth and flat by the constant flow. Farther down, the rock formed depressions, and as it neared the surface of the lake, the depressions became deeper and deeper. At the lake's edge, they were deep enough to resemble bowls.

Jake took a few tentative steps forward and peered down into the water. The bowls weren't limited to the outcropping; the entire lake, it seemed, was comprised of them, and all of them teemed with multitudes of fish. Untold numbers of them swam blissfully through the clear water, darting this way and that, diving into the depths, flitting so close to the surface that the silver light glittered from their perfect scales. They took no notice of Jake, even when he dropped to his knees and held his face so close to the water that the tip of his nose got wet.

The colors defied description, deep reds, and lustrous golds, and icy blues. They seemed to mirror the stars with their movements as if the sky and the lake were partners in a magnificent dance. Jake wanted to join, to dance with them, with the stars and all that lay beneath them, to dance to the song that burst from the sky like rain and filled him with quiet, intense joy.

Ursus barked, deep and resonant. The fish darted away, out into the expanse of the lake. Jake sat up. He wiped the water from his face and tried to blink it out of his eyes. Ursus stared down at him.

"Jake," he said, "Gordon is here."

Chapter Twenty-Three

A thin, yellow strand of smooth gravel separated the rainforest from the lake. It curved around them to their left, sloping upward until it met the trees. A pair of boulders had toppled, one on top of the other, leaving a small gap between them, now festooned with moss and the knobby edges of exposed roots, forming a small cave. Next to the cave stood Blue.

"There is a dog here," the horse said.

Jake followed Ursus across the strand, echoes of the star song still playing in his mind. When he reached the boulders, he bent down and inspected the cave mouth.

"Where? I don't see any dog."

"There," said Blue. "In the hole. I watched a dog go in."

It was barely large enough for Jake to squeeze his head and one of his shoulders through, but crawling all the way in was out of the question. There was no noise from inside the cave, no whimpering, growling, no scuffling of claws against the coarse, golden sand, only darkness and silence so profound that he began to wonder if Blue had been mistaken.

"Are you sure he went in there? What if all the shadows around these rocks were just playing tricks on you?" Jake said.

"A dog is here," said Ursus. "His scent is strong."

Jake hunkered down in front of the cave again, lying on his belly so that his face was level with the cave mouth.

"Hi Gordon. My name's Jake. Samuel sent us. I'm glad we found you, because we really need your help."

Jake received nothing for his trouble.

"I don't think he's coming out," said Jake. Frustration and disappointment gnawed at him. Jake had done exactly what Samuel asked. The cat had said nothing at all about what Gordon would do when they found him. Their meeting was supposed to be a happy one. Jake had played out the whole thing in his mind almost daily since they'd set out.

He had imagined Gordon trembling with pent-up loneliness and excitement at the sight of friendly faces so far from the Howl. He had expected a hundred questions. *Giver, how are you here? Will you rub my belly? Will you play with me? Who are your friends? May I join your pack?* He expected Gordon to accept their invitation with a *Come, follow me, I will take you there,* before taking up his place at the head of their little column. Together they would make everything right.

Jake risked slipping a hand inside but felt nothing more than the yellow gravel that covered the strand.

He slid it in a little further, testing the gravel with his fingers as he went, but he found nothing but empty space and more gravel.

"Jake," said Blue, "There is danger in dark holes."

Jake pulled his hand back out. "Not this one. I didn't feel a thing. Why would he go in there anyway? It's not like you were going to hurt him."

"The dog did not crawl in when he saw me," Blue said. "He crawled in when he saw you."

Jake backed away from the hole and stood up.

"You think he's afraid of me?"

"I do not know if he is afraid. He saw you and crawled in."

"He is afraid," said Ursus.

"Why would he be afraid of me? I'm not going to hurt him."

"In the dark, you have the shape of one of them," Ursus said.

"One of what? You mean a Malbinock? Gordon thinks I'm a Malbinock?"

"You have the shape of a Malbinock in the dark. That is what I know."

Anger, familiar and comfortable as an old shoe, bubbled up inside of him.

"Great! All this way, and he's afraid of me!"

Jake stomped back across the strand and stood at the edge of the lake. The stars, reflected in the water, flowed and rippled as if the sky and the lake were one, but Jake saw nothing of its beauty. They could do something about it, those stars, but they taunted him instead with their music, rippling against the horizon, cold and distant.

"I don't know what you want me to do!" Jake shouted.

The stars did not answer. Even the faint song had dissipated into silence.

"Tell me what to do!"

But the stars told him nothing. Jake sank down into the gravel and watched the lake. A slight breeze stirred gentle waves that slid soundlessly against the strand. Just beneath the surface, the fish swam. Jake wondered if there was a Calling-Place for them.

He looked up to find Ursus sitting next to him. Jake didn't hear him approach. The dog said nothing, and Jake felt a flush of shame for his outburst. For a while, he sat quietly, grateful for the dog's presence.

"Sorry," said Jake.

"You are the Giver. If you must howl, howl. If you must bark, bark."

"It wasn't supposed to be like this," said Jake. "I never thought he would be afraid of me. And if he's afraid of me right now because I'm shaped like a Malbinock, there's no way he's going to take us back to them."

Ursus dropped down to his belly, and Jake leaned against him. It was strange how natural it felt; as if it had been something he had always done. He felt the steady rise and fall of the dog's ribs against his back. The anger slipped away, and his body felt heavy and weak.

"I guess I can't blame the little guy," Jake said. "I mean, he was probably happy to see you and Blue. I bet you two were the first friendly faces he's seen in a long time. Then he sees me. I probably would have been scared too."

"He saw you and crawled into the hole," said Ursus. "That is what I know."

Jake slapped the sand and scrambled to his feet. "Maybe he's afraid of me, but he's not afraid of you. You can talk to him."

Ursus lifted his head from the ground.

"They are all afraid of me," he said.

"But that was before. You aren't like that now."

"He will be afraid. They are all afraid."

Jake pressed his hands into Ursus' head, just beneath the eyes. "No. Not all of them," Jake said. "There was one dog who wasn't. You remember. Nikola, or something like that. I don't remember, exactly. But that one dog wasn't afraid of you. She tried to help you. Now you have to try to help Gordon."

Ursus lay there for some time, staring into the undulating silver river that arched overhead. Jake sat beside him.

The stars continued their nightly dance above his head, and Jake could just make out the strains of their song. It was there, but faint, and no matter how hard he concentrated, he could barely distinguish it from wind rustling through the trees.

Ursus stood. "I will go."

Jake slipped across the strand and took refuge among the wide fern fronds at the edge of the forest. The strand was like a cliff that jutted out over the edge of the world. Stars dipped down from the heavens and found their way into the dark water of the lake, dancing in perfect unison with their counterparts above. Blue was only a silhouette against the sky, proud and noble, his head angled toward the mouth of Gordon's cave. Ursus joined him, another dark blot against the heavens. He stood for a moment and sniffed tentatively at the gravel just outside the cave's mouth. He backed away a few steps and then dropped to his belly.

He began to howl.

It was not the full-throated, deep howl that Jake had heard on the banks of the river. His voice was soft, high pitched, almost a whine. Had he not been watching, Jake never would have believed that such a sound could come from Ursus. There was meaning in it as well; something beautiful and profound, beyond Jake's ability to understand; mysterious and sad, a token of kinship that left Jake and Blue on the outside. It was the soul and spirit of the dog, all that a dog was, drifting in the sound of Ursus' cry, and Jake could do nothing more than touch the edges of it, and it filled him with a deep, penetrating sense of loneliness.

A small dog emerged from the mouth of the cave and stopped a few feet from Ursus' nose, his body indistinct against the heavens. Only his head appeared to have the shape of a dog; his body was a mass with no discernible legs or tail.

The little dog's movement reminded Jake of a pill bug, creeping along on a multitude of tiny legs that couldn't be seen unless the bug was turned over.

Ursus, for his part, remained still and silent, his massive head propped up on his front paws. Now Blue took a step forward and lowered his head, offering his snout for Gordon to smell. The little dog moved a few more feet and tentatively took in Blue's scent, sniffing around the horse's nose, lips, and chin. When the little dog finished his investigation, Blue stepped back again.

Ursus allowed the little dog to approach him. Gordon took in Ursus' scent as well, making a complete circuit of his body. Ursus remained still, doing nothing that might frighten Gordon back into the cave. Gordon turned around in a tight circle, twice, and then hunkered down against Ursus' massive left shoulder.

Jake experienced a twinge of jealousy. It was his spot that Gordon had taken. They seemed at peace, the three of them, and Jake was loath to intrude, though he resented the little dog for taking over his place at his friend's side. He wondered if it wasn't the first shred of peace Ursus and Blue had tasted since their arrival.

There was nothing for him to do but wait for day; approaching Gordon at night would only send him scurrying back into the hole. Jake leaned back and nestled into the soft soil, his eyes studying the endless shifting patterns of stars in the night sky. The song, only a whisper at first, increased in volume, and seemed to descend from all over the heavens, a soothing, joyful chorus that Jake ached to join, if only he could find the voice and learn the melody. He tried, but it shifted and whirled like the stars themselves, so that Jake could never get more than a few notes at a time before it left him for a new direction. He found it fascinating rather than frustrating, and he concentrated even harder.

He began to drift.

He heard the voices again, several of them, speaking at once. Men, women, perhaps a child or two, their voices intermingled and unintelligible, as if he had been dropped into the middle of a party where the guests all spoke a language different than his own. Gradually, the voices all fell silent, save three. Their voices were muffled as if they were speaking behind a thick door, but Jake didn't need to understand the words to know that something terrible had happened. One voice was a deep, soothing voice, ripe with concern and awful tidings. The other could barely speak; her voice was choked with heaving sobs. She was begging for something.

"I understand how hard this is. Really, I do. It's not something you have to decide this minute. But you have to understand that there's no brain activity, and that usually means—"

"No."

"Like I said, you don't have to decide anything this minute."

"You're not cutting up my beautiful baby."

"It's just something to think about. He could save a lot of lives."

"No! No! No!"

"Honey—"

"Don't, Brad. Don't you dare think it."

"Just listen—"

"Brad! We're not cutting him up. Do you understand?"

"Doctor—"

"I'm sorry. This has to be something you decide

together. Like I said, it's not something—"

"Stop talking like he isn't here! His heart is beating!"

The woman's voice dissolved into incoherent sobbing again.

"I don't think this is the right time, Doctor."

"Of course. Look, you're both tired. You should both go home. Sleep. You need to take care of yourselves, too."

When Jake opened his eyes, he saw only the wide, green fronds of the giant ferns through which passed a golden, dappled light. Voices echoed in his head, too distant to understand or recognize, and with them lingered a desperate sadness like nothing he'd ever felt. What he knew is that it wasn't his sadness, but someone else's, and only an echo at that, like warmth at the edges of a dangerous fire, not hot enough to harm but enough to prevent him from getting any nearer.

He sat up, brushing some of the fronds away from his face. The golden strand disappeared into gently lapping waves, the light sparkling across them as they washed against the gravel and receded back into the lake. With the waves came a deep, abiding sense of peace, pushing the sadness back into the depths of his mind. He took a deep breath, and the air was rich with the scent of dark soil and vibrant, healthy plants.

He stood up and left the cover of the ferns, making his way down the strand. The gravel was warm and smooth against his bare feet and gave way just enough to cradle them and make the walking easy. A little way up the strand, near Gordon's cave, Blue stood watch, while Ursus lay on his belly, his head resting on his paws. The light played over his coat with each breath, marking the regular rise and fall of his barrel chest.

Still nestled against Ursus, in the space Jake had claimed for himself, lay Gordon. His head and tail were hidden in a dark tangle of matted hair. From a distance, Jake couldn't tell which end was which. Next to Ursus, Gordon looked like a puppy, small and vulnerable. The little dog twitched a little and then was still again. Dreaming.

A few more steps, and Jake was almost close enough to reach out and stroke the little dog's tangled coat. He dropped to his knees and crawled. If he made himself small enough, maybe he wouldn't be mistaken for a Malbinock.

Gordon twitched again, and this time, a black tangle of hair lifted from the rest, and through it a pair of ebony eyes bored into Jake's. Jake looked away and then, slowly, returned Gordon's gaze. Gordon sat up on his haunches, more curious than afraid. Jake inched forward, expecting at any moment for Gordon to flee to the safety of the little cave, but he stood still, watching Jake, his head cocked a little to the side.

"Hey there," Jake said. Gordon made no reply.

"Don't you talk?"

Gordon cocked his head the other way.

"That's ok. I can do the talking. Ursus says I have too much noise in me. My name's Jake." He held out his hands, palms up. Gordon took a few tentative steps in Jake's direction. Jake stayed absolutely still, afraid that even a twitch would send the dog scampering back into the cave. Gordon's nose brushed cold and damp against his palm as he took in Jake's scent.

"See? I'm not one of them."

The little dog was close enough for Jake to smell him as well. Gordon stank of grease and burned rubber as if he'd been imprisoned in a diesel engine.

"You've had a rough time," Jake said. "I'm going to sit up now, ok?"

As he rose, Gordon retreated a few steps, eyeing the cave's mouth.

"Samuel told me to find you. He said you could help us. Do you remember Samuel?"

The little dog watched him silently, his head cocked to the side.

"You don't understand a word I'm saying, do you?"

Gordon sat on his haunches and blinked.

Ursus lifted his head. Jake scratched the big dog's muzzle. He fought down the frustration and disappointment welling inside him. There had to be a way for him to reach Gordon, to make him understand what they needed him to do.

"What did you say to him last night?" he asked Ursus. "I don't think he understands anything I'm trying to tell him."

Ursus thought for a moment. "He does not remember the Givers' noise."

"How am I supposed to talk to him then?"

"He does not remember the Givers' noise. That is what I know."

The frustration returned, hot and furious, and this time Jake couldn't contain it. He shot to his feet.

Gordon scuttled backward into the cave until he was swallowed by the darkness. Jake groaned and pressed his hands against the back of his head. He stomped through the gravel toward the water, muttering "all for nothing, we made this whole trip for nothing" over and over again.

The lake shimmered, its water a deep blue reflection of the sky. Beneath the surface, the fish darted between the submerged bowls, each intent on its own business. Did the fish know or care what the others did? Jake tried to imagine a Calling-Place for fish. Either there was a net somewhere, or the fish just leaped out of the water when they were called. Jake wasn't even sure if fish had ears at all.

He glanced at Blue, who watched him from across the strand. Ursus was watching him as well, but neither made any attempt to calm him. *If you must bark, bark. If you must howl, howl.* That's what Ursus would tell him.

If you must howl, howl.

Jake knew what he had to do. He returned to the mouth of the cave and sat down. He closed his eyes, pushing the warm gravel between his toes. Off to his left, Blue stamped the ground and shook himself. Farther out, a gentle breeze pushed the water against the shore in small waves. He breathed, and the air was cool and smelled of water and faintly of dog and horse.

He felt light, detached. The stars sang, distant and barely audible. But this time, Jake didn't strain to hear it. Instead, he added his voice.

His mind was like a curtain, opening to an empty stage, and onto that stage he poured all that he had done and seen and felt since Ursus pulled him from the river. How long ago had that been? He had lost count of the days. He saw in his mind a boy, angry and lost. Selfish. Sometimes cruel. He watched the boy, bursting with foolish pride, leading a pack of dogs through the forest. He watched the boy cower while the dogs fell, one by one, to the Malbinocks. He saw Sebastian, wide-eyed, pleading, before the darkness swallowed him while he stood by and did nothing.

The memories flowed past him, too much at once, tumbling over one another like the water over the falls. Samuel, his golden eyes shining, hunting. The foul-smelling pit in the rainforest, the soaring joy of the birds circling the Mountain.

And then he saw himself again, crouching by a small, dark opening in the rock. Ursus stood nearby. Blue had joined him. Their attention was not on him but on the mouth of the cave. Horse, dog, and boy all watched, waiting for something to emerge.

Shame twisted like a vice in Jake's heart. His song wasn't a dream but a mirror, and in the reflection was the truth. The truth was that he didn't deserve Gordon's help. He'd seen himself for what he was; a mean, petty, jealous, spiteful boy who cowered in the dark when his friends needed him the most. He couldn't take back what he had done but maybe could make up for it. Maybe he could make things right.

All he needed was for Gordon to point the way.

Gordon emerged from the cave, his tangled coat spilling from the shadows like dirty water. The little dog looked intently at the boy crouching near him.

Slowly, Gordon approached him. He sniffed the boy's hand and licked his cheek. Jake felt Gordon's tongue, warm and wet against his skin, and opened his eyes.

Gordon sat to his left, his head cocked to the side, tongue lolling from the side of his muzzle.

Jake smiled and gingerly ran his hand across the little dog's head. "I don't think I could ever be as brave as you."

Gordon stood and followed Jake's tracks down to the water's edge. For a while, he sat and looked out over the lake. Jake didn't hurry him. He stayed by the mouth of the cave, breathing deeply as if the peace were somehow dissolved in the air.

Then, without ceremony or fanfare, without even looking back at Jake or his friends, Gordon turned and walked up the strand, away from the Mountain.

Chapter Twenty-Four

They spent the rest of the day skirting the lakeshore, following the strand that offered the only separation between the lake and the dense rainforest on the other side. Night came, and still they walked. Clouds obscured the stars, leaving precious little light. It was only the contrast between the golden sand and his friends' dark coats that told Jake they were still ahead of him.

Jake finally called a halt when the clouds burst and a drenching rain soaked the strand. He and Gordon took shelter beneath Ursus and waited for the light to return. In the darkness, he listened to the rain's many voices; the hollow patter as it bounced against the fern fronds, the slap of its impact against Blue's back, the tinkling of rain against the lake like a million needles on a glass floor.

Despite the rain, or perhaps because of it, the odor of motor oil and burned rubber hung thick in the air around Gordon. For such a small dog, he took up a lot of room; Jake had to lean sideways to avoid a rivulet of water that poured down Ursus' shoulder. There was no room for him in his old spot, right beneath the big dog's chest where it was much drier, and so he did his best to keep out of the rain without touching Gordon's greasy coat.

He couldn't help the feeling that Gordon had stolen some part of Ursus for himself. It bothered him, like an itch on his foot that wouldn't go away no matter how hard he scratched. Even after he reminded himself that Gordon had been through something terrible, Jake could not push away the resentment that grew a little stronger each time he caught the pungent smell of motor oil in the damp air.

As soon as they caught sight of where the Malbinocks were holding Sebastian, Jake would send Gordon away. It was the right thing to do, considering what Gordon had already experienced.

It would be different if Gordon could talk to him. He could get to know the little dog, the way he knew Ursus and Blue, and they would be like a big family. But Gordon didn't understand anything he said. He only responded to Ursus, and it made Jake feel like he was the dog, and they the Givers, their words heavy with mystery and hidden meaning, known only to them.

Jake didn't like being on the outside. He fought the urge to slide out from underneath Ursus and take shelter under the fern fronds at the edge of the forest, but the profound darkness kept Jake hemmed in as surely as if it were made of stone. There was no telling where he would end up if he took his chances stumbling across the strand in the dark, so he leaned away from the miniature waterfall and waited for the light.

The rain blotted out the stars and drowned out their song, and Jake was left only with darkness and the rank scent of rubber and burning oil to keep him company. Doubts crept into his mind, whispering over the ever-present silvery rattle of rain on the lake.

We're never going to find it, he thought. And even if a miracle happened and they did, what could he do? He would fail like always, and he and all his friends would be caught, and then he would find out first-hand what the Malbinocks did with the animals they dragged howling into the shadows.

The whisper in his mind became a roar, loud enough to rouse him from his shelter beneath Ursus and into the darkness and driving rain.

"It is still dark," said Ursus.

Jake tried to come up with an excuse, but nothing came. He stood in perfect stillness as the rain soaked his clothes.

"Ursus, I—"

A keening desperate whimper tore Jake's attention away. It came from beneath Ursus. Jake's first fear was that they were under attack, that the Malbinocks had crept up, their noise masked by the rain, and taken Gordon without Jake even knowing it. He dove underneath his friend's barrel chest and searched the smooth gravel with his fingers.

Gordon was there.

"Gordon, it's ok," Jake said. "You're safe. No one is

going to hurt you." The dog's coat felt greasy and coarse, infused with sand and pine needles and bits of twig. Thick muscle lay beneath that, taught and shivering. If Gordon heard him, he made no sign except to crawl into Jake's lap and shiver against his belly.

The smell was almost unbearable. He felt Gordon's weight against his legs, surprisingly heavy for such a small dog. Jake stroked him, pushing away his own revulsion as he did so.

"It's all right, Gordon. We're here. Your friends are here. No one is going to hurt you ever again."

The words sounded hollow even as he spoke them. Gordon's shivering worsened, and Jake could no longer hold back his own fear.

"Gordon, don't die. Please."

Gordon's whimper became a whine and then a full-throated howl. Jake threw his arms around him and held him close, rocking him back and forth, whispering comfort, even as Gordon's paws raked his belly. Gradually, the howl trailed away into silence. Gordon's body grew still, and for an instant, Jake was afraid that the dog had slipped away in his arms.

"Gordon?"

He waited. He couldn't bring himself to shake him.

"Gordon?"

Jake's fear turned to welcome relief when he felt Gordon's ribs expanding, almost imperceptibly, against his legs.

"He's alive!" Jake said.

"He is here with us," said Blue. "When the light comes, we will follow him."

The awful weight of it settled on Jake and pressed on him until he could hardly breathe. He had no right. Sebastian and the other dogs were gone because of him. Gordon had done more than enough already when he escaped. Jake could ask no more of him.

"When the light comes," he whispered.

Gordon remained on Jake's lap until morning. When the light returned, Ursus stood and shook himself in a spray of water. Jake was already drenched, but the spray was enough to rouse Gordon, who rolled off Jake's lap and sat up. Jake watched the little dog, expecting to see some of the night terrors in his walk or expression, but Gordon seemed none the worse for his ordeal.

They set off with Gordon in the lead. Jake lagged behind, scanning the jungle for an opening. He saw nothing that would suit him; the routes he saw were wide enough that Ursus and Blue could follow, and Jake was sure they would when they noticed he was gone. Ursus had tracked him across the grassland for days; whatever head start Jake could get would not last long.

For such a small dog, Gordon could keep a brisk pace, and the jungle slid by on Jake's left. The lake sparkled on the right, but its beauty was little comfort. He was trapped, pinned between forest and water, as if he were heading down a narrow corridor toward a room he had no desire to enter.

This must be what the death penalty feels like, he thought.

The rain let up a little, but Jake hardly noticed the difference. It felt a little like a lukewarm shower;

colder than he would like, but not uncomfortably so. The gravel rolled, smooth and firm, against the soles of his feet. The foreboding in his heart deprived him of the peace that pervaded the place; every time he began to feel at ease, a glimpse of Gordon trotting along in front plunged him back into melancholy and a sense of inescapable doom.

Gordon turned away from the lake when they reached the edge of the rainforest. Moss, and then grass, sprouted among the roots in the open areas between the trees. Behind him, the Mountain still loomed, though it seemed a little smaller than it had in the morning.

Ahead of them lay a rolling plain covered in tall, wide-bladed grass. A few trees with broad leaves and thin trunks gathered in small clusters as if the grass had surrounded them and driven them into groups for protection. The blades were thick and waxy, unlike anything Jake had encountered before. While Gordon slipped through with little trouble, Jake found the going difficult. Eventually, he allowed Ursus and Blue to push their way through ahead of him.

The trampled grass tangled together and caught Jake's feet as if he were stepping through old fishing nets. On several occasions, Jake had fallen so far behind that Ursus had to stop and wait for him to catch up as if the grass was working against Jake on purpose, hindering his progress, sapping his resolve. While the grass clung to him, he would never be able to slip away.

On they trudged, their line stretching and shrinking like an accordion until even the trees shrank in the distance, and only spits of pale, yellow rock broke up the monotony of the grass. The rocks emerged from the grass regularly enough that Jake began to measure time with them. One rock after another, Jake kept count until the rocks began to look alike and Jake's count became little more than a guess.

One such rock had a fissure, a wide dark crack in the pale stone, like half-open jaws turned sideways, wide enough for him to enter but too narrow for Blue or Ursus.

A curious shiver ran through Jake as he passed it. Though the fissure beckoned him, the darkness carried with it a terrible foreboding.

He stopped. Ahead of him, Ursus and Blue forged on, unaware. He watched them for a moment, yearning to catch up. "I'll find you after," he whispered. "I'll find you all after and I'll never leave you again. Near and far is the same. That's what you told me. Near and far is the same. I'll find you and we will all be together again, safe. I promise."

He tore his feet from the tangled grass and slipped into the fissure. Cool darkness swallowed him, and the scent of damp rock filled his nostrils. The fissure was deep and narrow, opening just wide enough for Jake to walk without scraping the sides. Near and far, Jake thought. Ursus ran all the way across the grassland to find me. I can find him.

The slap of his feet against the smooth stone echoed down the passage. The air was cool and moist but not stale. Behind him, what little light there was gradually dimmed until Jake could no longer see his hand against the fissure walls. As he walked, he told himself over and over that he would see his friends again, but it sounded empty and hollow as his footfalls in the darkness.

If he stayed, Malbinocks would get them, and it would be his fault. Again.

He pressed on.

The passage sloped downward, and Jake lost all sense of distance and time. Only the slap of his feet and the gentle scrape of his fingernails against the stone assured him that he was still making progress.

Near and far is the same.

A scent, something vaguely familiar, filled the air. He moved slower, testing each step, and the strange, familiar aroma grew stronger.

Grease. Rubber. Rust. Moldy wood.

A junkyard.

Gordon.

The air smelled like Gordon. He froze.

He could see nothing. He dropped to his knees, his fingers passing lightly over the smooth stone, but he found nothing there to come alive and drag him away. Only the smell was there, pervasive and strong, and Jake knew it wasn't his imagination. There were Malbinocks somewhere ahead.

He didn't regain his feet but crawled instead, testing the ground ahead of him before he advanced. After a short distance, he realized that he had lost the wall, and with fear mounting in his chest, he crept on his hands and knees through open darkness. This couldn't be the hideout, he thought. Where are the dogs? Where are the cats?

Maybe there aren't any. Maybe they are all gone.

Jake tried to turn around and retrace his steps. The wall remained out of reach no matter which way he turned, as if it never existed at all.

"I want to go home," Jake whispered. But home was just a word, a thought shrouded in absent memories, meaningless. It would be enough just to find Ursus and Blue again.

He peered into the darkness as if his willpower alone could overcome the void. Somewhere overhead a tiny glimmer of light twinkled briefly before disappearing. He closed his eyes and opened them again, he saw it a second time. Hope welled up in his chest and tumbled from him in a half-sob. He scurried across the smooth stone on his hands and knees, looking up every so often to make sure the light was still there, guiding him.

The light grew stronger as he came closer. It no longer flickered but shone steadily in the stone sky above, and Jake realized that he could see his hands.

He climbed to his feet. The light, dim and silvery-gray, revealed a chamber of pale stone the color of old bones. A small crack high above Jake's head served as a natural skylight. A pool of brighter light traced an oval on the chamber floor.

He stepped into the pool and looked up. A sliver of blue marked the edges of a small crack in the vaulted roof. It was far too high to jump and probably too small for Jake's body. Around him, the pale stone loomed, and the odor of grease and rubber and metal hung in the air, somehow thicker and more pungent than before.

It was a stupid idea, he thought. *Of all the stupid ideas you've ever had, coming in here was the stupidest.*

Beyond the island of light that surrounded him, he could see nothing. The stone arched over him like a skull, forming the roof of his prison. The cave walls fell away well beyond the boundaries of his tiny world. He knew he couldn't stay; eventually, nightfall would come. But the darkness surrounded him like deep water, and Jake feared to wade back in.

He tilted his head upward and bathed in the light streaming down from the fissure. It felt warm and wholesome on his skin, like the feeling of flannel sheets on a cold morning just before he had to get up for school.

What lay beyond the pool of light was an impenetrable mystery no matter which way he decided to go. He envisioned himself falling into eternal nothingness. He imagined crawling until he forgot what he was supposed to be looking for, and the blind, cold tunnels became his home, and he became nothing more than an eyeless rat or a worm.

Fear kept him there, hovering on the light's edge. Nothing could budge him, not the thought of Sebastian's plea as the Malbinocks dragged him away or the sight of little Gordon creeping out of his refuge to lead them back to the place where the Malbinocks had stolen his voice. Even the certainty that night would fall, and the light would disappear was not enough to push him into the dark.

He stood there, ashamed of himself, held fast by the warmth on his skin. When the light vanished, the darkness would swallow him, suffocate him, hold him under until he lost the will to struggle. He did not know what would happen to him after that.

Out of the stillness, something breathed.

At first, he thought it was only an echo, only the sound of his breath bouncing off a faraway wall, mocking him. But he heard it again, and once more after that as he held his breath.

"Sebastian?" He whispered and took a step out of the light.

There was no reply other than another long, slow laborious breath. It was sick, whatever it was, and probably dying.

"Hold on," Jake called, "I'm coming." His voice echoed across the stone.

He crept forward until he could no longer see his hands and feet and then sank to his knees. He took one last glance behind him. The light beckoned him back, a smooth, silvery column, its warmth already faded from his skin.

Little by little, pausing every few feet to listen again for the breath, Jake closed in. It was close enough now that he could feel the first faint stir of air against his face. It was cool and smelled of rusted metal and greasy rubber.

"Hello?" he whispered. Up close, the breathing had taken on a peculiar hollow quality, as if the creature had gotten bigger as Jake crawled closer. Jake was seized with a sudden sense of dread.

"Ursus? Is that you?"

If it was Ursus, he made no indication, only

another breath and a faint squeak, followed by weak scratches against stone. Jake abandoned caution, expecting any second to run into whatever lay dying in the darkness.

He found nothing. Warm, dry air brushed past his arms and face as he grew closer, carrying with it the faint scent of grass.

Not a breath. An opening.

A way out.

Jake's relieved cry momentarily pushed away the silence, and he crawled forward with renewed vigor. Near and far is the same, he thought.

Something cold brushed against Jake's hand. The darkness was still absolute, and so he slid his fingers across the stone until he encountered it again, and he recognized the feel of it.

Baling wire.

Heart pounding, Jake resumed his advance, slower, sweeping the way ahead with his fingers. Pieces of wood and glass littered the floor until Jake could no longer move without crawling over them. A faint light appeared, and he could just make out the cave's walls. Icy fear caressed the back of his neck.

Don't look down, he thought. Don't look down.

He looked.

Jake's hands lay partially hidden in the deep layer of detritus that covered the cave floor. There were pieces of wood and bike parts, a cracked plastic pitcher that once belonged to a blender, computer cables wrapped around broken vacuum cleaners.

With a whimper, Jake struggled through the pile toward the burgeoning light. All around him, the pile groaned and squeaked as his weight shifted against it. Warm air rushed through the tunnel, fresh with the smell of grass and the promise of an open sky. The tunnel ahead turned sharply to the right, easily wide enough for Jake to slip through.

He kept his attention fixed on the light. It was a beacon. Despite the chaos beneath him, Jake clambered to his feet and sprinted the last few yards. He felt the warmth of the light against the side of his face for an instant and breathed deep.

For an instant.

A sharp, crushing pain engulfed his left leg. Then the tunnel fell rapidly away, as if the Malbinocks had turned the cave on its side and pulled it into the shadows like one of the dogs. Pieces of metal and plastic buffeted his body as he passed through the wreckage, and the light diminished into a small, distant square.

It wasn't until he stopped that he realized that something had wrapped itself around his leg. It remained there, squeezing. His leg throbbed, and his foot began to tingle as the thing wound itself tighter.

He turned over, nearly entangling his other leg, and fought with the snare. Jake tried without success to force his fingers beneath the cable to alleviate the pressure.

Jake's descent into darkness resumed with a jolt that drove the air from his chest. He tried to find purchase among the junk, but everything he grabbed pulled up out of the pile and came with him. He stopped a short time later as abruptly as he'd started. The cave opening was little more than a speck in the distance. He went back to work on the snare, but it held fast against his throbbing leg. The pain was becoming unbearable.

The groan of straining metal and the sound of grinding fingernails against rough stone forced him upright once again, but he could see nothing.

From somewhere ahead, a shadow emerged, and a tiny pinprick of light bathed the immediate area in a sickly shade of red. A reflection from the cave mouth, warm and distant, flickered briefly across the shadow.

A video camera.

"You're one of them," Jake whispered. He kept a tight hold on the snare, hoping to prevent it from tightening further.

The thing answered with a baleful groan.

"What did you do with Sebastian? What did you do with my friends?"

Then the thing was in his mind.

Jake could feel its presence, its curiosity. It wound through his memories, like a snake's tongue, icy, flickering.

"Get away from me!"

Jake grabbed the cable that held his leg and pulled with all the force in his body. The snare held fast.

Pain and fear got the better of him. He searched along the cave floor until his hands closed over something solid and rough. With a satisfying crunch, he struck his captor again and again until the red light went out and snare came free.

It wasn't enough. Jake rained blows down on the ground in front of him, lashing out in his fury until the object broke apart in his hands.

He sank to the ground, trembling.

All around him, the junkpile began to stir. The cave filled with the creak and groan of rusted hinges, the scrape of old wood against stone, the rustle of tattered fabric.

Jake fought his way through the pile, back to the tunnel where the light beckoned him. All around him the pile writhed. Now, instead of one presence in his mind, he felt many, all flickering, tasting, searching. With a strangled cry he threw himself across the last of the Malbinocks that filled the tunnel and into the warm light, following it on his hands and knees until he collapsed in a dense stand of tall, green grass. Above him, the sky shined an impossible shade of blue.

He stared straight up, unable to move. The Malbinocks were gone from his mind, save for a single word, an echo whispered over and over again.

Maker.

Chapter Twenty-Five

The grass resisted him. He didn't know where he was going, nor did it matter; he was headed away from the cave, and that was the right direction. He had a vague notion of retracing his steps, perhaps returning to the place where he had left Ursus and the others and picking up their trail. That notion faded quickly as he slogged through the unrelenting tangle around his feet.

Nightfall would bring the Malbinocks swarming from the cave, and they would be searching for him. That thought pushed him forward with renewed urgency. With enough distance, perhaps he could avoid them until morning, and then—

And then, what?

Without Gordon, he had no chance of finding the Malbinocks' hiding place, at least not quickly. While he wandered aimlessly, Sebastian and the other dogs would suffer as Gordon had. But Gordon was gone now, better off without Jake sending him back into misery and torture. He would be better off back at the lakeside in his comfortable den, falling asleep to the stars' song and the gentle lapping of the waves against the strand.

If he could get there.

Ursus and Blue would put up a fight, and perhaps even win, but the Malbinocks outnumbered them. At the very least, Gordon would be caught again. They would drag him into the tunnels and back to the horrors he and Samuel had escaped, and all the while Jake would wander, searching.

Near and far were not the same.

Jake pushed on. He felt the day slipping away, though the light gave no indication of how long he had been on the move. With each step his desperation and hopelessness grew. Leaving his friends hadn't made them or him any safer.

The idea began as a whisper, more of a feeling than a thought, like the strange thrill he might experience looking down from a high place, when the quiet urge to jump would sit in the back of his mind, easily ignored but impossible to completely dismiss. The idea grew, little by little, until the feeling formed into words.

You could let them catch you.

They would come, like a swarm of yellowjackets, searching the grass for him and not the others. They'd bring him to Sebastian. No wandering, no searching. Gordon and the others would be safe. A Maker would be worth more to them than a little dog.

Maker. The word confused him. Why call him Maker? He couldn't have made them; they were here before he arrived. Samuel and Gordon were their prisoners, and many of the dogs had already been taken. He must be important to them if they had a name for him, and he hoped it would be an advantage. He pushed harder through the grass. The more distance between him and the Malbinocks, the longer they would have to chase him, and the more time his friends would have to get away.

Though his body never fatigued, the monotony of forcing his legs through the tangled grass wore on him. There was nothing to see, no way to measure his progress, and no real objective. It would be easier to just sit and allow them to take him. But he thought of Gordon, trotting along near the ground, Blue and Ursus pushing along behind him, and Jake could not let them down. Him for them. It was a good trade.

Darkness was a relief when it finally came. The grass disappeared into shadow, and the stars emerged to begin their song. The music buoyed him. The grass caught the silver light on its edges and took on an otherworldly look as if the entire grassland had been plunged deep underwater. It was beautiful in its own way, but Jake had no time to appreciate it. In the distance, he heard the awful sound of metal against metal, and the music above faded into silence.

Jake knew he was surrounded, even though he couldn't see them. He felt their presence and heard the groans and squeals that marked their movement. He changed directions, but it was futile; wherever he went, the Malbinocks were ahead of him, their ring shrinking as they advanced. He could hear the violence in their movement through the tall grass, and the sound of their coming blotted out his own strangled breath. Then they were upon him, wrapping his ankles and wrists in wire. Agony gripped his hands and feet, and he felt the cold, snake-tongue probe in his mind again.

The Malbinocks dragged him feet first with his eyes toward the stars. He could see them occasionally through breaks in the grass, swirling overhead, silvery and beautiful and distant. Jake's sanity drowned in the cacophony that came with the Malbinocks' movement. The sounds around him melted together into a wild rush of squeaks and groans.

He didn't know where they were taking him or which direction he was going. He struggled at first, but struggling only made the wire dig into his skin and rub against the muscle and bone beneath, and so he surrendered, twisting this way and that as he skimmed across the flattened grass. The Malbinocks crowded around him, moving with purpose, their shambling gait no impediment to speed.

Ahead, the grass parted, and above his feet, Jake saw an outcropping of rock, pale yellow against the night sky. He clutched at the grass, tearing off handfuls as the Malbinocks dragged him closer to the stone. Conscious thought abandoned him, leaving behind only fear of the dark and of the terrible, oily stench that wafted from the deep. With a terrified cry, he fought, pulling on the wires that bound his wrists and ankles despite the pain. Twice he nearly managed to roll over, but one jerk on the wires was enough to keep him on his back.

A commotion behind him sent the Malbinocks that had been flanking him rushing back the way they had come. In his cloud of terror, Jake heard them depart, but the sound seemed distant and unimportant. Just ahead lay the mouth of the cave, open and hungry.

The tumult behind him worsened, and now only four of the Malbinocks remained, dragging him. The two that had his ankles disappeared into the darkness. With strength borne of terror, Jake pulled his knees to his belly and his arms to his chest. His wrists and ankles throbbed with cold agony. The wire pressed deep into his skin and rubbed against the bones in his arms and shins. With both hands, he grabbed at the wire wrapped around his right leg and pulled. The wire curled as he unwrapped it from his ankle.

A sharp jerk on the wires drove his upper body backward, and his head struck the ground. For an instant, he lay stunned. A Malbinock, his head a gasoline can, towered above him. It thrust the edge of a broken shovel blade at Jake's arm, missing him by inches. The blade sunk into the dirt, and the wire around his wrist tightened against it, pinning his arm in place.

Jake kicked out with his free leg, striking the Malbinock's leg just below the rusty hinge that served as its knee, and the creature crumbled on top of him. Broken but not dead, the Malbinock leaned against Jake's throat with a forearm of thick, cold metal. The acrid smell of gasoline filled his nostrils. His head began to throb with the same cold fire that gripped his wrists, and his body became heavy and sluggish.

Jake!

Blue stood over Jake, blotting out the stars. The Malbinock on top of him exploded into a shower of wood and plastic. Its head fell to the ground with a metallic clang, and Jake was free.

"Jake, this is not the way," said Blue. "We must run!"

Around him lay the broken bodies of the other three Malbinocks, the wires that secured him still trailing from their arms.

"Jake, we must run!"

He realized he was still lying on his back. He struggled to his feet. Pain coursed through his arms and legs, but he found that he could stand.

"Let's get away from here, Blue!" Jake dashed for the rock and climbed until he was level with Blue's back, and then threw himself on. Blue burst into a full gallop, sending dirt and broken pieces of Malbinock into the air behind him. Jake closed his eyes and buried his head into Blue's mane.

The ride wasn't long. As Blue slowed to a walk, Jake looked up to see Ursus standing tall in a circle of trampled grass. Near him sat Gordon. The Malbinocks were nowhere to be seen.

"We have to run," said Jake. "We can't stay here. They're looking for me!"

"This is not the way," said Ursus.

"We have to run!"

Every breath felt like an eternity, but Ursus did not move.

"Ursus, please! They're going to come back!"

"But this is not the way," said Ursus.

"There are many more," said Blue. "It is not safe to stay here."

"We'll find the way again," pleaded Jake. "But right now, we have to move."

The Malbinocks closed in.

"You can't fight them all," said Jake. "They'll get Gordon if we stay here. They'll get me."

"I will follow you," said Ursus.

Now they could hear the rustle of the grass, and the odor of grease and hot metal accompanied the mechanical clang of moving parts. Jake slipped off Blue's back and snatched up Gordon. He struggled briefly and lay still against Jake's chest. Ursus and Blue broke into a fast trot, shoving the grass aside for Jake. As fast as his legs would allow, Jake followed. The exertion cleared his mind. Shame and guilt crept in as his fear receded. Weariness settled on his back like a weight. Ursus and Blue began to edge farther and farther ahead.

"Guys, wait!"

Ursus stopped and turned.

"You must ride," said Ursus. "They are faster than you. If you run, they will catch you."

"What about Gordon?" Jake held Gordon up like a toddler, presenting him as if Ursus needed proof.

"Gordon must ride. If he runs, he will be caught."

Blue dropped down to his forelegs and allowed Jake to put Gordon on his back. The little dog wobbled a little, attempting to get his balance, and finally dropped to his belly. His eyes were wide open and he panted as if he had been running rather than Jake. Ursus dropped down to his belly.

"I will lift you," he said. Jake climbed on his back and Ursus stood. Jake leaped to the horse's back and wrapped his arms around Gordon. He pressed his legs and feet into Blue's flanks and the horse burst into a gallop, with Ursus a step behind.

Headlong they ran through the grassland. Behind them, the sounds of their pursuers receded into the distance. They fled, crashing through the thick grass until the stars vanished into the bright, deep blue of the daytime sky, and even then, they ran on. The grass became thin and sparse and finally disappeared altogether. The ground was hard and strewn with small rocks that clicked and cracked against Blue's hooves.

The elevation rose gradually until they found themselves at the top of a ridge, overlooking a maze of rocky outcroppings, riddled through with narrow gullies and canyons.

Blue stopped, and Jake slid from his back before helping Gordon down. The little dog sniffed around in a wide circle before sitting down on his haunches. He looked up at Jake expectantly, and Jake realized that the others were watching him as well, waiting for him.

And Jake had no idea what to do.

Chapter Twenty-Six

Rocky crags stretched out on either side as far as Jake could see. The ground was a jumble of broken rock. Not quite sand but treacherous enough to make the going slow if they attempted to cross.

Gullies and rills crisscrossed the land between Jake and the high, naked crags ahead of him. Ursus and Gordon sat on their haunches, watching him. Blue remained a few feet behind, his ears and nose in the wind, scanning for any sign of their pursuers. Since daybreak, the grassland, and now the rocky labyrinth before them, remained silent, save for the occasional whistle of wind and the rustle of the grass.

Though his body was none the worse for their harrowing flight, Jake's mind felt heavy and weary. The light drove away the terror that had gripped him in the dark, and now shame and guilt flowed in to fill the void. The dogs' expectant gaze made him feel even worse.

"This is my fault," he said. "We're lost because of me."

"Gordon can not find the way from here," said Ursus. "The way is behind us, in the thick grass."

"We can't go back there. They'll get Gordon if we try that."

"There are no Malbinocks now."

"Not right now, but what about when it gets dark? They know we're here. They're down there in their tunnels just waiting for nighttime. They could be below us right now."

"None have passed here for a long time," said Ursus.

"That's because they're in the ground. That's how they moved the dogs without a trail. I bet they have tunnels that reach all the way to the forest."

"It is not safe to stay here," said Blue.

"I don't think it's safe no matter what we do," said Jake. "That's why I tried to leave. I wanted to get so far away that I wouldn't put you in any more danger."

"Near and far is the same," said Ursus.

Jake pressed his palms against his eyes and sighed. "No, they're not. They're not the same at all. You should get far away from me where you can be safe."

"When we found you, we were not in danger." said Blue.

"That's not the point!" Jake said. "I woke them up! They wouldn't even be after us if I hadn't tried to get away. Doesn't that bother you?"

Jake paced back and forth while the others watched. He felt trapped.

"I will go with you," said Ursus. "I am a friend."

"It is not safe to break up the herd," said Blue.

"Break up the herd? The herd is way back there!" Jake pointed back the way they had come.

"That was not my herd. My herd is here. Ursus, and Gordon, and you, Jake."

The pain in Jake's wrists and ankles had faded, but the memory of it was clear. Blue came close, and Jake reached up and stroked the horse's broad neck. He was right. Jake wasn't strong by himself. They were a herd, a family. Alone, they were damaged, but their broken pieces fit together and made something far stronger, something better. Something worth keeping.

"I'm sorry I tried to leave you," Jake said.

"You are the Giver," said Ursus. "If you must run, run. I will follow."

"You are a friend," said Jake.

"I am a friend."

Jake threw his arms around Ursus and held on tight. He felt warmth beneath the smooth coat and breathed in the dog's scent. Ursus waited, patiently.

After a time, Jake let go. He felt light, as if a weight had been lifted from him. He looked out across the vast labyrinth of canyons.

"I guess we'll go in there," Jake said, pointing toward the broken crags.

"It is not the way Gordon came," said Ursus.

Jake shrugged. "We can't go back and pick up the trail. They'll get Gordon, and probably me again, if we try. Going in there is our only choice."

He searched for a little speech that would bolster their courage and their enthusiasm, but he was out of things to say. Blue and Ursus waited and watched while Jake stood at the edge of the maze.

He counted five possible entrances, and none of them looked particularly appealing. The rocks were the color of old blood. Wind and rain shaped the crags, marking their slow decay with rivers of sand and fine gravel. The place had a desolate, ancient look; any who had once called the place home had likely vanished a long time ago.

"Which way will we go?" said Blue.

"I don't know. Ursus, what do you think?"

"You are the Giver. I will go with you."

He looked again at the broken cliffs and tried to come to some decision, but without knowing what lay ahead, Jake could not make up his mind. Climbing was too risky; pebbles and chunks of broken rock lay in piles along the cliff edge. He scanned the cliffs, searching for potential routes to the top. All were rife with cracks and irregularities, but he saw nothing that would suggest a reliable route.

Gordon shook himself and trotted toward the nearest canyon.

"Gordon? Do you smell something? Is that the way?"

Gordon stopped and looked back. He blinked his eyes, yawned, licked his nose, and then proceeded toward the canyon at a leisurely pace, as if he'd taken the walk a thousand times before.

He didn't know if Gordon had remembered something or if the little dog had just gotten tired of waiting. Whatever his reasons, Gordon had chosen a path.

Jake followed him. "I guess we're going that way."

The rocks made the path treacherous, especially for Blue, who had to place his hooves carefully to avoid getting them caught or slipping against loose debris. The canyon meandered, never following a straight path for more than a few hundred feet. After a while, it began to branch out. Gordon chose the widest branches, and Jake wondered if somehow Gordon had rediscovered the path.

"So, you did find it," he said. "We're on our way again. Good boy, Gordon!"

"No dogs have passed this way," said Ursus.

"Well, he seems like he knows where he's going."

"He is following a scent. Not dog. Not cat. Not horse."

Jake paused, scanning the tops of the canyon wall. "Maybe there's something living in here."

"The scent is old."

"It's better than nothing. Let's just see where it leads."

Clouds drifted against the blue sky, and as the day wore on, they thickened to an ominous gray, so low they nearly skimmed the top of the canyon. Jake's apprehension grew; the clouds formed a misty roof overhead, blotting out much of the light.

"I smell rain," said Ursus

"It will come soon," Blue said.

Jake could smell it too; a scent that reminded him of summer, and lying on the driveway, warming up after running through the sprinklers with Sebastian. It had always been a pleasant scent, but there in the bottom of the canyon it felt like more of a warning.

"We have to find some higher ground," said Jake. "Gordon, we have to move faster."

With renewed urgency, they picked their way over the broken ground, pausing only occasionally to allow Blue to catch up.

Blue never complained, but the effort took a toll on him.

While the others could feel their way across the treacherous rocks, Blue could not, and the low light confounded him. Twice he nearly lost his footing, as the stones shifted beneath his hooves. All the while, Jake scanned the canyon for higher ground, but the walls were sheer and riddled with crevasses. Even worse, the ground ahead sloped steadily downward.

"Maybe we should try another way," Jake said.

The canyon walls rose high around them, and the clouds robbed them of all but the palest daylight. The pace slowed to a painful crawl. For balance, Jake moved like a bear on all fours, feeling the ground in front of him for a safe place to step.

The rain began in drops, small, and far apart. As they struggled forward, the storm gained intensity until the staccato patter of rain against the bare rock filled the canyon.

"Keep going!" Jake shouted, but it was no use. The downpour became a deluge, and rivulets of water poured between the rocks and washed over Jake's feet. He urged his friends forward with gentle shoves. They crept through the rising water until Blue suddenly stopped.

"Blue, we have to keep moving!"

Blue turned his hindquarters this way and that, throwing his weight to either side, heaving backward with all his weight. Despite the danger of being crushed by a hoof, Jake ducked low, searching the ground for the cause of Blue's distress. An instant later he found it; Blue's right front leg was caught in a fissure between two pieces of broken rock, and he was held fast.

The water swirled around Jake's chest as he dropped down near Blue's leg. He tried prying the rock loose, but it was far too heavy. Now the water flowed past his shoulders, rising steadily as the rain poured down in sheets, funneled into the canyon by its high walls.

"Ursus! Help!"

Ursus tried to dig out underneath the hoof, but the rock would not yield. Something wet and furry brushed past Jake's arm, and Jake snatched at it. It slipped through his grasp, but he snatched it again, and this time his grip held. Gordon thrashed in the water as Jake held him by the back leg. He managed to grab the other leg despite the little dog's struggles, and he pulled him in close, lifting him out of the water.

There was nothing else he could do. He lifted Gordon and placed him on Blue's back, with Ursus' help, before clambering up himself. He snatched up Gordon and held him close to his chest, gripping Blue's flanks with his legs. Gordon did not resist him.

The canyon had become a rushing, whitewater rapid. Blue began to sway as the water threatened to topple him.

"Blue! Hold on, Blue!"

"I will try."

Blue fought to steady himself, but it was not enough. Jake took a deep breath, closed his eyes, and waited for the water to close around him.

Then the swaying stopped. Jake wiped driving rain from his eyes.

It was Ursus.

His front paws braced against Blue's shoulders; the big dog pushed back against the water's force. Together, Ursus and Blue fought, as the rain washed through the canyon. Chunks of stone tore loose from the canyon walls above them and fell crashing into the flood, but Ursus and Blue held firm.

The rain eased and then stopped. Gradually, the water receded. Ursus dropped down to all fours, sinking to his belly, his lungs laboring for breath.

Jake slipped off Blue's back and landed in the water with a splash. It was still up to his knees.

"Ursus!"

He rushed to the dog's side. Ursus lay with his head half-submerged in the stream. He made no attempt to lift it, though the water came dangerously close to his nose. Jake stroked the dog's head.

"Ursus!"

Jake shook him, but Ursus remained still.

"Jake, I am still trapped," said Blue.

"I'm not leaving him!"

"Jake, I need help."

"Ursus, wake up!"

"Jake, it hurts."

Jake turned to Blue. "I am not—"

"Help him, Jake," Ursus said.

Jake could not contain his relief. It burst from him in a short, sharp wail, almost a bark, before the sobs came. He buried his head in the folds of Ursus's broad neck.

"Jake, you must help Blue. They are coming."

Jake lifted his head. "Who?"

But Ursus did not need to answer. In the distance, barely audible over the rush of water, came the sound of metal scraping against metal. For a moment, he just sat waist-deep in the water and listened to the sound of the Malbinocks closing in, the clank and squeals of their advance echoing balefully against the canyon walls.

"Jake!"

Blue's plea was enough to spur Jake into motion. He struggled to his feet and splashed through the water, now ankle-deep, to where Blue stood trapped. Through the shallow water Jake saw what was keeping Blue pinned. A thin, flat rock had snapped under the horse's weight, and his hoof was wedged between the two pieces, which were in turn wedged between larger rocks. He tried prying one of the pieces out, but it wouldn't budge. Frantically, Jake tried to dig underneath, but he found only bare rock beneath a thin layer of sand.

"Jake—"

"I'm trying!"

He fought down his panic and forced himself to think. He couldn't dig it out or pry it out. How could something so thin be so heavy?

"Jake, they are close—"

It was thin. It had broken under Blue's weight.

Jake snatched up a piece of rock and dashed it against the stone's edge. Blue whinnied in pain.

"Just one more hit," Jake said and struck the stone again. This time it cracked, and Blue tore his hoof from the trap. He backed away, limping on his injured leg. In the darkness, water splashed and with it the crunch of metal and wood upon stone. Jake hurried back to Ursus.

The big dog's breathing was slower, steadier, and he held his head off the ground, but the din of their pursuers pushed away any sense of relief Jake felt. He held Ursus's massive head between his outstretched hands.

"We can't stay here," Jake said. "I know you're tired, but we have to move."

"I will follow you," Ursus said, and he heaved himself upright. Water dripped in thin columns from off his belly.

Gordon remained on Blue's back. Hunkered down, he looked more like a filthy mop head than a dog. Jake reached up and grabbed hold of Gordon's front legs, but the little dog resisted. Each time Jake pulled, Gordon pulled back, and Jake let go for fear of hurting him.

"Gordon, we need you!"

"The scent is weak," said Ursus, "But I will track it."

They followed Ursus through the canyon, but Blue's injury and Ursus's fatigue made progress painfully slow.

"We're going to get caught," Jake said. "We have to move faster."

"I cannot move faster," said Blue.

It was too late. The first of the Malbinocks shambled into view. Jake grabbed a rock and hurled it at the creature's head. His aim was off, and the rock glanced off the plastic pipe that made up its shoulder. A second rock followed and found its mark. The Malbinock collapsed with a splash.

"Get a head start," said Jake. "I'll keep them back." Jake picked up another rock and cocked his arm back, waiting for the next target. It felt futile, but Jake could muster up no better plan. The fear that gripped him earlier returned, but the rock in his hand lent him a small measure of courage, and there was no shortage of rocks at his feet.

"You! You bring Badwatchers!"

Jake lowered his arm and searched the canyon wall. The voice was thin and reedy and spoke with a quick, sharp cadence that reminded him of a snare drum.

"I didn't mean to," Jake called.

"Mean to, not mean to. Badwatchers here. But you not Badwatcher."

Another Malbinock appeared, and Jake hurled his rock. He missed entirely. The second missed as well, and the shambling thing closed the distance. The rainwater gave it a filthy, oily sheen in the pale silver light that filtered through the clouds.

"You stay away from my friends!"

He snatched another rock from between his feet

and brought it down on the large can that served as the creature's head. The blow dented the can and sent the creature sprawling to the ground. Jake pounced on it and bashed its head until it was flat. The thing lay still. He crawled off, shaking with fear and rage.

It was no good. Five more emerged from the shadows, and Jake knew he could not take them all.

"You are not Badwatchers. I save. Follow!"

Jake cast about, but he still couldn't pinpoint the source of the voice.

"You come this way! Come!"

Together they followed the reedy voice. It led them deeper into the canyon, away from the pursuing Malbinocks. Blue did his best to maintain a hurried pace, despite the limp and the treacherous ground. Ursus brought up the rear. Every step seemed a labor for him. The din behind them reached a crescendo as the Malbinocks' numbers grew. Jake dared not glance back; instead, he focused on the ground in front of him. The grinding cacophony of the pursuit clawed at his ears. Hundreds of them, judging from the sound, and close enough that Jake expected at any second to feel a cold grip on his shoulder or ankle.

He never would have seen the path if the voice hadn't guided him to it.

"Look! Look here! You come!" The voice was no longer coming from above but from ground level and off to Jake's right, but Jake saw no path. From his vantage, it looked like nothing more than a crack in the rock face, only as wide as the length of his fingers.

"What is this? There's nothing here!" Jake said.

"It is there. You see. You see!"

Jake followed the voice toward the rock face. The crack was an illusion. As Jake moved closer, it widened into a cleft, and finally, into a small arroyo easily wide enough for Blue to pass.

"How did you do that?" Jake said.

"No time! You come, you come! Badwatchers close!"

Jake ushered Ursus and Blue into the hidden path while Gordon watched from his perch on Blue's back. Jake hazarded a glance behind him. Indistinct shapes shuffled though the canyon, their movement hindered by the broken rocks that littered the canyon floor. The sight of them froze his blood.

"Now climb. Climb!"

Jake could see no hill, only a flat path that meandered through a narrow ravine. Blue and Ursus had already disappeared behind a bend, and Jake hurried to catch up. Around the turn, the ground sloped sharply upward. Ahead, Ursus and Blue struggled up the incline. Blue had the worst of it. He lurched forward, hopping on his left leg to protect the injured right, but the hill forced him to use both. Behind him, Ursus dragged himself higher, his belly nearly scraping the path.

Jake snatched a rock from the ground, intending to smash the first thing that emerged, but nothing came. There was no one behind them, and the sounds of pursuit died off as they neared the summit.

"Why didn't they follow us?" he said, mostly to himself.

"Badwatchers not climb."

Above, the clouds cleared, and silver starlight illuminated the path ahead of them. It was just wide enough for the horse to pass, as long as he was careful, with only a few inches between his hoof and the path's edge. The path leveled off, and they emerged onto a flat, grassy mesa. Even in starlight the grass was strikingly green, a brilliant island of life in a world of bare stone.

In the center of the mesa was a small rise, nothing more than a bump in the flat expanse around it. A rivulet of water ran down the side and into a wide, shallow pool. Aside from the grass, there was no sign of any living thing.

Gordon allowed Jake to help him off Blue's back. The little dog dropped to his belly, as if welcoming the feel of solid ground beneath his feet once again. Stars swirled and danced; their light reflected in the pool. The air was cool and dry, despite the rain, and had a curious, dusty odor.

"Hello?"

Nothing.

"Thank you for saving us. My name is Jake. The big dog is Ursus, and the little one is Gordon. The horse is called Blue."

"Goodwatcher and horse. Goodwatcher and dog, together. Why come you here?"

The voice appeared to be coming from the vicinity of the rise, but Jake could see nothing stirring there.

"We're looking for our friends," Jake said. "They were taken by the Mal ... by the Badwatchers. We want to set them free."

"No dogs here. No horses here. You stay till light comes. Then go. Badwatchers hide in dark, move in dark. You move safe in light."

"Sounds like you know a lot about them."

"I know much. You stay until light, then go."

"You don't seem very friendly. Why did you help us?"

There was a slight pause.

"You bring Badwatchers to our safe place. Badwatchers catch you, they stay, look for more. Badwatchers chase you, they go away. We stay free."

"Well, do you have a name, at least?"

"Azrak."

"Sorry for messing up your hiding place, Azrak," Jake said. "But my friends are hurt. Do we have to leave tomorrow?"

"Light comes, you go. Or I call Badwatchers. Bring them back. Find new safe place."

"We're not going to hurt you," Jake said. "I told you, we're trying to save our friends. Wouldn't you do the same thing if you were me?"

"If you Azrak, you do same too."

"I guess we both care about our friends."

Jake took a few steps closer to the rise.

"I get it. That's why you're making us leave. You said 'our' and 'we'. You're protecting your friends. It's not that you're mean. You just love your friends. Well, it's the same with me, only it's my fault that my friends are in trouble. It was my idea to fight the ... well, you call them Badwatchers. The horses have another name for them. They call them Malbinocks."

"Badwatchers take my friends too."

Jake stopped when he reached the pool. The water lay mirror-smooth, and in its surface, Jake saw the face of a stranger. It was a boy, dressed in a dirty t-shirt and tattered jeans. The boy stared back at him with sad, blue eyes. Perhaps it was a trick of the starlight, but he seemed pale and thinner than Jake remembered.

"How you come here? No Goodwatchers here." Azrak's voice had lost some of its sharp edge.

"I don't know."

He told Azrak how he'd fallen into the river and about all the things that had happened to him since. Ursus and Blue made themselves comfortable in the grass, while Gordon lay down next to Jake, his back nestled against Jake's leg. The night sky swirled in all its glory overhead. But this time, Jake heard no music.

"Maybe it's a mistake, or an accident, or something else. I don't know. But there's something wrong here, and I have to try to fix it."

A shadow marred the silver reflection next to him. Jake turned.

Sitting next to him and gazing down into the pool was a rat.

Chapter Twenty-Seven

Azrak was nearly as long as Gordon. He was white with black, piebald blotches across his face and body. His eyes were black and narrowly-set, giving Jake the impression that Azrak was perpetually deep in thought. His scaly tail, nearly as long as the rest of his body, trailed out into the grass.

Other animals emerged from the rise. A large, gray rabbit followed a pair of guinea pigs, and behind them came a hamster, and finally, another rat.

"The rabbit is Drummerboy," said Azrak. "Two guineas, one Littles and one Speedy. Small one is Ahab. Brown one is Penny."

"You ... you're all that's left," Jake said. It wasn't a question.

"Only us left," said Azrak. "All the rest gone. All the mice gone. All the ferrets gone. Chinchillas all gone. Gerbils gone."

"What happened?" Jake could barely force out the words.

Drummerboy spoke up. "Warrens filled before. Long time past. Rabbit warrens, rat warrens, hamster warrens. Many warrens. Green hills. Good light. Grass. All friends. Rats and mice. Hamster and Guinea. Ferrets. All friends."

"Some others too," said Penny. She had a pleasant voice, high in pitch, but gentle and warm. "Ringtails and foxes come. All friends."

"Some go back to Goodwatchers, but many stay. Many not like being watched. Warrens better. Warrens free," broke in Ahab.

"Many hamsters, all friends, many tunnels under hill, light and grass above," said Speedy.

Jake tried to imagine the warrens as they had once been. It would have been an ocean of green, its hills like waves, undulating across the horizon. He imagined rabbits and all the different rodents flitting through the grass, in and out of burrows, reveling in the freedom beneath the open sky and beneath the rich green hills. No bars, no tubes, no plastic balls to control their movement, no electric lights forcing them from sleep, no hands reaching down to prod and stroke, no giant eyes to peer through the glass and no fingers tapping fearful drumbeats against the walls that kept them in.

"The mice gone first," said Azrak. "One day, many mice. Next day, only some. Hamsters and gerbils take empty tunnels."

"Mice think bad. Think we make them go," said Ahab. The hamster shifted, revealing a stump where his left rear leg should be.

"Mice stop being friends. Tell rats and rabbits and hamster stay away."

"Then mice all gone," said Ahab.

They were quiet for a bit. Jake didn't rush them; he wasn't sure he wanted to hear more.

"Our kind next," said Ahab. "Rats come take empty tunnels. We say no rats. We think rats kill mice and blame us. Hamster stop being friends. Our kind gone. Only Ahab left."

"Rabbits next," said Drummerboy. "We blame rats too. We do same. Rabbits go away. All but Drummerboy."

They told their story. The pattern was the same; disappearances, followed by distrust, and finally, isolation until eventually, they vanished completely. In some cases, there were one or two survivors. Most weren't that fortunate.

"Rats last," said Azrak. "We have none to blame. We blame each other. Black rat go with black rat, white rat with white, brown with brown. Black rat go, white rat go, brown rat go. I stay alone. Black rats say no. White rats say no. I look for rats like me."

"Did you find any?"

"I find only Badwatchers. I watch Badwatchers dig through warren walls, take rats, many at a time. Nowhere for rats to run. Rats block tunnels to keep out other rats. Only keep rats in. I watch. They take every rat, leave warren empty. Then I know. Then I feel sorry."

The rats did the Malbinocks' job for them. Fear divided them, distrust prevented them from communicating and restricted their movement. They separated into smaller and smaller groups, until taking them was as simple as breaking through the right wall and gathering rats or rabbits by the armful. With no tribe of his own, Azrak told of his weeks of wandering and hiding in the empty tunnels beneath the hills. After a time, Azrak was completely alone, and the Malbinocks ceased their searching and left the tunnels.

"How long were you down there?"

"Long time, short time, same."

"That's just what Ursus would say." Jake pointed to his friend, who lay on his side, his great chest rising and falling in a long, slow rhythm. Beside him stood Blue, his right front leg barely touching the grass.

Jake imagined what it must have been like searching lonely, empty tunnels for lost friends. Azrak may as well have been doing it for an eternity. Jake wanted to reach out and pull Azrak to him and hug him tight, but something told him Azrak wouldn't allow him to do it.

"And you didn't find anyone that whole time?" Jake feared the answer, but he had to know.

"I find Penny. Penny and the others." Azrak motioned to Drummerboy with his nose. "Now, no more rat. No more hamster, no more rabbit. Rat, hamster, rabbit, all same. Different, but same. Now only Drummerboy, Azrak, Penny. Only Ahab. Only Littles. Only Speedy. All same."

"Brown rats find out I still see friends," Penny said. "Brown rats make me leave."

"All of us. Not listen to others. Still trust. Still friends. Drummerboy remembered the flat water hill.

He came, we followed. We found Azrak later."

"Badwatchers chase. Penny and Drummerboy show me path. We find out Badwatchers not climb. Flat hill safe."

"Safe in light-time, safe in star-time," said Littles.

"Grass stop growing, hills break. Rains come. Wash away hills, leave rocks."

All around the mesa, the broken remnants of the warrens lay, chipped and misshapen as broken teeth. High above rolled the stars. They seemed terribly distant, unreachable, even if he stared into them. If the Malbinocks got their way, the grasslands would become a desert, the forest would die, its trees reduced to bare husks, reaching for the sky, thin and weak.

Jake couldn't think about it anymore.

"We'll leave in the morning," Jake said. "I hope I didn't ruin your hiding place."

"You safe here. Badwatchers not climb."

The breeze, with its strange, dusty smell, barely made a ripple on the pool. Jake closed his eyes and listened to the water bubbling out of the spring. The sound tricked down into his awareness, pushing away the weight of responsibility that pressed so heavily on him. He drifted. There was no music and no light, only silence and profound darkness. His body felt light and untethered, insubstantial as the breeze.

The voices erupted out of the void, bursting on his ears like rain on a window during a sudden thunderstorm. All but two of the voices fell away.

"It's been six hours, Mrs. Phillips."

"I don't want to hear this."

"Angie, we have to face facts."

"Brad—"

"He could save lives—"

"You're not cutting up my son!"

The voices fell silent, but Jake could sense their presence.

"Doctor, what are the chances—"

"Brad!"

"Doctor, please. What are the chances?"

A sigh and then silence.

"It's difficult to say. He was under the water a long time. I think it's unlikely that we will see any change in his condition. I'm sorry. We'll keep monitoring, but—"

"Go. Both of you, go. Please."

"Angie—"

"Let me sit with him. Go. Go outside in the hall. Let me sit with my baby."

Footsteps. A door closing softly. A mechanical hum, a rush of air, a beep.

"Jake. My Baby Bear."

It was the sad woman. She knew his name. Somehow, he knew she was smiling, and that her face was wet with tears.

"Come back to me."

And Jake wanted more than anything to do what the sad woman asked. But he was no more solid than a breath, and he could do nothing but listen. Her voice was close; so close he felt it more than he heard it.

"One misty, moisty morning, when cloudy was the weather, I chanced to meet an old man dressed all in leather. He began to compliment, and I began to grin.

How do you do, and how do you do? And how—"

Her voice trailed off into a desperate sob.

"Jake—"

It was not the voice of the sad woman. His body felt heavy again. He opened his eyes.

Ursus stood over him. Daylight flooded the mesa, the grass a brilliant green stain against the red rock. Azrak and his friends clustered around him. He sat up and blinked his eyes, trying to clear away the fog that had formed in his mind. It took him a moment to remember where he was and what he was doing there. His body felt ungainly and awkward, the way his hand might feel if he fell asleep on top of it.

Ursus seemed to have recovered from his battle with the floodwater. He sat tall; his head held high. Jake reached out and patted his paw. "Looks like you got some rest."

"It is good to lie on the grass again."

Jake understood. The scent of the grass and the gentle brush of the green blades beneath his feet revitalized him. The fatigue he had felt was only a memory. It was much the same for Blue; the big horse ambled over; his limp gone.

"Star-time is over," said Azrak. "Now you will go?"

"Go? Go where?"

"Away from safe place."

"I know, but where? We were following Gordon, but we lost the trail."

"You go. Safe place stay safe. Penny safe. Everyone safe."

"We're just supposed to wander around in these canyons until we get lucky and find our way out?"

Sitting on top of the little rise, Azrak gazed across the pool and out into the labyrinth beyond the edge of the mesa. In the daylight the canyons stretched, fragile and dangerous, into the distance. Against the backdrop of the canyons, the mesa and the little rise in the center felt small, almost insignificant. But for Azrak and his friends, the rise was home, pockmarked with openings large enough for Azrak and the others to enter.

"Azrak sorry. Safe place all we have."

"It's all right," Jake said. "I understand."

And he did. He could muster up no enmity against Azrak or the other rodents; in their place he might have done the same thing. He got to his feet. Gordon and Blue stood at mesa's edge, looking outward, and Jake headed toward them.

"How's the leg?" he said.

Blue lifted his right front hoof and set it down carefully. "It is better than yesterday. I can walk. But I do not think I can carry a Rider."

"And how's Gordon?"

Gordon glanced at him and cocked his head.

Azrak moved to the edge of the mesa, marking the path that led back down into the labyrinth. Jake and the others crossed the grass. When they reached Azrak, Jake stopped and knelt down, until his eyes were level with Azrak's.

"Thanks for helping us," he said. "I'm sorry we put you and your friends in danger."

"You brave Goodwatcher. Hope you find Badwatcher place and make friends free."

"Me too. I don't know how. Gordon was our only chance to find it."

"Always more than one way in," said Azrak.

"I hope you're right."

"Horse is not all better. You stay one more star-time, then go."

"We don't want to cause trouble for you," Jake said.

"No trouble. You stay one more star-time. Horse better. Dogs better. You better. Then you go."

"We will. I promise."

They stayed the day, lounging in the grass, looking out over the desolate remains of the warrens. Even stripped bare of its grass, the vast network of canyons retained a lonely beauty, as if the land was not dead but merely asleep, waiting for someone to awaken it.

By the end of the day, Blue's injury was completely healed. He trotted around the mesa, enjoying the exercise. Ursus, it seemed, had fully recovered from his ordeal as well. It did Jake's heart good to see his friends healthy again. With his friends better, he could face the prospect of leaving the mesa without so much fear.

The light failed and the world plunged abruptly into darkness. Jake expected the stars to be nearer than they ever had been, but they were strangely distant. They still swirled and flowed in celestial currents, but they felt diminished, their light pale and weak.

Jake could get no rest that night. While Blue and the others bedded down, he fretted over the approaching day. He had no idea where he would go, or what he would do. He closed his eyes and tried to drift, but the harder he tried, the farther away the stars felt.

A faint rustle, nothing more than the brush of a tail against bare rock, caught his attention. He opened his eyes. Azrak stood at the edge of the path that led down into the canyon. He looked around, as if to make sure he was alone, and then he vanished down the path.

Jake's first urge was to get up and follow. Instead, he woke Ursus.

"Azrak is gone."

Ursus thought for a moment. "It is his home. If he must go, then he must go."

"But what if he's up to something?"

"You are the Giver. If you want to track him, I will go with you."

"No, we'd have to leave Blue and Gordon behind."

Ursus laid his head back down between his paws and closed his eyes. Jake didn't try to rouse him again; Ursus would be no further help unless Jake decided to move. The dog rolled over on his side, and Jake leaned against his giant chest. The dog's long, slow, regular breaths calmed him.

The light had not yet returned when Azrak appeared once again at the edge of the path. The night's exertions had taken a visible toll on the rat; he moved slowly, trudging across the grass. After stopping at the pool for a moment to clean his face, the rat slipped into the shadows near the rise and disappeared.

Jake said nothing about it in the morning. Azrak and the others turned out to wish them well. Jake thanked them and led the procession across the mesa.

"Thanks for the help," Jake said.

"Azrak glad to help."

Jake wasn't sure if he believed him.

They left Azrak and the other rodents at the top of the mesa and began the descent. The path curved around, hugging the cliff edge, barely wide enough for them to comfortably walk. Blue had the most difficulty; the loose rocks forced him to take the descent extremely slowly.

There was no trace of the Malbinocks. Jake expected they would be gone, but it was a relief nonetheless. Above, the sky was a clear, cloudless blue, and light filled the canyon. The bright light revealed numerous hidden branches, each of them wide enough for Blue, and each leading in a different direction. Jake surveyed the path ahead of them. None of the paths seemed more appealing than any other. Each was bordered by high, sheer walls, and each one was littered with treacherous piles of sand and red rocks.

Jake thought about marching back up the mesa and confronting Azrak. There was nothing out in the canyons at night except Malbinocks, and no reason that any animal would want to make contact with them. Jake and his friends could have used a few extra days to scout out the area and perhaps find a path forward, but the rat wouldn't have it.

The rat's insistence on their leaving so soon was suspicious. Azrak should have learned his lesson; the rodents' refusal to help one another led to their downfall, but Azrak had just done to Jake what the other rats had done to him.

Jake considered going back and taking the mesa

by force. No hamster or guinea pig was big enough to challenge even the smallest of his companions. But he thought of Penny, clinging desperately to the last patch of peaceful ground, shunned by the other brown rats for showing kindness, and he knew it was out of the question.

"We have to pick one," Jake said. "Back or forward, what's it going to be?"

None of his companions had an answer.

"Come on. Somebody must have an idea."

"I will follow you, Jake," said Ursus.

"You are a Rider," said Blue. "Riders know where to go."

"Gordon?"

Gordon, of course, said nothing. He sat next to Blue, his head cocked slightly to the left.

"Let's keep going straight," Jake said. "If it ain't broke, don't fix it."

It was something his dad said a lot, and somehow saying it made him feel a little better. His companions offered no objections. Jake shrugged his shoulders and stepped off. The others followed suit.

"Not that way."

Azrak sat on a perch high on the cliff face. "Way blocked. Rocks fall, make pile."

"All right, we go that way, then," Jake said, pointing to a branch that led off to the right.

"Not that way. Gets small. Horse and big dog no get through."

Before Jake could choose another path, Azrak disappeared through a narrow cleft in the rock, reappearing a short time later at ground level. It startled Jake to see Azrak so close.

"How did you do that?"

"Many ways in. Many ways out."

Jake pointed to the canyon in front of him. "Well, which way is out?"

"You follow," said Azrak. He headed for a branch that curved off to the left, without looking back to see if they were behind him. Jake hurried to catch up, gesturing for the others to join him. As he picked his way among the jumbled stones, Jake fought with a terrible foreboding. Azrak moved through the rocks with the kind of ease that comes from long familiarity. It would be easy for Azrak to lead them down a dangerous path, only to leave them at a crucial moment. The others did not appear to share his concern, though Jake made no attempt to ask them. Whatever the rat had in mind for them, they would face it together.

All around, the canyon walls gradually closed in, as if the land itself was trying to swallow them.

Chapter Twenty-Eight

They walked through winding canyons, sometimes wide enough for the four of them to walk abreast, other times narrow enough to force them into single file. What did not change was the rock. It was the same dull, red color, brittle and hard to the touch. Jake's shirt, coated with fine dust kicked up on the trail, changed from dirty white to dull orange, as if he'd been playing in a bucket of old nails.

Azrak never hesitated. He moved at a steady pace, yet slow enough to ensure he didn't lose anyone. At each branch, he forged ahead, never pausing to consider an alternate route, as if he'd taken the trip a hundred times. Where was the rat leading them?

The twists and turns in their path left Jake hopelessly disoriented. If it was Azrak's plan to lead them into a dangerous place and abandon them, it was working. If he were separated from the dogs, Jake would never be able to find his way back. They might be able to find him but they would still have to contend with flash floods and Malbinocks. Blue and the dogs were focused on Azrak, watching him for direction, paying little attention to Jake at all. His mood went from nervous to resentful at how quickly the rat had taken over.

Thanks to Azrak's careful choice of paths, Blue was managing a good pace. The route was much less punishing than the one Jake had chosen the day before. Azrak had everything in hand.

It seemed a little too perfect.

Jake tried to shake it off. All the proof he had said otherwise. If Azrak wanted them to be taken by the Malbinocks, he could have just stayed hidden and watched as the Malbinocks overwhelmed them with numbers and dragged them off. But he had risked his own safety and the safety of his friends by leading them to the mesa.

But Azrak was the same rat that had barely given them time to catch their breath before sending them off into the maze. Try as he might, Jake could not dismiss the feeling that Azrak was leading them all into a trap. But he followed along with the others, keeping his suspicions to himself. He spoke little, afraid that if he talked, Azrak would know that Jake was on to him.

"Come," Azrak said. After the long silence, the rat's squeaky voice startled him. "Safe place near for dark-time."

They followed Azrak beneath a stone arch, through a narrow passage, and into a deep cul-de-sac that opened to the sky. The walls curved outward to form a natural stone bowl. Other than the opening they had come through, there seemed to be no other way in or out.

"This place doesn't look safe to me" Jake said. "If it rains, we'll all drown in here."

"No rain coming," said Azrak.

"How do you know that? Yesterday that storm came on pretty fast."

"No rain is coming," said Ursus.

"Fine, but if they come for us, how are we going to get out?"

"Big dog go there. Lie down, block opening."

"What, so they can drag him off?"

"Big dog too big. One Badwatcher fit, others behind. Not strong."

There was a certain logic to it, but it didn't make Jake feel any better.

"Sounds like you have all the answers. Ok, fine," Jake said. "We'll stay here. Hopefully it doesn't rain and drown us all before morning." He looked for the highest spot he could see, on a small rise just to the right of the opening. It only put him a few inches higher than the others which only frustrated him more. He sat down with his back to the cliff face and folded his arms in front of his chest. The others hunkered down as well.

Ursus blocked the entrance with his body, while Blue stood a few feet away. Gordon nestled against Ursus' shoulder, in Jake's spot, and Jake scowled. Azrak curled up on the opposite side of the opening, his head pressed against his long, scaly tail. If they noticed Jake's foul mood, they didn't acknowledge it.

You're the Giver, Jake said to himself. If you must fold your arms, fold your arms. If you must grump,

grump. Unless some rat comes along and then, who cares what you do? But Ursus was already asleep, his barrel chest rising and falling steadily. Gordon slept too, in Jake's spot. It would have been easy for him to slip in next to Gordon and rest his back against Ursus, but his pride wouldn't allow it. Some small part of him wanted it to rain, for the cul-de-sac to fill up like a giant bathtub, just so he would be right. But the sky remained clear, and when night fell a while later, and the stars burst into their glorious dance, Jake still hadn't moved.

He pretended to close his eyes. Azrak would probably make his move soon, and Jake would be there to catch him. Through the haze of half-closed eyelids, Jake watched the rat rest peacefully. The high walls kept out any breezes, and overhead, the stars danced in silence. The air was clear, but Jake could hear no music, as if he'd finally gone beyond their reach.

Now was not the time to worry about it, when the real danger slept a few feet away. The light, reflecting from Azrak's white coat, was just enough to keep the rat illuminated. When Azrak decided to sneak away, Jake would be ready for him.

He passed the time calling up broken memories of his home and his family. He tried to picture his mother, to hear his mother's voice, but he could remember nothing. Here and there he had bits and pieces of his father —a single throw from a game of catch, a fishing pole by the river, a chance to hand his father a wrench while he worked on Jake's dirt bike. But his mother was a blank. In his mind, it was as if she never existed at all. Her absence left a subtle ache in his heart.

Azrak twitched. His nose came up, and he gave one furtive glace on either side. What he saw must have satisfied him. He rose to his feet and quietly scurried to where Ursus lay across the narrow opening. He crept toward the dog's hindquarters and, in one smooth motion, disappeared. Jake leapt to his feet and dashed to Ursus, kneeling down next to the dog's massive head.

"He left us," Jake whispered.

Ursus rose and sniffed the ground in front of him, disturbing Gordon in the process. "He came this way," Ursus said.

"I know. I just watched him leave. I'm going to follow him."

"I will go with you."

"No. Not this time. Maybe Azrak is trying to trap us, but he's right about the door. If you stay in front of it, Blue and Gordon will be safe. I'll follow him and find out what he's trying to pull, and then I'll come back and we'll decide what to do."

Ursus moved aside so that Jake could pass. He crept into the passage, seized with a savage glee. Whatever Azrak was planning, Jake would put a stop to it. The stars provided just enough light to guide him through the rocks that littered the canyon floor. He saw no sign of Azrak.

Jake emerged into the canyon they had been following for most of the day. He dropped down low, scanning the broken rocks for signs of Azrak.

Something white crept across dull, red rocks, moving steadily away from their camp inside the bowl. Jake crouched low and followed. A memory, fleeting but distinct, flashed through his mind. He remembered a crisp, fall morning, cold enough to see his breath, the sun only a promise on the horizon. Dad led the way, through a stand of stunted white pines, to a place where the birds sat hidden in a clump of hawthorns. It came and went, just a flash of scent and color, vanishing as quickly as it had come.

Jake got a good look. Azrak—as he suspected.

Jake stalked him, eager to catch him in the act, eager to show the others that they had been duped. It was a rat after all. Rats had a bad reputation for a reason. They hid in walls and destroyed everything they touched; what they couldn't chew up they used as a bathroom, spreading diseases wherever they lived. And they were no better here than they were at home.

Azrak lifted his head, silver light catching his whiskers as they twitched. Jake threw himself to the ground as Azrak glanced in his direction.

A short time later, the rat crept into a narrow defile and disappeared.

Jake clambered to his feet and ran, hunched over, across the canyon, throwing his back against the wall near the entrance to the defile. Inching over just enough, he turned his head to peer inside, but he saw nothing; the wan starlight wasn't enough to penetrate the darkness.

Jake couldn't see, but he could hear. He squatted down and closed his eyes. The only sound was the slight scrape of dirty cotton against stone and the rush of air through his nose as he breathed. He heard nothing else for a long while. Then, in the distance, he heard the faint squeal of moving metal.

He heard it again, closer than before.

A few paces away, a large chunk of rock had fallen from the canyon wall and tumbled to the bottom, landing with a sizable gap between itself and the cliff face. Jake slipped into the gap and hunkered down.

Now Jake was sure. Azrak had sold them out.

He had to warn his friends that the rat was a traitor. He slid around behind the stone, intent on making a run for the passageway, but it was too late. Jake counted twelve of them, shambling over the broken rocks. Some were hunched over as if they were looking for something small among the stones. A rat, perhaps.

A squeak, unnaturally loud between the sheer rock walls, seized the Malbinocks' attention. The echo made it difficult to pinpoint the source, but the Malbinocks cocked their misshapen heads toward the defile. The twelve formed a half circle, tightening as they closed in on the gap that marked the defile's entrance. What was Azrak waiting for?

The squeaking stopped. The Malbinocks stopped as well, holding their positions, probably waiting for Azrak to give up Jake and his friends. Azrak was the last of his kind for a reason. He must have been the craftiest rat of them all.

And now Jake had fallen into his trap.

He felt a peculiar glee about being right. Next time, maybe Ursus and the others wouldn't be so quick to follow just anybody.

Another squeak pierced the silence, but it didn't come from the defile. It echoed across the canyon from behind. Jake turned, nearly losing his balance in the process, and peered into the darkness. The Malbinocks turned as well. Four of them broke ranks and began to pursue whatever lay behind them, while the others closed in on the defile.

The rat was leading them straight to Ursus!

Jake broke cover, scrambling across the scree toward the four Malbinocks that followed the rat's last signal. He picked up a rock and moved toward them, arm raised.

A blaze of white flashed past the Malbinocks' legs. One of them snatched it, but it was gone almost as soon as it appeared, and the Malbinock came up empty. Azrak appeared again, this time between the two in the center. In their haste to grab him, they collided. Their bodies tangled together and in their violent struggle to free themselves, they collapsed, a writhing, screeching mess. The remaining two made no attempt to help. Their attention was on Azrak, now sitting, clearly visible, a few feet in front of them. They attacked together, but again he eluded them.

Jake froze in plain sight, struggling to make sense of what he was watching. The rat flowed like water among the stones, vanishing and reappearing as if by magic, leading the remaining Malbinocks on a fruitless chase until they, too, collapsed in a writhing mass of wood and copper pipe and metal banding. The screeching and groaning sounded oddly human, as if the sound of their tangled bodies were giving voice to their frustration.

A heavy thump from behind broke him of his reverie, and he turned just in time to avoid the tines of the broken rake the Malbinock was using as an arm. Jake tumbled sideways, landing hard amongst the rocks. Searing pain lanced through his left forearm and down into his fingers.

The remaining eight Malbinocks lumbered toward him. He rolled away as the rake came down again, the steel tines shattering a rock near his head, so near that pieces of it peppered his face. He tried desperately to regain his feet.

Azrak appeared, and the Malbinocks abandoned Jake and attacked the rat as if seized by a sudden madness. They groped and swatted, snatched, grabbed, but their efforts came to nothing. Two more of the creatures fell, and those that remained pursued Azrak in a frenzy.

"Jake. Why you come?"

Jake didn't have an answer. Azrak watched him for a second, his black eyes fixed accusingly on Jake's.

"You go back to friends. I come later."

And then he was gone.

Jake did as he was told. He ran, his arm still tingling from the fall.

Chapter Twenty-Nine

The last few hours of the night were the longest.

Jake was afraid Azrak would not return and perhaps more afraid that he would. He hadn't confided his suspicions in anyone, but Azrak knew. Azrak had looked into his eyes and seen the truth.

If he didn't come back, they would be lost, stranded in the middle of a labyrinth of bare rock, just waiting for the next rainstorm to come and wash them away, or for the Malbinocks to catch up with them. It would be no less than Jake deserved, but he couldn't wish that on his friends. And so he waited, watching the entrance to their camp as if his life depended on it.

He knew watching would change nothing; if Azrak chose to abandon them, there was nothing Jake could do. But that wasn't the thought that kept his gaze fixed on Ursus and the narrow passage beyond. It was another.

What if Azrak couldn't return?

There was no question that the rat could take care of himself. But he was used to working alone, and Jake's presence had upset his plan, forcing him to improvise. Jake could not bear the thought that Azrak had been captured. It was that thought that made the minutes drag on like lifetimes, and made the canyon walls feel like a prison.

A rescue was out of the question. There was no way Ursus could track Azrak and protect Gordon at the same time. Going alone was no good either; it would take only a couple of turns before Jake was hopelessly lost.

When day finally broke, Azrak still had not returned. Ursus stood and shook himself, a cloud of red powder billowing around him.

"It is day," he said.

The words "Azrak is not here" were left unspoken, but they hung in the air nevertheless. Jake stared at the narrow crevasse. Light streamed in and gave the red rock an eerie glow. Overhead, the sky shone blue, but there was no guarantee it would remain that way.

"Blue, how is your leg?" asked Jake.

Blue took a few tentative steps, and then walked at a normal gait. Jake could see no trace of his limp.

"It looks like it really is better."

"It does not hurt," said Blue. He reared and stamped a few times, and then stood, relaxed. If they did decide to travel, Blue would not slow them down. Jake was glad for Blue's sake, but outside of the bowl, the labyrinth continued, unabated, in every direction. Malbinock patrols and treacherous rocks awaited them no matter which way they decided to go.

"There's no point in staying here," Jake said. The others did not object. He led his friends out of the crevasse and back into the main canyon. Perched on his hind legs at the top of a boulder was Azrak. A wash of shame battled with joy and relief in Jake's heart. He closed his eyes and sighed. Azrak glared at Jake from high on his perch.

"I'm sorry I doubted you," Jake said.

"You look," said Azrak. He darted his head back and forth, up and down. "You look. You see."

Jake did as Azrak told him. It was the same bare, red rock it had been the day before; lonely, barren and bereft of life. None of the rain that had nearly washed them away remained, and air felt as dry as the ground beneath Jake's feet.

"Jake not trust Azrak. Azrak not trust rabbit. Azrak not trust mouse. Azrak not trust guineas. You look. You see." He gestured again at the dry, dusty canyon.

"This is no trust. Warrens gone. Friends gone."

Jake could think of nothing to say.

"I had Goodwatcher," Azrak continued. "My Goodwatcher called Zoey. She gave good food, clean water, warm bed. Big nest. Zoey take Azrak out of big nest and Azrak ride on Zoey's shoulder. Zoey love Azrak. Azrak love Zoey too. But Azrak get pain in belly. Goodwatcher Zoey take Azrak to other Goodwatcher. Goodwatcher poke Azrak with sharp claw, Azrak fall asleep, wake up here."

"Azrak miss Goodwatcher Zoey. Azrak want see Zoey again."

"She sounds like a nice person," Jake said. "I'm glad she gave you a good life."

"She give good life, then take pain away. This why Azrak help you."

"I'm sorry," said Jake. "Do you think you could give me another chance?"

Azrak sat for a moment. His eyes were unfocused, trained on something far away.

"Follow," he said. He vanished from the top of the boulder and reappeared a few seconds later next to Ursus. Without another word, he slipped nimbly across the scree. Ursus, Jake, and Gordon followed. He moved with the same deliberate purpose as he had the previous day. Through narrow channels and high-walled canyons, they wended their way over the broken rocks.

Jake had no idea what awaited them when Azrak finally stopped. At the very least, he was certain Azrak wasn't leading them into a trap, and that made the going easier.

As they navigated through the labyrinth, the air began to change. It felt drier, and the strange, dusty scent that hung in the air intensified. It made Jake think of old newspapers stacked in a forgotten corner, of library books no one read, of clothes in the back of the closet, hidden behind broken umbrellas and old board games. But there was no promise of discovery, only the dry, wasted smell of unwanted things.

The click-clop of Blue's hooves on the broken rocks sounded with the regularity of a metronome. Even the breeze died, and the air felt as close and dry and dusty as the inside of an old chest.

Ahead of them, the canyon came to an abrupt end. A tall ridge blocked their path, and the canyon no longer branched out but instead widened, until they emerged into a broad, desolate valley. Azrak bore to the right. For a while he followed a path parallel to the ridge.

"Is that snow?" Jake said, pointing to the top of the ridge. The red rock looked as if it had been coated with powdered sugar.

"Snow?" Azrak said.

"It's like ice, but fluffy."

"Azrak not know snow. Not know ice."

"It is not snow," said Blue.

They skirted the base of the ridge until they came to a cave. The opening was gigantic, easily large enough for all of them to fit. Inside, the way lay shrouded in darkness. Jake shuddered.

"Way out," Azrak said.

Jake didn't relish the notion of venturing into another tunnel. The strange scent pervaded the air now, so thick it dominated every breath he took, and it seemed to be coming from inside the cave.

"What's in there?" Jake said.

"Azrak never go look."

Jake turned to his friends. They stood in a close group facing him. He ran his hand across Blue's nose, and gave Ursus a scratch on the chest. He knelt down and stroked the top of Gordon's head.

"I have to do this," Jake said. "But you don't. I couldn't have gotten this far without you, but maybe it would be better if I went on by myself. I don't care what happens to me, but I do care about you. I never had better friends. Go back to the lake, back where the fish are. That was a nice place."

"I am a friend," said Ursus. "I will go with you."

"You are a friend. You are the best friend a kid could ever have. But you don't have to do this."

"I will go with you."

Blue pawed at the red gravel with his hoof. "It is not safe to break up the herd."

"Azrak go too," said the rat.

"You? But what about Penny and the others?"

"Penny need Azrak, Drummerboy need Azrak. But other rats need Azrak more. Azrak come. Azrak help."

Jake fought back tears and turned to Gordon.

"Gordon—"

Gordon disappeared into the darkness of the cave.

"Guess that's my answer," Jake said and followed Gordon inside. The cave remained tall and wide, its sides smooth, burnished by sand and wind. To Jake's relief, the tunnel was really nothing more than a thick, deep arch. The ground sloped down gently and then began to rise again, and they emerged into blinding, white light.

Jake blinked his eyes and they adjusted to the brightness. Red rocks, beaten down by wind, tumbled across a flat plain, covered in a thick layer of white dust. The dust lay in drifts across the landscape. It swirled into the air at the slightest disturbance, billowing like smoke. Far into the distance, thin, yellow shapes thrust up, pale yellow against the grey sky.

"Guess this is the way," he said, but without much enthusiasm.

"No dogs have come this way," Ursus said. "No cats. No horses. None have come this way."

"That's where we have to go." Jake pointed across the expanse. He looked at his hands, already coated with dust, giving his skin an ashen, pale cast. He shuddered and tried to wipe it off on his shirt, but that was already coated as well, and rubbing his hands against it only made it worse. The sight of his pale hands unnerved him, and he couldn't bring himself to begin the march.

"It is not good to linger in one place," said Blue. "We will be safer if we walk." He eyed the mouth of the cave, and his restless hooves stirred up white clouds around his legs and belly.

Jake was in no hurry. The dust and the dry, foul air repulsed him. If there were anyone else at all to take his place, Jake would have given up the task without a second thought. But there was no one else. Jake stood at the mouth of the cave as if it were a precipice, afraid to take a step.

Sebastian and the other animals were out there, somewhere beyond the white expanse. Cy, Serafina. Hundreds, perhaps thousands of others, yearning for a chance to be free again. Jake looked over the white desert and wondered why it had to be him. Not a fireman, or a soldier, or a police officer. Not a scientist. He wasn't strong, or brave, or smart. Most of the time, he wasn't even very nice.

"We have to stay together," Jake said.

"I will stay close," said Ursus.

"Blue, you should carry Azrak." Jake approached the rat, but Azrak took a step back.

"Rats not ride horses."

"Today you do," Jake said. He picked Azrak up and set him on Blue's back.

"Do not worry, little rat," said Blue. "I have never lost a Rider."

Azrak pressed his belly against Blue's back. "Too high," he said.

"You can ride on my shoulder, then," Jake said. He plucked Azrak off Blue's back and draped the rat across his shoulders. Azrak curled gently against Jake's neck. "Better?"

"Is good," said Azrak.

Jake could think of no words of encouragement or advice. He set his sights on the strange, yellow objects in the far distance. It was a goal, at least, and he hoped they could move fast enough to reach it before the darkness came. If nothing else, it promised some shelter. He took a deep breath and stepped out past the mouth of the cave. Another step followed the first. He didn't look back.

Chapter Thirty

The dust was not as deep as Jake expected; it had blown into drifts against the ridge, but out on the open plain it was barely deep enough to cover the top of his feet. The going was easy; the ground was flat and free of rocks, but walking was more of a labor than it had been anywhere else, as if the plain sloped imperceptibly upward.

Even if he couldn't see a slope, he felt it as if someone were adding grains of sand to a bag attached to his back each time he took a step. Ursus and Blue plodded along beside him. He thought of asking Blue for a ride but decided against it; Azrak would be reluctant, and Jake didn't want to burden the horse with extra weight. If the walk was sapping his strength, it was probably doing the same to the others. It was certainly adding to Gordon's burden; the little dog pushed along through the dust several paces behind.

"Blue, how are you doing?" Jake asked.

"I can go farther."

"Do you think you could carry Gordon for a while?"

"I will carry him."

"Keep going. I'll bring him."

Jake did not stop their progress. Instead, he doubled back to Gordon, and to his dismay found that the going was no easier in the direction they had come. The discovery frightened him, but he said nothing about it to the others. When he reached Gordon, he picked him up.

"You feel like you gained some weight." It took extra effort to return to Blue and, with Ursus' help, lift Gordon onto his back. Azrak hadn't moved a muscle since they set out, and Jake felt the rat's weight settling heavier against his shoulders. Still, he didn't ask Azrak to get down, afraid he would vanish in the dust.

The strange, distant shapes became larger and more distinct, though Jake could still not make out what they were. His shoulders ached with Azrak's weight. Jake tried to ignore the fatigue in his legs and ache in his neck. He envied Gordon, riding carefree on Blue's back while Jake plodded through the dust alongside him.

Ursus padded along without complaint. Jake envied him as well; his long legs carried him over the dusty hardpan without apparent effort, and he alone had no one to carry.

There were many more of the yellow objects than Jake had originally seen from the mouth of the cave. They rose out of the ground on thin stalks, pale yellow against gray-white expanse. Some had bulbous tops, while others were truncated, spiky and irregular, as if someone had broken them off.

The trek across the desolate plain was exhausting, and all Jake wanted to do was drop Azrak to the ground, sink down next to him and close his eyes. Not now, he told himself. Not out here in the open. He could rest later.

"Come on, guys. We're almost there," he said. Jake grew impatient. His legs burned with the effort of keeping up with his larger friends. He put his head down and watched his feet take one pitifully small step after another, stirring up little puffs of white dust with each footfall. When he glanced up again, his eyes widened. The strange objects, so distant from the ridge, were close enough that Jake understood what they were.

"They're bones," he whispered. "A whole forest of them."

He bent down and scooped up a handful of dust. He relaxed his hand and let the dust flow over the meaty edge of his palm and drift back to the ground. The dust had taken on a yellow cast, the same pale yellow as the bones that sprouted out of the earth like trees.

"This is not a good place," said Blue.

At long last, they reached the first of the bones. They jutted from the ground at odd angles, forming impassable thickets. Jake and his friends skirted the edge looking for shelter, but the forest was an unbroken tangle.

"No good, no good," whispered Azrak. His voice was faint, and heavy with despair. Azrak hadn't walked more than a step, and he spoke as if he were ready to die from fatigue.

"Look, if you want to go back, you're more than welcome—"

It was when he tried to glare at Azrak that Jake saw the bones for what they really were. He caught a glimpse, just at the edge of his vision, of the skeleton of a gigantic lizard. It was larger by far than the five of them combined, or had been in life. Its body curled upward, braced by its tail, the massive head staring toward the sky through large, sightless eyes. One of its forelegs stretched out ahead, its bony claws reaching for something above it.

Jake studied the bones. It wasn't an illusion; the lizard was there, its body bent almost perpendicular.

"Jake, there is no shelter here. This is not a good place to stop," said Blue.

But Jake couldn't take his eyes off the lizard. It was trying to tell him something, something important, but he couldn't understand.

"What happened to you?" Jake whispered.

"Azrak already tell."

"No, not you. The lizard. Look at it."

Azrak shifted on Jake's shoulders. "Azrak not know lizard. Show."

"Right there." Jake pointed to the skeleton, amazed that the rat could miss it.

"Nothing there. Only bones."

"You can't see an animal in there? Blue, what do you see?"

"Danger."

"Ursus, do you see it?"

"Nothing has come this way. Not cat. Not horse. Not rat."

The message, if there was one, was meant for Jake alone. It made him sad to see the lizard's bones, searching, yearning, grasping, and finding nothing. He closed his eyes. When he opened them again, he knew.

The lizard was trying to escape. Locked into a cage and forgotten, it waited. For a long time, it waited, while the emptiness in its belly grew, and its flesh withered, and no one came. No one opened the locked door, no one looked in. The last drops of water evaporated from the drinking bowl, and still it waited, waited until the emptiness was too great. Outside the door was food, was water, was life. With its last breaths, it grasped at the top of the cage, and then was still.

The lizard was not alone. All around him they emerged, dogs chained to trees, locked in garages and closets, horses packed in tiny barns to starve, rabbits and guinea pigs left in backyard hutches to freeze in winter and bake in summer, unable to eat or drink, yearning for comfort and finding none. Kittens stranded on the side of a busy highway, their cries drowned in engine noise and car exhaust. There were others, burned into the forest, but Jake couldn't bear to look at them all.

He reeled with the terrible, empty futility in their dead eyes. He ached for them, for all of them, for their hunger and their loneliness. He hadn't the energy to weep for them. All he could give them was a whispered, "I'm sorry". He meant it, meant it with everything left in him, but it did nothing to relieve the helplessness that radiated from every yellowed bone.

"Jake, look! Jake see! There!" Azrak pointed with his paw.

A path lay before them, one that had gone unnoticed. He was sure it hadn't been there a moment ago, but there was no mistaking it now. It led deep into the tangled forest before curving out of view.

Jake led the way; his shoulders stooped with something more than the weight of the rat. The others followed, and Jake could feel the hollow eyes of the dead, watching him depart.

Chapter Thirty-One

The little light that reached the forest floor played across the bones and washed the place with a sickly, yellow hue. Jake could no longer make out the skeletons of individual animals, but he felt them all around him—hungry, cold, and empty. Underfoot, the dust was nothing more than a fine powder, a thin patina over the hard-packed ground. He stopped briefly to allow Azrak to slide off his shoulders. The rat gazed at the tops of the bones, illuminated brightly beneath the sky.

"Bad place."

"We have to keep moving," Jake said. But his legs felt heavy, even without the burden of carrying Azrak. Ursus and the others hesitated.

Jake relented. "Fine. I'm tired too. Let's rest here for a little while."

"This place not for rats," said Azrak.

"It's not a place for anybody," Jake replied. "But I don't think a little rest will hurt us."

"I will stay with you," Ursus said. He waited until

Jake sank down at the base of one of the larger bones, and then Ursus sat beside him. Blue stood on the other side, scraping the ground with his hoof. He shook himself and snorted. Jake looked up and noticed that Gordon was still on the horse's back. Getting up was far more difficult than he expected, as if his legs had grown shallow roots into the ground and by standing he'd rip them out.

"All right, Gordon," he said, stretching his arms to coax the little dog off Blue's back. But Gordon would not budge.

"Gordon, come on." Jake tried to pull Gordon from Blue's back, but Gordon resisted him, and Jake didn't have the energy to keep fighting.

"I can carry him," said Blue.

Jake was too tired to argue. "Suit yourself, then."

He sank back against the yellowed column. It felt cold against his back. His feet were cold as well. He shivered and tried to stand, but the cold had bled into his bones. Heat leached from his body like water being squeezed out of a sponge, but Jake felt no particular distress. He and his companions had walked as far as they could. It was a well-earned break for all of them. He leaned his head back and closed his eyes.

Somewhere in the twisted depths of the forest came the sound of voices. He'd heard them before, spoken words tumbling over one another like drops of water over the falls. He was no longer frightened or confused by them. Gradually, the voices fell away until there were only three. They were familiar to him as well.

"Angela—"

"Please, Brad. Just one more night. One more. And if he doesn't—"

"The doctor said—"

"I don't care what the doctor said. I don't care. You have to give this to me, Brad. You have to."

The voices died away. A faint, electronic hum filled the space between them.

"Brad, it's all right. It won't affect his ... there aren't likely to be any significant changes if we wait until morning."

"In the morning, then."

A door closed.

"Brad, I want him back. I want my beautiful boy."

"We'll stay with him all night."

The sad woman began to sing.

"One misty, moisty morning ..."

Jake opened his mouth to sing, but the words would not come. A strange tightness in this throat would not allow it. The sad woman's voice grew more distant.

"When cloudy was the weather ..."

There was such sadness in her voice, such pain, somewhere out among the bones, and Jake wanted very badly to go to her, to find out what he could do to help.

"I chanced to meet an old man dressed all in leather ..."

Jake's body felt as if it were covered in wet sand. He struggled. Twice he slipped, landing against the thick column.

"He began to compliment ..."

The voice was faint, only a whisper, a breeze among the bones where none should be. He tried again to regain his feet, and this time he did not sink back. One hesitant step and then another, and though he could not feel his feet, he knew that he was walking. It felt oddly like floating, but he could hear the gentle tap of his soles against the hard ground.

"And I began to grin ..."

"How do you do—" Jake sang. It came out as a whisper, a croak. "How do you do?"

The forest fell into silence.

Darkness surrounded him. Only a few pale shafts of silver starlight filtered down through the tall bones. Nothing looked familiar. The path was gone. He stood in a small clearing, littered with shattered stumps jutting from the ground like rotten teeth. Jake could still hear the echoes of the sad woman's voice in the air. She was close by, she had to be, but Jake could see nothing.

"Hello?"

Nothing.

"I want to help you."

Silence.

He felt a tug on the cuff of his jeans, and then another. He peered into the darkness by his feet and felt around with his hands, but there was nothing near him. Another tug, and then another followed. Frustrated, he dropped to his hands and knees, feeling around in the darkness for his assailant.

A sharp pain lanced through his scalp. Whatever

had been tugging on his pants, had taken hold of his hair. The force of the tug pulled him off balance, and he tumbled forward on his belly. He rolled over. A heavy, warm mass settled on his chest, and something tickled the skin on his cheeks and jaw. He shook his head and opened his eyes to find Gordon sitting on top of him.

"Gordon? How did you ... Where am I?"

He struggled to sit but only managed to prop himself up on his elbows. His body tingled, barely obeying him, as if he'd been lying in the same spot for many hours. Gordon licked his face and tugged on the tattered collar of his shirt. Jake squinted, bleary-eyed.

He hadn't moved a muscle. A few feet away, Ursus lay on his side, and Blue stood a short distance beyond that, his head drooped down so low his snout almost rested in the dust. Gordon ran in a circle and then returned to attack Jake's collar once again, shaking his head as he pulled. The bones loomed over them, ominous, sickly yellow columns blotting out the stars. He had dreamed it, the voices, the sad woman, all of it. She was out of his reach again.

The sad woman's voice was gone, only the echo of a memory that was painfully real a short while ago. His elbows gave out on him, and he slumped back down on his back, watching Gordon pull frantically on his shirt sleeve and collar.

"What's gotten into you?" He sat up. A layer of dust ran down his chest and settled in small drifts in the folds of his shirt.

"How long—"

A coating of dust lay over Ursus and covered Blue's back as well. Jake's tried to think, tried to remember.

There were people talking, a woman singing. But they were gone, or they had never been there in the first place. Once again, he struggled to get to his feet. His arms and legs were leaden, and his mind felt as if it had been caught in a whirlwind that slashed through his memories and left nothing in place. He stood, swayed, and would have fallen again if Gordon hadn't grabbed the bottom of his shirt and pulled backward. For a few seconds he stood there, tottering between Gordon and the cold ground.

He blinked his eyes. His head cleared.

They had to move.

He staggered across the clearing to where Ursus lay. He knelt and shoved the big dog's shoulder. Ursus did not budge. He tried to rouse Blue, grabbing his ears and shaking them gently.

"Blue, you have to wake up. Blue! Blue!"

Blue raised his head. Jake could see his reflection in the horse's huge, brown eyes. His face looked rounded, distorted, his eyes unnaturally wide with fear.

"Blue. The herd. It's in trouble. We have to move!"

Blue blinked and snorted. "Freya was here," he said. "Standing in the open. I heard her call. I tried to get away, but I could not run fast enough. I felt a pull on my ears. Now I am here."

"Help me wake up Ursus."

Jake shook him while Blue pawed at his muscled flank with his hoof, and Gordon tugged at his ear.

"Blue. Bite him."

Blue stopped pawing at Ursus' flank.

"Bite him on the nose. Hard."

"He will be angry."

"He'll get over it."

Blue hesitated, then gave Ursus a half-hearted nip.

"That's not enough!"

"I am afraid."

"If you don't, he'll become a part of this place!"

But Blue could not bring himself to do it. Jake took a deep breath, and then he bit down, hard. Ursus rolled, gathering his paws under his body, and a low, baleful growl rumbled from his chest. Jake scooted away on his backside. Ursus bared his fangs, his eyes focused not on Jake, but on some unseen enemy. He was the Ursus of the life before, fearsome and savage, locked in the death-grip of a long-dead memory.

Jake grabbed Ursus by the ears, and the dog snarled, his fangs only inches from Jake's face. He felt the dog's hot breath wash over him, but he did not let go.

"Ursus," he said, "You are a friend. You came all this way with me. Come back! Come back!"

Jake felt a twitch in Ursus' ears, and Ursus' eyes cleared. He sank into the dust. Jake stepped back, trembling. Ursus shook himself and struggled to stand. He failed the first time, dropping roughly to the ground.

"I am a friend," he said, and tried again. This time he managed to stand, though his back legs wobbled and his head sank so low his snout traced lines in the dust between his paws.

There was no time for celebration. "We have to move," Jake said. "I think if we stay here any longer, we won't be able to leave."

He pressed forward, navigating between the bones. After a few steps, he stopped.

"Where is Azrak?"

They found him curled up at the base of a large bone, fast asleep. Jake didn't attempt to wake him. Instead, he lifted him gently and placed him on Blue's back. Azrak barely stirred as he was being moved.

"There's no time to wake him up right now. We have to get moving," Jake said.

They resumed their march. For Jake, each step was a chore. The cold ground chilled his feet as if he were walking on ice. He forced one foot forward, and then the other, his pace painfully slow. The others fared little better, content to plod along behind him. Silence pervaded the place, and the air was thick with the smell of bone-dust.

On through the night they trudged. Jake was so weary, he pulled himself along the shattered remnants of fallen bones, and the cold drove up from his heels and into his ankles and calves, threading through bone and muscle toward his knees.

Jake concentrated on walking, until the silence smothered him and he could no longer stand to be wrapped in it.

"One misty, moisty morning, when cloudy was the weather, I chanced to meet an old man dressed all in leather ..."

But that was all he could remember.

The sound of his own voice lifted him, and his steps came easier.

"Hey, Blue," he said. "What is the nicest thing you remember? From your old life, I mean. Before you came here."

Blue did not answer.

Jake turned, worried that the horse would not be there, but Blue plodded along behind him, Azrak still lying limp between his massive shoulders. Asking Gordon would be fruitless, and trying to remember things would probably just cause Ursus pain, and so Jake found himself alone, even in the company of his friends. But try as he might, he couldn't abide the silence for more than a few steps.

"I'll tell you my favorite memory," he said. "I remember ... well, I don't remember who it was exactly, but he was serving me breakfast in bed. Only it wasn't my bed. It was a lot bigger. There was somebody else there too, eating breakfast with me. I don't remember who it was. I think it was the sad woman, the one who was singing to me earlier." his voice trailed off. It hurt him to think about her.

"I do not know your sad woman," said Ursus. "No Givers passed this way."

Jake did not stop talking. He pulled all of his fragmented memories from his mind and gave life to them, making up the details that remained hidden. In his words his life before became idyllic, filled with laughter and joy and contentment. He talked about hunting deer in the woods, about paddling a canoe through the sleepy currents of the river behind his home, of days spent at school with his friends. They talked about bike rides and games of tag and about movies he'd seen, books he'd read. He told them about how he once backed his dad's truck out of the driveway when he accidentally put it in neutral, about how he and Sebastian went on a six-hour walk because they made a wrong turn, about riding out thunderstorms in stifling, moist heat beneath a thick blanket, about sipping hot cocoa on a Monday morning, watching the snow fall in drifts deep enough to keep the school bus at bay. And as he talked, he pressed forward, ignoring as best he could the numbness that had crept up past his knees.

"There was this one time," Jake said, but he could no longer remember. The other memories were gone too, as if by thinking about them he'd used them up, like logs on a fire, but even the ashes were hidden from him. He searched the recesses of his memory for anything; a song, a smell, a touch, but he could find nothing. Whatever energy had sustained him drained away, as if the dam that had held it in place had burst, and he was left empty again.

"There was this time," he said, hoping that something would emerge, but nothing did. All that he remembered began when Ursus pulled him from the river.

"Jake."

It was Ursus. His voice was deep and strong again.

Jake stopped, and Ursus padded up to his side.

"They are near."

Jake strained his ears, listening for the sound of Malbinocks, but there was only silence.

"Malbinocks? Where?" he whispered.

"Not Malbinocks. Dogs. Cats. Others. They are near."

Jake saw nothing but the thicket of bones and a few dim stars peeking through the gaps. He held his breath and listened.

Carried across the night air was the faint but distinct sound of a howl.

Chapter Thirty-Two

Guided by the distant howls, they passed through the Forest of Bones. The sound was terrible, unnatural, unlike anything Jake had ever heard. It was both deep and piercing, as if it came from the throat of a gigantic, wounded animal, larger even than Ursus. Sometimes the howls would stop, leaving Jake in suffocating silence.

The spaces between the bones grew larger as they plodded through. The bones themselves were also thinner; most were barely the width of his head, and many had fallen, as if blown down by a strong wind. The ground became spongy. Small, sickly patches of green moss appeared around the bases of some of the bones. It crept across the length of the ones that had fallen, slowly, inexorably devouring them.

There was something awful about the moss, creeping across the yellowed surface of the fallen bones, consuming, but giving nothing in return, wiping away the last traces of something that once breathed and perhaps had joy. Death was not black but pale, sickly green splashed across a field of faded yellow. Death was bones and dust and numbing cold. The finality of it frightened Jake, and his fear pushed him forward.

A dull, stinging pain replaced the numbness in his feet as if he were walking on needles or broken glass. It spread to the tips of his fingers as well, creeping slowly through to his palms. He checked his hands and feet but found nothing out of the ordinary. His skin had grown pale, almost translucent, but there were no cuts or scrapes to be found.

"There is something ahead," said Blue.

Jake searched the breaks in the forest. In the distance lay a jagged, dark mass that stretched across the horizon.

"It looks like mountains," Jake said.

"It looks like danger," said Blue.

"We could both be right."

"The dogs are there," said Ursus. "Dogs. Cats. Others."

A loud groan broke the silence, calling them.

"Guess that's where we're going." Jake rubbed his feet to soothe the pain.

A short while later, they left the last of the bones behind them. Ahead lay a plain, carpeted with the same foul, green moss that covered the fallen bones. The lethargy that had gripped Jake faded, and as it receded, pain took its place, growing more intense as they made their way across the plain. It wasn't enough to prevent him from moving, but it invaded his mind, nagging him, until he could think of little else but getting rid of it. Jake tried to think of something else but even his memories of the Howl and of his trek across the grassland felt strange and distant as if they had happened to someone else.

It wasn't long before the cool, numbing sleep in the white dust became a pleasant memory, and deep in the recesses of his mind, Jake began to entertain the notion of returning there, letting the dust cool the terrible burning in his hands and feet. Perhaps he would hear the sad woman singing to him, and he could follow her into the cold—

"Jake."

He came to his senses. Ursus was there, his brown eyes boring into Jake's.

"That is not the way."

Jake blinked and shook his head. The steady throb in his hands and feet had not subsided. He looked past Ursus. Instead of the dark ridge, distant bony spires dotted the horizon.

It would have been easy if he were alone. It would only be a short walk, and then he could go back to sleep. But if he kept walking, Ursus and Blue would follow him, and Azrak, still asleep on the horse's back, would have no choice. Gordon would come as well, confused, trusting, and the five of them would sleep until their bodies were covered in the white dust and lost forever.

If he were alone, it would be easy.

"Jake."

He turned around. There was the dark ridge, closer and taller, the strange howls louder and clearer.

Jake took one tentative step and then another. His feet left deep, wet impressions in the moss, and an oily liquid flowed from the ground and collected between his toes. Wherever it touched, it burned. The dark ridge rose from the plain far faster than it should have, growing taller and more massive as they moved toward it.

Then the darkness lifted, as if someone had pulled a cover away, and Jake saw what lay in front of him. It was not a ridge but a wall.

A wall made of buildings.

It looked like an angry giant had scooped up all the buildings in the world and piled them three or four high in a rough line across the bog. Some of them were huge; barns large enough to house twenty horses, high school gymnasiums, courthouses. Wedged in among the barns and the box stores were houses, churches, offices, car showrooms, garages, sheds, warehouses, and bus stations, all held together by nothing but their weight. They seemed to have been placed at random, with no thought as to which side should be up. Some were completely upside down, while others rested on their sides. Some were at an angle, wedged tightly against the surrounding structures.

Jake approached the wall and ran his hand along the wood siding. Flakes of faded red paint disintegrated against his fingers, but the wood itself was solid. Prying off boards would be impossible; he couldn't get so much as a fingernail between them.

The wall cut the bog in both directions, and Jake could not see where it ended. He tried to visualize, to comprehend the enormity of it, but it was too much. The sight of it repulsed him. It lay like a sore on the land, a terrible, spreading rash. Jake sank down at the base of the wall and peered into the sky. The buildings, stacked one on top of the other like gigantic bricks, stretched upward, curving away from him until the top was lost from view.

He thought of the Malbinocks, spindly, skeletal things, shambling across the bog. It must have taken them hundreds, even thousands of years to build something as massive as this. What could the five of them do against creatures who could build buildings and then stack them on top of each other? There must be millions of them here, waiting until the darkness to build and feed.

What could the five of them possibly do?

He felt his friends' eyes on him. Though they said nothing, Ursus and the others stood off to the side, waiting for Jake to tell them what they would do next. A boy, a horse, two dogs, and a rat, each one exhausted. When night came, the Malbinocks would pour out of their hidden tunnels and swarm over them, dragging them to whatever terrible fate awaited them on the other side of the monstrous wall.

The groaning began again, loud enough that Jake could feel the vibration through the wood. It startled Blue and Gordon, who both took a few steps backward. Only Ursus seemed unmoved. Then the groaning stopped abruptly, and in the silence came a muffled crash, followed by another, far in the distance.

"That sound," Jake said, "It isn't the dogs and cats. It's the wall."

"They are near," said Ursus.

None of his friends offered any other suggestions. They waited a few feet behind him, trusting him to find a way. He felt them watching, their expectations settling on him like a wet jacket. *The Giver knows all,* Ursus would say. *I will go with you.*

But there was nowhere to go. The wall loomed over them and split the plain, and Jake could see no way to get over it or around it. The only way, it seemed, was to go through. But that meant doubling back until they found the entrance to a tunnel. Ursus and Blue would have to stay behind because there wasn't enough room in the tunnels for them. Jake felt trapped, as surely as if he were on the other side of the wall. The yellowed spires of the Bone Forest loomed in the distance like prison bars, marking the limits of his vast cage.

"When night comes, it will not be safe," said Blue.

"I know. I'll figure something out."

Jake stared past Blue and Azrak, back across the vast expanse of powdered bone toward the warrens, and he thought about the sad woman. He couldn't help her, or Sebastian, or any of the other animals that lay trapped behind the wall of buildings.

"They will come for us," said Blue. "The Malbinocks will come."

"They have not passed this way. But they are near," said Ursus.

Gordon snuffled along the edge of the bog, where it met the wooden siding.

"Gordon, what are you looking for? There's nothing there," said Jake.

The wall groaned again; this time close enough to shake the bog beneath their feet. The shock startled even Ursus, and all of them retreated. The sudden movement jostled Azrak, sending him dangerously close to sliding off Blue's back. The foul bog water soaked through Jake's pants and settled, cold and oily against his skin.

Azrak stirred.

"Azrak?"

Carefully, Jake took Azrak off Blue's back and settled him into his lap. The rat was still fast asleep.

"He moved," Jake said. "I felt him move."

The others gathered around. At first, Azrak remained quiet, and only the slight rise and fall of his chest assured them he was still alive. Then his body twitched, and his eyes fluttered open.

Jake's relief was tempered with guilt.

"Take it slow, Azrak. You've been asleep for a while." He ran his fingertips across Azrak's back. Jake could feel the bones through the rat's coarse hair.

"Feet hurt. Tail hurts. We come to Badwatcher place? Where are others? Azrak saw others. Where are warren friends?"

Jake thought for a second. "They were never there, Azrak. It was the Bone Forest. It did the same thing to us. We all fell asleep too, except for Gordon. He saved us."

"No friends?" Azrak inspected his tail and his front paws.

"They're not here. You dreamed them."

"Tail hurts. Hurt not a dream."

"No. My hands and feet hurt too." Jake rubbed his hands together.

Azrak climbed out of Jake's lap. His first steps were tentative, wobbly.

"Be careful."

Azrak looked at the wall. "Badwatcher place. We go in now. Find others."

"There's no way in," Jake said.

"Always way in. You look. You see."

"I looked," Jake said. "There isn't."

"Jake not look," said Azrak. "Jake looks, he finds way in. Always way in."

"I did so!"

The wall groaned as if in pain, and another tremor shook the ground.

When the shaking stopped, Azrak slogged through the sodden, filthy moss toward the wall.

"You should take it easy," said Jake, but Azrak did not slow down.

"Azrak, it's dangerous!"

"It is not safe here," said Blue.

"See? Blue agrees with me."

But the rat moved on, undeterred. By the time he reached the wall he seemed almost normal again, skittering against the wooden siding, testing, probing for an opening. Gordon joined him, snuffling along the seam where the building and the bog met. Neither appeared to be having any success.

"I told you. There's no—hey, wait."

The wall had changed. Where there was only siding before, a door had appeared. Oily water dripped from the lintel and ran down the outside of the doorframe. The oily stain extended past the door and down the length of the wall, stopping at a half-submerged brick building a few yards away.

Jake ran his finger across the newly exposed siding, tracing a white streak through the oily water. It burned his skin, and he wiped it on the front of his jeans. He tried the door, but it was jammed shut. Even a hard kick from Blue's hind legs couldn't dislodge it.

"I don't think the Malbinocks built this," Jake said. The thought brought him a measure of comfort. "I think it just comes up from underneath. I bet if we look, we could find a broken window or something."

Jake led the way, energized by his discovery, but apprehension grew with each locked door they found. Gordon kept his nose in the turf until his little snout was slick and shiny, covered with the oily bog water. Jake tried to urge the little dog along, but Gordon would have none of it, searching every inch before moving ahead. Finally, he stopped and began digging furiously into the turf until only a pair of stubby legs protruded just beyond the edge of it, covered in bits of rancid moss.

"Gordon?" Jake reached out and patted the little dog's back flank. Gordon turned around, glanced at Jake, and then returned to his work.

Jake could barely recognize him. The little dog's fur was saturated with bog water and plastered against his body, revealing a thin, almost emaciated frame.

"Gordon—"

Gordon scratched twice and then sat on his haunches.

Jake hunkered down and peered into the newly dug hole. Released from the turf, the fetid aroma forced its way into Jake's nose and lay stinging on his tongue. Eyes watering from the foulness of it, he explored the inside of the hole with his arm. It was narrow, barely large enough to admit him, but he would fit.

"I go. You stay," said Azrak. "Rathole not for Goodwatcher."

Jake stopped him with a gentle hand on his back.

"No, Azrak. You're not strong enough."

"Azrak strong. Azrak brave."

"Can you turn a doorknob?"

Azrak hung his head.

Gordon dropped to his belly and wriggled toward the hole as well, but Jake stopped him.

"No, Gordon. This has to be me."

Jake had never been more afraid. He turned to his friends.

"If there's a way in, I'll get in there and open the door. We'll probably be safer inside there than we will out here. Once we get inside, we can camp out for the night. Then tomorrow, we can start looking for dogs and cats." He tried to keep his voice from shaking.

"I will stay here," Ursus said.

"If this doesn't work, go back to the forest and find Samuel."

"I will stay here."

Jake looked at his friends, one by one. They watched him expectantly. He didn't share their confidence. The hole, black and fetid, lay like a hungry mouth in the bog. He wished more than anything that he could send someone else but his friends were depending on him, and the thought of letting them down was the only thing worse than the filth that awaited him in the hole.

It didn't seem right to say goodbye.

"Guess I better go."

Jake dropped to his belly and squirmed into the hole. The stench was so thick, it had its own texture, gritty and foul, as if every piece of moldy cheese lingering beneath old refrigerators and every bit of spoiled meat hiding behind old stoves had been swept up and dumped in his path. He could feel it working his way underneath his fingernails and into the crevasses of his ears. He crawled, elbow over elbow, through the muck, wishing with each pull that he could turn around and go back, back to the fragrant, peaceful woods and sit by the waterfall painted with silver starlight, back to the lake and the sound of water lapping gently against the pebbled shore. But he thought of Gordon's small, frail body and matted fur. He thought of Ursus and Blue exposed against the vastness of the wall. He thought of Azrak, who would have gone in his place if Jake had allowed it. He thought of Sebastian, and Cy, and Sarafina, and Jake could not leave them.

Jake's elbows sank into the putrid mash, slick, greasy clothes glued to his skin. The world closed in around him, pinning down his arms, and so he became a worm, undulating, pressing inch by inch through the narrow passage. Gradually, it pressed closer and closer until he could barely move or breathe.

In the distance, he saw light.

He tried to call out, but he couldn't speak. Conscious thought abandoned him. He was left only with a desire to be free of the darkness and the stench, a hunger to reach the gray light that hovered just past his reach.

The hole closed tighter around him, engulfing him until the light was nothing more than the cold, distant twinkle of a star. With one last effort, he wrestled his arm free and stretched out his fingers. They struck something solid and rough. Greedily, his hand closed around it. He pulled, struggling against the filth and the darkness and his own paralyzing fear.

The darkness yielded. He emerged from the hole through a space between wooden boards just wide enough for his shoulders. The air smelled of cigarettes and old food, though the fetid, oily scent of the bog water lingered in his nostrils. Dust motes swirled in rays of pale light that leaked through a window covered almost to the top with black mud. Thick beams rose from the wooden floor, disappearing into the shadows. Cardboard boxes lay in haphazard piles, some of which brushed against the ceiling.

The floor was solid and cold, and the feel of the wood against his skin reassured him. For a few seconds, he lay on his belly and breathed in the stale air.

I'm in, he told himself. I'm in.

From below him, leaking through the gaps in the floorboards, came the unmistakable sound of voices.

Chapter Thirty-Three

Pungent, dry dust billowed up and hung thick in the still air. For a second, Jake froze. He waited for the sound of footsteps, but there were none. The voices continued unabated. They spoke in sharp, clipped tones as if they were angry, but the words themselves were muffled by the floorboards. Jake felt his way through the labyrinth of cardboard and plastic wrap, searching for a way out of the room.

The door was just around the pile of boxes, at the bottom of a short flight of stairs. Long ago, it had been painted white, but the paint had faded to a pale yellow.

He listened carefully to the voices. Ursus and the other animals spoke directly into Jake's mind, but this was different. It was real sound, welling up through the gap underneath the door, enticing him and repulsing him at the same time. He drank it in, quenching a terrible thirst he hadn't realized was there, and for a time, he stood on the first step, his eyes closed, listening. It didn't matter that he couldn't make out a single syllable or that the voice carried with it a sharp, vindictive bite. The voices meant that he wasn't alone in the vastness, that someone else shared his confusion and anger and joy.

He waited, hoping that the anger would relent, and there would be laughter or sadness in the voices. Before he made himself known, he'd make sure their anger wasn't directed at him.

But what if it was?

He needed a weapon.

Jake searched through the spilled boxes, looking for something he could use to defend himself if the need arose. Whoever had packed the boxes had done it thoughtlessly; old clothes, books, dinnerware, bicycle parts, plastic gloves, picture frames, shoes, and other things Jake didn't recognize flowed from the boxes and spread across the bare floor. Beneath him, the angry tirade droned on.

Head down, he combed through the detritus, searching more with his fingers than with his eyes. The angry voices below continued their tirade. Their anger fueled Jake's desperation. He tossed objects to his left and right as if he were looking for some lost treasure buried deep in a closet. With each moment, his apprehension grew. An old dress shoe shot across the room and landed hard against a pile of boxes. A glass pot lid suffered a similar fate.

He didn't know exactly what he was looking for, and that added to his frustration. The words came with difficulty; something blunt, solid, for pounding. A hammer. A sharp thing, for cutting. Scissors. The words sounded foreign, alien, as if he was hearing them for the first time. Not scissors. Something else. A knife.

He rifled through stacks of paper, old clothes, pliant, soft, crushable things, and still the voices downstairs droned on. Jake wondered how they could even breathe. He redoubled his efforts, shoving aside bits and pieces until his shoulder thumped against the bottom box in a tall stack, sending a mountain of cardboard crashing on top of him. Most of the boxes missed their mark, falling just past his right arm, but one landed squarely against his back, shoving him into the floor and knocking the breath from his body. Jake lay stunned, the box still half on top of him, and he expected the sound of footsteps rushing up the stairs. But no one came, and the tirade continued.

When he was certain no one was coming, he braced himself and pushed up to his knees. A heavy box teetered precariously on his back, dumping off as he pushed up. A new pile of fresh detritus added to the existing layer.

In the new pile, Jake's hand brushed against something cold and smooth. A flicker of recognition passed through his mind. He reached for it, and his fingers closed around a curved piece of polished wood. Each finger nestled in its own separate curve as if it had been made to rest there. Attached to the wood was a cylinder of cool, smooth metal. The word burst into Jake's mind.

A gun.

Jake could not remember what it did, but it felt heavy and solid. His index finger slid easily against a curved piece of metal that jutted out from the underside of the cylinder. A dim memory kept him from squeezing too hard. Something bad would happen. He turned it over and over in his hand, and the weight of it, the cool, smooth wood against his palm, made him feel strong, as if just holding it was enough to keep anyone from hurting him.

He took a deep breath and scrambled over the pile of boxes toward the door. The boxes hadn't fallen down the short flight of stairs, and the landing was clear of debris. The knob turned easily, without so much as a squeak, revealing another set of stairs, and as the door opened, the voices tumbled in like water from an overflowing cup.

"Shut up! I'm tired of hearing you every night!"

"You're doing that on purpose!"

"I'll teach you. Come here!"

Jake held the gun out in front of him as he descended the stairs. With each step downward, the light from the attic window faded. The darkness felt like a hungry animal, swallowing him by degrees, driving him closer to its belly. The darkness was more than the absence of light. It was something real, solid, sinister, pushing into his eyes and sinking into his lungs as he breathed, and all the while, the murmuring voices drifted upward from out of the gloom; angry, sharp, and unrelenting.

"You need a lesson in manners, boy."

"Oh, you want to play games? You want to play games? Ok. We'll play."

Jake continued down the stairs, though every

muscle in his body and every thought in his mind screamed for him to go in the opposite direction. Step by creaky step, as the voices got louder and the light failed, Jake kept moving. There was no other choice; eventually the darkness that surrounded him would spill out of its prison and find him, wherever he was. Facing it, at least he knew it was coming.

The voices grew louder but less distinct, as if more people had arrived. Everyone talked at once, drowning each other out, obscuring individual words, until only the emotions behind them were recognizable. Anger dominated them, but there was also disgust, and something worse, a sickly-sweet false kindness.

"Hello." Jake's voice was weak, and the word barely squeaked free of his throat. "Are you trapped here? I have a way out."

The murmuring continued, unabated.

"My name is Jake. What is this place?"

"There you are!"

The voice sounded so close that Jake expected to feel a warm breath in his ear. He jumped sideways, lost his footing, and tumbled off the stair. His back glanced off a wall, and he fell, shoulder first, tumbling down the next step. He came down hard on his left arm, and pain shot up into his shoulder. He tumbled again, landing on his back, sprawled full-length, and lay still in complete darkness. His left arm throbbed in time with his heartbeat. He closed his fingers around the gun's grip.

"You stupid little pest. I knew I'd find you here!"

It was a woman's voice, gravelly and shrill, as if

she were accustomed to yelling. As soon as it came, it disappeared, lost in the cacophony of other voices.

"But I came in through a hole. Were you watching? What are you doing down here?" Jake tried to keep his voice steady. He didn't want to anger the woman further.

"I'm going to teach you, you ignorant little thief. You're going to learn. Even if I have to beat you to death to make it stick."

Jake sat up and scooted backward. It was the woman again, her voice booming down from high above him. Jake instinctively drew his knees toward his chest, forgetting all about the gun still clutched in his right hand.

"I didn't steal anything," he croaked.

"Oh, now you're just doing that to spite me. Well, guess what? It worked. Come here. Come here now!" The voice was no longer overhead but somewhere off to his right, and it wasn't the woman. It was the voice of a younger man, angry, spoken through clenched teeth.

"Doing what? I don't even know who you are!" He cast about again for the stairs but found nothing. The floor under his fingers felt like rough, unfinished wood.

"You like that? You like that smell? Come on. Get a little more. Get a good whiff of that in your nose. Maybe you'll learn."

Jake took a deep breath through his nose. The air was cool and dry. It smelled of dust, mingled with a faint scent of oil and rubber.

"Check this out."

The voice was that of a teenage boy, low and conspiratorial.

"Check what out? Why are you acting like this?" Jake's left arm throbbed, and he hugged it against his chest.

"Put it there. Right there, right behind him. Watch when he turns around."

Jake's back was already against something solid, but the voice made him turn around nonetheless. He brushed the back of his hand against the object he'd been leaning against. It was smooth and flat, slightly curved inward where he'd leaned against it, creased where the inward curve began. It was a cardboard box, completely unremarkable as far as he could tell, like the ones he'd encountered upstairs.

"It's just a box. Are you even talking to me?"

Cruel laughter burst from the roiling chaos. Pleasure without joy, the laughter of those who enjoy watching the misery they cause. But Jake wasn't any more miserable than he'd been a minute earlier, and the laughter, raucous as it was, felt misplaced. It melted back into the whirling storm, mingling with the thousand other voices that spoke at once, and their words blended into a vile, discordant mockery of the star-song, and Jake tried not to listen. He was afraid he might hear his own voice, already joined in.

Jake understood.

He was by himself but not alone. Though the speakers weren't there with him, they were real nonetheless, their words spoken in anger, or frustration, or sadistic pleasure, only to be forgotten an hour later. Forgotten, but not gone. Sent away.

Stored.

Changed.

All around him, the Makers droned on, their everyday cruelty swirling like a hurricane around him, tiny, thoughtless abuse played out thousands of times, draining away in foul rivulets until it ended up in the cold, dusty darkness beneath the wall. Carelessness, greed; heedless, stupid waste, it all ended up here, a mountain of it, a constant pressure forcing itself ever upward until it erupted out of the ground and formed the wall.

And somewhere, sometime, Jake's voice had echoed against dusty cardboard boxes and forced the wall a little higher. Of that, he had no doubt. He was as sure of that as he was about the number of fingers on his hands and the toes on his feet, and with that knowledge came a profound remorse, made worse by the finality of it. It was done, his voice already a part of the walls and the floor, and he could do nothing about it.

Something moved.

It was no voice, but a scrape; heavy, solid, and nearby. That scrape was followed by another, and the smell of oil, rubber, and metal filled the room.

Jake rolled over to his hand and knees, searching in spite of the pain for the stairway. The gun clanked against the floor like a hoof, heavy and reassuring. He crawled around in circles, searching, but the stairway was nowhere to be found. Instead of a solid wall, he found another cardboard box, followed by another. Each turn brought more obstacles, a labyrinth with walls that seemed to shift as he navigated past them.

Between the thumps of the gun and the gentle brush of his jeans against the wood came the awful groan of metal grinding against metal, the scrape and crack of wire tightening around pieces of timber and plastic. The sounds of labor were all around him, Malbinocks being born, taking their first clumsy, tentative steps, the din an agony to Jake's ears.

One by one, he felt them reach out, the snake-tongue flicker of their minds searching, hungry.

They found him.

Maker!

Maker!

Maker!

"No!"

Jake scrambled backward until a wall of cardboard stopped him. He felt the column buckle and collapse on top of him, showering him with refuse and half-filled boxes. His retreat accomplished nothing; he could feel the infant Malbinocks in his mind, seeking him like a newborn calf seeks its mother. He could feel their need; their hunger burned hot and immediate, relentlessly driving them.

The collapse of the boxes left Jake hopelessly lost. He struggled over the mound of refuse, sliding across stacks of paper and banging his knees into pieces of plastic and glass, a flood of broken and worthless things that wiped away any mental map he had created.

The Malbinocks clamored through the maze as well, colliding with boxes and with each other, struggling to be the first to reach him, to taste firsthand his misery and pain. Closer and closer they came, as

Jake retreated. Finally, he collided with something solid and could go no further.

A wall.

With a cry of relief, he began to feel his way along it, certain it would lead him to the stairway. Something tightened against his ankle. A terrible, searing pain traveled like liquid fire up his calf and past his knees.

"Let me go!"

But the Malbinock did not obey. It drank deeply, squeezing his ankle like a sponge, and lapping up the agony.

Jake tried to drag himself away, and he heard the hoof-thump of the gun against the floor. The polished wooden grip felt smooth against his palm. He raised it and pulled the trigger.

He heard no sharp crack and felt no recoil, nor did he smell the pungent scent of smokeless powder. The only sound was a slight whoosh. For an instant, his heart sank, and a low, guttural moan escaped from his lips. The only thing the gun had produced was a small, blue cone of light that emanated from the barrel.

He smelled smoke. The grip on his leg got tighter.

A burst of heat and light washed over his face as orange flames raced up the side of a nearby box. The flames washed the room in orange light, sending Malbinocks skittering for the shadows. Jake felt the grip on his leg loosen as the Malbinock tried to disengage, but it was too late; the wooden spindles that made up its left arm caught fire, spreading into its torso.

Free of its grip, Jake made his escape, retreating across the pile of refuse. The fire spread across the boxes, and a thick curtain of smoke took shape near the ceiling, descending downward like a storm cloud. The Malbinock, now engulfed in flame, flailed around; a hideous, misshapen man wreathed in a shifting, bright orange skin. It staggered around, dying, touching off smaller fires as it went.

The fire grew hotter and higher, its light quickly masked in the thick, black smoke that dropped like a curtain from the ceiling. The stairwell was nowhere in sight.

Panic seized Jake, and he crawled away from the fire, knocking over boxes and struggling through their contents, while the fire burned hotter and the smoke dropped down so low, he had to crawl in his belly to see the path ahead of him.

The room shuddered. Jake felt the jolt through his body, short, sharp, like a giant's footstep. Smoke stung his eyes, and the roar of the fire washed over the muttering voices and drowned them.

Jake crawled with his right arm and his legs, tucking his left against his chest. The smoke lay around him like a hot blanket, smothering him. He searched the room once more through eyes blinded by tears, as the air around him began to sting with heat.

Jake saw a light to his left. He blinked twice to clear his eyes, and it was still there, a cool, gray rectangle, spilling over the lowest step in the stairwell, only a few feet away. Jake staggered to his feet and ran through the smoke, falling headlong against the staircase.

Up the stairs he crawled, toward the light, terrified the flames would catch him before he reached the attic, ignoring the searing pain, until the attic door emerged half-open from the gloom, spilling light and hope across the top of the staircase. He dove through, slamming the door behind him. The window itself was visible through the thin pall of gray smoke that hung in the air. Where there had once been only a crack, a two-foot gap now lay between the top of the window and the dank moss that marked the ground level. The rest of the window was still obscured by layers of black, spongy mud.

Smoke poured beneath the attic door and pooled in great, roiling clouds against the inside of the vaulted roof. Jake's mind raced. The window was the only way out, and it was impossible to open.

"Ursus! Blue! I'm down here!" Jake pounded against the window with his palm. There was no answer from outside. The smoke thickened and lowered, inching toward him.

He turned the gun around and struck the window as hard as he could. It cracked but didn't break. He struck it again and again. The crack lengthened, but the window held. Now the smoke was just above the top of the windowsill, the air noticeably warmer.

In the corner of the window, a small, white face appeared.

"Azrak! I'm down here! Help me!"

Azrak disappeared, and Jake wasn't sure if the rat had even seen him. He pounded on the window with all his might, and the cracks spread out like a spiderweb. The smoke dropped lower, until only a thin, horizontal sliver of light remained.

"Ursus! Blue!"

Then the sliver across the window winked out, all at once, as if someone had thrown a switch, and Jake was once again plunged into darkness. He sank to his knees, crying out to his friends until fear, and fatigue, and hopelessness silenced him.

Something struck the window with an impact heavy enough for Jake to feel through his knees. With a sharp crack of splintering wood and glass, the window disintegrated, buried under an avalanche of mud.

Jake never saw it coming.

The mud felt like a living thing, snatching the gun from his hand and dragging him across the attic floor. He came to a stop among a pile of boxes, his legs buried in heavy, thick sludge. Some of the smoke cleared, and the room was bright enough for Jake to see. The mudslide left a deep cavity where the window had been, wide enough to pass through, the slope gentle enough to easily climb. But climbing was the least of his worries; the mud covered him to the bottom of his ribcage, pinning him to the floor.

He dug frantically into the mud throwing gobs of it sideways to splatter against the boxes. His left arm was useless, and exhaustion sapped what little strength remained in his right. His digging slowed, and his fear grew. He imagined the fire climbing the stairwell, orange flames wreathed in black smoke coming for him. But the muscles in his arm burned and refused to obey when he tried to dig faster.

Something blotted out the light from the window, and then Ursus was above him. Two swipes of his massive paws were enough to free Jake's legs.

"Fire is near," Ursus said. Jake had never heard such urgency in the dog's voice. He followed Ursus to the window, but just as he was about to clamber up the muddy slope, he caught a glint of metal to the side and remembered the gun. He slogged through the mud and found it, lying against a heap of old magazines.

"Jake! Fire!"

Jake snatched up the gun. The weight of it in his hand gave him courage, despite the burning fatigue in his right arm and the throbbing pain in his left. He stumbled over boxes and up the muddy slope. A blast of cool air hit him as he emerged from the shattered window into the daylight. Fetid ooze coated his clothes. He crawled a short distance from the building and collapsed into the moss.

Chapter Thirty-Four

Jake lay still, his eyes closed. Despite the smell, the cool dampness of the moss was welcome after the heat, smoke and dust inside the wall. He opened his eyes. Ursus and the others stood a short distance away, watching him. Above their heads, smoke trailed into the sky. It poured from the open window and leaked from invisible gaps in the siding, drifting upward until it converged in a billowing, black column high above their heads.

Now that he was free of it, the smoke gave him a deep satisfaction. It was the first useful thing he'd done since he arrived on the riverbank. It felt good to finally hit them back. To him, the smoke was an accomplishment, and he smiled as he watched it drift into the gray sky and disappear.

Tongues of flame licked the outside of the window, and white steam mingled with the smoke as the fire baked off nearby moisture.

"This way no good now," said Azrak. He pushed up

next to Jake's leg, and Jake laid a gentle hand on the rat's back.

"We can't go back in there," Jake said.

"Too much fire. Find new place. New way in."

"No. I mean, we can't go back in there at all."

Jake stood up and pointed at the place where the wall emerged from the turf. "Down there. That's where the Badwatchers are born."

He told them about the voices, about the senseless cruelty that echoed in the darkness, the chorus of petty evil that spawned the Malbinocks, but he doubted they understood. It was like trying to describe the desert to a fish.

"Dogs and cats are near," said Ursus. "Their scent is strong."

"Yes," said Azrak, "Always a way in. We look. We find. A better way. Easier way." The rat seemed smaller against the roiling column of smoke. It boiled out of the windows of the upper floors, obscuring the wall in a gray curtain.

Jake thought of the Malbinocks burning in the oily blackness below ground. He savored their pain, and it was even sweeter knowing that he was the one who had caused it. He'd only killed a few of them, newborns at that. He rubbed his ankle and smiled. If it felt that good to kill a few of them, how much better would it feel to kill them all?

"I have another idea," Jake said. He held up the gun.

"Don't worry. It's not a real gun. It just makes fire. Watch."

Jake pulled the trigger, and a blue flame burst
from the muzzle, hovering at the end. All the animals
took a step back, except Gordon, who made a full
retreat and hid himself behind Ursus.

"We're not going to find a way in. We're going to
make a way in. And we'll kill every last one of them
while we do it." He looked at the flame, dancing on the
barrel, inches away from his closed fist. Azrak slinked
away, joining Gordon.

Jake watched the flame, made brighter against
the backdrop of black smoke. The flame was power.
With it, he could destroy anything.

He was a Maker.

He could make fire, make buildings disappear
in smoke, make his enemies burn. Now they would
feel afraid, crouching in their dark tunnels, and the
thought of them cowering filled Jake with savage joy.

He moved with purpose across the short distance
that separated him from the wall of buildings, towards
a section of the wall untouched by the smoke. He would
light that section, then another, all the way down the
line until the entire wall was alive with fire. He could
see it in his mind, the vast, raging wall of flame sending
a curtain of black smoke to blot out the sky. It would
burn for days, weeks perhaps, and when it was nothing
but ash, he would root out what was left of them in
their tunnels and burn them too.

"This is not the way." Blue trotted across the bog,
insinuating himself between Jake and the wall. "There
is danger in fire."

"Dangerous for them," Jake said. He tried to walk
around Blue, but the horse moved with him.

"Fire will not take a Rider. It runs where it wishes to go."

"Why burn?" Azrak said. "We come to bring home dogs. Bring home cats. Bring home guinea, mouse, rat and rabbit. Why burn?"

"Guys, look around." He pointed at the vast bog, and the Bone Forest beyond. "Nothing else is going to burn. We set the whole wall on fire and kill them all at once. No more disappearances. We can all live happy. Don't you want those things gone? What about you, Ursus? Don't you hate them? If I kill them all, everyone will be free."

"You are the Giver," said Ursus. "If you wish to burn, burn. Givers know what to do."

"See? Ursus agrees with me," Jake said. Once more, he tried to get around Blue, and once again, the horse stopped him.

"Blue, step out of the way."

"Jake—"

"I said get out of my way!"

Blue hesitated and took a step back.

"Good," said Jake.

The soggy ground beneath Jake's feet grew unnaturally warm. A groan, almost too low to hear, escaped from the column of smoke, as if some gigantic beast was trying to claw its way out.

The ground shook. Blue backed away, leaving the way open for Jake to approach the wall.

"Jake, it is not safe here."

Jake hesitated. The lighter remained in his hand, but the flame had gone out. He pulled the trigger again and the flame reappeared. The sight of the flame gave him courage again, and he took another step toward the wall. Another deep groan rent the air, followed by an ear-splitting crack. Steam rose in fetid tendrils around Jake's feet.

"Jake! It is not safe!"

The shaking grew worse, and Jake had to fight for balance.

"What did I do?" Jake whispered.

Another sharp crack sent them all into a retreat. The rumbling under their feet intensified, rattling windows along the wall. A low, grating sound added to the din, and the rooftop dropped into the smoke and vanished. A sharp tremor in the bog threw Jake into the moss. From the ground, he watched, afraid that he'd awakened something beneath the wall, and any second it would rise out of the fire and drag him into whatever pit it had crawled out of. He curled into a ball and covered his head with his arms.

A tremendous boom blew the smoke outward, and with it came shards of wood and glass tumbling end over end through the air. All around him he heard the thud of shattered wood impacting the bog.

The rumbling stopped, and an unnatural quiet settled over the landscape. Jake uncurled his body and propped himself up on his knees. The column of smoke dissipated gradually until only a few wisps remained. Jake gaped.

The section of the wall he'd crawled under was completely gone. Jake looked around for the others. None seemed to be injured. Gordon had dug into the moss so that only his head was showing, and Azrak had tucked himself in the hollow between Ursus' foreleg and chest. Blue stood to Ursus' right, his hooves stamping nervously into the turf.

"Where did it go?" Jake stared at the gap, astonished. Where several houses had stood, stacked one on top of the other, there was nothing but a partially flattened roof. What little debris there was lay scattered in a wide arc around the newly formed gap in the wall. Wisps of smoke and steam trailed upward from the edges. It merged into a haze that hovered above the flattened roof like a raincloud.

Ursus approached the roof and sniffed the air.

"There is still fire."

Jake joined Ursus and put a hand on the tar shingles. They felt cool to the touch. The haze carried the stink of the bog into the air and obscured the view of what lay beyond.

"Doesn't feel hot to me."

"There is still fire."

"Good. I hope they all burn."

Jake's fear receded. He looked again at the collapsed roof, sloping gently upward to an apex near the middle of the gap. Burn it all, he thought, one section at a time. The trick was burning them from within. He climbed up on the shingles and sidled along the adjoining wall. The shingles felt like sandpaper against his bare feet. He found what he was looking for only a few steps ahead.

A piece of the wall had been torn away, exposing the inside. Jake caught a glimpse of cardboard boxes, stacked like the buildings in the wall, their corners crumpled under the weight.

"See?" Jake said, pointing to the opening. "There's always a way in."

He stepped up to the opening, his heart filled with a dark, vengeful glee. He held the gun high, at ear level, as if he were marking off paces for a duel. He pulled the trigger, enjoying the metallic click and the whoosh of the flame that leapt from the barrel and danced on its edge.

Burn it all, he thought, from the inside out. Every box, every piece of junk, every voice. Especially mine.

He crouched down and peered through the gash in the wall. The light, thin and weak in the haze, penetrated only a few feet into the room. Beyond that were shadows dark enough to hide his enemies. He had to be careful. The boxes right inside the door would do for a start.

He reached out with the gun, its barrel still alive with blue flame, and aimed it toward the boxes just inside the wall. Before the flame touched the box, a scuffling noise behind him made Jake pull back. He quenched the flame and turned around.

"Ursus, go on back. It's going to get dangerous, and I don't want you to get caught—"

Out of the haze emerged a dog. It crawled on its belly, dragging itself across the rooftop. Jake recoiled in horror. It was not so much a dog as the skeleton of one, with its skin still stretched across the bones. It might have been a Great Dane once, with a glossy white coat, dappled with spots of black across its back and legs. Now, it was a mottled gray. Its eyes, hollow and glassy, stared beyond Jake, into some dream or memory. Other than the scrape of its toenails on the shingles, it made no sound.

The gun slipped through Jake's fingers and landed with a thud against the roof.

He approached the dog slowly, bent at the waist, his palms out in front to give the dog something to smell. It was an effort to keep his eyes open, to not turn away. The dog made no move to attack or escape. It lay against the shingles, staring into the haze. When Jake reached its side, he crouched down and laid his hand against its head, between the sagging flaps of skin that had once been its ears. Its head was cold, and its coat barely separated Jake's hand from the dog's skull.

"Hello," Jake whispered. He tried to say more, but the words bunched up in his throat, and all he could manage to say was, "I'm here."

He ran his hand down the dog's neck, his fingers traveling over the vertebrae, feeling each bump. Shame and sadness overcame him. He could think of nothing to say, no words of comfort or hope that would do anything to ease the dog's suffering. He stroked its emaciated back, trying not to think of his own voice, echoing in the darkness somewhere beneath them.

Thump, thump, thump.

The sound startled Jake. At first, he thought it was coming from underneath the roof, a half-burned Malbinock looking for a way out. He looked behind him and found that wasn't the case at all.

It was the Great Dane's tail, wagging, skin and bones tapping lightly against the shingles.

Any desire for revenge Jake had been harboring vanished. His thoughts tumbled over each other like rocks in a landslide. Still time, still light ... where are the rest ... get him out, get him out, there are others—

Get them out.

"Stay here," he said, but it was hardly necessary. Aside from its tail, the dog made no attempt to move. Jake half ran, half slid down the roof, deeper into the haze. Indistinct shapes appeared, growing clearer as he got closer. Finally, the haze cleared, and Jake could see what lay ahead.

Beyond the collapsed roof stretched a vast, broken wasteland. Piles of smashed wood, crumbled plaster, drywall, copper pipes, and electrical wiring mingled with pieces of shattered furniture, old clothes, and toys, and mattresses, stretching down a long slope until it vanished into the distance. The wall rose like a dam to Jake's left and right, leaning inward. Far off to his left, a house teetered and fell, smashing into a gigantic pile of crushed beams and siding.

"They are here," said Ursus.

Jake didn't hear Ursus approach, but he was grateful for his presence. He laid his hand against the dog's shoulder. Solid and warm, a relief after the Great Dane.

"I don't see anything," he said. He swept the horizon again, searching for movement. The wasteland was still and silent.

"They are here. Many dogs. Cats. Others."

Jake cupped his hands to his mouth. "You're free! Here's a way out!" He pointed behind him, toward the Forest of Bones.

"You can come out now!"

Clouds gathered overhead. A cold breeze flowed through the gap, whistling through the tangle of wood and wire. A short distance into the morass, a piece of cloth flapped like a flag against a sheet of metal.

Jake stood on the edge of the roof, unwilling to go beyond it. It felt to him like walking into an ocean.

"You're sure they're here?"

"They are here. Many dogs, many cats. Others. They are close."

"If they're close, they can see there's a way out. Why aren't they leaving?"

"They are afraid."

"Afraid? What for? I'm here to help them."

"They are afraid. That is what I know."

Maybe they're afraid of the gun, he thought. But it didn't make any sense; there's no way they could see it against the dark shingles, and no way they could know what it did to the wall. But he could think of nothing else that might scare them. Certainly not him, a scrawny boy covered in mud and soot. He scanned the area around his feet, hoping to catch a glimpse of a tail, or eyes, or a paw.

Jake's frustration turned to resentment. He paced back and forth across the roof, glaring out into the waste.

"What's wrong with you? I came all this way to help you! Come here, now! Don't you understand? Don't you even care anymore? You're free!"

A few feet out, he saw his distorted reflection in the sheet metal. He stood at a slant, his body bent at a strange angle, one arm longer than the other, misshapen arms flailing wildly as he shouted into the waste.

He could easily be mistaken for a Malbinock.

Chapter Thirty-Five

He stood for a while, transfixed by his own warped reflection. Him, but not him. The version of Jake that stared back at him was put together all wrong, and all that was wrong was magnified in the dents and curves until that was all he could see. If the animals were afraid, as Ursus said, maybe they had a reason to be. If he had set the wall on fire from the outside, the wasteland would have caught fire as well, and all the animals he set out to save would have burned along with the Malbinocks.

Jake retrieved the gun. Its solid weight had given him courage in the dark, but now he could hardly bring himself to touch it. He took it to the edge of the roof and threw it as far as he could into the waste. It traced a high arc across the sky and landed out of sight.

"See? I'm a friend!"

He returned to the Great Dane and knelt in front of him.

"Tell them," Jake begged, "Tell them I'm a friend. Tell them we're here to help."

The Great Dane looked into Jake's eyes, but it made no sound but the rapid thump of its tail against the asphalt shingles. Curiously, it seemed a little better. Not healthy by any stretch, but its eyes were clear, its coat thicker, the markings on its back and legs a little more distinct.

Nevertheless, it didn't make any attempt to help.

Jake ran his fingers through his hair. It was knotted and full of grime, the way Gordon's had been when they first met him.

That was it.

"Ursus! Tell them just like you told Gordon. They'll listen to you!"

Ursus had been facing the waste, sitting on his haunches, and sniffing the air. He sat up a little straighter and raised his head to the sky. His howl came from deep within, plaintive and vibrant. The gap seemed to act as a megaphone, sending his howl across the waste like an avalanche, full of sadness, empathy, and love. As beautiful as it was, Jake could not touch it; it was not meant for him, and he longed to experience the whole of it. Ursus finished his howl, but the sound seemed to linger, hovering above the waste as if it were unwilling to leave.

Nothing stirred.

"Try again, Ursus. They'll listen to you. I know they will!"

Ursus howled again, and the sound wrenched Jake's heart. As Ursus called out, Jake scanned the refuse for any sign of movement, any indication that Ursus was getting through to them.

Ursus began to trail off, his howl almost complete. Jake wasn't sure he could bring himself to ask for a third. At the very least, Ursus deserved a chance to rest.

Another voice joined Ursus. It was pitched higher, almost a squeak, but it rang through the gap, clear and crisp, like the first rays of light on the morning after a storm when the world shakes off a cast of dull gray and blazes with color. Though it wasn't meant for him, Jake could sense its meaning.

Hope.

Gordon slipped through the haze, still howling, and took his place next to Ursus. Together, they sang. Jake caught fleeting glimpses of meaning, the feel of soft grass, the sight of bright, blue sky, the scent of cool, dark glades, and the spray of a silver waterfall.

Ursus' howl grew louder and more confident, his voice merged with Gordon's in a haunting, ghostly harmony, their memories laid bare and hurled out into the waste. Jake sat down at the edge of the roof, closed his eyes, and listened. Azrak joined him, curling up in his lap.

"They come. They come!" Azrak cried.

Out in the distance, something moved, darting in and out of sight among the broken boards and rusted pipes. Too small to be a dog or a cat. Jake leapt to his feet, almost spilling Azrak into the waste. Gradually, the thing got closer. It was a hamster, skittering through the junk, its coat stained gray as if all the color had been drained from it.

"Hello, I'm—" Jake said, but before he could get out another word, the hamster shot past, raced across the shingles, and disappeared into the haze. Another followed soon after, this time a mouse. It shot past as well as if it didn't see Jake or the others at all. By twos and threes they came, guinea pigs, rabbits, rats. They all rushed past without so much as a sidelong glance, their little paws scratching against the shingles like the first drops of rain.

Drops became a trickle, then a flood. Cats joined the rush, and finally, dogs, a raging torrent of fur and paws, and all the while, Ursus and Gordon sang, calling them to freedom. Their howl was taken up by the escaping dogs, and the song took on a life of its own as if the waste itself had joined them.

The Great Dane rose. The other animals had been flowing around him, like a river around a rock, and they were careful to avoid him. He waded through the throng, his bones moving visibly beneath his skin, and approached Jake. The two stood, eye to eye, a tiny island of peace in the deluge. Jake could think of nothing to say. Then the dog gave Jake's cheek a single lick. His tongue was dry and thin, like a piece of fine-grit sandpaper, and Jake gently stroked the Great Dane's ears.

"Go home," Jake whispered.

The Great Dane turned, gave Jake a single look back, and then joined the other dogs in flight.

Jake pressed his back against the gap wall. A strange peace had settled over him, a quiet sense of satisfaction and gratitude. Along the way, he had often thought of what he would do when he found them. He envisioned himself marching at the front of a vanguard of dogs and cats, a conquering hero. He envisioned moving among them, feeling their reverence for him and basking in it as he might bask in warm sunshine after a swim. Back at the Howl, they would add his name into their song, praising him.

Now, watching the animals flow past in a vast procession, those daydreams felt empty and small. What he felt right then, the warm, gentle elation that settled bone-deep in him and radiated to his fingertips and toes, was pure, unblemished love, love for every one of the animals that surged past him on their way back to freedom.

It was enough.

"Jake!"

It was Blue, standing along the edge of the deluge, stamping his hooves against the churned, blackened moss. "Jake, watch how they scatter! They will not be safe if they are alone!"

Blue was right. Once clear of the gap, the animals ran aimlessly, with no sense of purpose except to get away, like ants fleeing a disturbed nest.

"Ursus! Gordon!"

The two stopped singing. Their voices were barely missed; the song had spread throughout the waste, and Jake had to shout to be heard.

"Tell them to follow Blue!"

"I will tell them," said Ursus. He waded through the throng, and bounded off across the bog, howling as he went.

"But I am here," Blue said, "To lead, I must be ahead."

"That's right," Jake said. "You have to lead them out of here. You're the biggest and the fastest."

"I will lead them." Blue hunkered down. "Climb on my back. We will go now."

"Let's get Azrak and Gordon first."

Jake motioned Azrak and Gordon to him. Azrak came, but Gordon, cut off by the escaping animals, stayed put. Jake picked up Azrak and put him up on Blue's back.

"Azrak, you rest. We'll need you to guide us through the warrens."

"Rest, yes. Then we see grass again," Azrak said. He settled himself down between Blue's shoulders.

Jake waded into the press of dogs and cats. He expected to fight his way through, like wading across a swift stream, but the animals avoided him, and it felt more walking on a windy day. He snatched up Gordon, and carried him back to where Blue and Azrak waited, and placed the little dog on Blue's back.

"Now you climb, Jake. Climb! We all go! Leave Badwatchers to starve!"

Yes, thought Jake, throwing himself over Blue's back. They'll wake up and look around, and there won't be anything in the cupboard. Jake could picture them, wandering around in the dark, searching.

Jake's eyes widened, and he slid off Blue's back and leaned against the horse's ribs, his arms pressed against his head.

The dark. How could he be so stupid?

When night fell, the Malbinocks would pour out of the wall and right through the gap, running down the weakest and slowest first, and then, one by one, taking the rest of them, dragging them back into endless misery and pain.

"Climb, Jake, climb!"

There was nothing he could do about it, no way to keep the Malbinocks from swarming across the bog and snatching them all up when the light failed. Blue could outrun them, but the rest would be left behind. He closed his eyes and once again saw Sebastian dragged into the shadows, pleading with Jake for help. An hour of freedom, maybe as much as half a day, and then whatever head start they had would vanish.

"Tell them to follow Blue, Gordon."

Gordon barked and sat happily next to Azrak, tongue lolling off to one side. Jake took the little dog's muzzle in his hands and scratched around his eyes and ears.

"You're the bravest dog I've ever met," Jake said. "Now you can go home, back to the lake."

Gordon barked again and licked Jake's cheek.

"It is your turn, Jake. Climb on. I have never lost a Rider."

"I'm not going," Jake said.

"Why stay? Why stay? Climb! Come with Azrak!"

"I have to make sure we get them all out. I'll follow as soon as the last one is free. Now go, Blue!"

But Blue didn't move. "It is not safe to split the herd," he said.

"You're right, it's not," Jake replied, brushing his

hand against Blue's flank. "That's why you have to lead them."

He pointed to the fleeing animals. "That is your herd, Blue. Lead them out. Don't let them split up. I'll find you when we get back to the grassland."

Still, Blue hesitated.

"They are my herd," said Blue.

He gave Jake a long look and then stood up and galloped away, churning giant chunks of moss into the air. Jake watched them until they shrank into the distance and disappeared.

"I'll find you in the grassland!" Jake shouted. Gordon answered with a sharp howl that remained in the air long after they were gone.

It wasn't really a lie, Jake told himself.

But deep in his heart, he knew that it was.

Chapter Thirty-Six

There are so many, Jake thought. Dogs, cats, and rodents streamed from the gap. While a few still peeled off and ran whichever way they chose, most stayed together, forming a long, meandering line across the bog. Jake watched the horizon, looking for the cloud that would mark their arrival at the Bone Forest.

All his friends were safe, heading back toward the grassland and the deep green forest, far from the rank, greasy bog, and the horrors that lay beneath the wall.

All he had to do was delay the Malbinocks until the following morning, and his friends would stay that way. He studied the gap, watching dogs and cats file past him.

What he needed was a fire. Light and fire were the only things the Malbinocks feared. A fire—large enough to keep them back but small enough to be controlled.

He kicked himself for tossing the lighter into the waste. Even if he was willing to risk the trip into the vast pile, the odds of finding the gun were almost zero.

He caught a wisp of smoke drifting up from below the collapsed roof and watched it dissipate into the air.

Maybe he didn't need the lighter after all.

Jake set to work, dragging boxes, clothes, furniture, anything he thought might burn, and piled them a short distance away from the gap. His left arm still ached, but he did his best to ignore it. There would be time to rest his arm when they were all safe from the Malbinocks.

The pile had to be in the right place. Too close, and the animals wouldn't chance going around it. Too far away, and it would be useless to contain the Malbinocks behind the wall. As he dragged boxes, he searched through them, keeping a watch for matches or lighters. His search formed a trail of junk between his pile and the wall.

As the pile grew higher, Jake's search became more and more desperate. He began dumping the boxes when he reached the pile, digging through the rubbish, searching for anything that would help him. Even a single match would have been welcome, but there were none to be found.

Despite that, he was impressed with the pile. In only a short time, he'd managed to build it taller than he was, a miniature brown Mountain newly risen from the bog. The animals wound their way around it without giving it a single look. Back and forth he went, piling boxes as fast as he could go, with nothing but faith that he would be able to light it when the time came.

And then, he found it. Stuck in the bottom of a box was a book of matches, its corner wedged beneath the packing tape. With a shout, he snatched the book of matches from their hiding place, admiring them as if they were made of diamonds. He tore one out and flipped the book over to expose the striker. His hands felt numb, his heart pounded, his mind a whirlwind. He pulled the matchhead across the red strip.

The match caught in a puff of smoke and sulfur, flared for a moment, and went out. He tried another one, with the same result.

"Come on!"

He pulled a match from the back row instead, but he pulled a little too hard. The matchbook flipped into the air and flew in a lazy arc to Jake's left. Fingers outstretched; he dove. The book danced against his fingernails and tumbled into the bog. Jake went after it, landing on his knees. He felt its stiff, square outline against his knee, softening in the ooze.

He stared at his pale, thin hands. He wondered, with vague, dull curiosity, if there was any blood in them and why, at the moment he needed them the most, they had failed him. Small, bony, weak hands. Worthless. One match was all he needed, one out of an entire book, just one, to give the animals he'd accidentally rescued a chance to get away.

One match.

Past his hands were his knees, bent and pressed deep into the soggy moss, surrounded by filthy bog water. He looked at the gray sky and the junk which had somehow shrunk from a mountain into a dirty little pile, and at the dogs and cats struggling through the mud because Gordon had given them his promise that they would be free again.

He thought of running until the darkness bore down and brought hungry Malbinocks to snatch him from behind. He thought of standing and fighting, of forgetting the lost matches and finding some other weapon, to kill as many as he could before they overwhelmed him. He thought of both and did neither.

Just as Ursus said. Near or far. All the same.

A flash of silver-gray broke up the monotony of the moss, and Jake saw the foreleg of a dog, darting from the river of animals and behind the useless little pile of boxes before Jake could get a look at it.

"You're going the wrong way," Jake said, without conviction.

Out from behind the boxes stepped Sebastian.

Jake could not move or speak. There was no mistaking him; Sebastian was thinner, his coat flecked with grime, and dust, and splotches of paint, but it was him.

With joy, fear, and relief so profound he couldn't form Sebastian's name, Jake threw his arms around the dog's shaggy neck. Sebastian wriggled, his tail flailing behind him. Jake held his friend for what felt like a long time.

He cupped Sebastian's muzzle in his hands. "It's so good to see you, but you can't stay here. Go back to the Howl and wait for Brad-Hun."

Something brown protruded out the side of Sebastian's mouth. "Hey, what is that?" When Jake reached out to grab it, Sebastian released his jaws and out tumbled the gun.

"Toy smelled like Jake," Sebastian said.

"I think you just saved them," Jake whispered, picking the gun off the ground. Beads of dirty bogwater dripped off the end of the barrel and dropped back into the moss. "I think you just saved everybody."

He pulled the trigger. It sputtered before the flame emerged, gloriously blue and constant.

"We can go back to the forest? Play, and sleep, and howl, and wait?"

"Yes, Sebastian."

"I will go. Jake will go too!"

"I have something I have to do here, just for a little while. You go ahead. I'll find you. Follow the other dogs."

Sebastian did a full turn and then sat down on his haunches. "I will wait. Jake will do his something and then we will go to the forest together."

"No, Sebastian. You need to go, right now, as fast as you can, and don't stop until you get to the forest."

"And Jake will come?"

"Of course." Jake managed a weak smile. "I came here, didn't I?"

"Jake does not belong here," Sebastian said. "Come to the forest. We will go together."

"Go now," Jake said. He pointed toward the dogs, winding in a steady stream toward the horizon. "Do what the Giver says."

"I will go now."

"You're a good dog, Sebastian."

"I am a good dog. I will go to the forest and wait."

Sebastian gave Jake a long look, then sprang past him, vanishing around the boxes.

Jake peered into the distance, trying to catch a glimpse of Sebastian's silver-gray coat, but his friend was gone. He pulled the lighter's trigger and watched the flame sputter into life. He put the flame a few inches from the corner of a box, but he brought it no closer than that.

He looked up at the pile he'd created. It was hopelessly inadequate, barely taller than he was despite the many trips into the wall. He could go back in there ten more times, and it wouldn't change a thing. What he needed was an extra day, and he didn't have it.

The flame hovered near the corner of the box for a few more seconds before Jake doused it and put the gun back into his pocket. Just inside the breach in the wall he'd seen some broken chairs, along with some rakes and broom handles. They'd burn longer than boxes, and it wouldn't take long to get them back to the pile.

He quickly made the short trip back to the breach and ducked between the boards, giving his eyes a moment to adjust to the dim light. Sure enough, in the far corner lay a pile of broken furniture. End tables, as it turned out, rather than chairs, with wooden spindles for legs, all of which were snapped off and piled underneath the flat tabletops. Next to them was a bundle of garden tools—rakes, hoes, and shovels, along with a few brooms and a mop, bound together with a length of baling wire.

The tabletops looked a lot more substantial and would probably burn longer, but the tools would be easier to carry. Jake chose the tools, wrapping his arms around the thick bundle of wooden handles. He dragged them to the opening and then ducked between the boards, pulling the tools after him, his mind wrestling with the problem of getting the tabletops into the pile. There were three of them, but if he stacked them—

Darkness fell.

Chapter Thirty-Seven

The scurrying of paws against the shingles tapered off and then stopped altogether. Jake drew the gun and pulled the trigger. The flame gave off a weak glow that barely penetrated the darkness. The roof was empty. With the darkness came an ominous silence, as if the entire world had hidden in a closet, hands over mouth, waiting for something fearsome and inevitable.

Somewhere in the distance rang the piercing, industrial groan of rubbing metal. In the quiet it felt much louder, like a single bird calling out on a still morning. Others joined in until the air was filled with the sound of their movement, punctuated by the sounds of dogs and cats in distress. Jake winced at the sound; sharp, anguished cries that ended abruptly and didn't return.

As the Malbinocks emerged, Jake felt their presence in his mind, their dim consciousness a host of snake tongues flickering, searching, anticipating a good meal. Their anticipation turned to confusion and then to anger.

Jake snatched up the bundle of tools and dragged it across the roof. With one hand it was slow going, and the scrape of the handles against the shingles carried through the gap, announcing his presence. Despite his terror, Jake did not relinquish his grip on the tools, dragging them, step by step, toward the edge of the roof. As he pulled, he listened to the Malbinocks converge on the gap, so loud that Jake could not hear his own prayers, whispered out loud between haggard breaths.

The edge of the roof was only a few feet away, and then the long slog through the moss, churned into a black, treacherous mess by the escaping animals. He hazarded a glance back to see how close the Malbinocks had come. He froze in place and nearly dropped the gun.

Hundreds of Malbinocks crowded into the gap, following Jake as closely as they could, their bodies barely visible in the tiny, weak light from the gun. Jake felt like he was staring up at an avalanche. The bundle of tools slipped from his arm and landed near his foot with a sharp clank.

"Stay back," Jake stammered. He took a step backward. The Malbinocks advanced, lingering just on the edge of the light.

"I have fire." He brandished the gun. The flame wavered. "I burned down these houses with your friends inside, and I'll burn you!"

He took another step back.

The Malbinocks packed into the gap, a hungry, impenetrable wall, pushing toward him.

He stepped back again, and his foot sank into the moss.

The flame sputtered a little.

"Stay back!"

The Malbinocks moved forward.

Jake glanced behind him. He could just make out the edges of the pile. The roof creaked as the Malbinocks pushed closer.

He pointed the gun at them. The flame was smaller, its tip rounded and dim.

"I'll burn every single one of you!" he shouted.

But the flame no longer frightened them. They moved closer now, inexorably, as Jake stumbled backward into the bog.

The pile was close enough to reach if he ran for it. He would have one chance to light it before the Malbinocks caught up to him. One chance. He took a deep breath and steeled himself.

He turned. Hovering in the darkness were two large eyes, alive with the reflected light from the gun.

Ursus stepped past him.

A low growl rumbled from his throat, so strong Jake could feel it in the moss beneath his feet. From the depths of the growl came Ursus' voice.

"I am called Ursus at the Howls. I do not fear you. My teeth are sharp, my jaws strong."

"Ursus?"

"I will make you show your bellies. I will tear your throats."

"Ursus, no!"

Ursus stopped at the edge of the roof. He stood like a sentinel, his body taut as a spring, head erect, ears folded back. In the dim light, he seemed to stand larger as if he'd grown, commanding the gap with his presence. Noble and terrible, he held his ground, strength and courage incarnate. In the shadows beyond the gun's weak light, the Malbinocks inched forward.

Ursus stopped growling, and in its absence hung a dreadful silence. You don't have to do this, Jake thought, but the words would not come out. Muscles rippled beneath the dog's black coat. Ursus leaned forward, the movement almost imperceptible.

No—

The world exploded into motion as if all its pent-up energy had been released at once. Ursus sprang into the shadows and met the Malbinocks mid-charge. Jake made for the pile, ankle-deep mud sucking at his bare feet. Behind him, a battle raged, heavy thuds and the splintering of wood and the staccato of makeshift feet swarming across the roof.

Near senseless with terror, Jake reached the edge of the pile. The flame from the gun barely illuminated the ground in front of him, the heap of boxes barely distinguishable from the dark emptiness beyond. Only a small dome of flame remained at the end of the gun barrel, a blob of blue light clinging to the metal. Jake held it to the corner of a box.

"Light. Light!"

A thin, gray wisp of smoke curled over the edge of the box. The corner glowed red, and a tiny flame emerged and danced above the cardboard. The flame wavered, and then lengthened, as if newly awakened from a long sleep.

Ursus howled. Abruptly, it ended, the silence punctuated by a loud, heavy thump.

"Ursus!"

Jake cupped his hands and blew on the flame. It shivered, then bent away from him and grew, feeding on the life Jake breathed into it. It spread outward and upward, fluttering audibly as the box blackened and shriveled into ash. When it spread to the box above it took on a life of its own, fully grown and hungry.

"Ursus, hold on!"

Orange-tinged light pushed back the darkness. The Malbinocks fled, leaving the gap littered with their broken bodies. They had been torn apart with such violence that Jake could not tell one from another. Splintered boards and fragments of old furniture lay in drifts festooned with baling wire and electrical cords. Smashed bits of plastic, useless power tools, swatches of tattered clothing, rusted car parts, and a host of other objects lay in piles, obscured in shadow.

And in the middle was Ursus.

He lay on his side, blanketed to the shoulder in the broken remains of his enemies. Jake shoveled them aside, piling the pieces into a mound until Ursus was uncovered. He laid a trembling hand on Ursus' ribs, praying that he would feel his friend breathing. Ursus' skin was warm and a little damp, and beneath that, Jake felt the weak rise and fall of his breath.

"The fire is going." Jake pointed to the burning boxes. Ursus stared uncomprehending into the darkness. A burst of orange sparks exploded into the night sky as a part of the pile collapsed in on itself.

Beyond the firelight's arc the Malbinocks waited, chittering like feral rats, their awareness flickering through Jake's mind.

He tugged at Ursus' paw. "Come on. It's not that far away. You can make it."

Ursus made no effort to move. His paw was heavy in Jake's arms. He laid it down gently.

"It's safe by the fire. They can't get us there. All we have to do is make it to morning."

Jake brushed a fragment of wood from Ursus' head.

"Why did you come back?" He sank to his knees and looked into Ursus' eyes. Ursus didn't reply, nor did he have to. Jake already knew the answer to his question. He laid his arm over the dog's neck and buried his face into Ursus' warm coat and brushed a palm over his forehead.

"I won't let them get you," he whispered. "We're going to make it to the morning. You and me."

Jake snatched up two long pieces of wood and returned to the fire. He shoved them into the flames until the ends ignited. The feel of the solid wood against his palms and the heat against his face gave him courage. He held them out as he struggled back through the bog, waving them enough to keep the flame alive.

The Malbinocks fell back at the sight of the approaching flame. Jake caught a glimpse of them, climbing over one another to avoid the light, wave upon wave of them. The hungry fought with those trying to escape the light, and the sound of their struggle rolled through the gap in the wall.

Jake held the middle of the gap, waving the torches until, half-consumed, they dimmed, and no amount of waving could bring them back. He retreated then, casting the smoking remnants into the bog before finding two stout axe handles that looked like they would burn well. He wanted to stop and reassure Ursus, but there was no time. The Malbinock's deafening clatter followed him back down the roof.

The fire burned lower. It consumed the boxes, and now it was their contents that burned. The flames flickered lower but steadier, still throwing out heat and light, and for Jake, hope.

With the axe handles he stirred the fire, sending the scorched remnants that remained at the edges into the center. The flames leapt up again, brightening the bog. The axe handles caught fire, and Jake returned to the roof.

The fire dimmed by the time he reached the center of the gap, but the axe handles burned brightly and the Malbinocks retreated past the firelight's reach. Jake felt their hunger, the chittering sound in their joints elevated to a high-pitched buzz, a swarm of angry insects looking for a way out of the trap.

He held them there until the axe handles burned low, and he retreated again, back to the dying fire.

Twice more he returned to the gap with fresh torches, holding back the ravenous tide of Malbinocks hiding in the gloom, and each time he retreated to the fire's safety, it burned dimmer. During his retreats, he managed to grab a few boards to toss into the fire, but it wasn't enough.

As it weakened, the Malbinock tide came in stronger, lapping closer and closer to Ursus before being driven back again into the dark by the light from Jake's torches. When he crossed the bog for the fifth time, he looked back, and the fire was gone. Only a few embers lay in a broken circle like fallen stars.

The Malbinocks' hunger filled his mind, their anticipation palpable, their deafening shriek vibrating the roof under his feet.

Jake knelt next to Ursus. The torchlight was pitifully weak, barely illuminating a pale circle with Jake and Ursus at its center. Beyond, the Malbinocks quivered, the eagerness in their bodies a collective scream. The wave of a torch sent them scrabbling backward.

With the torches in his hands, Jake could only study his friend's face, commit it to memory, the strong set of his massive jaws, the nobility in his cheekbones and forehead, the sad kindness in his eyes.

His eyes!

In Ursus' eyes, there was recognition.

"The fire's out," Jake said. Ursus said nothing. Jake held a torch where Ursus could see it.

"This is all that's left."

Jake bent his head until it touched Ursus' smooth coat. "Thank you for pulling me out of the river. And thank you for coming with me. I never had a better friend."

One of the torches guttered and faded out, its presence marked by nothing but a dim, red glow. Jake stood up and swung it hard. It whistled through the air and struck something solid, breaking into a hundred pieces, red embers that slipped into the shadows and died, too cool to ignite the detritus around them.

"I'm sorry," Jake said.

When the second torch faded, Jake threw it at the Malbinocks. A shower of sparks lit the sky above them for an instant, and then the world plunged into darkness.

Chapter Thirty-Eight

Morning did not come.

When the last spark faded, the Malbinocks poured over Jake in a wave of wood and wire. They tore into him, their grip burning ice cold through skin, flesh, and bone. Jake's screams were lost in a vast chorus of euphoric groans and squeals. Under him, around him, over him, their bodies a gluttonous shroud smothering breath and hope.

The Malbinocks fed. All that he was, the Jake that passed effortlessly between worlds, all his memories and emotions, the essence of him drained away, drawn into the creatures that squeezed him like a sponge. He vanished from the outside in, the cold working its way through his veins until he could feel nothing. Not numbness, but nothingness; his body was melting ice.

In an instant, or an eternity, Jake would be gone, his energy and essence broken apart, consumed, waste heat, the groan of metal against metal, a temporary fix, enough to give the Malbinocks a little more time to hunt and feed again. He would be nothing, without even a dried husk to mark his end, less even than a dead fly on a windowsill.

He saw, or rather, felt his end, true oblivion, and he cried out, one last time searching for something to grasp, something that the hungry, mindless evil could not touch.

Through the darkness, he heard an answer. Faintly at first, then stronger. It was a voice, singing, high-pitched and off-key, as if the singer were fighting tears.

One misty, moisty morning
And cloudy was the weather
I chanced to meet an old man
Dressed all in leather

Jake could feel nothing. He had no limbs to reach out, and so he sang. Though he had no memory of learning them, the words came to him as if he'd known them and sung them a thousand times,

He began to compliment
And I began to grin
How do you? How do you?
How do you do again?

The melting stopped. The Malbinocks no longer fed on what little was left of him.

He was a spark, a mote of dust, drifting alone along dark currents, unaware of where they were taking him. But the pain was gone, and that was enough. Perhaps they had eaten their fill, or light filled the bog before they could finish. An instant or an eternity passed. Near and far were the same. He listened, trying to hear the song the stars sung on clear nights or the sad woman's quavering voice, but they were too distant to hear, or they weren't singing at all.

He settled and became still.

Another instant, another eternity passed.

The darkness was no longer complete.

Points of light appeared, first one and another, filling his vision, swirling in great eddies like the gentle lapping of waves on a beach, and with them, the song. It flowed through him, enveloped him, cradled him, invited him to add his voice to theirs.

But he did not know what to sing. He lifted his voice, and it was strong, but there was no harmony. Beneath the calm and the peace there lay a sadness. It was not grief or fear, but a wistful disappointment that, though he knew the words and had found his voice again, he was not ready to sing.

Someday he would.

But not now.

Something held him back, and unless he could give his voice fully to the song, he could not sing it.

Not something. Someone. Through the myriad entwined voices that swirled in perfection around him, he heard her, whispered but clear, calling to him, begging him to follow.

He did. Gradually, the song receded, and he longed to turn back and surround himself in it like a warm blanket on a winter morning, but he could not. Not yet. Not until he could add his voice. There was more to do before then. As the song faded, the voices descended into a confused babble before fading away. The stars winked out, one by one, until Jake once again lay in quiet darkness.

"One more minute."

"Angela—"

"Just one, Brad. Please. One more."

"It's been an hour. We have to ... Angie, honey, he can save other lives."

"I don't want him to save other lives, Brad. I want my baby. I want my Jake."

Another voice broke in. Quiet, professional, sympathetic. "Maybe it would be better if you waited out—"

"No. Do it, fine. You do it. You let my baby die. But I am not leaving him."

Silence and darkness, warmth. His body was a long-abandoned house, and though it felt familiar, it no longer felt like it was entirely his. He explored it from the inside, gradually becoming aware of the tips of his toes and fingers, arms and legs, his belly, heart, and brain.

Above him, the sad woman's muffled sobs drifted down, mingled with an electronic ping and a hissing sound like air escaping from an inflated balloon, and the subdued conversation between two men that was happening somewhere near his feet. He could hear their voices, but he couldn't understand what they were saying. One of the voices was calm, level, matter of fact. The other was tight, like a stretched rubber band, his words clipped, as if the speaker was out of breath.

Aside from his ears, nothing worked. Jake couldn't close his mouth or open his eyes. Though he could feel his body, he couldn't move it. His chest rose and fell with mechanical regularity, but it wasn't something Jake was doing. Drifting free had been a lot easier than this; he felt like a prisoner in a cell made of meat and bone.

"I'm ready," said the sad woman. She squeezed Jake's wrist. Her palm was warm and damp, her grip desperately tight. Fingers moved around his mouth. He felt the pull of tape against the skin around his lips, and something smooth and warm slid against the inside of his throat and across his tongue. It didn't hurt, exactly, but it felt strange, unnatural, and he was glad when the last of it slipped across his front teeth and was gone.

His mouth closed on its own, and he felt much more comfortable. The whooshing sound stopped, and the strange, electronic ping fell silent. The sad woman's grip relaxed a little. She stroked his cheek and ran her fingertips through his hair.

"How long will it take?"

"Not long. He isn't aware of what is happening, so he won't suffer."

Jake's chest burned, and his fingers tingled. Something was missing, something important. It had to do with the balloon sound, the machine that was breathing for him. Someone had turned it off.

Guess it's my turn again, he thought.

Jake breathed. His awareness returned fully, all at once, a shock like ice water against his skin. The air he inhaled brought with it the sharp, antiseptic smell that reminded Jake of the dentist's office—all plastic, rubber, spray cleaner, and old coffee. Other sensations returned as well, gravity, cold, and the awareness of time passing, the urgent need to take a second breath, and then a third. He felt the light weight of the blanket against his chest and the padded mattress beneath him and the cool air that leaked beneath the blanket and brushed past the soles of his feet.

"Did his chest just move?"

"It's normal. It's called 'agonal breathing'. It happens when the body begins to shut down—"

"It moved again."

"Angie—"

"Brad, I swear! He's breathing!"

"That can't be."

"Look for yourself!" the sad woman said, her voice pitched high, as if she were begging.

A blast of cold air settled on his skin as the blanket and sheets were swept aside. The cold disk of a stethoscope pressed against his chest, first in one spot, then another. He kept breathing. The tingling in his toes and burning in his lungs subsided.

"It's not possible."

"What? What are you saying?"

"He's breathing. His heart is beating. I don't understand—"

"Oh, my God! Jake! Come on! There's another one. Come on!"

He could feel the sad woman's warm breath in his ear. Her grip on his hand was almost painful.

Jake wanted to hug her and tell her it was going to be all right, she didn't need to be sad anymore, but his body was heavy and his throat was a dusty, dry tunnel searching for air. The best he could do was squeeze her finger.

But that didn't make the sad woman happy. She wailed; her sobs so intense that Jake could feel them through her grip. Her tears dripped against Jake's chest and ran down his ribs, soaking into the thin sheet.

"Jake, if you can hear me, squeeze my finger again."

He wasn't sure he wanted to. The first squeeze made her even sadder than she'd been before, but he wanted to please her, so he squeezed her finger a second time. Immediately he regretted it; the sad woman's wails lingered in the room after her breath failed her. A mad bustle of voices and footsteps surrounded Jake. Gentle hands moved him this way and that, pinching and poking with a strange urgency. Low voices issued terse commands, spoken so quickly that Jake couldn't understand what was being said. Then the sad woman's finger tore away from his grip, and her voice was lost in the commotion.

Frightened, he forced open his eyes. The light blinded him at first, and then indistinct shapes loomed in and out of his vision. He blinked. Two women in blue worked over him, and beyond them, her head just visible above the silver bar that ran the length of the bed, was the sad woman.

She was pretty but tired. Her eyes were red and puffy, her cheeks glistening with tears. She looked familiar to him. He'd seen her before, a long time ago. Before.

Before what?

"Stay, baby. Stay." Though she spoke in a whisper, he heard her clearly through the chaos. Jake felt a stab of regret. He had done something, something terrible, and that was the reason she was so sad. He tried to think, to remember, but it was like trying to see through a cloud. Shapes, perhaps, shadows, but nothing clear. He remembered a river, and dogs, and ice, but it was all jumbled in his head.

"You said he was gone." Jake couldn't see the speaker, but he bit into the words like he wanted to break them into pieces. "You said there was no brain function."

"There was no brain function."

"You were going to harvest his organs!"

"Bradley Phillips! Not now." The sad woman's sharp command silenced the entire room. For a moment, the room was quiet save for the occasional electronic beep and the sound of his own, raspy breath pushing past his parched lips.

"Let's talk about it in the hall, Mr Phillips."

"Fine."

The door opened, and the sound of activity drifted in from the hallway before being silenced abruptly by the click of the closed latch. Now it was only Jake, the sad woman, and one other dressed in blue, who busied herself pressing buttons on a white box above Jake's head. The sad woman grabbed his hand, holding it tight between hers.

"Jake. Promise me you'll stay. Squeeze my hand, baby. Promise."

Jake looked into her eyes, and he wanted more than anything else to take away the pain that lay behind them. Whatever he'd done, he would fix it, and she could be happy again. He squeezed her hand and tried to whisper, "I promise," but the words would not come. The squeeze was enough to make the sad woman smile through her tears, a broad smile that reached clear to her eyes.

Chapter Thirty-Nine

Jake slept.

The sleep was luxurious and restful, as if he'd been awake for weeks and finally got the chance to go to bed. Every time he woke, the sad woman was there, sometimes sleeping herself, sometimes watching him closely, as if she feared he would disappear if she took her eyes off him.

His breathing came easier, and his body warmed and began to obey him again. Aside from a sore throat and cracked lips, most of his body felt all right. Every so often, a woman dressed in blue would come in and poke him, before scribbling on a clipboard, tugging on the various tubes and wires, and then writing on the clipboard again.

The sad woman hadn't moved. Jake watched her. Her chin rested on her upper chest, her eyes closed, her breath slow and regular. Though Jake had never seen one, he thought she looked like an angel.

"I'm sorry," he said. His voice was raspy and weak.

Jake barely recognized the sound of it, as if it were being spoken by someone else. The sad woman opened her eyes.

"I'm sorry," he said again. The sad woman's eyes filled with tears.

"Sorry? Sorry for what, honey?"

"I made you sad."

"I was sad because I thought I wouldn't see you again."

"Did I run away?"

She shook her head and smiled. "You had an accident."

"What kind?"

"You fell in the river."

"I don't remember," he said. He stared up at the tiles over his bed. "I don't remember anything."

She brushed the hair away from his forehead. "The doctor says it's normal. Rest, and it'll come back. You'll remember when you're ready."

"What if I don't?"

The monitor above his head pinged a little faster.

The thought of the dark, of icy wire wrapped around his wrists flashed through his mind, and he shuddered.

The sad woman pushed aside some wires and snuggled against him on the bed. Her body was warm and soft against his back. She smoothed his hair and brushed her slender fingers across his cheek.

"Try to sleep. I'll be right here. When you wake up again, the doctor said it would be ok for you to try some food."

"I am hungry."

"Sleep a little more. Later on, we'll try some food."

Jake closed his eyes. He was still afraid, but the sad woman pushed the fear away and made it feel distant and small.

"Could you sing me a song?"

"Of course I will."

The sad woman took a breath and sang.

You are my sunshine,

My only sunshine.

You make me happy—

"No, not that one."

"You don't like it?"

Jake tried to sit up, but the sad woman's gentle pressure kept him lying down. The last thing he wanted to do was hurt her feelings again. "It's not that. I was just ... I was hoping you'd sing the other one. The one you sang to me when I ... when I was away."

She sang again, and this time, it was the right one. Memories flooded his mind, and there, lying next to him, was his mother. Jake reached for her, buried his head against her chest, and cried until he fell asleep.

Chapter Forty

Jake stayed in the hospital for observation for several days. During his stay, he discovered a truth about grown-ups that he'd never noticed before. The truth had always been out there, hanging like the fireworks on the Fourth of July for everyone to see, but Jake had never paid close enough attention to really notice it. Lying in the hospital bed gave him plenty of time to get a good look.

The truth was that adults only pretended to have things under control. They worked hard to make other people think they understood things and knew what to do, but half the time they didn't, and they just made it up as they went along.

The doctors decided it was the temperature of the water that saved him and that if he'd fallen into the water any other time of year, he probably would have died. The water, they said, slowed his metabolism—whatever that was—enough to preserve him until his body recovered and started working on its own again.

That's what they told him. Well, sometimes. They also told him that he had actually died and that it was a miracle he was sitting up, eating, and talking. Either it was cold water or a miracle, but the grown-ups never chose one. They seemed perfectly willing to bounce between the two depending on who they were talking to.

The day after Jake first opened his eyes, he got to watch himself on the local news.

"And tonight, some good news for a Washington County family who nearly lost their ten-year-old son. Janet Myers has more. Janet."

The screen cut to a woman in a blue dress who looked more like she belonged in Sunday School than walking across a bridge. Jake didn't recognize the bridge or the reporter.

"It wasn't far from here that ten-year-old Jake Phillips was playing near Baskahegan Stream. On that fateful day, he fell through the thin ice and became trapped underneath. Rescuers rushed to the scene, but by the time they pulled him out, he had already spent thirty minutes under the ice. Though they were able to revive him, there seemed little hope of recovery. Jake was transferred to Eastern Maine Medical Center where he lay in a coma, his body being kept alive by machines. Three days passed before Jake's parents made the agonizing decision to let Jake go."

Watching his own news story was like listening to his parents talk about him while he was still in the room. At least this time, he wasn't in trouble. The story cut to a taped interview of Jake's dad, still wearing his work clothes and the battered, green John Deere hat that never seemed to leave his head.

"Well, at that point, it seemed like the right choice. We thought if he could save other lives, then some of Jake would live on."

There was a strange, haunted, faraway look in his dad's eyes, one that Jake never wanted to see again. To Jake's relief, his mother didn't appear in the interview. The scene cut back to the reporter.

"Doctors removed Jake from life support at approximately 4:30 yesterday afternoon. Jake's family gathered around him, expecting a tragedy. Then, a miracle happened."

They cut to one of the doctors. Jake hadn't bothered to learn their names.

"Well, normally, in a case like this, with no brain function, the body tends to shut down rather quickly without mechanical help. In this case, we saw a very abrupt resumption of autonomic brain activity, and the patient began to breathe on his own almost at once. Frankly, I've never seen anything like it in all my years practicing medicine. The human body has amazing recuperative powers if given the chance."

"Doctors speculate that it was the cold water that preserved Jake's body, slowing down his metabolism and his need for oxygen, which allowed rescuers and medical professionals to get him on life support during that critical first few hours.

"Miracle, or Medicine? That's a question for experts to decide, but for a young Washington County family, the answer is clear. I'm Janet Myers for WAGM news."

To Jake, it felt like medicine. Every few hours, a nurse or a doctor or a counselor would come in, and he'd have to answer the same questions. They would ask him how he felt, what he remembered, where he lived, what he liked to do for fun. At first, Jake gave honest answers, but after a while, boredom set in, and he tried to think of more creative things to say. A short, dark-haired woman with round glasses came in with a set of flashcards, and Jake told her that God had personally sent him back down to be an example to other kids because he was such a good boy. He told an older man with silver hair and a curly beard that for fun he liked to spend lots of time in the water. The old man asked him if that was why he decided to go swimming. Jake told him usually he'd wait for the ice to melt, but it was taking too long. The man laughed. He didn't stay long, and Jake was sorry to see him go.

He spoke with Jake's mother on the way out, and Jake distinctly heard him say the word "normal" several times before the old man finally departed. Being under observation in the hospital was like having kindergarten in the waiting room of a doctor's office, except that in the hospital, they changed the teacher every few hours, and there was no snack time or recess.

On the fourth day, Jake's mother brought in a bag filled with a change of clothes, and a few minutes later, he was riding a wheelchair through sterile, cream-colored halls toward the elevator. Nurses and doctors wished him well and made him promise not to come back anytime soon.

His parents were all smiles on the ride home. They sang along to songs on the car radio and stopped at the McDonalds in Lincoln for lunch. He pretended to enjoy it, but the food balled up into a sticky paste in his mouth and resisted when he tried to swallow it. He had to take each bite like a pill, forcing it down with soda. It took two cups of Mountain Dew to get through the entire thing, and then they got back on the road.

The world slipped by through the car window, and Jake fought with a terrible sense of disappointment. He knew each house and business they passed; he'd seen them all countless times, but there was something wrong with them, something not quite as he remembered.

He realized it was the color. The entire world looked as if it were the subject of an old photograph, worn and faded, the way a picture looked when it was left in the sun too long. Along with the color, the sounds were strange too, poor imitations of how the world ought to sound. It was why he couldn't enjoy the food and why he gave up looking out the window on the way home and instead closed his eyes and thought of his friends.

He thought of the last time he'd seen them, running into the stampede of escaping dogs and cats, disappearing into the throng without a backward glance. He thought of Sebastian, and Gordon, and Blue, with Azrak perched on his broad, strong back. He tried to remember the grassland and the forest, but even his memories felt muted. Try as he might, he couldn't visualize the colors, or hear his friends' voices in his head, or take in the scent of the rainforest or the waterfall. But most of all, he thought of Ursus.

His family had a party in his honor. Cousins, and grandparents, and uncles, and aunts—people he had seen only a handful of times in his entire life descended on their house. Jake did his best to be friendly and polite, mostly for his mother's sake, but he couldn't help notice how much noise was in them all. Until Mom shooed them away, they hugged him and peppered him with questions. What was it like? Did he see anything? Did he talk to Jesus? Did he hover over his body?

They speculated about how everything would be new and fresh and exciting because of his second chance, and how proud they were that he was so tough and such a fighter and how they would come over more often because life was so short. Over Dad's barbecue, they argued about politics, and sports, and music, and movies, and television shows, and cars, and fishing, and deer hunting, all at the same time, their voices overlapping in a confused babble.

If his mother hadn't stopped him, he would have gone to the hollow and waited there until the family had said their goodbyes and the house was quiet again. He was glad when the last truck bumped over the rutted driveway and departed.

After a week, the quiet became oppressive. Each day, the memories of Blue and his other friends faded, and he couldn't bear the thought of losing them completely. He dragged his old art set out of the closet, one his grandmother had sent him for his 8th birthday, and he spent his days drawing the woods and the Mountain where the wild animals hid in the high canopy and peered out from the maze of roots. He drew the golden grassland, constantly frustrated by the dull, faded colors and his own lack of ability. He tried to draw the Calling-Place, but he gave up, unable to do it justice.

But mostly, he drew Ursus. Over and over again, until the black marker faded to gray and the crayon was nothing more than a nub between his thumb and fingers, he drew his friend as if drawing him could take away the glassy emptiness in his eyes and the stillness in his paws, lying broken among the heap of dead Malbinocks in the dark. Jake knew it couldn't, but he drew anyway. While he drew, he felt like his friend was somewhere close by, present, but just out of sight. It wasn't enough, but it was all he had.

One night, Jake was awakened by the sound of dull creaks that stopped as soon as he opened his eyes. He peered across the floor, searching for a source. Neither of his parents had even mentioned the state of his room since he got home, and living in it for a week had made it messier than it had ever been. His floor was a sea of chaos, and among the broken toys, old games, dirty clothes, plates with half-eaten slices of pizza, were nooks and crannies where shadows bred and lurked. He turned on a flashlight and held it against the floor, terrified that he'd brought them back with him. He waited up all night, relieved when the first gray sunlight penetrated the curtains.

He spent the whole of the next day cleaning his

room, much to his parents' surprise. Jake wondered whether it was "normal", but he didn't ask.

That was when the nightmares started. Just flashes at first, a glimpse through the window at a shambling, man-like figure silhouetted in the moonlight. He would wake up every night screaming, still feeling the cold pressure of Malbinock wire against his wrists and ankles as they nourished themselves on his agony.

It didn't take long at all before his parents whisked him off to a psychologist. The one they chose was a thin man with a wispy blond beard and black-framed glasses. He sat next to Jake on a couch in his office. Jake didn't want to talk to him, but somehow, after a few minutes, he found himself telling the man, who insisted on being called Doctor Nick, about the dreams, and how he felt so out of place, even in his own house.

"You ever hear of a metaphor?" The question came after a long period of silence, startling Jake, who had been trying to remember Ursus' voice.

"No."

"Well, it's a fancy word. A metaphor is kind of a code. It's a way to work something out without having to really face it directly. Now these creatures ... these Malbinocks ... they're dragging you down into the dark, suffocating you?"

"Yeah. No. Well, sort of."

Dr. Nick nodded. "Have you thought about where you might have felt that before? Sometimes a traumatic event can stay with you, and your mind has to come up with ways to deal with it, to process it. That's how we learn. What you're going through is completely normal.

Think these dreams might be about what happened to you in the river?"

Oh, God, Jake thought. At least he didn't throw in anything about miracles.

Nick scribbled something on a piece of paper.

"I'm going to prescribe two things. The first thing is some medication to help you get through the night without those dreams. That way, you'll be ready for the second thing."

"What's the second thing?"

"You're going back to school. I think it's important for you to embrace everything life has to offer, and you can't sit around in your room, waiting for it to start. You have to take the first step, and I think the first step is to go back to school."

Jake was surprised to discover he wasn't angry about it. In fact, it was a relief. Mom and Dad both agreed it was for the best.

The first day back was strange. The class treated him like he was made of glass, and even Precious Peter made an effort to welcome him back. His ordeal had earned him a certain notoriety. Before he was just Jake Phillips, the troublemaker, but now he was Jake, 'the kid who died.'

He found out it wasn't just adults at the hospital who were making things up as they went along. Apparently, it was all grown-ups because his teacher gave him a folder full of worksheets and told him if he completed them, he'd be all caught up with the rest of the class. The folder was pathetically thin, and Jake wondered if the class had spent the last month having parties every day, just waiting for him so he wouldn't fall behind.

He still didn't like schoolwork. Times tables and spelling words and understanding nonfiction passages and learning the rivers of Maine didn't seem all that important, but the reasons for not doing it seemed even less important, and so he sat in his old seat and concentrated on his work. They had a meeting about him after the first week. His mom was pleased to find out that Jake's newfound focus was very normal. It almost made Jake laugh.

The weeks and months rolled on. Faded green leaves grew thick on the birches and the aspens, and the last of the snow that hid in the woods melted away. Jake floated through his days at school and his appointments with Doctor Nick, going through the motions and saying the right things and making sure he stayed very, very normal, while inside he felt like a lost balloon, drifting helplessly in the breeze through a faded landscape, unable to soar and unable to land.

On the last day of school, his teacher sent him home with a framed certificate that read "MOST IMPROVED STUDENT—JACOB PHILLIPS" in elegant script. He gave it to his mother, who promptly hung it on the wall next to a photo of him and Sebastian.

"He would be proud of you if he was here," she said. "And you did so well that you don't need summer school. You have the whole summer to do whatever you want."

Jake smiled and accepted his mother's hug. She still looked at him like a rare treasure every time he came through the door.

He hoped it would stay that way.

Chapter Forty-One

It was time for bed, and Jake stood alone in front of the bathroom sink, his pill resting in his left hand. He stared at it, a tiny white dot in the middle of his palm. A paper cup filled with water sat at the edge of the sink. For reasons he couldn't explain, he left the pill in his hand instead of popping it into his mouth. He hadn't had a bad dream since Doctor Nick started him on the medicine.

Doctor Nick was like all the other adults, making it up as he went along. The nightmares were normal. The way he cleaned his room and did his homework and stayed quiet and the way he ate his peas and tied his shoes and combed his hair. All very normal after trauma. Of course, he was also special, and his miracle gave him a second chance at life, and not many people got a chance like his.

Jake turned the pill over. There were tiny letters and numbers stamped into it.

If not many people got a chance like his, how did Doctor Nick know what "normal" was?

Usually, his mother stayed in the bathroom until he swallowed the pill and washed it down with the water, but sometimes she got distracted. That night she'd given him the pill and filled the cup and then left while he was brushing his teeth, promising to come up in a little while and check on him.

He picked up the pill and held it between his thumb and forefinger, rolling it back and forth like a tiny wheel until it left an impression in his skin. It was better without the nightmares, waking up screaming, soaked with sweat, searching his bed for chunks of wood and pieces of baling wire. After the pills, he didn't have to keep his foot pressed under a chair leg to keep himself awake at school. It was better.

The medicine helped him stay asleep, but it didn't do anything about the things that left him lying on his back, studying the animals drawn in crayon and taped to the wall next to the bed. The drawings were all he had left of them; their memory faded until they were nothing more than names, poorly written beneath their portraits. Ursus and Blue, Samuel and Gordon and Azrak, Serafina, all just names, words carved on paper tombstones that whispered about the friends he'd left behind, but without the comfort of memories.

"How are you doing, Jake?"

His mother never gave him orders anymore. She treated him like an expensive dinner plate, every touch gentle, every word carefully spoken. He took one last look at the pill.

"I'll be right out," he said.

He tossed the pill into the toilet and watched it drift downward, turning end over end until it settled on the bottom. He flushed it away, and over the sound of the water he heard the thump and creak of his mother's feet on the stairs. He grabbed the glass of water and drank it down, finishing the last of it as his mother leaned around the door and peeked in.

"Ready for bed?"

Jake nodded.

She didn't ask about the medicine. Jake was grateful he didn't have to lie to her. She wouldn't have ordered him to take another pill, but he would have done it on his own to keep her happy. She followed him into his bedroom and watched him climb into bed as if it were a miracle. When he was all settled, she turned out the light.

"Good night. I'll see you in the morning." She kissed his forehead.

"Good night, Mom."

She smiled, her face radiant, angelic, as if she was looking at the most beautiful thing in the world for the first time. After a moment, she left the room, closing the door behind her.

That night, Jake had a dream.

In the dream, he was a bird, his feathers white as cloud tops, his spirit bursting with joy and profound relief.

He flew.

It had been ages since he felt the freedom of the sky, and he relished each beat of his wings and savored the rush of air across his feathers. He soared over a rainforest of rich, deep green that blanketed the ground. From the center of the rainforest rose a vast mountain of yellowed stone. The rainforest grew up the side of its wide base until the sides grew too steep, exposing the yellow stone that rose to a sharp peak, just visible through a veil of mist.

He wasn't alone. All around him flew others, their plumage brilliant against the deep blue of the sky. They reveled in flight, as he did, soaring high above the cages, beyond the fleshy fingers dangling like worms through the bars, the sharp stink of bird-filth welling up from sodden old newspaper. Here, there was only the sky and the Mountain during the day, the shelter of the tall trees at night, the crisp, fresh wind, and the beating of wings in flight.

Freedom.

Deep in his heart he knew he was only borrowing the birds' joy, but it didn't stop him from embracing it. He climbed into the azure sky and then dove back through the flock, unbound by time or gravity or fatigue, and then back up again until he could see nothing but the open, unblemished sky.

He peeled off from the flock and dove straight down until the vast, undulating carpet separated into individual trees, their leaves quivering in the breeze. He dropped down beneath the canopy and flitted between wide trunks and over branches, avoiding them without any conscious effort.

Somewhere ahead, a waterfall tumbled from high on the Mountain, a great, rumbling, penetrating roar that permeated the air with sound and the scent of damp rocks. He plunged into a cloud of cool mist, and then he was through, the vast waterfall churning beneath him. He dove down until the tips of his wings nearly skimmed the turbid water before climbing again into the treetops, darting between the branches, until the waterfall's roar receded into a deep, peaceful silence.

The forest ended, its border a strand of silver pebbles bordering a lake. He followed it for a while. In the distance, two figures sat at the water's edge, looking out into the water, where flecks of living gold and orange and blue danced, flitting here and there with a beauty that rivaled the stars. As he got closer, he saw that the companions were not humans but dogs.

When he reached them, he landed on a low branch, just behind them. On the left was a Great Dane, white with black spots along his back and sides. Next to him was a Scottish Terrier, his black coat so hopelessly tangled that he looked like a mop with legs. Side by side they sat, quietly watching the gentle waves lap up the strand, just touching their front paws.

Jake watched them for a while. Just before he took to the sky again, the terrier turned his head. Their eyes met.

The little dog looked at him for a moment, his face a picture of deep, peaceful satisfaction. Then, slowly, he turned his gaze back to the lake.

Jake beat his wings and rose back into the air. He flew over them, skimming the lake before banking sharply upward, until the lake was no more than a blue ribbon far below.

He flew on until even the Mountain shrank, and below him lay a landscape of rolling, grass-covered hills. He descended in lazy circles, closer and closer to the hilltops. The hills were dotted with holes, and from them emerged rabbits, hamsters, and other rodents of all sorts, darting among the grass, only to disappear again through another hole. There was no division among them; all seemed perfectly content to share the warrens together.

With no convenient landing spot, Jake flew on. Some of the creatures looked up, watching him with interest as he passed them.

Before him stretched a vast, empty grassland. Jake pumped his wings, gaining speed until the grass was nothing more than a light-green blur. When he passed a band of horses, he slowed down, and before long, the grassland, now a brilliant shade of gold, was speckled with animals. Most were horses, but there were also cows, goats, donkeys, and, farther on, cats and dogs. Some were alone, others in pairs or small groups, but all together, free in their own way as Jake was in his.

One horse caught his eye. On his back rode a large, piebald rat, and they galloped across the grassland, practically racing Jake as he flew. Though the horse galloped at full speed, the rat never flinched, so comfortable there, he might as well been sitting on solid ground. There was something wonderfully familiar about them, and he slowed his flight for a short time, matching the horse's speed, before climbing back into the sky.

He flew on, over the golden grass, over the wide, dark expanse of the river, and into another forest. Dappled green light filtered through the canopy, and as Jake flew, a feeling of joy and anticipation came over him. His destination lay just ahead. Here, Jake passed dogs and cats, sharing the woods without rancor, their ancient animosity forgotten.

The land gradually rose in elevation. The air grew colder, and broad-leafed trees gave way to evergreens. He followed the land up until the slope flattened out into a wide plateau, where dogs and cats lazed by a pool fed by a waterfall. At the plateau's edge, he landed on the branch of a large pine and watched the scene below.

A border collie tumbled with a much heavier Rottweiler, their game a raucous, gentle ballet, while nearby another dog pranced and bowed, eager for his own turn. The cats paid them no notice, aloof and absorbed in their own feline musing.

Jake looked out across the plateau, giddy with anticipation, but nothing changed. The animals did not even waste a sidelong glance at him. He began to wonder if he'd flown too far or not far enough.

"Jake."

It was the first voice he'd heard, and it sounded as vast and forceful as the waterfall, filled with wisdom and majesty. There beside him on the branch was a cat, his chest a snowy white, his sides and back as gold as the grassland beyond the river.

"He is not here," Samuel said. His words were like an icicle in Jake's heart.

"But we beat them. Everyone is free," said Jake.

"The Malbinocks are weak. They will hunt again. But right now, we are one. Rat, guinea, horse, cat, dog.

All are the same. Someday, they will forget. Many will go to the Calling-Place, and new ones will come, and the Malbinocks will hunt again."

"Where is he, Samuel? Where is Ursus?"

"He is not here."

"I want to see him again!"

"You will not see him here."

Jake couldn't cry. His bird body would not allow it, so he expressed his grief in flight. Through the canopy, he left the forest, the river, the grassland, all of it far below. Up and up he went, until the sky darkened and stars emerged, one by one, from within the deepening blue.

Though he was as close to the stars as he had ever been, even when he drifted to his mother's voice, their song was faint and distant, a half-remembered dream. He flew toward them anyway, not to join them, but to beg them. If anyone knew where Ursus was, they would. He flew until his wings ached, and the stars told him nothing.

Up, up he went until the stars burst around him in an explosion of color. He was no longer flying but falling. His wings and feathers were gone, and he felt the cold wind rush past his bare skin.

Lights like stars burned below, fixed in place. They dimmed as he fell, and to his left, he saw the sunrise. The world spread out like a map. Trees, streets, and the roofs of houses rushed toward him. Terrified, he closed his eyes and threw his hands out reflexively against the coming impact.

He felt only a light thump, and a gentle creak

escaped from somewhere inside his mattress, as if he'd done nothing more than turn over in his sleep.

He opened his eyes and sat up. Sunlight blazed around the edges of his curtains and landed in long, bright lines on the bedroom floor. He touched his legs, his belly, his head. All were exactly as they had been when he closed his eyes the night before. His relief was short-lived when he thought of Ursus. Whatever the second death was, Ursus had suffered it, and it was more than Jake could bear. He rolled his face into his pillow and sobbed, squeezing the pillow around his head until he could barely breathe.

There was a knock at the door. It was his mother's knock, quiet and tentative.

"Jake?"

He heard that familiar tremor in her voice as if she were afraid that this time, he wouldn't answer.

"Yeah, Mom," he said. He tried hard to push the grief out of his voice. There was no reason to worry her.

"Are you all right?"

She opened the door. Jake wiped his eyes on his forearm, but it was too late. It didn't fool her. She sat down on the edge of the bed and felt his cheek and forehead with her palm. Her hand was cool and soft.

"Nightmares again? But the medicine's been helping. What happened? You took it, didn't you?"

Jake shook his head. "Not a nightmare. At least not like the other ones."

She looked at him. There was relief in her face, and joy, as if she were seeing him again after a long absence. It was the same look she had every morning since he came home from the hospital. He wondered if someday, it would go away, and everything would go back to the way it was before. He hoped not.

"Want to talk about it?"

Jake shook his head. If he tried to talk about it, he'd have to think about Ursus, and that would just make him cry.

She drew him close and held him for a long time. Jake drew in her warmth and let it wash over him. The hurt was still there, but while his mother held him, it was bearable.

"If you come out, Dad's got something in the living room that might make you feel better." She kissed the top of his head.

"What? What does he have?"

"You'll have to go take a look."

Curious, and grateful for anything to take his mind off the dream, Jake let go of his mother and slid out of bed. The wood floor chilled the bottom of his feet.

"Mom, what is it? Tell me."

She smiled and pointed at the door.

Jake opened it and peered into the hallway, still dim at that time of the morning, and padded across the runner that lay down the middle of the floor. The smell of bacon and coffee wafted through the hallway, and on the television, there was a heated discussion about who would win the Heisman Trophy. None of it provided any clues.

He stepped into the living room. On the sofa, his dad sat, a large, satisfied grin on his face. It was an expression usually reserved for birthdays and Christmas morning. At his feet was a large, brown cardboard box.

"Morning, Jake."

"Mom said you had something."

His dad smiled. "Maybe."

In Dad talk, that meant, "yes".

Jake pointed. "In the box?"

"Could be." Dad's smile broadened.

Jake approached the box and lifted the flaps. As he leaned over to look inside, his gaze was met by a pair of innocent brown eyes, new but somehow familiar. The puppy spun around in the box and barked. Muscles rippled beneath a coat of black hair that carried an iridescent sheen when the light played over it.

The pup barked again, deep and resonant, and then tumbled out of the box and into Jake's lap. The sound of the television and his father's voice faded into the background. Jake held the pup in his arms, eyes closed. He breathed in the pup's scent and felt a warm, wet tongue against his cheek, followed by the gentle sound of snuffling against his ear.

He opened his eyes, and the world's colors were rich and deep again. For a long time, Jake held the pup in his arms, afraid that if he let go, it would disappear. Eventually, the pup wriggled out of his grasp and launched into a boisterous, headlong sprint around the room.

"Well, at that price, I had to get him." Jake realized that his dad had been talking for a while. He looked at his father, unsure of what to say.

His dad pointed to the pup. "So, you think we should keep him?"

It was a silly question, but that was part of the fun. Jake nodded.

"I was hoping you'd say that. I guess you'll have to come up with a name for him."

Jake smiled, watching the puppy dash in circles around the room.

He already had a name picked out.

About the Author

Michael LaReaux was born and raised in California. After an idyllic suburban childhood, he served six years in the military before earning his degree in Creative Writing from CSU Hayward. He splits his time between Maine and worlds of his own creation, where he is free to be a self-sacrificing, heroic combination of Humphrey Bogart and Superman. He lives in an old farmhouse with his wife, two rambunctious dogs, and a very destructive cat.

Dive into the
Stormbird Community

...where story develops deeper, stronger connections to transform the world.

Stories about our world, and our relationship with nature, have been told by wise souls and changemakers for countless generations. We've gathered around campfires and sat under the limbs of mighty trees to be nurtured by their wisdom. Story is how we've shared moral tales, empowered ourselves with knowledge, and paid hope forward into the future.

Our authors embody the spirit of those changemakers. They write with reverence, wisdom, and inspiration about the places, plants and animals, habitats and ecosystems of our shared home—*Earth*.

There is no better place to connect with these stories than through the Stormbird Community. We will gift you eBooks and other content that stimulate your mind and heart. In a new philosophical place we call The Gathering, we'll connect you directly with our brave authors and other bold thinkers. We'll invite you into exciting discussions, but we'll also listen and allow you to explore.

Dive into the current of Stormbird's stories and soar with them, *like feathers in the wind.*

www.stormbirdpress.com

Stormbird Press is a proud signatory to the United Nations SDG Publishers Compact. At the time of publishing this title, our focus in on contributions to *SDG 13: Climate Action, SDG 14: Life Below Water, SDG 15: Life on Land,* and *SDG 16: Peace, Justice and Strong Institutions.*